By Frenzy I Ruin

USA Today Bestselling Author
Cora Reilly

Copyright ©2024 Cora Reilly

All Rights Reserved. This book or any portion thereof may not be reproduced or used in any manner whatsoever without the express written permission of the author except for the use of brief quotations in a book review.

This is a work of fiction. All names, characters, businesses, events and places are either the product of the author's imagination or used fictitiously.

Subscribe to Cora's newsletter to find out about her next books, bonus content and giveaways! (corareillyauthor.blogspot.de/p/newsletter.html)

Cover Model: Anthony Patamisi
Photographer: Michelle Lancaster www.michellelancaster.com
Cover Design: Hang Le

Aurora Scuderi spent her childhood and teenage days doing one thing—loving Nevio. Until one fateful moment, he breaks her heart without a second thought. Leaving Aurora with her broken heart bleeding in her hands. Fleeing Las Vegas is the only way for Aurora to heal—forget Nevio and that night. But a man like Nevio can't be shaken off that easily. The hunter in him was awakened.

Nevio Falcone is darkness. It seeps from his pores. It's where his monster comes out to play to satisfy its cravings. Until he starts to crave something other than carnage: the one woman he shouldn't pursue—Aurora.

What Nevio craves, he ruins. He told her to keep her distance. Now it's too late to run away. Consequences be damned.

FAMIGLIA
(NEW YORK)

BROTHERS

LUCA VITIELLO — **ARIA SCUDERI**   **MATTEO VITIELLO** — **GIANNA SCUDERI**
  MARCELLA AMO VALERIO   ISABELLA

ROMERO CANCIO — **LILIANA SCUDERI**   **RYAN TREVISAN** — **CARA BARESE**   **CASSIO MORETTI** — **GIULIA RIZZO**
  SARA FLAVIO INESSA   MAXIMUS   PRIMO   DANIELE SIMONA GABRIEL

OUTFIT
(CHICAGO)

DANTE CAVALLARO — **VALENTINA ARESCO**
  ANNA   LEONAS   BEATRICE

DARIO FABBRI — **BIBIANA BONELLO**   **DANILO MANCINI** — **SOFIA MIONE**   **ROCCO SCUDERI** — **MARIA BRASCI**
  UNNAMED   LUISA   ORLANDO   ALDO   ROCCO SCUDERI JR.   RICCARDO

CAMORRA
(LAS VEGAS)

BROTHERS

REMO FALCONE — **SERAFINA MIONE**   **NINO FALCONE** — **KIARA VITIELLO**   **SAVIO FALCONE**   **GEMMA BAZZOLI**   **ADAMO FALCONE** — **DINARA MIKHAILOV**
  NEVIO GRETA GIULIO   ALESSIO   MASSIMO   CATERINA   LUNA   ROMAN

FABIANO SCUDERI — **LEONA HALL**
  AURORA   DAVIDE

By
Frenzy

I Ruin

Prologue

Aurora

Hate and love are closely related. Both can take your breath away and immobilize you with their intensity. They represent the ultimate of human emotions. They should be complete opposites, divided by a vast chasm of other less potent emotions, but they aren't always, and where Nevio was concerned, they definitely weren't for me. In my case, love and hate were like toxic lovers, dancing their destructive tango inside my body.

I didn't think they could exist beside each other. Yet they did. Love and hate played tug of war with my heartstrings, draining me with the constant backlash I felt.

I loved Nevio Falcone for almost half of my childhood and teenage life until I realized that I needed to learn to hate him if I wanted to get away unscathed.

Though that wasn't even an option anymore.

Not physically.

Not mentally.

Nevio could hurt me far worse than he already had.

I knew I needed to stop him.

But I wasn't sure if I could.

The worst thing? A part of me didn't even want to try. A part of me wanted to risk heartbreak and pain just to be with him. A part of me was as addicted to our roller-coaster ride of hate and love as he was to his nightly hunts.

Maybe that was Nevio's special power, to make you long for something that could potentially destroy you.

I was in love, but I wasn't blind.

Nevio embodied pure destruction, and somewhere along the way, I'd become collateral damage.

Nevio

Sometimes I wanted to hurt everyone, but there were certain people I always wanted to save a little more than I wanted to hurt them. Save them from me. The problem was that every day, I was a little less sure who held the reins, me or the monster. A monster who reeked of blood and sought carnage.

Maybe I was delusional when I thought there was a difference between the monster and me.

Chapter One

Nevio

Nevio 19 years old

I'M NOT SURE WHO STARTED CALLING MASSIMO, ALESSIO, AND ME the Unholy Trinity. Maybe Savio. He had a canny talent to come up with nicknames. For as long as I could remember, my twin Greta had been Dollface, and I had been PIA (pain in the ass—naturally). And that was long before I'd made good on the name and taken the first girl anally.

I suppose the name was fitting, though any comparison to anything church-related was certainly classified blasphemy, considering what the three of us were up to at night.

Music blasted from the speakers of my all-black Dodge Ram. All black like our clothes, from our steel-toed boots to black cargo pants, leather cuffs, bandannas, balaclavas to our weapons, even up to the blades.

All black like our souls. Though I loved the flash of a silver blade and how it mirrored our victims' panic on occasion.

The inside glowed red from the dashboard and the small LEDs in the center console and doors. Even my headlights had a red tinge.

The red because of the blood that would soon stain our skin and clothes. My pulse sped up in eagerness, thinking of the scent and soft texture.

Massimo often rolled his eyes at the excessive symbolism, as he called it, something he attributed to the institutional church as a way to mesmerize the masses. Still, he'd never worn anything but black on our raids, and it certainly wasn't because of peer pressure. He wasn't receptive to that shit.

I turned off the asphalt road onto a long dirt driveway. Huge signs that said "No trespassing," "Armed response," and "Spring-Guns" welcomed us. Hell yes.

Massimo tossed his balaclava onto the back seat. His dark brown hair, several shades lighter than mine, was pressed against his forehead. He gave it a quick toss so it fell more freely. I stifled laughter. Not vain, my ass. "Out here, we won't need to hide our faces, I reckon," he said.

My own balaclava was pushed up on my head, keeping my hair out of my face. Unlike Massimo, I fucking hated it if I had strands in my eyes, which was why I kept it shorter than his, though we both kept our sides and back trimmed. "It's not a matter of need but fun. People freak out when they don't see our faces."

"They freak out when they see your face. It screams crazy-murdering motherfucker. That doesn't leave anyone unaffected," Alessio said from his spot beside me. One of his legs was propped up on my headboard. His hair was as long as Massimo's, but because of the wave in his, it always piled atop his head in a fucking surfer-boy style. As if emo boy would ever use a surfboard—except perhaps to smash in someone's head with it. "Who is it tonight?"

Alessio had a Robin Hood complex. While he liked the hunt and kill, he needed a reason for it to make peace with his conscience. He was always wary when it was my turn to pick our targets, though I mostly made sure that they had a track record.

"Killing them will give you all the cozy feelings. Don't worry."

"Meth house," Alessio said the moment I parked the car in front of the hut. It really wasn't more than that anymore. Through the open windows, the stench of cat urine and rotten eggs was a clear giveaway of what the house occupants were up to.

One of the half-ripped-off shutters of the window on the left moved. I hit the gas, and the car jerked forward. A round of shots hit my truck bed, and from the sound of it, it was bird shot. That would cost a fortune to fix.

I gritted my teeth. "Next time we visit meth heads, we're taking your car. The nice victims don't try to tear your car apart when you pay them a visit."

Alessio rolled his eyes at me before he aimed out of the car and fired a few shots with his semi-automatic. I hadn't come here to shoot someone by accident. The fun was over too quickly.

Guns had their time and place, but not during our nightly raids. That was pure sensation. I needed to feel and smell blood, not fucking gunpowder.

I parked the car around the corner, then pushed open my door and got out. With my head ducked, balaclava still on top, I ran along the building wall until I reached a back door. A glance over my shoulder confirmed that Alessio and Massimo were on my heels. They both had their guns drawn, but I only had my sawtooth combat knife in my hand. It was my newest purchase, and I was eager to try it out. I kicked in the back door. Stealth didn't make sense anymore.

Now, maximum fun was to be had.

I stepped into a filthy kitchen where nobody had cooked anything in a while, considering the dirty pots piled high on the stove. Moldy sandwich bread and processed cheese were the only food items in the place, and I had a feeling these assholes were still eating them. Since they were high on drugs, mold probably was the least of their worries. The stench was a nuisance; garbage, mold, something sweetly rotten. I probably had to drag these assholes out for the torture, or I wouldn't even smell their dirty blood.

Something creaked to my right, and a narrow door to a storage chamber swung open. What looked like a zombie with missing teeth and frizzy bleached hair staggered toward me with an ax. Grinning, I ducked under the dismal swing of the ax, then rammed my knife upward into the rib cage of my attacker and ripped it out after a twist of my wrist for maximum damage. Blood spurted out, and I jerked back to avoid it—there was good blood and bad blood, and this was the latter—but droplets still hit my throat and chest. The body staggered toward me in its death-fight. I pushed to my feet and shoved it away from me. It toppled backward and onto the floor with the sound of crushing bones and a wheezing kettle.

Now that it wasn't in motion, I could see my attacker was a woman, her age hard to guess because of the state her body was in from years of drug consumption. Her bathrobe opened wide, laying her bare. Her tits and pussy lips looked like the floppy ears of a basset hound, and most of her skin was covered in blisters I very much guessed were some kind of sexually transmitted disease. "Fuck," I muttered and quickly moved to the sink to wash the blood off my throat. I didn't have any open wounds yet and hadn't touched her blisters, but I didn't want to take any chances. Then I rushed into the doorway, which led to a hallway with a staircase leading down into a dark basement.

"Genital herpes and syphilis. Don't touch her," Massimo said.

"Thanks for the advice," I muttered and motioned at the blood all over my clothes. Uncle Nino would have to do my blood work later. Again.

It would require plenty of additional blood spill to get me into the mood for after-torture sex, which was a long-established tradition I'd hate to part with only because of saggy crack-whore tits.

"I meant Alessio."

Alessio gave us both the finger before he draped the rug over her body. I shook my head but didn't comment. I was used to this by now. If he started saying a prayer for our victims, he could go on solo killing sprees.

"You shouldn't have killed her. She's probably a victim of circumstances."

I snorted. "She was trying to split my skull with an ax. Every perpetrator has a sob story in their past, so cry me a river. Fuck, even I'm probably a victim of circumstances. Promise me you won't cover me with a dirty rug if I get killed." Alessio stared down at the body. "And she's too young to be the crack-whore you want to find."

Massimo gave me a wary look. Since Alessio had found out that Kiara and Nino weren't his biological parents, he'd been staring at every junkie as if she might be his mother. My guess was she was rotting somewhere in the desert.

A shotgun slug tore away pieces of the wooden doorframe with an earsplitting bang right beside me. Massimo and I dropped to our knees, and Alessio threw himself into the storage chamber. At least he had enough sense not to throw himself on the corpse. Kiara wouldn't be impressed if he got syphilis.

"Now stop mourning the whore and help us catch these assholes so the fun can get started," I snarled, losing my fucking patience. He'd always been more compassionate than Massimo and me, but the news about the whore who pushed him out of her vagina had really set him off.

I crawled toward the doorframe and poked my head into the hallway. The shot couldn't have come from the basement, even if the rummaging suggested people were down there. A head peeked out of the doorway across from us. An ugly-ass redheaded guy with the same blisters all over his face like the dead crack whore. I really hoped these idiots hadn't all inter-bred like fucking rabbits. If they all had syphilis, I'd have to wear a full-body condom to torture them. What a waste of opportunity.

That was the problem if you picked the lowest scum of society as your victims. Fuck Alessio's conscience. Next time, we'd hunt someone who knew the basic rules of hygiene.

I wanted to feel blood on my skin and not smell like a rubber duck for hours. Alessio barreled past us. I tried to reach for his leg to stop his manic move—those were usually my specialty—but missed him. Redheaded guy stepped out and aimed a shotgun at him. Alessio threw his cyclone knife at the guy, which pierced his eyeball. He tipped backward and fired a shot that tore a hole in the ceiling. More splinters rained down on us.

"Fuck it, Alessio. That's one less to torture. I'm not the one who'll share a victim. You and Massimo can do that," I growled.

"Cry me a river," Alessio said with a laugh. "Wasn't that what you said?"

I shoved to my feet and checked the guy, but of course, he was definitely dead. Alessio pulled out his knife, and blood shot out of the eye cavity. Clanking from downstairs distracted me from my disappointment. Massimo, Alessio, and I crowded around the steep staircase leading down into a basement. Judging from the rough walls, it had been hammered into the ground by someone who didn't do this professionally.

"Seems like a tomb," Alessio said.

Massimo put on his thinker face. "Could be a trap. And we're making us vulnerable by climbing down the ladder."

"We could try to drive them out with teargas," Alessio suggested. "There's still some in the trunk."

"We don't know if there's a second exit. There could be a flap door, and they could get away," I said.

"What's your suggestion?" Massimo asked warily.

I peered down into the basement. The staircase was so steep, it was practically a ladder, and the floor wasn't too far down.

"Don't—" Massimo began, but I didn't let him finish. I squatted down and jumped into the basement.

With a grunt, I landed on my feet, stirring up dirt. Two guys stared at me dumbfounded, the same ugly fuckfaces as the guy from above. They had been busy packing up their drugs. I flung my smallest knife at the one closest to me and impaled his right hand, which had been going for the gun on the table in front of him. Then I pushed to my feet and barreled toward them, colliding with the second. I heard another thud suggesting Massimo or Alessio had jumped after me. I knocked the guy out and heard another grunt behind me. Massimo had knocked out the other guy.

Commotion in the back of the basement set me in motion. A third victim. Tonight was Alessio's lucky night. He wouldn't have to share.

When I reached the end of the basement, I saw long legs disappear through a flap door, then the rope-ladder vanished too. I sped up and catapulted myself up so my fingers grabbed the wooden frame of the flap door.

Another ugly redhead stared at me with wide, stunned eyes. Those stupid brothers had definitely all banged flappy-pussy-zombie. He clutched the rope-ladder in his blistered hands, then his gaze darted to the shotgun at his feet.

"I skewered the ugly bitch from above. I hope she wasn't your squeeze." His head shot up, and I gave him my most manic grin.

He reached for the gun, and I hoisted myself up. The moment I was above ground, I aimed a kick up. The shotgun flew from redneck's hand, and a shot barely missed his head.

Phew.

He stared at me panicky, his mouth ajar.

"Run."

He staggered back, almost stumbled over the ladder, before he dropped it and fled. I shook my head. Next time, I'd pick decent victims. These motherfuckers were so pitiful. Where was the challenge?

"What are you doing?" Massimo called up from below, dark brows drooping in disapproval.

"Trying to have some fun."

"Don't let him escape. There are booby traps down here. He could ignite them from afar."

I sighed but sprinted after the guy. Within a minute, I had caught up with him. No fucking challenge. I kicked him to the ground and dragged his dizzy ass back to the meth hut. By now, Alessio and Massimo waited in front of the house with the two other assholes at their feet.

"We'll torture them here. I don't want their diseased corpses in my car," I said.

Two hours later, I got my predicted outcome. Cutting them up was hardly any fun. And on Massimo's insistence, we'd covered up with protective suits.

When we were done, I perched on the truck bed and smoked my usual after-torture cigarette. It didn't have the intended effect. I still felt restless.

"Don't mope around," Massimo said.

I glowered. "This was a mess. I'm not a fucking crime scene cleaner." I motioned at the blood-covered protective suit I'd tossed to the ground.

"Let's go grab some tacos. I'm starving," Alessio said.

I threw the cigarette on the ground and stomped it out. "I don't know about you, but the only thing I'm hungry for is a decent kill. You can bury your faces in guacamole if you want, but I'm going to find another motherfucker to kill."

Alessio and Massimo exchanged an exasperated look.

"You need to learn when it's enough," Massimo said, sounding like our fathers.

"Not in this lifetime. I want blood, and I'll get it. You can come along, or I'll drop you off at Taco Bell. I don't fucking care."

I climbed into the car. I knew where I was going. I'd had a backup kill on tonight's list anyway because I'd anticipated this miserable kill-fest.

I put the address into the GPS while Massimo and Alessio argued. When they got into the car, I knew they'd come along.

"We'll join you," Massimo clipped.

Alessio looked pissed.

"It'll be fun. He's a former prize boxer turned attorney causing trouble for the Camorra."

"We're not in it for the fun but because Massimo wants to keep you in check. We're your babysitters."

I grinned. "Good luck."

Chapter Two

Nevio

The night had been rough—rougher than usual. Our victim had escaped because I had a sick penchant for hunting and had allowed him to run. We almost hadn't found him.

Massimo sent me a disapproving look. Even with sunglasses covering his eyes, I knew that was what it was from the downward tilt of his mouth and even sharper contours of his cheeks. He was royally pissed at me. He would never risk one of our targets getting away. Not because the police would arrest us—our fathers would get us out immediately—but because our parents weren't fond of our nightly adventures. Especially if the victims weren't pre-approved.

When Dad had caught us last time, he'd threatened to split Alessio, Massimo, and me apart and send us to work for Underbosses in different states.

The hunt had been fun, though, even if it took until the early morning hours.

"You know she's checking you out again?" Alessio said in a bored tone. Like Massimo, he was stretched out on the lounge chair beside mine, with dark glasses over his eyes.

"Who?"

"Aurora."

I glanced over my shoulder at the spot where Carlotta and Aurora tanned on sun lounger at the other end of the pool. Aurora was indeed looking my way, a glass clutched in one hand, but she quickly jerked her head around, then casually looked back and gave me a forced smile. She didn't notice her glass tipping over and spilling its ice-cold contents all over her front. She let out a shocked scream and dropped the glass—luckily unbreakable thanks to Kiara's overprotective nature—on the ground, so it spilled its remaining contents everywhere. Her drink had been red—probably some awfully sweet fruit concoction—and left red splatters all over her white bikini. It was the first time I saw her in a bikini. Up until this point, she'd worn bathing suits or swim trunks and tank tops.

Of course, it would go *this way*.

Aurora jumped up from her sun lounger, probably to clean up. Her breasts bounced up and down in the triangle bikini top. She filled it out nicely, and the red juice trailing down the valley between her breasts reminded me of blood, which made the sight even more appealing. I dragged my eyes away before my thoughts got carried away. I'd spilled blood last night, and Rory was off-limits.

"It looks as if you got a visit from Aunt Flo," her younger brother Davide cackled, pointing at her ass. The back of her bikini bottom was indeed red in a very compromising way.

Aurora glanced my way, her face turning beet red. Despite her tan, her naturally pale skin blushed easily and very frequently. Pressing her lips together, she whirled around, her blond ponytail whipping through the air before she rushed over to the house with a mumbled, "I'll get a mop."

Carlotta, who'd watched everything with a concerned look, followed her, as could be expected.

Massimo watched her leave with intense interest. She wasn't in a bikini. Of course not. Yet the modest bathing suit didn't seem to diminish Massimo's fascination in the slightest.

"They won't return soon. Aurora will probably cry, and Carlotta will give her a pep talk. Give it an hour," I said.

Aurora was amazing with a skateboard and athletic skills in general, but she had a horrible talent that made her a complete fool of herself around me. Greta thought it was because she had a crush on me. I *knew* it was the case. The problem was Aurora liked a version of me that was pretty much only the PG version. But the real Nevio wasn't even R-rated. A movie about me would be banned because of excess violence and craziness.

Massimo frowned. "I don't care when they return."

Alessio scoffed. "He wasn't talking about *them.*"

"I wish it had been blood that would have elevated a pitiful display to a slightly entertaining one," I mused as I stretched out again with my arms crossed under my head.

Alessio released a sigh. "Don't mess up."

I cocked an eyebrow at him. "I have absolutely no interest in Rory. She reeks of innocence. Her clumsiness even triggers my protective side. It's not sexy. I don't do pity fucks."

"You don't do pity anything," Alessio muttered. "As long as she doesn't accidentally fall on your dick, everything's good."

"It's more likely that I accidentally fuck you in the ass, asshole, all right?"

"Then my cyclone knife is going to impale you."

I shrugged. "That'll only get me off sooner. Pain and pleasure, nothing beats that."

Massimo got up from his chair with a shake of his head. "I need to clear my head. Every second of your nonsense talking makes me feel dumber."

"You should wait with your water show until Lotti returns. I'm sure she'll appreciate how your muscles glisten when they're wet," I said.

He gave me the finger, then dove into the water in perfect form.

Aurora

I stormed up to my room, utterly furious at myself. Soft steps followed me.

I didn't stop until I was in my room. When Carlotta closed the door, I began to tug my bikini from my body. The red juice on the white fabric really made it look as if I had my period. My eyes burned with mortification, even if it wasn't the case. I'd spent days working up the courage to wear a bikini. Not because I was shy about my body but because it simply wasn't my usual style, so it was a given that everyone would notice.

I had wanted Nevio to notice, but not like this, though.

"We should return. Don't make a big deal out of it. If you downplay the situation, the boys won't care. They probably don't either way. They don't feel embarrassment like we do," Carlotta said in her reasonable voice.

It was one she had to use often when Nevio was concerned.

I nodded, even if I really didn't want to go back down there. It wasn't the first time I'd acted like a clumsy cow around Nevio, but that didn't make it easier. "Why am I like that?" I asked angrily.

Carlotta shrugged.

I grabbed a familiar sporty bathing suit from a drawer.

"Put on another bikini," Carlotta said.

I raised an eyebrow. "Lotta, are you trying to turn me into a sinner?"

I sometimes teased her about her prudish bathing suits and gym clothes.

"It's not sin. I just feel more comfortable if my most private areas are covered up. But it would draw even more attention if you switched back to your old style only because of a little accident."

I grabbed the second bikini I owned, a turquoise piece that brought out the blue in my eyes, according to Carlotta.

Carlotta gave me a thumbs-up, then she checked her own reflection. Her bathing suit was modest with a high neckline, though I knew it was mostly to cover up her scar. She still managed to look effortlessly sexy.

She took my hand, and we headed back downstairs. Pretending nothing was up, we headed straight to the pool and jumped in. The cold water cleared my head.

When we emerged, both Carlotta and I were laughing.

By Frenzy I *Pain*

Davide popped up right beside me, startling me and tried to dunk me. Despite him being three years younger than me, he was already stronger and taller, and managed to push my head underwater. Carlotta fell victim to Nevio's little brother, Giulio, who was only seven but a force to be reckoned with.

I spluttered when I managed to resurface after almost a minute.

Carlotta coughed somewhere behind me, then screeched again.

Through blurry vision, I saw Nevio and Massimo dive into the pool. Shortly after, Nevio was by my side and dunked my brother with a devious grin.

Massimo helped Carlotta, but his intervention looked less fun. He grabbed Giulio by the throat and shoved him away. "Be careful. Carlotta has a heart condition."

Giulio rubbed his throat and poked out his tongue at his cousin, then dashed off and began to splash Alessio, who'd remained on the lounge chair.

Davide followed suit, leaving me with Nevio. "All good?" he asked, then his eyes dipped lower. I glanced down and flushed. A tiny sliver of my nipple peeked out. I quickly tugged my top back into place. Something on Nevio's face made me feel hot and not from embarrassment.

"I'm fine, really. I won't have a cardiac arrest from a bit of water play," Carlotta said, looking embarrassed. Massimo seemed to disagree, judging by the stern look on his face.

"Young love must be sweet," Nevio muttered.

"Yeah," I agreed. Our eyes met, and the heat in my cheeks intensified. Nevio searched my eyes, and I couldn't look away. I had no hope that he couldn't see my stupid crush on my face.

Alessio flung himself into the water with an ass bomb, dousing Davide and Giulio.

Water splashed Nevio and me in the faces too.

"Water battle!" Nevio shouted.

Before I knew what was going on, Nevio hoisted me onto his shoulders, and my thighs hugged his neck. Stunned, I stared down at his black crown.

"You should wait this out," Massimo told Carlotta who grudgingly moved to the edge and lifted herself out of the pool. I sent her an apologetic smile, but she only gave me a thumbs-up.

"I want to fight her!" Davide shouted.

I sent him a dark look. He'd been annoying as hell recently. Mom said he was going through hormonal changes, but so what? So have I for the past few years, and I was never this annoying.

"Kick his ass, okay? I count on you," Nevio said, peering up at me, his white teeth on display in a challenging grin. My heart picked up, and I grinned in turn. "Oh, I will."

Davide climbed on Alessio's shoulders while Massimo played referee.

"No hair tugging," Massimo said sternly to my brother, who would definitely try that move. "Alessio, Nevio, you can kick and punch each other. No off-limit areas."

"Finally, some good news," Nevio said.

Alessio pointed his fingers like guns at him. "You better watch your balls."

Massimo let out a whistle, and the battle was on.

Eventually, I was out of breath, and we settled on a draw after Davide and I had both landed in water about two dozen times. I sank down beside Carlotta, who handed me a towel. My chest heaved with every breath I took.

Nevio sent me another grin from the pool. "Good job, Rory."

I smiled back and nodded.

"Now look at me," Carlotta muttered, and I did. She smiled. "See, you can act normal around Nevio. This is a good start."

"It was fun." Then I sobered. "I'm sorry you had to sit on the sidelines."

"Don't be. I'm used to it by now. Diego is even worse than Massimo."

"Massimo is really concerned about your health," I said teasingly, looking over at him. He was chatting with Nevio and Alessio in the pool. My eyes halted on Nevio who ran his fingers through his wet hair before he hoisted himself out of the pool, biceps flexing, his trademark grin on his face. It wasn't one that made you want to smile because you realized that something was lurking behind it.

Carlotta jabbed her elbow into my side. I quickly dragged my eyes away from him. I wasn't sure why I had such a hard time ignoring Nevio. The magnetic pull he had on me was sometimes terrifying.

Chapter Three

Aurora

My sixteenth birthday was right around the corner, but Mom cradled me to her side as if I were a little child, and I didn't protest. This felt like the last moments of our lives. Fear clogged my throat, and my heart pounded wildly in my chest. Mom kissed my temple, her arms around my body tightening even more as wheels squealed before us and a metallic crash sounded. Through the windshield, I saw the car with Remo and Nino and their families smashed against a shipping container.

I cringed, and Mom's hold on me became painful.

We were in an industrial harbor area of New York, I wasn't sure where exactly. During my few visits in New York over the years, I'd never really gotten the hang of the city's outlay. We jolted against our belts when Dad hit the brakes.

"Heads down," he shouted before he ducked out of the car with his gun drawn. Gunshots rang out, and another crash sounded.

"Get out of the car," Adamo said as he exited and held the door open for us. His wife Dinara, who had been sitting beside me, got out first, pulling the gun she was carrying. I was glad they had decided to leave their young son Roman with his grandfather for this trip. That way at least he was safe.

Mom and I were unarmed. I knew Mom had practiced shooting with Dad but I had never seen her with a gun apart from that, and I had only held one once or twice. There had never been a moment where I'd felt unsafe in Las Vegas. I had never liked the feel of a weapon in my hand and considering the tremor in my body I doubted my aim would have been good in a situation like this.

We hid behind an overturned van. A trail of blood led around it where Dad had dragged away the driver.

In the distance I could see more cars approaching, black limousines. Probably reinforcement for the Famiglia who was attacking us. I still couldn't wrap my head around it. These men shooting at us were married to my aunts. We had been here for a wedding. How could they do this?

I felt sick as I watched my family fall apart. I hadn't seen my aunts and cousins in New York very often but since losing my grandmother, the only grandparent I'd ever met, it had been the only extended family I had. Now they would disappear from my life too, if we survived this.

Considering the number of Famiglia cars heading our way, I didn't have much hope for us. I hadn't considered dying yet. I'd sometimes worried for Dad's life when he hadn't returned in time and Mom's worry had fueled my own, but I had always felt safe.

What if these were the last minutes of my life?

"Everything's going to be okay," Mom whispered. "We'll be safe either way. They don't hurt women." Even as she said it, Mom's gaze moved to Dad, and fear overtook her face.

Maybe we were safe, or as safe as a woman could be in our world, but Dad and the other men would definitely die.

An image of Nevio flashed in my head. He'd stayed home with the rest of the Unholy Trio, just like Savio and his family, and my brother Davide.

By Frenzy I *Pain*

A van barreled toward us and stopped with squealing tires. The sliding doors jerked open, making my body clamp up with trepidation. How many more Famiglia soldiers would ambush us? But it wasn't an unfamiliar face I saw. Nevio got out of the van. My eyes grew wide with relief, then utter shock when I noticed the woman in his hold. He was pressing a knife against her throat. Even from afar, I immediately recognized my aunt Gianna. She looked scared. I only knew her as a feisty, loud-mouthed woman so seeing her like that really drove the seriousness of the situation home.

I couldn't believe Nevio was threatening her life, but then again, maybe this was our only chance to get out of here alive.

"Stop!" Matteo roared. The Famiglia stopped firing and so did our side.

"Surprise, motherfuckers," Nevio shouted with a wide grin. I'd seen several versions of his grin, but tonight, illuminated by several headlights in an eerie way, I got a glimpse of how people felt that were terrified of him. There was something unhinged, wild, and hungry about him. I wasn't sure if he'd care that Gianna was a woman.

He pulled Gianna along as he walked toward Remo, Nino, Adamo and Dad. She struggled against his hold but it was futile. One look at Remo's face told me he hadn't known Nevio was here. Nevio had always been bad at following rules, even when they came from his father, the Capo of the Camorra.

After him, Massimo jumped out, and then Alessio with my cousin Isabella in his grip. Isabella's already wild mane was all over the place, her glasses were broken and she looked as if she'd cried. I tried to catch her eyes, maybe show her somehow that it was going to be allright, even if I was the last person who had any control over the outcome of tonight, but she never looked my way. The way we were hidden behind the van, she probably couldn't even see us.

"If you touched a single hair on their heads, I'm going to make you regret the day you were born," Matteo growled. I only knew him as the funny, easy-going husband of Gianna. I'd always loved his jokes. It was difficult to see him as the enemy all of a sudden.

I still felt pity for him for having to watch Gianna and Isabella being taken, and I felt guilty because part of me was relieved.

Nevio flashed his teeth at Matteo and briefly touched Gianna's hair. She tried to escape his grip, but he pushed the knife against her throat as a warning once more. "I don't regret anything yet."

I'd never seen Nevio or my father in action as Made Men. I only knew their domestic side. It was easy to forget that it was only a small part of them.

"Isabella, Gianna, are you okay?" Amo called. I briefly glanced his way. He was the reason we were here, the reason things escalated. My gaze next moved to Greta. Her eyes were on him with a look I could feel deep in my gut and in my heart. Her face expressed what I sometimes felt when I looked at Nevio. Longing and wistfulness.

Her feelings for Amo, and his for hers had led to the conflict between the Famiglia and the Camorra. Love could be a destructive force.

Suddenly, Matteo stormed toward Nevio and had to be stopped by Luca. "The fucker hit you!"

My eyes registered the bruise on Gianna's face. I sucked in a sharp breath, but I simply couldn't imagine Nevio slapping my aunt. It wasn't his style…

"I'm afraid that's not true," Nevio said as he walked over to his father. "Sorry, Dad. I disobeyed, but I simply couldn't resist ruining a wedding. If I'd known it would come to this…" He chuckled and exchanged a look with Massimo and Alessio, looking like this was the greatest night of his life. He wasn't scared at all. He'd walked into danger as if it meant nothing, as if his life meant nothing, as if death and pain meant nothing.

"You're going too far," Matteo said quietly.

"Too far?" Remo snarled. "You attack me and my family while we're guests in your territory. Never talk about honor to me again. I'm the master at playing dirty, Vitiello. You just opened the fucking Pandora's box."

Nevio peered down at Gianna and sucked in a deep breath. "I smell war." He laughed as if this was good news. War.

"Leave my territory. We're even. And let Gianna and Isabella go right now," Luca said.

Remo scoffed. "Even? Plenty of Famiglia blood will be spilled before I'll consider us even, Luca."

"I think Alessio took a shining to your daughter," Nevio kept provoking.

By Frenzy I *Pain*

I stopped listening to their power play. I clutched Mom's hand, wishing there was something we could do to stop the men. It was too late to stop a war, even I knew that, but we could all leave alive today. I didn't want people I knew to die. I didn't want to have to watch them die. Maybe that was selfish, but the idea tore at me. Especially if I considered that someone I loved might kill someone I cared about.

A gasp sounded somewhere and suddenly Greta was running toward the water. Her face was determined. No sign of fear even as she flung herself into the Hudson and disappeared under the black surface.

"Greta!" Several screams rang out and people began running. Nevio released Gianna and rushed toward the water to save his twin.

Nevio flung himself into the water seconds later and Amo followed after checking the water's surface for Greta. Both of them were willing to risk it all for Greta. Remo and Serafina rushed toward the edge too, calling Greta's name.

Mom wrapped her arms around me as if she was worried that I'd run there too. I was too frozen to move, by everything that had happened. The gunshots had ceased.

Dad and Adamo stayed close to us while Nino and Remo ran toward the water's edge.

Amo pulled Greta out of the water and began CPR, soon after she opened her eyes. Nevio watched everything with a heaving chest and stormy expression from the side, dripping wet.

Even from a distance I could see his struggle, his fear for his twin's life, his hatred for Amo. Mom brushed a few strands from my face. I could feel her shaking, which was surprising because my own body was wrecked by tremors.

I wasn't sure how much time passed, but soon Dad led Mom and me away toward a van. We all got in. Greta was wrapped in a fluffy white towel and huddled against her mother Serafina. The drive was rough. Even though, the Famiglia had allowed us to leave, I still feared another attack.

I'd always felt like I had all the time in the world. Everyone had always said to me that I was still young and had my entire life ahead of me, but today had shown me how quickly things could change, how unexpectedly a life could end. There was still so much I wanted to do in my life, so much I hadn't experienced yet, I was terrified I might never get the chance.

When we got out of the car, we were at an airport and a private jet was waiting for us. I held my breath until we were in the air.

It was silent in the airplane except for the low murmurs of the male members of our family. Their faces were a mix of anger and determination, and I knew they were already discussing revenge plans. More blood would be spilled. Life as I knew it was over. All because of two people who loved each other in secret. I'd thought it was romantic, now I realized it was tragic.

I reached for my necklace with the gold charm of a skateboard. Carlotta had discovered it in the shop window of a jeweler for pre-owned pieces a few years ago. I'd bought it and since then it had felt like a token, something I always carried with me no matter where I went. But my hand came up empty. I glanced down. My neckline was bare and I was in my comfy pjs. At night was the only time I ever took off the necklace and put it on my nightstand. I must have left it there in the hotel room when we'd fled from the ambush. I swallowed.

There was no way I could ever get it back. My suitcase with my clothes was lost too but because I had to dress to impress at the wedding, I didn't pack anything that was dear to my heart except for the necklace.

My heart felt heavy. Over the years, I'd always touched it when I needed encouragement or a bit of luck.

I pulled my legs up against my chest and rested my chin on my knees. My eyes burned and the back of my throat clogged up. I wasn't sure if this was only about the necklace. I fought the raw emotions that tried to claw their way out of me.

Greta had almost drowned, had lost the man she loved, yet she wasn't crying. She looked composed in her typical, far-away Greta way. And Kiara who had her head bandaged because of a headwound wasn't wallowing in self-pity either. She was chatting quietly with Alessio and Massimo, making sure they were okay in her typical motherly way. I doubted they would suffer nightmares from this. Knowing them they would soon start making plans for payback.

I didn't want to be the one to make a scene.

I turned my face toward the window, hoping to hide my tears if I failed to suppress them. In my peripheral vision, I registered movement, but I didn't turn, expecting Mom. I was afraid she'd hug and console me because then the tears would definitely flow freely.

"Worst wedding of all time, don't you think?" Nevio asked, his voice dripping with sarcasm.

I sniffed and cleared my throat. "Definitely." The wedding had felt off from the start, not because I'd picked up on any danger, but because it had been obvious that Amo wasn't marrying the person he wanted. Luckily for once I could stop myself from saying something embarrassing and didn't bring up my observations about love to Nevio. "But it'll make history."

Nevio's mouth twisted with anger. "Oh it will. But if I'd planned an ambush like that, I would have done it properly. Not in the aftermath of a wedding but at the party. Bloody weddings are far better than the standard."

I looked at him. "Some think weddings and funerals should be sacred."

"Nothing's sacred anymore, Rory." He looked toward Greta, something dark passing his face before he looked back at me. I'd never talked about it with Nevio, but it had been obvious from the start that he didn't want Greta to have feelings for Amo.

I nodded slowly. "I thought you were supposed to stay in Las Vegas." His father had forbidden Nevio from joining the festivities to avoid a scene. And Nevio did indeed cause a scene but one that saved us.

A smirk pulled at his lips. His eyes reflected a darker emotion that didn't match the casual twist of his mouth. "I suppose it's good that I'm bad at following rules."

"You think your dad's going to punish you?"

"He better not. We saved the day."

They really did. I wondered how Gianna and Isabella were feeling. After Greta had jumped into the water, chaos had erupted and I'd lost sight of my aunt and cousin.

"But why were you in New York? You couldn't possibly have known that there would be an ambush. Did you want to crash the wedding?"

"Never. Amo deserves to be married to that witch. But I was hoping for a bit of entertainment afterward. New York is full of opportunities."

I gave him a doubtful look. "That would have caused trouble."

"Trouble found us without my help."

"You saved us tonight but I have to admit I was really scared for Gianna and Isabella. I was worried you'd hurt them."

"Right. You are related to them."

I nodded. "I guess I won't see them anymore."

"They're blood but blood doesn't mean shit if your family tries to kill you."

I bit my lip. Of course, that was true, but I doubted Gianna and Isabella, or any of the other women in the Famiglia had known about the ambush plans.

"The Famiglia played dirty and so did we."

I imagined how Gianna and Isabella must have felt. "Would you really have hurt them?" I wanted to believe that Nevio, Massimo and Alessio had only put on a show, that they they wouldn't have hurt Gianna and Isabella no matter what had happened.

Nevio's smile hardened and his eyes gave me an answer before his mouth did, "If you go into war as a player, you need to be willing to play it to the end. A bluff is a risk, especially if so much is on the line."

I nodded. It wasn't the answer I wanted, but it was the answer I'd expected. I knew Dad, too, would have done anything to protect Mom and me. "I'm glad you didn't follow the rules. It was really scary. I thought we'd all die."

Nevio shook his head. "This was a good reminder to stay on our toes. It won't happen again. You don't have to worry, Rory."

The way he looked at me with absolute conviction, I believed him.

"It's tragic. This must be hard for Greta."

"That's what you get when you let emotions run your life."

Chapter Four

Aurora

A week had passed since the disastrous wedding. I relived the car chase every night, the panic and fear, but my nightmare always ended with Nevio sweeping in like a dark knight and saving us. Well, in my dreams he saved me, carried me off in his arms and then kissed me.

Carlotta gave me an amused look. "You're daydreaming again. Only you can turn a nightmarish event into an anti-hero tale."

"Anti-hero?" I said. My cheeks burned as I once again regretted telling Carlotta about my dream even if we usually shared everything. Carlotta didn't have a crush on anyone, and she'd never really had one. Maybe that was why she couldn't understand my inability to act like a capable human being the moment Nevio was around.

She opened her eyes wide, as if her big green doll eyes weren't already striking enough. "He's not the hero in this story, or any story, Rory, even if your dreams say otherwise."

"Shhh," I hissed, glancing over my back at the guys. Nevio, Alessio and Massimo perched on the banister at the top of the half pipe and watched how my brother raced down the pipe with a howl. Then Giulio followed, as usually doing a stunt that was still too hard for him and slammed into the pipe. He seemed to see Davide as his role model, often forgetting that my brother was much older than him.

Giulio's knee and elbow were burst but he got up with a grin as if nothing had happened. Nevio gave him a thumbs-up. Then our gazes met, and he rolled his eyes at his own brother. I grinned and shrugged then quickly looked back to Carlotta.

She pressed her lips together and sent me a look that said "get-a-grip". Being around Nevio used to be easier. I'm not exactly sure when it became a major effort for me not to make a fool out of myself. The first time it really hit home that I was hopelessly and embarrassingly in love with him was in the night of Greta and Nevio's eighteenth birthday when she snuck into my bathroom and Nevio later followed. Even Greta noticed it that night and that said a lot about my inability to chill around him considering Greta wasn't overly perceptive when it came to emotions.

Since then, I had to pay extra attention to act normal around Nevio and I'd obviously failed once more judging by Carlotta's expression.

I grabbed my skateboard and climbed up the pipe. Skating always cleared my head. And no matter how stupid I acted around Nevio, it never affected my skateboarding. I was cool as a cucumber when I threw myself down the ramp.

I reached up for my necklace, then realized that it was no longer there. Today was the first time I skated since I'd left it in New York. The first day that had felt almost normal since war had become our new normal. I lowered my hand and released a small sigh. Normal had never been harder to achieve.

I made a mental note to talk to Greta today. I'd been caught up in my own trauma and knowing her tendency to deal with problems herself, I hadn't wanted to push her into a girl-talk she probably didn't even want.

I briefly caught Nevio's gaze who was no longer in deep conversation with the other guys but watching me intently. This was the first time we hung out together since that day. He too seemed oddly normal.

I gave him a brief nod then focused on my skateboard and the ramp. I let myself drop, my feet firmly on the board. The air tore at my ponytail and T-shirt, tugging it from my dungarees. I raced up the other end of the ramp and did one of my favorite tricks, one I always got right no matter how bad of a day I've had, a backside nosepick.

I did a few other tricks I was really good at. Today was a day for my comfort tricks. I preferred to work on the more advanced tricks on feel-good days or with less people around, especially the noseblunt slide was still giving me major problems so I needed to be in the right mindset for it. I had a feeling it would take a few weeks for me to reach that mindset again.

When I finished my routine without a hiccup, Nevio let out a whistle and applauded.

"Show off," Davide muttered, but his expression told me he was actually proud of me.

I gave a small shrug. I hadn't meant to brag. This wasn't a difficult routine for me but I couldn't help but grin at their praise.

It had taken a long time for me to feel comfortable on a skateboard but more importantly in a skate park. I had been the first girl in our circles with an interest in skating and always felt like the odd one out when I'd joined the boys. Many had made teasing remarks, as if me being a girl made it impossible to be good at skating. Boys in our circles were often caught up in the Middle Age with their thoughts. Nevio, however, had never made a big deal out of me skateboarding. He treated men and women the same way, from what I heard even when it came to his kills. It was a thought I didn't like to dwell on.

Maybe Nevio had that opinion because his dad always said "women should stop thinking and acting like the weaker sex if they don't want to be treated that way".

Carlotta smiled broadly. She joined me at the skate park most days, even if she didn't skate herself. Her brother Diego considered it too risky because of her heart condition, though she hadn't had any troubles in a long time. I thought Carlotta wasn't too sad about it anyway. She was a girly girl, who preferred art, dancing and music to most sports.

I perched on the rail beside her again.

"This is how you impress a man," she murmured and nudged my shoulder.

"Because you know so much about men," I muttered with a small laugh.

But she had a guy watching her with rapt attention all the time. Like now. Massimo's gaze was attached to her. He didn't look like he was fawning over her or madly in love, but really I doubted Massimo was even capable of that expression, but his intent observation spoke volumes. Carlotta had never even flirted with him. They talked a lot, or rather argued about pretty much every topic under the sun because their viewpoints were on opposite ends of the spectrum, but that seemed to have done the trick.

Maybe showing Nevio the cold shoulder or even fighting with him on occasion would do the trick for me too, but so far I hadn't managed the necessary composure around him. It wasn't even that I was throwing myself at him or flirting, I was just being an embarrassing klutz.

It wasn't really surprising that Nevio wasn't into that. Few people were attracted by clumsiness I assumed.

I wasn't sure what Nevio's type was. I'd never seen him with a girl, but word of mouth said he hooked up with them frequently at parties. Carlotta and I hadn't been to one yet. Nothing had really made me want to go.

It was a warm summer evening about two weeks after the attack in New York and war had broken out between the Camorra and the Famiglia.

The atmosphere was strange at home and it was even worse at the Falcone mansion.

I packed my sunglasses and a spare bathing suit into my beach bag. I'd spend the evening at the pool with the Falcones. Davide had already gone over there an hour ago to hang out with Giulio. Except for Greta I'd be the only girl there today, and she and I had never been close friends. Now that things with Amo had gone downhill, she was even more closed off. I hadn't even managed to talk to her yet. Not to mention that she wasn't fond of water.

When I entered the kitchen, Mom ate sushi with a fork, still not having gotten the hang of sticks yet, spearing every roll as if it had offended her while she read over a police report about the arrest of one of her clients. Dad would be working all evening and I would eat pizza over at the Falcones so she had the evening to herself, which usually involved work if she wasn't having a girls' night with Serafina, Gemma and Kiara.

A perpetual worry line had taken habitat on Mom's forehead since the war declaration.

I sank down across from her and put my bag on the ground. I'd overheard Mom and Dad talking in hushed voices in the living room almost every evening in the last two weeks, but neither of them had shared their concerns with me.

Maybe I wasn't an adult but I was a good listener.

Mom looked up from the report and glanced at her watch, a beautiful Cartier piece Dad had gifted her for Christmas. "Aren't you meeting the other kids?"

"They won't care if I'm late." I cringed inwardly at how bitter I sounded. I loved hanging out with the Unholy Trinity and the other Falcones, but I always felt a bit like the fifth wheel if Carlotta didn't join me. Giulio and Davide hung out together even if they weren't the same age, and the Unholy Trinity was a tight unit anyway. Then there was Greta. We chatted when I was over there but I could feel that she felt comfortable on her own and so I always worried she only hung with me because I'd be lonely otherwise.

Mom pursed her lips. "Do you want me to call your Dad and ask him to talk to Diego about allowing Carlotta to come?" Dad was Diego's boss, who worked as an Enforcer under him.

"No, don't. Diego is having an overprotective streak because of the war. He'll calm down in a week or two. I'm fine."

Mom nodded slowly but I could see her concern. I hadn't sat down to talk about myself and so I quickly changed the subject. "What about Dad, is it hard for him that he won't be able to see his sisters again?"

When Dad had first joined the Camorra, he hadn't been on speaking terms with his sisters, because all three had married into the Famiglia. The rest of his family, the Scuderis, were still in Chicago where Dad had been born but he never spoke of them. It made me sad that our family was so tiny, even if the Falcones felt a bit like an extended family. It was different. I'd always loved seeing my aunts and cousins in New York. Now that wouldn't be possible anymore.

"Your father is very focused on guaranteeing our safety at the moment. He and the Falcones have to put new security measures in place now that attacks could happen at any time."

I didn't feel in danger. Las Vegas had always been a fort, the ultimate safe place, and I still couldn't imagine that the Famiglia would attack us here. "He doesn't have time to think about what that means for him and his sisters."

I gave her a doubtful look.

She smiled. "I always forget how grown up you are. Your father has high guards around his heart, like most men in this world, and he has never fully lowered them for his sisters after their reunion. I think that makes it easier for him to handle the situation but it's still not easy."

I nodded. "Sometimes I wish I was like Dad in that regard, that I could shield my heart so easily."

"It's not just bad if you have a big heart, Aurora. You're a very loving person, don't let anyone take that from you. I love that about you."

I rolled my eyes but at the same time my heart swelled.

Mom watched me closely. "Are you sad because you can't see your aunts and cousins anymore?"

I gave a one shoulder shrug, suddenly emotional. "Are you?"

Mom had gotten along really well with my aunts Aria, Liliana and Gianna, and considering she had no more family of her own, I could only imagine how hard this must be for her.

"I'll miss them," she said softly, giving me a sad smile. "I know it was hard for you when Grandma died, and now you're losing even more people you care about."

I looked down at my feet. Dad had never liked Grandma because of her drug problems and how poor of a mother she'd been for Mom, but I'd mostly felt pity for her and enjoyed spending time with her on good days. "It's okay. I'm going to be fine. We have the Falcones. It's almost like having a big family."

Mom nodded but I could see the hesitation in her eyes. "Your dad sees them as family, well sort of, but I think you and I have a more nuanced look. Or do you think of Nevio as something like your cousin or brother?"

My eyes widened in alarm. "No," I said, disgusted by the mere idea. My feelings definitely weren't anywhere close to being sisterly.

Mom smiled knowingly and I flushed. I rose to my feet. I didn't want to discuss Nevio with Mom or anyone except for Carlotta for that matter.

"Crushing on guys who are unattainable is a safe and good way to discover your emotions," Mom said.

My mouth fell open, and my face burned even hotter. "I know I'm not Nevio's type, Mom. Thanks for rubbing it in."

Mom took my hand. "That's not how I meant it, Sweetheart, but you and Nevio obviously won't happen. I think you know that, right? You're sweet and caring and have a huge heart, but Nevio…" Mom trailed off. "Let's just say your dad and I would be terribly concerned if there was the possibility of you and Nevio seeing each other."

I tugged my hand from her grip. "Like you said, it's just a silly crush. Nevio sees me as a little, stupid sister, not more, so don't worry."

I grabbed my bag and quickly left before Mom could say more that would upset me.

"What's up? You look like you're going to bawl," Davide said the moment I arrived at the pool.

I glared at him and sank down on a vacant sunchair. Nevio floated on an airbed, sunglasses over his eyes while Alessio and Massimo played waterball.

Luckily none of them paid attention to my brother's comment or me. The only person who seemed to notice my distress was Greta. She sat on a chair under an umbrella over to the left, and was reading a book. Or had been. Now her dark eyes were locked on mine.

She gave me a tight, little smile before she returned her gaze to the book, but it was obvious that she wasn't actually reading.

I pushed to my feet and walked over to her. "Is it okay if I sit here?" I motioned at the vacant chair across from her.

She put down her book on the table and nodded. Her dog Momo, a white fluff ball, was curled up on her lap. Her Rottweiler Bear wasn't around. "Where's Bear?"

"He's been even more protective of me lately so I'm keeping him up in my room when others are in the garden."

"You mean when Nevio is around," Alessio added as he walked past us.

"He doesn't like any of you," Greta said gently, but firmly.

"I once read that dominant dogs have trouble with other alphas. He sees them as rivaling predators in his territory," Davide piped in.

I pursed my lips, then turned back to Greta. "Dogs are sensitive to emotions. He probably senses your distress," I made sure to say this in a bare whisper so the nosy guys wouldn't overhear this part of the conversation too.

Greta stroked Momo's fur, her dark eyes flashing with wistfulness, even pain. So far I'd only dealt with unrequited love, which was already difficult, but Greta's love to Amo had been returned and then ripped away. I imagined that was a thousand times harder, especially if you had to watch the person you loved marry someone else.

"Nevio sees this whole situation as confirmation of something he's always believed: that love is stupidity. An emotion that weakens you, while hatred makes you stronger," Greta whispered. The way she looked at me tightened my throat.

I shrugged as if it didn't matter.

"So even if Nevio had feelings for you, which I don't know because it's not something he'd admit even to me, he'd fight them as a weakness."

I bit my lip, my eyes slanting to Nevio, who kept throwing glances our way despite being in a match against Massimo.

Greta went to bed early, without eating pizza but the rest of us settled on the grass across from the huge trees where Massimo and Nino had attached a canvas so we could watch a movie outside. I shivered. It was chilly tonight and my still damp hair only intensified the sensation.

"Rory," Nevio called, pulling his sweater over his head and tossing it at me.

By Frenzy I *Pain*

I caught it before it could hit me in the face. I put it on without protest, trying not to smell the fabric.

"Gross," Giulio commented. "I wouldn't want Nevio's sweat all over me."

"You're lucky I'm too old to rub your face all over my axle," Nevio said, baring his teeth.

I stifled laughter at the disgusted look on Giulio's face. "Alessio did that once."

"Because you were sniffing in my personal stuff."

I grinned. Huddled in Nevio's sweater, I watched the movie. It was past midnight when Davide and I finally headed home.

"Wait," Nevio called.

I stopped and turned to see him jogging after us. He probably wanted his sweatshirt back, which I was still wearing. Davide hovered close to me like my personal bodyguard and I almost rolled my eyes. I couldn't help but wonder if Dad had given him a secret mission to watch Nevio and me.

Nevio stopped beside us and gave Davide a questioning look. "Go ahead. I don't think Rory needs a bodyguard on our premises."

"She's not supposed to be alone with boys."

Nevio scoffed. "Get lost."

"Go," I said firmly. "Don't be ridiculous."

Davide made a face but he finally walked off. At thirteen, he still often switched between utterly childish and surprisingly adult behavior.

"Sorry," I said with an embarrassing laugh.

Nevio stared at the spot where Davide had been with a dark look then he shook his head and gave me a sardonic smile. "I bet your mom told him to keep an eye on me."

"No way." My voice came out completely false sounding.

Nevio's smile broadened. "I know I'm the ticking bomb here. They all want to make sure you aren't in my vicinity when I go off."

"That's not true." I motioned at his sweater. "I forgot to give this back to you." I began to pull it over my head but felt my shirt being dragged up with it. Of course I'd manage to get tangled in a sweater. A warm hand brushed my skin and tugged at my T-shirt, keeping it in place while I pulled the sweater over my head. My cheeks burned from the time inside the sweater and embarrassment when I met Nevio's gaze. He was still holding my T-shirt. I stared down at his hand. He released the fabric. I handed him his sweater to break the silence. "Here."

"That's not why I ran after you," he said with a smirk.

"No?"

He reached into his pants and pulled something out, which I couldn't make out because it was hidden in his fist. He held it out to me and uncurled his fingers.

My eyes widened in surprise. It was a skateboard necklace, very similar to the one I'd lost.

"You must have left it in New York."

I swallowed. "Yeah. Everything went so fast…I left it on my nightstand." I cleared my throat as the events of that night flooded my memories. "I didn't think you paid attention to my jewelry."

"It was a strange piece of jewelry, hard not to notice," he said with a chuckle.

I nodded. Wearing a skateboard around your neck and loving the sport had given me the tomboy stamp, though I loved "girly" things just as much as throwing myself down a halfpipe.

"Eventually the events from that night won't bother you anymore," Nevio said.

"Do they bother you?"

Nevio smiled a ghost-smile. "Chaos and destruction run in my veins. I don't mind bloodshed and fighting."

"I know," I said. "But that fight was different. Greta was there. She jumped into the ocean."

Something dark passed Nevio's eyes. "Yeah, that put a damper on the night."

I rubbed my arms. This time the outside chill wasn't responsible for the shivers raking my body. My heartbeat picked up as I remembered the fear I'd felt that day.

"You are safe in Las Vegas. War won't reach us here. And remember, I'll always be there to save the day with a crazy stunt."

I couldn't help but smile.

Nevio pushed his hand with the necklace over to me. "Take it. It's for you if that wasn't obvious before. I see you trying to grab the thing all the time. You're obviously attached to inanimate objects."

I swallowed and took it gingerly. "Why?"

"I don't know why you're attached to things. I'm not emotionally attached to jewelry."

"That's not what I mean. Why—"

Why did you buy it? This was such a sweet thing to do that my heart wanted to put more meaning into the gesture than it probably deserved.

"I know what you mean." Nevio shrugged. "It's odd. You're not you without it."

I bit my lip. So he found me odd? "Thanks. That's really nice of you."

Nevio clucked his tongue. "Don't spread any false tales. Nobody will believe you if you say I'm being nice."

I tilted my head, regarded his face in the dark. "Can you put it on?"

Nevio took the necklace and reached around my neck. Goose bumps rippled across my body when his fingers touched my skin. We stood really close. This was the perfect moment to kiss. It was almost too perfect, like in my fantasies, and really romantic. Nevio dropped his hands and leaned down to my ear. "This is a gift between friends, Rory. Remember the warnings your mother tells you about me. A mother's instinct rarely lies."

He stepped back and turned around without another word, stalking away.

I stood there for several minutes dumbfounded.

Chapter Five

Nevio

One year later

I wasn't sure who had first compared me to a black hole who swallowed even the brightest light. Probably Massimo who always knew shit like that and used it to piss me off.

Greta was inherently good. She helped animals, never used violence. Fuck, she didn't even eat meat, eggs, milk or fucking honey. *Honey.* Because the poor bees were exploited or something ridiculous like that.

Yet, she'd set a man on fire last night. We'd always been close, but over the last year since Amo had wed that bitch Cressida and war had come down on us, she'd spent even more time with me. She'd often seemed distant but she'd been by my side and I'd taken that as a good sign.

Fuck me. Being around me had obviously finally taken effect. I would have never thought Greta was capable of hurting anyone.

I sat on a chair next to our pool in the twilight of the early morning

By Frenzy I *Pain*

hours, taking a smoke and trying to understand how my peaceful twin could have burned someone alive. That was something I would do, something I *had* done. I ran a hand through my hair. I still smelled of smoke and burning flesh. It was one of the smells that was the hardest to get out. It wasn't my favorite either. I preferred the freshness of blood to the charcoal scent. If I wanted a barbecue, I could throw a few steaks on the grill.

The sound of a window opening drew my attention to the Scuderi mansion. Aurora peeked out of her window and waved at me, her blond hair like a halo in the dark.

Aurora meant light, and like my sister, Aurora was good too. She always asked others how they felt, truly cared about their emotions, and gave me concerned looks when she thought I was hurting, even if that was never the case.

Aurora had sought my closeness. I'd always kept her at a distance, mostly because she'd seemed too young, too innocent for what I had in mind. The last year I'd been busy with war, with Greta, with trying to control my deep need to maim and kill Amo Vitiello so ignoring her crush on me had been easy. But recently I'd caught myself thinking about Aurora, even fucking dreaming about her. About her smile. About how she threw herself down the half pipe. About how she made even dungarees seem like a valid fashion option.

But I was a fucking black hole, drawing in any source of light with my irresistible pull, only to extinguish it and tinge it in blackness.

I could only imagine what Massimo would say about my analysis, about my abundance of symbolism. But dammit, I was right.

I'd ruined Greta even if she'd had years to grow immune against it. Eventually I'd pulled her down into my black hole.

It would be the same with Aurora. I already had Greta on my conscience, if you could call my shaky moral compass by that name, I didn't want to add Aurora to that list.

There were so many women out there I didn't give a flying fuck about, enough to spend several lifetimes fucking. I definitely wouldn't entertain thoughts of one of the very few I minded hurting.

I stifled a groan when the patio door opened and Aurora stepped out in a white bathrobe. Speaking of symbolism…

She headed straight toward me, probably thinking I needed company and consolation. The only thing that would console me for a little while right now was a good torture session, preferably Amo, and then an angry revenge fuck with a woman from the Famiglia.

"Hey, I saw you sitting there from my window," Aurora said unnecessarily.

I nodded and took another deep pull.

She wrapped her arms around herself and tilted her head as if she was trying to see through my protective layer. "Mom and Dad refused to tell me what happened, but I gathered it was something about Greta. How is she?"

I grimaced and tossed my cigarette to the ground then stomped it with my boot. "She set a guy on fire. She's in her room now, trying to come to terms with it."

Aurora's eyes grew huge and she sank down on the lounge chair beside me. She stared at me as if she was hoping I'd take the words back. "She would never do that. I just can't believe it."

I chuckled sardonically. "That's what happens if you hang around me too often. My darkness rubs off. It's more contagious than syphilis."

She shook her head. "That's not how it works. And you're not dark."

I cocked an eyebrow. "Rory, ignorance can be a blessing but it can also be dangerous."

She bit her lip, a deep frown lining her forehead. "It's not about you. It's about what she went through this last year, with losing Amo and all. Don't blame yourself."

My lips curled with contempt at hearing that loathed name. He was definitely responsible for the shit show, too, and he'd eventually pay for it, but that didn't mean I wasn't to blame.

"I just came outside to tell you I'm here if you need someone to talk. Alessio and Massimo might not always be the best choice for every topic. I can keep a secret, you know that." Her voice was gentle and beckoning, and she put her palm on my hand hesitantly. I could feel it shake slightly. I frowned down at it, at the intimacy, at the way I actually didn't mind it. For a moment I let it sit there, warm and soft against my night-cooled hand.

Then I pulled it away, building a barrier between us. "I'm fine. This is nothing a good killing session can't cure."

"Everyone has moments of weakness."

I scoffed. "Aurora, stop trying to normalize me. I'm not like most people. I won't ever be a victim in any scenario. I'm someone who turns other people into victims. If you want to save someone, do yourself a favor and don't pretend I'm misunderstood and not fucking bad."

Aurora nodded and got up, shoving her hands into the pockets of her bathrobe. "My offer stands," she said softly before she turned and walked back to the Scuderi mansion.

She didn't often show that side around me, but she could be stubborn. I liked that side of her.

Aurora

Almost eighteen, about another year later

It was the first time I was back in New York in two years. The last time we'd all attended my cousin Amo Vitiello's wedding to a woman who had later been killed by Nevio for hurting his twin, Greta. It hadn't been a pleasant wedding. I still had nightmares about how the Famiglia had lured us all into a trap and attacked us.

I often woke from the sound of gunshots. It had been my first personal encounter with violence, the first time I'd really feared for my life. It had also been the day when my infatuation with Nevio had turned into something even more, something that was hard to put into words.

Nevio had saved us that day, in his very own way. Ruthless and brutal, how most people perceived him, but apart from the lust for violence I had seen something else in his eyes that day: love and concern. Not for me, for his twin Greta, but seeing those things had made me yearn to see the same emotions in his eyes for me one day. Foolish, I know.

Now Greta and Amo were married. There was peace between the Camorra and Famiglia again. War hadn't lasted long but its effects still lingered in the deep distrust and animosity both sides felt for each other.

Greta was a beautiful bride and her happiness over marrying Amo was obvious. But what really brought tears to my eyes was the look in Amo's eyes when he looked at her. Pure unrestrained adoration gleamed in them. He was so very obviously in love with her. Nobody could doubt his feelings after a look at him. I wondered if anyone would ever look at me like this.

My gaze slid to Nevio in the first row beside his parents and younger brother. He looked as if this was one of the worst days of his life. Letting go of his twin was hard. Nevio seemed so full of darkness and need for destruction that many didn't think he cared about anyone but he had trouble letting go of the people he cared about. Greta was at the very top of this list.

I had attended several weddings in my life so far. As the daughter of the head Enforcer, it was part of my social duties. But this was the second tensest wedding of my life. The first had ended in war, and this one would end war for good. But suspicion and wariness saturated the air. I hadn't seen my aunt and cousins in so long, and still hadn't had a chance to talk to them. Their faces reflected forced joy, but beneath it I could see the same tension I felt. A wedding mere months after the peace treaty couldn't be as free and joyous as a celebration like that warranted.

Especially Isabella was someone I wanted to talk to. She and I had always gotten along well, and I really hoped that was still the case. Luckily, she sat at my table. The parents of the groom and bride had to share a table, which led to quite a few very intense staring matches between Luca and Remo, and I was glad I wasn't actually sitting at the table. It didn't help the tension between those two that Nevio looked ready for trouble. He hated that Greta married Amo, but so far he'd behaved.

At our table there were my aunts Gianna and Liliana with their families, and following etiquette Nino and his family should have sat there too, but Matteo had threatened to stab both Massimo and Alessio with a "fucking" butter knife as rumor had it and so other arrangements had been made. I had to admit I was relieved on Isabella's behalf. I could only imagine what it would do to her to spend an entire evening at a table with the very people who'd kidnapped her and threatened her life.

Nino and his family now shared a table with Adamo and Savio and their families. I was pretty sure Kiara had had a serious conversation with both Massimo and Alessio before the wedding because so far they had both done their best to avoid any contact, even with their eyes, with Isabella and Gianna, though the latter looked ready to start a new war.

I leaned over to Isabella who sat beside me. Her maroon curls framed her face wildly and I noticed she made sure to use the curtain of her hair to shield herself from the table to our right, where Alessio and Massimo were sitting. We hadn't gotten the chance to talk yet, except for a few brief pleasantries because of the wedding schedule.

When Nevio had kidnapped Gianna and Isa to save us, I'd been relieved, had admired his bold move. I had avoided thinking what this had done to Isa. For me Alessio, Massimo and Nevio didn't pose a danger, and I wasn't scared of them, but Isa didn't know them very well, and if I was being honest, knowing their reputation, I wasn't sure if they wouldn't have hurt her to get their message across.

Mom began chit-chatting with Liliana and Gianna about mundane things like yoga in an attempt to avoid any touchy subjects, and the list was very long…

Still the atmosphere was difficult. Matteo wasn't really interested in conversation with Dad, and busy glaring alternately at Massimo and Alessio, or Nevio, who apparently hadn't gotten Kiara's memo to keep his head down. Luckily, Maximus and Dad seemed to get along decently, and chatted about Maximus's various tattoos all over his body. Especially Davide's interest in the many tattoos fired the conversation up. Davide, of course, had to show off his recently acquired Camorra tattoo. Dad had insisted that he was inducted on his fourteenth birthday despite Mom's protests, and Davide had run around like the king of the world ever since.

"Are you going to college?" I asked Isabella when the dinner conversations finally started. She was turning nineteen soon so she must have finished high school last year.

She turned to me. "No, I still need to finish high school. I took a break after certain events."

I flushed. So much about not putting your foot in your mouth. Mom sent me a concerned look and Gianna looked less than pleased about our conversation. Nobody had told me college was on the list of banned topics.

"Uhh… sorry. I—"

"But I'm going to attend Columbia University this fall. I'll sign up for Creative Writing. I think it'll help my writing career," she said firmly, completely ignoring my apology and our mothers' worried looks. She pushed her glasses back up her nose, and gave a small shrug.

"Wow. Creative writing? That's really cool. Have you already been accepted to Columbia?"

She let out a small laugh. "No, the application window isn't even open yet. But let's be honest, I'll be accepted." She glanced at Matteo. "I'm a Vitiello." It was difficult to read her emotions.

"True," I said. "How long have you been writing? You never mentioned it before."

"Well, our contact has been sparse in recent years." She pursed her lips and widened her eyes.

I laughed. "That's one way to put it."

"But I have been writing short stories pretty much all of my life. I never considered taking my writing seriously, but after the war broke out, I started writing novellas and novels, and it's what I want to do."

"They are really good," Sara piped up. I looked at her in surprise. She had quietly chatted with her two younger sisters while her brother Flavio had joined the conversation of the men.

Isabella scrunched up her face comically. "You called them disturbingly dark."

Sara's cheeks turned red. She looked pale and thin. I remembered how she'd been before the war, before something happened and she married Maximus instead of a man she'd originally been promised to. If I hadn't known those two were husband and wife, I wouldn't have guessed it. Sara mostly angled her body away from Maximus and he was obviously careful to keep his distance too. They seemed like strangers. No, not strangers, because they obviously both carried baggage that concerned the other. I had asked Dad about it but he'd refused to talk to me about it. I couldn't imagine that Maximus was violent toward Sara, even if he looked absolutely capable to do so with his muscles and tattoos, and considering his job, he definitely was capable of excessive violence too. Romero, Sara's Dad, would have never tolerated it.

I bet Nevio knew about this. He'd avoided me like the plague, ever since I'd offered him my help if he ever needed someone to talk. I hadn't pushed him after that because I didn't want to appear clingy and honestly,

I was just over it. Trying to understand Nevio was a 24/7 job I didn't want to waste my time on right now.

"They are dark and poignant. People will love them."

"But you didn't," Isabella said, without sounding offended or accusing.

"I prefer more uplifting literature, but that's a personal taste and doesn't say anything about the quality of your work."

"You have to let me read one of your books," I said. "I can handle dark."

Davide snorted. "Since when?"

"Stop eavesdropping." I rolled my eyes at him, then turned back to Isabella. "Ignore him. He's being intolerable since he became a Camorrista."

Her smile was a bit stiffer than before. "I'm sure you can handle the dark. You spend a lot of time with the Unholy Trinity, after all."

I wasn't sure what to say to that. I felt an apology on the tip of my tongue, but I doubted she wanted one from me.

After dancing with Dad and Davide, who annoyingly enough was already taller than me, I looked around for a sign of Nevio. I'd really love to dance with him, but I didn't see him anywhere. Alessio took Davide's place as my dance partner, looking like he'd rather be somewhere else.

"You don't have to dance with me if you don't want to," I said as he put a hand on my lower back.

"Some things are inevitable," he said.

I raised my eyebrows. "Thanks."

He gave me a tight smile. "I'm sure you'd rather dance with someone else, even if that choice is highly problematic."

"I don't know what you're talking about," I said defensively.

"You know, Rory, I don't like to get involved, but I have one piece of advice for you that you should consider. Get Nevio out of your fucking head. The faster, the better. On his good days Nevio is a psychotic asshole, on his bad days he'd make your worst nightmares look like a piece of cake."

I tried to end the dance, but Alessio held me in an iron grip. "I wonder what he'd say to one of his best friends talking like that about him."

"He'd agree with me. Nevio knows what he is, and he has no intention of becoming a better version of himself, trust me."

"Thanks for your advice, but I'm not a little kid."

"Where's Isabella?" Alessio asked suddenly.

"Why?"

"None of your business."

"Then I don't know."

Alessio glared down at me, but then Valerio took over, and our conversation ended abruptly. Soon after, I didn't see Alessio anymore. I hoped he knew what he was doing. I doubted Isabella wanted to talk to him. I managed to slip away from the festivities and began roaming the corridors of the hotel. The entire place had been rented for the occasion, so the only people I met were other wedding guests or employees of the hotel. I didn't see Alessio or Isabella anywhere, but eventually, I spotted Nevio on the floor, smoking. He looked as if he was ready to tear down the place. Maybe Alessio was right. Maybe it was best for me to stay away from Nevio. But this wasn't about my crush. This was about a friend helping another, and Nevio looked as if he definitely needed help today.

Chapter Six

Aurora

I DIDN'T BOTHER REMINDING HIM OF THE NO-SMOKING POLICY OF the place. He knew.

His body tensed briefly, then he slanted me a hard look, but at least he relaxed.

"Are you okay?" I asked.

He'd removed his tie and speared it with his knife and impaled it into the hardwood floor. His jacket had been tossed to the floor beside him. His sleeves were rolled up to his elbows, revealing his muscled arms and the Camorra tattoo.

"I came here to stop myself from starting a bloody wedding. Although, that would have been an improvement."

I stopped beside him, unsure if I should sit down or stay where I was. Did Nevio even want me around? "Greta looks happy."

Nevio took the cigarette from his mouth and moved it to his forearm. He hissed when the glowing tip touched his skin.

I dropped to my knees. "Don't!" I reached for the cigarette and gasped when my fingertip touched the still hot tip. I jerked away. Nevio extinguished the cigarette then grabbed my hand and inspected my fingertip, which started blistering. I sank my teeth into my lower lip from the burning sensation.

He shoved to his feet and pulled me up as well. After he'd picked up his knife and stuffed it into a holster at his belt, he took my hand again and led me away. I wasn't sure where he was taking me. "There's an ice dispenser," I pressed out as we passed a room with one.

"Too cold. The water should only be slightly colder than room temperature."

We arrived at the spa, and Nevio turned on the faucet in the women's changing room. As soon as the cold water hit my finger, I felt a moment of relief, but then the burning returned.

"What about you?" I asked, nodding toward the blister on his forearm. It must hurt worse than my wound, considering he'd touched the cigarette far longer to the spot.

"I think this is only the third time I've seen you in a dress," Nevio mused. I had opted for a teal-colored, long V-neck dress. It showed a little cleavage but was still modest. Dad wouldn't have let me wear it otherwise. I shrugged. "It's a wedding. Even I don't wear overalls at weddings."

Nevio released my hand. "It'll still hurt for a few days. Next time, don't get between me and a cigarette."

"You shouldn't hurt yourself."

Nevio gave me a challenging smile. "Why not? I thought I could have some fun at this wedding."

"Burning yourself is your version of fun?"

His smile became darker, and my belly dropped in the most unexpected way, my body flooding with heat. Why was a glimpse at Nevio's sinister side having such an effect on me?

"I have different versions of fun, Rory. None of them are feasible at this wedding. My father made himself very clear about that."

"Can't you just have fun like other people?" I asked, cringing at how

Goody Two-shoes I sounded. Nevio's answering eyebrow-arch confirmed it. He motioned for me to follow him through a white door saying "pool."

He held it open for me, his eyes on me the entire time as I swished past him in my dress, and even as I found myself in the massive indoor swimming pool area of the hotel, I could still feel his gaze resting on my back. The look in his eyes wasn't one I'd seen before, and I couldn't decipher what it meant.

"Then let's have fun like normal people, Rory. Maybe you can teach me a thing or two about it. I can't wait," he said in a low voice as he stepped around me, his arms making a sweeping motion like a ringmaster handing the arena over to the next show act.

I blinked up at him, feeling on the spot. Nevio was only three years older than me, but so often, I felt like a stupid little girl around him. A world of experience and darkness lay between us.

"We…" I looked around, and my eyes finally settled on the serene water surface. "We could go swimming."

Amusement crossed Nevio's face. "Do you hide a bathing suit beneath your dress?" He lowered his voice further, and a hint of condescension entered his tone. "Because I doubt you mean skinny-dipping."

Swimming naked with Nevio? The mere thought made me flush and sweat. I'd often fantasized about this, but now that an option had presented itself, nervousness overcame me.

Nevio chuckled. "I'm joking, Rory. Don't get your virginal cotton panties in a twist."

Embarrassment and anger mingled in my body. "Someone could come in. We could swim in our underwear." I gave a shrug as if it wasn't a big deal. That was pretty much like being in a bathing suit, right?

Nevio raised one eyebrow and stepped back, beginning to unbutton his shirt, revealing a body that had featured in my darkest fantasies. Muscles and scars, so much strength. Nevio wasn't just appearances, not like many posers and fitness models on social media. Every bit of muscle served a purpose. Impressing others was only the cherry on top. I knew because of the fight trainings I'd watched. So far, I hadn't been allowed to see a real cage fight, though.

I pushed off my high heels. Then I reached for the zipper on the side of my dress. My belly flipped when I pulled it down and slipped the straps off my shoulders. Tugging at the dress, my strapless bralette, almost the same color as my dress and adorned with lace, came into view. I was glad I'd convinced Mom to go underwear shopping with me for the wedding because my underwear drawer had been filled with the aforementioned virginal white cotton panties. I'd have hated to confirm Nevio's suspicions. I wanted to surprise him, to show him that I was more than tomboy Rory. I was a woman who knew what she wanted, even if she had trouble showing it in a non-embarrassing way.

Nevio watched me as he opened his belt. I hoped he couldn't see my fingers shaking as I pulled down my dress the rest of the way, revealing the teal-colored floral lace panties. The lace wasn't really sheer, but suddenly, I was worried about how much Nevio would be able to see of me. Did my pubic hair shine through? I'd trimmed it and it was dark blond, so maybe it wouldn't.

I straightened even as my body flooded with heat and the desire to bolt. Nevio was already only in tight black boxer trunks. I motioned at the pool, hoping my skin wasn't as red as it felt. "Ready to jump in?" My voice sounded strange to my own ears, a little rough and scratchy.

Nevio came up to me, and I wasn't sure what to do with my arms. I crossed them loosely over my belly, completely overwhelmed by the situation. Why was I acting like this? I'd been in a pool with Nevio countless times before. My bathing suit didn't really cover much more. But it had been different. We'd never been alone, and underwear just held a different level of intimacy.

Nevio dove into the pool headfirst in perfect form, barely stirring up the calm surface. I stepped closer to the edge, shivering when my toes touched the water. It was colder than expected, and immediately my skin pimpled. I scanned the elegant pool landscape with the white stone columns and view over New York.

Nevio's head emerged from the water, and he tossed it back, sending droplets of water flying. A few wet, black strands fell into his face. His dark eyes took me in, and I wished I knew what was going through his head. "Your body will get used to the cold."

I sank down on the edge and pushed my legs up to my knees into the water. I was a warm water kind of girl. No cold showers or ice baths for me.

Nevio swam over to me, and I braced myself, worried he'd pull me in.

Instead, he grabbed the edge and pushed himself up, catching me completely off guard. "I was really considering killing off some Famiglia asshole when you found me. As always, Rory, you make your name proud, bringer of light in the dark." His biceps flexed as he pushed himself higher until his face was level with mine. My heart stopped, only to pound harder a moment later. Rivulets of water ran down his forehead and cheeks, over the curve of his smirking mouth. Would he kiss me?

But his lips passed my nose, and he pressed a kiss to my forehead. He exhaled before he dropped back into the water with a splash. Cold droplets hit my face. They didn't help with the heat in my cheeks.

A kiss on the forehead.

I wanted to scream in utter frustration. And bringer of light? I knew Dad also saw me as inherently good, a light in their dark world, which was why he and Mom had picked my name, but I didn't like to be seen like that. It put a massive burden on my shoulders to live up to their expectations.

"I didn't know we were having a water party," Alessio said.

My head swiveled around to where he stood in the doorway. His eyes met mine, and he raised an eyebrow. I pushed off the edge and lowered myself into the water. I needed to cool down. If it hadn't ruined my hair, I would have dunked my head too, but that would be difficult to explain to my parents.

"What happened to you?" Nevio asked, swimming over to the spot where Alessio stopped near the pool's edge.

I hadn't noticed before, but Nevio had a point. Alessio looked ruffled. His dark-blond hair was all over the place. His shirt buttoned the wrong way, with a few missing buttons. And his fly was open. He hadn't looked that way when we'd danced.

"Uhh," I began, but Nevio was quicker. "Don't release the kraken on us, all right?"

Alessio looked down his body but didn't seem the slightest bit embarrassed about his predicament. He gave Nevio a pointed look. "As long as you keep your kraken in check, we should be fine." He popped open the button, then kicked down his pants and got out of his shirt before he too jumped into the pool, not bothering to be careful.

Water flew everywhere and barely missed my hair. I'd definitely get in trouble with my parents tonight. I could feel it. Though maybe I could say it was my way to keep the wedding peaceful. Nobody could argue that a wedding without Nevio and Alessio was far likely to escalate.

The guys exchanged a look that made it clear whatever had happened to Alessio wouldn't be discussed with me around.

I swam toward the closest ladder.

"Where are you going?" Nevio asked.

"I should probably return to the party. Mom and Dad will wonder where I am. I don't want to get in trouble."

I climbed out, grabbed my dress from the floor, and quickly rushed into the changing room. I locked myself in, then let out a shuddering breath. A kiss on the forehead, as if I was ten. I was almost eighteen, but Nevio treated me like his little sister. God, did he really see me as his kid sister? I closed my eyes. Taking a shuddering breath, I opened my bra. It was too wet. There was no way I could wear it under my dress. The fabric of my dress fell in ripples over my chest, so it shouldn't be too obvious that I wasn't wearing anything beneath.

I got out of my panties too but wrung them out, then put them back on even if the sensation of the cold, damp material was awful. I simply couldn't imagine returning to the wedding without panties. The material clung to me in an uncomfortable way, but I still put on my dress.

When I stepped out of the changing room, Nevio was waiting in front of it. I touched my heart.

"You're dripping," he said, his eyes on the floor.

I followed his gaze. Indeed, a few droplets of water gathered at my feet. The panties were still too wet.

"Your dress will be soaked as soon as you sit down."

I cringed. That would look as if I'd peed myself. Nevio stepped up to me. "Just get out of your panties. Nobody will know. Your dress is long. It would look suspicious if you dripped water all over the floor under your dress."

I stepped back into the changing room and got out of my panties as well, then returned with my bra and panties in hand to Nevio. I had left my purse at the table, so there was nowhere I could put my underwear.

"Here, let me take this from you. I can get rid of them later."

Nevio took my bra and panties from me, catching me off guard.

I swallowed, unable to get past the fact that Nevio was holding my panties. Again, I had dreamed of that moment several times, but never like this. Not even close. A hysteric laugh crowded in my throat.

Alessio appeared beside us at that moment. I knew he interrupted us on purpose. What was it with his savior complex? Since when was he so concerned about me being around Nevio?

He glanced at my underwear in Nevio's hand and then at my face. "You realize how your father would react if he saw Nevio with your underwear."

"Dad doesn't know what kind of underwear I own," I muttered, annoyed.

Nevio gave me a wink before he walked back to the pool with my underwear.

"You're very bad at following advice," Alessio murmured in my ear.

Nevio regarded us with narrowed eyes as he sank down on the edge of the pool and put my underwear on the floor beside him.

"I'm only bad at following bad advice."

I quickly left the pool area, and after catching my breath in the hallway for a moment, I decided to return to the party. When I entered the ballroom where the festivities took place, I felt on the spot, even if nobody paid me close attention. Just the knowledge that I wasn't wearing underwear was enough to turn me into a jumpy mess.

I hurried to our table and sank beside Isabella, who scribbled in a small notebook but stashed it in her purse when she noticed me. "You look flustered," she said curiously.

"So do you." Her cheeks were flushed, and her freckles stood out more than usual, plus her hair was no longer in an updo.

We stared at each other for a few heartbeats before we both nonverbally decided to change the topic and switched to my plans of working as a nurse.

We obviously both had secrets we didn't want to share.

Nevio

"I hope you're not thinking about keeping that," Alessio said with a nod toward Rory's underwear as he strode toward me.

"For someone who looks like he had a wedding fuck, you're terribly ill-tempered."

"And for someone who sees Rory as an almost sister, you're awfully interested in her panties."

"For someone who pretends to see her the same way, you're awfully invested in her possible sex life." I pushed to my feet and looked him straight in the eye. "Maybe your concern stems from a carnal desire, my friend."

Alessio laughed. "Don't turn this on me. We both know I don't see Rory that way."

"Me neither," I said with a shrug.

"You used to be a better liar. You need to work on that before you become Capo."

"You sound like a Consigliere," I taunted.

"But I'm not, and I won't be. Some things aren't meant to be. I'm not fit to be a consigliere. I know my limits. Maybe you should start considering yours."

"Limits are there to be broken down."

Alessio shook his head. "Not every limit. Some limits are worth being honored, especially if they are meant to protect the people who deserve our protection."

I rolled my eyes. "I'll behave, but don't pretend you're against becoming Consigliere because you want to protect others. You're being a prissy because of completely irrelevant circumstances."

"Blood isn't irrelevant."

"The only time I care about blood is when it runs over my hands and fills the air with its metallic scent."

Alessio chuckled. "You're the craziest fucker on this planet."

"Not crazy enough to get it on at a Famiglia wedding. You know they honor their virgins."

Alessio didn't say anything.

I let out a whistle. "Don't tell me you really banged a virgin?"

Still nothing. Alessio had a good poker face if he wanted to. "You're being awfully secretive about this."

"Let's go back to the party."

I shook my head with a chuckle. Knowing Alessio, he'd probably fucked some neglected MILF, not an honored virgin. Always working on his karma.

I got dressed, and then I grabbed Rory's underwear. Under watchful eyes, I tossed away her bra, hoping he hadn't noticed how I'd stuffed her panties into my pants pocket. I'd long given up figuring out the reasoning behind my actions, so I didn't even try this time.

It was three in the morning when I finally gave up on sleep and decided to leave the hotel before I accidentally killed a Famiglia soldier and caused another war. I needed to let off some steam. I particularly needed to keep my mind busy and as far away from what Amo and Greta were currently up to.

I short-circuited a motorbike I found in the underground parking of the hotel and left the premises with smoking tires. I didn't care if this was one of the Famiglia's bikes. There was a high chance that this belonged to either Matteo, Maximus, or Marcella's biker boy, all of them people I loved to piss off in whatever way I could. Stealing a ride for the night was one of the lesser transgressions I could commit, considering the rage I was feeling. I bought a bottle of cheap vodka on the way to a part of the city where most people didn't want to be stranded at night. Those were usually the places where the most fun could be had. I doubted Luca would get his panties in a bunch if I killed off the scum of his city. And if he did. Oh well.

Two hours later, I sat in a puddle of warm blood on the dirty floor of a biker meetup. Beside me on the ground, a biker took his last gurgling breaths, blood spurting out of his chest and throat wounds. I dropped my phone on the floor after I'd told Fabiano to pick me up. His voice still echoed from the speakers, but I wasn't listening.

I tried to count how many I'd killed, but it was a mess. I regarded the samurai sword in appreciation. It was my first time using one. I should probably thank the owner of the pub for having it on his wall. But I suspected he was among the chopped-up bodies around me.

Most of the events after I'd stepped into the establishment were blurry or blacked out. Sometimes when my fury rose too high and my blood lust took over, I became too frenzied to remember details.

I hung my head, the alcohol really taking effect now that my adrenaline and blood lust had ebbed away. I was battling unconsciousness. Dammit. The sound of police sirens made me tense.

"Fuck it," Fabiano muttered as he stepped inside, pushing a chopped-off calf out of the way with the bottom of the door.

I lifted my head to meet his gaze, even if it felt too heavy.

Fabiano stood in the center of the bar, still in his wedding suit, and he looked royally pissed.

Chapter Seven

Nevio

I grinned crookedly as Fabiano turned around himself to take in the full scope of the mess. "I thought you'd bring Luca along. Doesn't honor dictate it?"

Fabiano slanted a look over his shoulder, grimacing. "Luca is the groom's father. He shouldn't have to deal with *this* tonight."

"You came without a watchdog from the Famiglia?" I asked.

"He came with me," Matteo said as he stepped up to Fabiano, with his manic shark-grin.

Fabiano stalked over to me, trying not to get blood on his beige leather shoes. No chance.

"You should have worn other shoes," I said, pointing at my black dress shoes. They were probably ruined too, considering how squishy the inside felt, but you couldn't see it at first glance.

"Thanks for the advice. I don't know why I thought you'd act halfway human on a night like this."

"You mean the night Amo fucking Vitiello takes Greta away from us?"

"He'll probably take her virginity too," Matteo said with a hard smile.

I tightened my hold on the samurai sword and was about to push to my feet. But Fabiano kicked his heel down on the sword at an angle that broke the blade apart. Now, I held a short zig-zag sword in my hands. "I can still kill him with this, probably even create a messier and more painful result."

"Messier than this fuck show?" Fabiano growled, looking like he wanted to stab me with the samurai sword. He looked even more murderous than Matteo, come to think of it. He grabbed my arm tightly and jerked me up. I let him because I was fucking tired and just wanted to nap. "Drop the sword," he hissed, and I did even that.

He began patting me down and pulled green panties from my pockets. His eyebrows rose. For a moment, I considered asking him if he knew who those belonged to, but I'd already had enough fun tonight.

"If you fucked one of our women, I'll really enjoy slicing you up," Matteo said, who kept his distance from me, probably because he worried he'd actually choke me with his bare hands if he came close, though that move was more Luca's style.

"The only fun I had tonight was this." I motioned around myself. "But I'd be up for a post-kill fuck if you have someone in mind."

"Nobody wants to fuck you in the state you are in," Fabiano growled, dragging me toward the exit. Again, a stupid comment lay on the tip of my tongue. It wasn't self-preservation that stopped me, though. Funnily enough, I didn't want to talk like that about Rory, even if it was in jest.

"You can thank me later for getting rid of the police," Matteo said as we passed him.

"Thanks. That's what family is for. If you ever feel like causing a bloodbath in Las Vegas, ask me. I know the best spots."

"You'd probably try to kill me in your manic bloodlust, so no thanks."

I couldn't promise it wouldn't happen, so I didn't say anything.

Fabiano pushed me toward a black limousine and shoved me onto the passenger seat. He got in behind the steering wheel and didn't say anything for a couple of minutes before it burst out of him. "What the fuck is wrong with you? We all thought you'd grow out of this shit."

I chuckled. "How do you grow out of being a killer?"

Fabiano slanted me a look. "If you're always giving in like this, it'll control you. As a Capo and a man with a loving family, you need to be in control of it."

"That's why I'll never have my own family, because I don't want to control it."

"Don't want to or can't?"

I looked out of the window. Fuck if I knew.

"If you can't, then you should stick to your words and stay a lone wolf."

Aurora

The next morning at breakfast, Nevio looked as if he'd had a rough night. I didn't know details of what had transpired, only that Dad had to leave some time in the middle of the night to pick up Nevio, and he'd been in a foul mood when he'd returned.

Nevio's dark expression probably wasn't the result of a rough night, though. The upcoming bloody sheets show definitely had something to do with it too.

The Famiglia had established their tradition of showing the bloody sheets after a wedding night again recently, mainly to appease their conservative members. I had never witnessed a bloody sheet presentation before. Mom had always ensured we were somewhere else if one had transpired after a wedding we had attended, but in the Camorra, it rarely happened.

Today, I had decided to be present. I had to admit I was a bit curious about how these things were handled, and I wanted to see how Nevio handled it.

Eventually, Amo and Greta entered the room hand in hand, and a few women from the Famiglia presented the sheets. Embarrassment crawled up my neck when I saw the red on white. I was infinitely glad that the Camorra didn't follow this tradition.

"It's a barbaric tradition," Mom said, her cheeks red and disgust twisting her lips.

"That's the Famiglia for you," Dad said.

I really wasn't sure if Dad had reason to bash the Famiglia. The Camorra was barbaric in its own way, and I knew that many of the conservatives in our circle expected bloody sheets too, even if it wasn't officially approved of by the Capo.

Suddenly, a knife with a burning napkin attached to it hurtled through the room and pierced the sheets, which caught fire immediately. A few seconds later, they were completely aflame, and the fire alarm was set off. Cold water splashed down on us and everyone around.

I sucked in a sharp breath, my pulse picking up. The sound of laughter turned my head to where Nevio, Alessio, and Massimo were obviously celebrating. Nevio's eyes met mine, and he gave me a wink. This reminded me of yesterday, how he'd simply taken my panties. Had he thrown them away?

Why would he keep them?

We'd been back home in Las Vegas for a week, but tonight was the first time I would spend with the Unholy Trinity again.

I'd texted Greta a couple of times, and she'd seemed happy, but Nevio had been impossible to grab, so I wasn't sure how he was handling the separation from his twin.

Carlotta was allowed to spend the night at my place, so she and I went over to the Falcone premises around the time of our agreed meeting. We were supposed to have a movie night in Greta's former ballet studio, which had now been transformed into a cinema and gaming room with a pool table, dartboard, and a retro pinball machine. The guys were already inside when we arrived, spread out on the comfy armchairs in front of the TV. Carlotta and I shared the loveseat. Nevio was laughing at something Alessio had said. At first glance, he seemed perfectly at ease, but something in his eyes told me that wasn't the whole story.

As usual, we watched an action movie. Despite multiple discussions, they refused to watch anything that held a hint of emotional depth.

Usually, Diego picked up Carlotta at ten at the latest. He was strict with the curfew, but she was allowed to spend the night at my place today. At some point during the movie, I must have dozed off because the next thing I remembered was lying in near darkness with the TV off and without Carlotta by my side.

A shadow fell over me. My heart rate picked up.

"You missed the best part of the movie," Nevio said from above me.

I squinted up at him. He was half bent over me as if he was about to pick me up.

We were the only people still in the room. "Where's Carlotta?" I asked, sitting up in full concern mode. I would have smashed my forehead against Nevio's if he hadn't moved back quickly. The amused twitch of his mouth made me curse myself inwardly. This would have been the perfect moment for a kiss, right? And I messed it up. Well done, Rory, you stupid klutz.

"Massimo is carrying her over to your house. He didn't want to disturb her beauty sleep."

"Oh," I said hesitantly. Was that okay for Carlotta? Diego would definitely throw a fit if he found out.

Nevio stood. "She's safe, don't worry."

He held out his hand and pulled me to my feet, bringing us close once more. And again the realization that we were alone in the studio crashed into my head.

His pondering face was close to mine and slowly morphed into a mischievous expression.

"Your dad found your panties in my pocket when he picked me up on the night of the wedding."

"What?" Utter horror mixed with mortification flooded me. "Did you tell him they were mine?"

Nevio cocked an eyebrow, on the verge of laughter judging from the twitch of his mouth.

Of course he hadn't. We wouldn't be standing here if he had. "He would have kicked your ass."

Nevio smirked. "He would have tried to kill me. He was pissed off at me anyway."

I nodded, still trying not to freak out over the fact that Dad had found my panties in Nevio's pocket. Then another thought struck me. "Why did you have them with you anyway? You were supposed to throw them away."

"Must have forgotten, was a busy night after all," he said with a shrug, as if it was everyday business to carry my panties around in his pocket, and nodded toward the door. "Come on. I'll take you home."

I tried to figure out if he'd told the truth, but I didn't want to make a bigger deal out of this than it was. Nevio had probably seen hundreds of girl panties in his life. Why would he care about mine?

"I walk our premises alone all the time," I said, then wanted to kick myself. If Nevio wanted to spend more time with me alone, I should be the last person to argue.

"Strange things happen all the time," Nevio said ominously.

We left the studio together and strolled over the lawn toward my home. Two windows were still illuminated, the living room where Dad or Mom were probably still waiting for my return, and the other was my bedroom window.

"Will you and the rest of the trio go out tonight?" I asked curiously. It wasn't even midnight yet, so I suspected they still had something more entertaining to do than watch sleeping girls.

Nevio looked up at the night sky with a sly smile. "I think the night is ripe with opportunity, so yes."

I wondered if that meant they would head to a club or go out on one of their raids. The first time I'd realized what they did at night—or the basics of what they did—I had been utterly devastated and shocked, though I wasn't even sure why. Dad had always told me that the Unholy Trinity was dangerous—not for me, thank God—and that I shouldn't let them pull me into their trouble. I followed Nevio's gaze up to the sky, wondering what exactly drew him to the night, to the darkness.

"I like how peaceful nights are," I said softly.

Nevio smirked. "Of course, you do, Rory." He drew in a deep breath as if he was sniffing the air for a trail. "I like how much potential for havoc the darkness holds. The same night sky, two very different perspectives."

I didn't know what to say to that, so I nodded. Once again, it felt like a simple conversation attempt had brought even more distance between us. The back door to our patio swung open, and Dad waited in the doorway.

Nevio tipped an invisible head. "Where's Massimo?"

By Frenzy I *Pain*

"At your mansion," Dad said and motioned for me to come in. I stepped up to his side. "Thanks for taking me home."

Dad glanced between Nevio and me. "Always the gentleman," he said dryly.

Nevio grinned at him, waved at me, and left. Soon, his tall form disappeared in the shadows.

"Carlotta is up in your bedroom with your mom."

"Okay," I said with a tired smile.

Dad was watching me in a way I couldn't quite place, and I was too tired to try. Trying not to embarrass myself in front of Nevio had taken enough out of me.

When I arrived at my door, Mom just pulled it shut. "There you are. Carlotta is getting ready."

Mom pressed a kiss to my cheek, and I slipped into my bedroom. I turned off the main light in favor of my dimmed down night-light, then I perched on the windowsill. It didn't take long until three shadows moved across the lawn, dressed in black. They carried backpacks, and Alessio wore a black balaclava. A shiver passed my spine.

"I don't know why they have to do this at night when they're already doing so much for the Camorra during the day," Carlotta murmured when she came up behind me.

I'd often asked myself that question too. "Maybe it's the thrill of the forbidden."

"I wonder if this is more Nevio's doing, and Alessio and Massimo just join him out of solidarity."

I pursed my lips. "Alessio and Massimo aren't innocent bystanders either."

"I know," Carlotta said softly, but I could hear that she disagreed.

I had been surprised when Mom and Dad had agreed to let me go to Roger's Arena on a fight night. For a long time, even my argument that Davide had been allowed to go for a while had seemed invalid in comparison to their need to protect me. Dad was overly protective of me, but in this case, I was certain that Mom had been the one who had been against it more. She loathed the cage fights and was anxious weeks before Dad's fights. They had become less frequent in recent years, but on occasion, he and the Falcone brothers still showed their strength in the cages.

"Are you sure you don't want to ride with us?" Mom asked again as I put on my favorite white sneakers in our entry hall.

"She'll be fine, Leona," Dad said with a hint of amusement. "Let her soak up the pre-fight atmosphere with the trio."

Mom sank her teeth into her lower lip. "I'm just worried they're already too caught up in their fight mode and will be reckless."

"It's a short drive, and I'm sure Massimo will be the one driving." Dad went over to Mom and grabbed her shoulders, rubbing them lightly. "Relax. You're tenser than on my fight nights."

I giggled. "Mom, you realize I won't be in the cage tonight, right?"

Mom huffed. "You two shouldn't gang up on me. And trust me, Aurora, seeing a fight on screen and seeing it live are two very different things."

I had watched only one recorded fight a couple of days ago. It had been one of Dad's old fights, and it had made me squeamish. Not because of the blood—I had no trouble with that, but the brutality with which Dad had acted had unsettled me. I only knew a different version of him. I could only imagine how much more impressive it would be to see a live fight, especially as I'd heard stories of how brutal the fights of the trio were.

My phone beeped with a message from Carlotta.

On my way.

I smiled in relief. I had worried that Carlotta would bail. She wasn't too fond of blood and definitely didn't enjoy fighting as much as her sister, Gemma, did, who had had fight training when she was our age. Diego would drive her to the fight, though. He was in the arena more than any other Camorrista because of his wife, Antonia, who had inherited the bar from her father, Roger.

I got up and regarded myself critically in the mirror. It had probably taken me way too long to decide what to wear to an event where nobody would be dressed up or pay attention to what I was wearing. Eventually, I'd settled on tight black jeans and a burgundy off-the-shoulder crop top.

"It's cool inside the arena. You should put a cardigan on," Dad said pointedly.

Mom rolled her eyes. "It's sweltering in there. She'll be fine."

I bit my lip, close to laughing. The doorbell rang, and Dad opened it after a look at the camera. Nevio stood in front of the door. It was the first time someone other than Carlotta picked me up at my door. Usually, I went over to the Falcone mansion when I spent time with the trio. This felt oddly like a date, even if I knew it *definitely* wasn't.

Nevio was dressed in black pants, a black tee, and black sneakers, nothing out of the ordinary, and his grin wasn't as tense as I would have expected on the night of a fight.

Dad appeared behind me and put a hand on my shoulder. His expression was hostile. He acted as if Nevio and I had a date, and he had to scare him to behave. My cheeks warmed, and I nudged his side inconspicuously with my elbow. What was his problem? He could see Alessio and Massimo in the car in front of our house. This definitely wasn't a date.

"Get Aurora to the arena safely."

Nevio didn't seem overly concerned by Dad's threatening undertone. "Massimo is driving, and I don't need road rage to get me in the mood for a bloody fight."

Dad shook his head, one corner of his mouth pulling up in a way that suggested he knew.

"Come on, Rory, before your dad delivers a few more threats he picked up in chick flicks." Stifling laughter, I stepped up beside Nevio and followed him to the car. He opened the back door for me so I could climb in. Now this really felt like a date. A date with his two best friends along for the ride…

"We'll arrive shortly after you," Dad said as a way of goodbye, making it sound more like a warning than a mere piece of information.

"Not if Massimo races through every red light on the way," Nevio shouted as he closed my door, then hopped into the passenger seat. Dad gave him a look that suggested he would join his opponent in the cage tonight and give him a thrashing.

Nevio waved, and with squealing tires, Massimo pulled the car away from the driveway.

I looked back to see Dad still watching our departure. He was pissed.

Nevio turned up the music, something about a "pelvis being on fire," which made me pull a face—because of the lyrics and the melody.

"A good night for a fight," Nevio mused, his arm propped up on the rolled down window as the wind tore at his hair.

Nevio didn't seem to be in fight mode. He was relaxed and in a joking mood, as if we were heading to a party.

I was surprised that he didn't take this fight seriously. Massimo was silent and focused. Maybe that was because he was driving, but I had a feeling it had more to do with his fight, and Alessio had earphones in, and his eyes were closed. That was how I imagined someone to look who was about to get into a potentially life-threatening fight. It happened a few times a year that people died in the cage, and in recent years, the number had grown. From what I heard, it was mainly because of Nevio's fights.

Massimo parked the car in one of the designated spots in front of Roger's Arena. I had to admit I was nervous about tonight. I didn't want to embarrass myself in front of everyone. I hopped out of the car, and Nevio joined my side, strolling along like this was business as usual. A few customers stood outside of the bar to smoke, and they mustered us curiously as we passed them by.

"Nervous?" Nevio asked as we headed toward the steel door of Roger's Arena. I'd never been inside before, but Carlotta had told me many stories because she had accompanied Diego there during closing hours on occasion to visit Antonia.

I gave him an embarrassed smile. "Shouldn't I ask you that question? I'm not going to enter a cage for a brutal fight."

Nevio flashed me a grin that was full of eagerness. "Are you nervous before you step on your skateboard?"

"No, but it's not the same."

"Why? Fighting is in my blood. When you step on the skateboard, you risk your health too."

"The risk is low. You know you'll get hurt when you step inside the cage. It's inevitable. If I perform a trick well, I definitely won't even suffer a bruise." I had had a few harder falls in the past, but nothing too bad, not even a broken bone so far. My brother, though he'd been skating for fewer years, had already suffered a broken arm and rib. Of course, he sometimes acted like a lunatic, which made accidents more likely.

By Frenzy I *Pain*

"I don't mind getting hurt, and I know my opponent will be far worse off than me."

There wasn't a bouncer at the door. I suppose if you entered the arena intending to cause trouble, there would be many willing participants to teach you a lesson you wouldn't soon forget.

"It's more unsettling for spectators to watch Nevio fight than for him to actually do it," Alessio muttered as he stepped up to us. It was the first time he'd taken his earphones out, but an air of concentration still surrounded him.

Nevio opened the door for me and winked at Alessio. "That's just how I like it."

Chapter Eight

Aurora

When we stepped inside, my breath halted. The bar was filled to the brim with guests, mainly men. Every table was occupied and even the booth along the concrete walls. People who hadn't found a seating place stood against the walls to watch the spectacle as well. The wall beside the bar was decorated with red neon tubes encircled with barbed wire that said words like Blood, Sweat, and Courage. The stench of smoke, sweat, and alcohol carried in the air. Some guests smoked inside, so I wasn't sure why the others had fled outside to do so. My eyes were drawn to the huge fighting cage in the center. The mesh looked like chicken wire, but I knew it was much sturdier to withstand the impacts. Two men and a referee were inside of it as the first fight of the evening was about to begin.

Nevio threw his arm around my shoulders with a teasing smile and took a deep breath. I was momentarily startled by his closeness, especially in such a public place. Even if this was a solely friendly gesture, people in our circles loved to draw the wrong conclusions and spread false rumors.

"This is the scent of pure adrenaline. Isn't it intoxicating?" Nevio asked in a low, compelling voice.

I drew in another, slightly deeper breath, and was once again hit with the odor of sweat and alcohol. I gave Nevio a doubtful look.

I spotted Carlotta in a booth with Diego. Antonia was at their table too, but you could tell from her stressed expression that she was on the jump to get back to work behind the bar. Her cocktails were famous, so she was definitely needed back there.

Carlotta spotted me, her eyes darting between Nevio and me, then his arm around me, before she waved me toward them.

"Do you need to get changed?" I asked the guys.

"Not yet," Nevio said. We all headed over to Diego and Carlotta. Dozens of gazes followed us, and I could see that many of them lingered on Nevio and me. Rumors would definitely be floating around soon. Just what I needed to get Dad off my back.

"You realize people will think you're staking your claim on Aurora, right?" Carlotta said the moment the guys and I arrived at the table.

I gave her a shocked look. She was usually such a calm person, but Nevio really brought out the tiger in her.

Nevio bared his teeth. "Let them draw whatever conclusions they want. That's not my problem."

"But it's Aurora's. If guys think she's yours, nobody will approach her parents to ask for her hand."

Nevio let out a laugh. "How about you worry about your own untouchable status because it's firming up." He looked at Massimo, who had his eyes on Carlotta with a look everyone around would understand as possessive.

Carlotta flushed as she glanced at her brother Diego, who'd listened to everything with utmost interest. "No stake-claiming whatsoever, understood?" he growled at the guys, then briefly smiled at me before giving the guys another stern look. "I'm going to talk to a few people. I assume you'll be around until your fights."

"Sure thing," Nevio said, drawing me closer to his side. I knew it was meant as a friendly gesture, but under everyone's attention, I still blushed as if he'd kissed me. Diego didn't comment, only left with a shake of his head. It felt good to be pressed up to Nevio's muscled body like that. The back of my head touched his pec, and his fingers were hot against the bare skin of my shoulder.

We all slipped into the booth and ordered drinks, but I was distracted by the whistle of the referee that announced the start of the first fight. I watched with parted lips as both opponents stormed each other like crazy rhinos and began to pummel each other with fists. Blood spurted out of the mouth of the man on the left, but it didn't stop him, even when he spit something on the ground.

"That was his front tooth," Nevio said with a nod. My lips curled in disgust.

"Not bad," Alessio added.

Carlotta sent me a slightly nauseated look. I gave her a shaky smile. Worse than the sight of the blood and brutality were the sounds of a fist or foot hitting another person. The first fight was over within fifteen minutes. The winner grinned his missing-tooth smile at the masses, covered in blood and sweat. His opponent needed support from a friend to get out of the cage. He shook his head at the nurse who offered to check on him. The Camorra employed several doctors and nurses for the fights and the Made Men who got injured on duty.

"A fight shouldn't be over before one of the fighters can't stand," Nevio muttered with a disgusted twist of his mouth.

"If every fight ended fatally or with serious injuries, Antonia wouldn't find fighters for the fights anymore," I said. Dad had mentioned how difficult it was to find people who agreed to fight Nevio.

"You underestimate the number of desperate souls out there," Alessio said.

Maybe. I remembered how Grandma had been on her bad days, when she needed more drugs than Dad had rationed for her, when her despair streamed out of her every pore. She probably would have entered a cage too if it promised relief.

Two hours later, it was Nevio's turn. He didn't bother going into the changing room. He simply got up and pulled his T-shirt over his head right beside me. My eyes did their usual routine of scanning his abs, pecs, biceps, and of course my insides warmed at the sight.

I'd never really paid close attention to the tattoo on his back. It was impossible not to look at it of course. the grotesque smile of the Joker (just the mouth, not the rest of his face), the "Why so serious?" in blurred red letters, followed by a long string of crossed out HAHAHAHA. I was fairly sure there had been less crossed out haha-ha's the last time I'd seen Nevio without a shirt. Alessio leaned over to me. "It's his tally list."

I pursed my lips. "Of won fights?" I asked, but I didn't remember any fights since I'd last seen his back. Maybe he counted test fights as well? The number of H and A seemed too low for that, considering how often Nevio had fight training with Massimo, Alessio, and the other men of his family. On the other hand, he always had strong opponents, so even as someone with his talent, he couldn't always win.

Nevio walked toward the cage at a relaxed pace, every muscle in his back flexing in the most tantalizing way, and even though his fight shorts were loose, you could see his firm ass in them. Some people pointed at the tattoo on his back, and their expressions varied from impressed to concerned.

"Not quite," Alessio said. "It's the number of people he killed. He only got the tattoo this year, but he remembered every fucking kill of his life. Not bad for someone who doesn't remember the last party."

I blinked, swallowed, my gaze darting between Nevio's back and Alessio's amused face. Was he pulling my leg?

"I'm not joking," he said. His expression suggested I needed a reality check.

"He's not," Massimo said matter-of-factly. My gaze found Nevio again, but from a distance, and at my current angle, I had no way of counting just how many crossed-out letters there were.

"How many letters are there?" I asked quietly.

"Every vertical line of each letter stands for a kill. So one H equals two kills."

"What about the horizontal cross-out line?" I asked a bit tonelessly. As if it mattered. There had been many letters on Nevio's back, even more vertical lines. Way too many.

"They're just for fun, no meaning," Alessio said. "You probably shouldn't count next time you see him close-up." He smiled strangely. "Or maybe you should."

Carlotta shook her head with a disgusted expression, then narrowed her eyes at Massimo. "Do you have a tally list too?"

Alessio chuckled and shook his head.

"I don't require one," Massimo said with an expression that suggested he wasn't sure why Carlotta would even ask.

"He has a mental one."

"And you?" I cocked an eyebrow. "You three always hang out together. I doubt you're only sitting by while Nevio and Massimo kill people." I lowered my voice for the last part as if anyone in this arena didn't know they were killers. The noise level had risen up to painful dimensions when Nevio climbed up the steps to the cage, so I doubted anyone could eavesdrop anyway.

"Oh, I'm not any better or worse than those two, but I'm not the one smooching with you girls."

Massimo gave him an exasperated look.

The door to the changing room opened, and Nevio's opponent stepped out. He was sturdier than Nevio, very muscled but not as defined. A bit of fat had accumulated around his belly. He had a thorn crown inked into his bald skull and a huge skull with Jesus on his chest. The marks of the staking were also tattooed into his wrists and ankles, and his smile was on the verge of insanity.

"He looks crazy," Carlotta whispered, appalled.

"He is clinically insane," Massimo commented with a casual shrug as he leaned back in the booth.

"Should he even be here then? He can't make rational decisions in his state."

Massimo regarded Carlotta with furrowed brows. "Fighters don't have to be sane."

Alessio chuckled. "By society's standards, none of us are sane considering our murderous tendencies."

Carlotta looked truly concerned. She lightly touched Massimo's forearm. "Still. I feel sorry for him."

"He thinks he's the incarnation of Jesus, and he attacked a couple of priests because their sermon suggested otherwise," Massimo said.

Carlotta's eyes widened, and she looked at the man, who'd by now reached the cage. "Wow."

"Would you prefer to go outside with me while Nevio fights?" Massimo asked quietly.

I exchanged a look with Alessio, who rolled his eyes with a dry chuckle.

"I'll be fine," Carlotta said with a shaky smile.

"Just tell me if you need to go out."

Stifling a laugh, I turned back to the cage, my belly twisting with nerves. Nevio's opponent was insane, and insanity could be dangerous. People developed incredible strength if driven by madness. When the man entered the cage, I realized just how much taller and broader than Nevio he was. He was half a head taller than Nevio, who was already 6'4, and he had probably at least sixty pounds on him, though looks could be deceiving. Nevio was all muscle, and those weighed more than fat. Still, fear filled me as I watched the man cross himself with a too-wide grin.

Nevio leaned against the cage with crossed arms and regarded his opponent with condescension. He didn't look concerned in the slightest.

"This will be a long fight," Alessio muttered, supporting himself on his elbows and blowing out a long breath.

"You think the guy can beat Nevio?" I whispered.

Massimo shook his head. "No. But Nevio usually toys with these kinds of opponents."

His relaxed stance changed the moment the referee left the cage and locked the door. I still couldn't detect a sign of nervousness. He looked hungry and lethal, his dark eyes locked on his opponent with a deadly determination that sent a chill down my spine. Then one corner of his mouth darted up, but this smile—if you could even call it by that name—reminded me so much of the Joker smile on his back that my belly fluttered anxiously.

"I'm divine. Bow at my greatness!" the man shouted.

Nevio pushed himself away from the cage. "First, I'll shut you up."

The man barreled toward him with a fervor that had the entire cage rattling and shaking under the force of his heavy steps. Nevio sidestepped the attack and aimed a kick at the man's back, sending him flying against the cage. He whirled around, a wound at his head bleeding, and Nevio's bare foot hit him under the jaw. The crack of the bone echoed through the arena.

Carlotta raised her palms in front of her face, but I couldn't take my eyes off the equally brutal and grotesque display.

Massimo and Alessio had been right. Nevio did indeed play with his opponent, kicking and beating him hard, choking him, only to let up and give him time to breathe and recover for another futile attack. Instead of staying on the ground and playing dead like any sane person would have done, the guy attacked Nevio every time, mumbling unintelligent things as he did.

After almost forty minutes, I could see Nevio growing bored, so he aimed a brutal kick against the man's head. He toppled backward, making the whole cage shake as he collided with the floor and blood spread under him.

Carlotta jumped up, squeezed past me, and rushed outside, followed by Massimo, who gave Diego a sign that he would handle the situation. However, unsurprisingly, Diego still followed them outside.

The referee raised Nevio's arm above his head as Nevio stared down at his opponent lying at his feet with a look that made it clear he wanted to finish him. To be honest, I wasn't sure if he had already succeeded. A doctor and nurse rushed into the cage and began treating the guy.

"Maybe you won't believe it, but this is still the tame version of Nevio's monster," Alessio murmured.

I tore my eyes away from the cage to meet Alessio's gaze.

"Still no second thoughts?"

I pursed my lips. He chuckled and shrugged.

The clang of the cage door drew my attention back to the cage where Nevio was climbing down the steps. He didn't return to the changing room, though. Instead, he headed straight to the entrance door and went outside. The doc and nurse administered CPR, then let up.

By Frenzy I Pain

"Another one for the tally list," Alessio said.

"I'll check on Nevio," I said apologetically. "Are you okay here by yourself?"

Alessio gave me a grin. "Don't worry about me."

Nevio

I stalked past Massimo and Diego, who were trying to console a distraught-looking Carlotta. What had she expected? I bet Diego had told her enough horror stories so this fight couldn't have been a surprise. I wasn't in the mood for this shit.

I didn't stop until I reached the back of the building where the dumpsters were, far away from damsels in distress. There I leaned against the wall and stared up at the night sky. It never really got dark in the city. The lights masked the sky's true blackness, making it appear less all-consuming than it was.

I chuckled and ran a hand through my sweaty hair. My heart rate had already come down. Fights like this rarely kept up my adrenaline for long.

They weren't satisfying. I liked the thrill of the hunt, the panic of an unsuspecting victim, the freedom of torturing someone to death by whatever means that struck my fancy that day. Cage fights were tame entertainment for the masses. They weren't what I craved. They were like a small tease, a minuscule starter that only made you hungry for more.

Fuck, I wanted to maim and kill. I hoped Alessio and Massimo were still in the mood for a raid after their fights.

Soft steps sounded. My head whirled around, the hunter jumping at the chance of having a quick fix, but my eyes landed on Aurora. She hovered near the corner of the building and watched me with concern-filled eyes. "Are you okay?"

Another carnal need reared its head, one I'd never felt around Rory. One I'd never allowed myself around her. She took a few steps toward me. My eyes took in her elegant shoulders, narrow waist, and defined belly. Then I dragged my gaze back up to her face.

It was so full of innocent worry for me that I got a fucking grip on myself. I really needed to head out for a hunt.

"Is he dead?" I asked.

"Yes. They tried CPR, but it was futile," Aurora said quietly. There was no judgment in her voice, no drama or pity either.

I nodded. I'd known the last kick would do him in. I'd hoped it would give me a greater sense of satisfaction but no.

Aurora came closer and stopped in front of me, holding out a tissue. "I forgot to pick up a towel on the way. But this is good for his blood on your face."

"I don't see where it is," I said. Not that I cared if I had his blood on my skin. I'd been covered in people's blood from head to toe before. It was half the fun of torture.

"Do you want me to clean your face?" Aurora asked, holding up the tissue.

"Sure." I watched her closely as she gently touched the tissue to my cheek, then my chin and forehead.

"Do I have something on my face?" she asked with a nervous laugh, her blue eyes searching mine.

"Always the wrong emotion."

Her brows pulled together. She lowered her hand with the tissue. I shook my head with a dark chuckle and straightened from the wall, bringing Aurora and me closer. "Always compassion, understanding, concern…" I trailed off because the other emotions I sometimes caught on her face were even more dangerous.

I touched two fingers to her cheek and bent down until our lips were almost touching. Aurora froze, her eyes widening, lips parting. Hope shone on her face. Hope for what? The only thing I could give her was a hard fuck against this wall with my fingers around her throat. My pulse quickened, my heart beating faster than during any moment of my fight tonight.

"One day, there's going to be hate on your face when you look at me, and that'll be the right emotion, Rory."

I kissed her cheek right by the corner of her mouth. The scent of her lip gloss, like my favorite cookie dough, filled my nose. I pulled back. Rory's eyes darted all over my face in utter confusion.

Someone cleared their throat, and I stepped away from Aurora, then headed to Diego who watched me wearily. When I tried to pass him by, he grabbed my forearm. "This could have been Fabiano instead of me."

By Frenzy I *Pain*

"I guess we're lucky it wasn't," I murmured with a hungry smile. Because tonight I wasn't sure if I would have held back the monster even against someone who I had known all my life. Diego shook his head and released me. He glanced at Rory, who was still standing by the dumpsters, and watched us in confusion.

Diego had the look of someone who had been forced to witness a ninety-pound bulldog lick a baby because the parents thought the beast could be tamed.

I turned and headed into the night. I wouldn't wait for Alessio and Massimo. I needed the hunt now.

Chapter Nine

Aurora

With Nevio, it always felt like I was taking one step forward, only for him to push me two steps back. I hadn't talked to Carlotta about Nevio's cryptic words after the fight. I wouldn't have talked to anyone else either, but Diego had mentioned what he'd seen to my father. Of course, he had. He was always protective of Carlotta and seemed to think he could shove his nose into my business too.

Mom and Dad had both confronted me after we'd returned home from the fight.

"Diego shared something he witnessed tonight," Dad had said gravely as if he were talking about an inexcusable crime.

I hadn't processed my strange encounter with Nevio yet, so being confronted by my parents about it came as a shock.

"Sit," Mom said, motioning to the kitchen chair across from them.

I sank down, trying to keep my face in check. It had been a near miracle

By Frenzy I *Rain*

that I was allowed to attend the fight. If I gave the wrong answers now, I'd never be allowed to go anywhere fun, and I definitely wanted to attend an upcoming party the Unholy Trinity had mentioned.

"Diego has an overactive imagination. I'm surprised he doesn't force Carlotta to wear a chastity belt." I felt a bit guilty for talking about him that way. He was an okay guy and was trying to raise Carlotta as well as he could with their parents dead.

Dad narrowed his eyes at me. "He caught you in the back alley with Nevio. And I quote, his lips almost touched hers when I walked in on them."

"Almost," I said with no little amount of scorn. For one, I was really mad. Mad at Nevio for this ridiculous kiss. After the one on my forehead from the wedding, I'd hoped next time would be a decent kiss—mouth on mouth. "Nevio kissed my cheek because I'd cleaned his face with a tissue. If his lips came close to mine, then it was because it was dark."

Dad raised one eyebrow. "It wasn't too dark for Diego to see it."

"What do you want from me? Nothing happened between Nevio and me, and nothing will. He kissed my cheek. That's it. You always think the worst of Nevio. You seem to know him better than I do, so do you really think he'd only kiss my cheek like a good boy if he were interested in me?" That last sentence hurt a little because I wondered the same.

"She has a point," Mom said, and I could have hugged her.

"Maybe. But I still want you to be careful around him. If I think something is going on between you two, I'll sell this damn place, and we'll move to another city. I'll ask Remo to let me work as enforcer in LA or San Francisco."

I rolled my eyes. "Dad, please. Nothing will ever happen between Nevio and me."

"Is this too much?" I asked as I turned around to show Carlotta every angle of my outfit for the party.

"I wouldn't say there's any part of this outfit that's too much… of fabric," Carlotta said, then giggled at her own joke.

I glanced down at myself. This outfit was the sexiest I'd ever been. I had opted for a white blouse that I'd tugged up with a knot so I showed my belly. The top buttons of the shirt were also open to show a little cleavage, and I wore a leather mini skirt that I'd found in the back of Mom's dresser. I wished I could ask her when she'd worn it, but that would probably be too suspicious. Better wait until after the party.

"Is it too sexy?" I asked.

While Carlotta had chosen a short summer dress for the occasion that showed plenty of curves and leg, it looked cute on her and not too sexy. I was worried I would look like I was trying too hard.

She pursed her lips. "You should feel sexy in it. That's the main objective."

"The main objective? Massimo has rubbed off on you."

She tugged a strand behind her ear. "He uses it on occasion when we discuss our different viewpoints."

I rolled my eyes. Those two were flirting in the weirdest way. But who was I to judge?

"I feel sexy, but also a little like I'm not me. Which is good if I want to catch Nevio's eyes since good ole me isn't doing the trick." If he kissed me on the forehead, cheek, or hand tonight, I'd seriously lose my shit around him for the first time. I was done with this.

"You shouldn't have to be someone else to attract someone, Aurora."

I shrugged. "Seems to be my only option right now."

"No, it's not. You could just show Nevio every version of you. In the past few years, you've become someone different around him. You don't show any sass or answer back to him. You're tongue-tied around him. That's the problem."

I sighed because I knew Carlotta had a point. I really wasn't sure what to do about it, though, since my mind seemed to go blank with him around.

"I'll start with this outfit, and maybe my brain and tongue will come around by tonight."

A knock sounded, and Gemma poked her head in. My heart almost jumped out of my chest, thinking it was Mom. If she saw me in this outfit, she'd probably not allow me to attend the party. I'd fought too hard for my parents' permission to lose it now. She slipped in, and her eyes widened. "No way can you go out like that."

"Are you channeling your inner Diego?" Carlotta asked pointedly.

Gemma gave her an annoyed look. "I'm just being realistic. If Fabiano sees Aurora like that, he won't let her go. Should I be worried about who you want to impress?" Gemma narrowed her eyes at me.

"In this day and age, girls can dress sexy for themselves, Gemma. We don't need or want to impress boys anymore," Carlotta said.

"You act like I'm sixty," Gemma said, then raised her eyebrows. "Since when is she so argumentative?"

"Since she argues with Massimo on a daily basis."

Gemma tilted her head in curiosity, and Carlotta sent me a shut-up look. She usually shared everything with Gemma, so I was surprised she hadn't mentioned her endless arguments with him to her sister.

"His viewpoints are impossible. I have to argue with him," she said with a shrug. She was good at making this seem like nothing. Her nonchalance was impressive, and I needed to learn from it.

"All right," Gemma said slowly. "Do what you want, but you better put one of your overalls on as cover before you leave this room."

My overall. Everyone always pretended I wore them all the time. I had plenty of different clothes in my wardrobe. And I definitely wouldn't go to a party in them! I grabbed one of my overall dresses, put it over my party clothes, and tugged my blouse down to cover my midriff.

"If I'm supposed to do your makeup and hair, we need to hurry," Gemma reminded us.

Fifteen minutes later, we left my room. Dad wasn't home yet, which was good because I still expected him to retract his permission at any moment. Mom only briefly checked my outfit and told me to be careful. Carlotta and I followed Gemma to her and Savio's wing of the mansion. Gemma had set up a table with plenty of makeup and a chair in front of it. There were also snacks. I half wished we'd actually stay for a girls' night. I wasn't really a party girl, which was probably why I'd never been to one. I liked dancing, but I preferred doing it in a different atmosphere. The relaxed parties at the race track, when I'd babysat Roman for Adamo and Dinara, were nice and chill, but I wouldn't back out now and risk looking like the biggest Goody Two-shoes in front of Nevio and the other guys.

Carlotta popped a few chips into her mouth while Gemma began to do my makeup.

"Do you want fake lashes?" Gemma asked eventually, holding up an assortment of lashes.

I quickly shook my head. I'd once worn fake lashes, and they'd driven me completely crazy.

When Gemma finished our makeup, it was already time to leave.

"Be careful, okay?" she said firmly.

"Massimo, Nevio, and Alessio will keep an eye on us. Nobody will bother us with them as our bodyguards."

"Pardon me when I'm not convinced these three will keep you out of trouble."

"You're breaking my heart, Gemma," Nevio said from his spot in the doorway to the patio.

We all jumped, not having heard him approach.

"Turn down the creep factor, will you?" Gemma muttered, causing Nevio's grin to widen. "And you don't have a heart I could break."

Nevio looked from Gemma to Carlotta to me. "How come Gemma looks like she's about to go to a party, and one of you looks like she's attending a picnic in a park, and the other looks like she's hitting the half-pipe?"

I flushed immediately. Then kicked myself in the butt because I wanted to follow Carlotta's advice and not be a goddamn punching bag around Nevio. "What's your fashion style called? Out of the morgue?"

Nevio cocked an eyebrow, his answering grin giving me heart palpitations. He let his gaze move down his body, and my eyes followed as if drawn by an invisible force. He was in a tight black tee with a black leather jacket and black cargo pants that fit enough to show off his trained body, especially his booty. I knew because he'd worn these pants around me before. Black boots rounded the outfit off.

Nevio motioned at his watch, which also had black carbon on a red face. "Time to leave. Come on, girls."

Carlotta and I followed him down into the basement. He led us through the corridors until I lost my bearings. I rarely went down here anyway, but I had a feeling most people would have lost their orientation by now. "Why are we down here?"

"Because we want to get you to your first party in style!"

We moved through a hidden door behind a shelf and eventually arrived at a steel door. Nevio entered a code into the keypad, and it opened with a groan. Behind it was a tunnel. The steel door closed behind us the moment we stepped through. A massive steel gate was in front of us, separating us from the rest of the tunnel. It smelled dank and as if someone had emptied their bladder close by. A motorcycle leaned against the wall inside the gate.

"What is this place?" Carlotta asked with a wrinkled nose.

Graffiti covered the walls, and puddles littered the ground. The tunnel had a sort of oval shape, and it wasn't very high in this part. There were maybe three hand-width between Nevio's head and the ceiling.

"There's a labyrinth of tunnels beneath Las Vegas. More than a thousand homeless live there. It's also a hub for criminal activity of course."

"Camorra operated?" I asked.

"Nah. This part of the underworld is not directly controlled by us, which is why some individuals come here hoping to keep their profits to themselves."

"So your dad doesn't care?"

"As long as it's not a big part of business, he thinks people who live like rats should be treated like one. The only time the Camorra intervened was when your grandma tried to purchase drugs down here away from your dad's watchful eyes."

I swallowed hard. Dad and Mom had never mentioned anything. It was disconcerting that Nevio knew more about my family than I did.

"Is it dangerous down here?" Carlotta asked, rubbing her arms.

"Definitely. During flash floods, you need to seek a high spot or drown. If you're referring to the people living down here, they won't bother us."

Nevio grabbed the motorcycle and entered a number into another keypad, so the gates in front of us swung open.

"Girls, choose your spot," he said, motioning at the bike. He sat as close to the handlebars as possible, leaving little room for us. We'd really have to press together.

Carlotta looked horrified.

"I know you've ridden on a bike with Massimo before, but I suppose you have a lower tolerance for feeling up my six-pack than his," Nevio mused, then jabbed a thumb to the spot right behind him. "That's your place, then." He flashed his teeth at me. "You can hug Rory."

I wasn't sure if he was insinuating that I didn't mind touching his six-pack. If so, he was right, though this wasn't how I envisioned it. I perched on the bike behind him. "What am I supposed to do with my legs?"

"Keep them off the ground," Nevio said.

I had to press my crotch against Nevio's ass and press my front against his back so Carlotta had enough room to sit. I wrapped my arms around Nevio and pressed my palms flat against his stomach. My cheeks burned, and heat flushed the rest of my body at our closeness. I could feel the hard ridges of his six-pack through his thin tee. Every part of Nevio was hard. Well, almost every part of him. The thought made my cheeks heat furiously. I'd often dreamed about running my fingertips over his abs and down to the delicious V I often saw when he trained or when we were at the pool together.

Carlotta slung her arms tighter around my waist when Nevio started the engine. The sound carried in the tunnel and amplified until my ears rang from the roar.

Carlotta let out a little screech when we jerked forward, and then I heard nothing but the wind rushing in my ears and the angry roar of the motorcycle as Nevio weaved past dirty puddles at a maddening pace. I wasn't sure how he even knew where to go or how he could see anything ahead of us in the unsettling darkness of the tunnels, which the small headlights could hardly penetrate. I supposed he and the rest of the Unholy Trinity had spent plenty of time down here over the years, which was easily as unsettling as the tunnels themselves.

On occasion, I caught a glimpse of life in one of the tunnel branches, flashlights or fires, tents and moving shadows. Headlights in the distance made me tense. But I realized they weren't directly pointing at us and not moving. A car waited at the opening of the tunnel. We drove up a slope and finally hit open air. Nevio hit the brakes and brought us to a standstill beside the car: his Dodge Ram.

Carlotta still clung to me even when Nevio turned off the engine.

Massimo hopped out of the car. Alessio remained seated in the back with his arm propped up on the open window.

"Fuck him playing the gent," Nevio said in a low voice to me when Massimo helped a shaking Carlotta off the bike. "Damsel in distress never worked on him before."

By Frenzy I *Pain*

I laughed. "I think Lotta doesn't have the stomach for rides like these. It was intense."

"But you do, skater girl," Nevio said. Did he sound impressed?

Carlotta stumbled toward the car, and for a moment, I was sure she'd throw up, but then she squared her shoulders and climbed into the back seat with Massimo.

"You have to ride in the front with me. It seems Massimo has to play doctor."

I got off the bike, trying not to show that my legs felt like rubber too. I had actually enjoyed the ride more than I'd thought, but I wasn't used to the speed in combination with the stench of sewerage.

Nevio opened the door for me in a rare act of chivalry and held out his hand, palm upward in a mocking gentleman's gesture. I stifled a grin and took his hand, then climbed into the passenger seat.

I turned around to Carlotta. She still looked pale, and suddenly, I worried about her heart. "You okay?"

She gave me a small smile. "Yeah. Just a bit squeamish."

I nodded then turned back and tugged down the suspenders of my overall dress before I shoved it down my body. Luckily, the RAM was a beast of a vehicle, so I had enough room to move. Eventually, I kicked it off and knotted my blouse over my rip cage, then popped open the three top buttons.

"What's going on here?" Nevio asked, and I noticed his intent gaze on me. He still hadn't started the engine.

"This is my party outfit. The overalls were just my disguise."

"Makes you wonder what else you're hiding beneath the sweet tomboy attitude," Nevio mused.

"Is this ride going to take off any time soon?" Alessio asked impatiently.

Nevio tore his eyes away from me with an air of annoyance and started the car. As with the bike before, he raced again. "Provisions are in the center console."

I opened the console and found an array of tiny bottles inside. Everything from vodka over Jim Beam to Jaegermeister. The only non-alcoholic option was Red Bull.

"Jaegerbomb for me to get my blood pumping," Nevio said.

"And for me," Alessio said.

"Jim Beam," Massimo said.

"You're driving, Nevio," Carlotta said. "What if you cause an accident?"

Nevio motioned at Massimo. "I forward this question to my legal defendant." He glanced at me. "Jaeger Bomb."

Massimo turned to Lotta. "Considering Nevio's high tolerance for alcohol due to years of consumption, it's highly unlikely that a drink, especially mixed with an energy drink, will influence his driving skills negatively. His style of driving is a danger under any circumstances."

"Thanks," Nevio said dryly. I opened the tiny bottle of Jaegermeister and the can of Red Bull for him.

"Take a gulp from the can," Nevio said.

I did without thinking about it even though I hated energy drinks. I frowned.

"Now, there should be room for the Jaegermeister." I poured the alcohol into the drink, then handed it to Nevio.

In the back seat, Massimo and Carlotta were caught up in an argument about the dangers of drunk driving. "Now to the second part of your statement. Consequences of a car crash would be minor for us. Our car is massive, and legal consequences are unlikely."

"But other people could be hurt."

Massimo's expression made it clear that wasn't his concern. "At this time of night, it's unlikely we'd crash into a family."

Carlotta shook her head, hopefully realizing the futility of arguing about conscience with Massimo. "It's still irresponsible."

"You know what? Make that a double Jaegermeister without the bomb. I need to get drunk ASAP," Alessio drawled. I bit back a laugh. Listening to Massimo and Carlotta could be tiring. I handed him two bottles, then picked one for myself. I'd never tried Jaegermeister. I rarely drank alcohol at all.

"Don't get drunk on my watch," Nevio warned. "I have every intention of not remembering a single thing tomorrow morning, so you need to keep your wits about you."

"I'm not here to babysit you," I said indignantly, congratulating myself inwardly for the hint of sass in my voice.

"You're supposed to keep us safe," Carlotta added.

Nevio snorted. "*Lotta*, everyone knows you're here with us. You'll be safe, even if all three of us lie passed out in our own vomit by the end of the evening."

Carlotta sent Massimo a critical look. "That won't happen," he said. "I don't make a habit out of getting drunk or stoned. That's Nevio's job."

"Alessio gets drunk too," Nevio said as he parked on the lawn in front of a massive mansion. I didn't even know whose party this was. A rich kid from Las Vegas who was probably buying drugs from the Camorra.

Everyone got out of the car, but Nevio stopped me when I wanted to climb out too.

"If I see you drinking too much, I'll have Massimo drive you and Carlotta home. End of story."

My eyes grew wide with surprise. "What?"

He opened his door and jumped out before he faced me again. "You heard me, and I'm being serious, so be a good girl, Rory."

Chapter Ten

Aurora

This was the first time Carlotta and I went out with the Unholy Trinity, and I hoped it would be a memorable experience. The guys let us enter the building first. The white marble lobby was already crowded, people mingling with drinks, laughing and chatting. Though it was loud, the source of the ear-splitting music came from the living room where people were dancing and crammed together like sardines. Despite this being a huge house, the number of people attending this party surpassed even its capacities.

While Carlotta's and my entrance was met with mild curiosity or assessing looks from the girls, and appreciative or even flirting looks from the boys, the atmosphere shifted the second Massimo, Alessio, and Nevio stepped in close behind us. We became invisible to the boys, especially when Nevio pulled me against him to murmur, "Remember to behave.

Massimo will keep an eye on you and Carlotta." He pressed a kiss against my temple and was off.

Another one of those annoying friendly kisses!

He left me a little dumbfounded once again, and before I could retort, "Only if you do."

Nevio headed straight for a room at the end of the big lobby, a kitchen from the looks of it, and the admiring and nervous gazes of almost all the girls followed him.

Alessio chuckled dryly, still beside me just like Massimo and Carlotta. "He's like a black hole."

I gave him a blank stare, my brain not catching up, especially as the droning bass made clear thoughts difficult.

"He's referring to the strong gravity of a black hole."

"Even light doesn't have enough energy to escape its pull." Alessio gave me a meaningful look, then he followed Nevio. Maybe he didn't notice, but his pull wasn't so much worse.

Massimo stayed and led us past the gawking masses toward the kitchen. By the time we arrived, Nevio and Alessio were already gone, probably with alcoholic provisions, of which the kitchen had an almost unlimited array. Massimo went over to one of the fridges that must have been set up for this occasion since they barred part of the kitchen counters and took out a can of 7up for Lotta and a can of Mountain Dew for me before he grabbed a Corona from a basket filled with ice for himself.

Because of her heart, Carlotta never drank. She'd once tried a sip of champagne at a wedding, and Diego had gone completely berserk. Since then, she steered clear of it. I didn't usually drink either because I just didn't like the taste and didn't tolerate much, but I guessed that had more to do with my lack of training when it came to alcohol than my general taste.

I took the can from Massimo and took a gulp. Maybe I'd have a drink later, but to start, it was probably a good idea to keep my wits about me. I wanted to get a feel for the party first before I risked getting tipsy.

The other people in the room gave us curious looks, especially Massimo's presence as our massive shadow. He ignored them and stoically drank his beer. His black polo shirt revealed the tattoos on his arms, which seemed at odds with his nature. Then again, it didn't.

"You don't have to play our bodyguard if you prefer to hang out with Nevio and Alessio, or *someone else*," Carlotta said.

I leaned against the counter, allowing the beat to fill me up and watching my friend's interaction with Massimo. The way she had said someone else had made it clear she meant someone female, at least for me.

Massimo narrowed his eyes slightly and glanced into the living room, which could be seen through the round arch connecting the two rooms. "I know most of these people, but I don't want to spend time with any of them, nor do they appreciate my company. Alessio and Nevio can entertain themselves and usually do in an annoying way."

Carlotta nodded toward a group of girls who were watching us, and especially Massimo through the open French doors of the kitchen. "They seem interested in your company."

I was distracted by something in the living room, so I stopped listening to their conversation, which would probably soon end in a debate anyway. Nevio chatted with two girls, sipping from a vodka bottle. He looked utterly bored, but the girls were definitely interested. Alessio danced with a girl, though she did most of the dancing, and he mostly nodded along with the music. I wasn't sure how he wasn't suffering a heatstroke in his hoodie.

Maybe I could get Nevio to dance with me since even Alessio was on the dance floor, doing what could be generously labeled as dancing.

I gave Carlotta a look, my eyes darting to Nevio, and she answered with a small nod, knowing my plan even if she probably disapproved of it, considering her wariness of Nevio. I pushed away from the countertop.

"Where are you going?" Massimo asked.

I rolled my eyes. "Into the living room to dance. People saw me enter the party with you, so I doubt anyone will bother me, and if they do, Alessio and Nevio are there to protect me."

"I wouldn't count on Nevio. He's already drunk one-third of his bottle, and he'll finish it by midnight."

"Does he always drink this much?" I asked.

"At parties, yes, especially since Greta has moved to New York. Being around so many people makes him murderous pretty quickly, and the alcohol mellows him out."

I nodded as if this made sense. I had caught the occasional glimpse

By Frenzy I Rain

behind Nevio's smirking mask and seen how much he missed his twin. He had a heart, but it was well-guarded. I headed for the living room. The music rang in my ears, and I had to resist the urge to cover them with my palms. Alessio danced toward me, barring my way and leaving me no choice but to engage in a quick dance with him, though that was only for show of course. "Not a good idea, Aurora."

"What's your problem?"

"Remember the black hole?"

"I've known Nevio and you all my life. You act like I'm an oblivious bystander who'll be shocked by the skeletons in Nevio's closet."

Alessio smiled condescendingly. "You know us by day."

"It's dark outside now," I muttered, glancing past him to Nevio, who perched on the backrest of a long leather sofa while both girls stood closely in front of him.

Alessio shook his head, then danced backward, briefly lifting his hands, palms outwards to signal defeat. I walked around him and headed straight for Nevio, even if my heart hammered hard enough to do lasting damage to my ribs.

Now I wished I'd actually had some alcohol to boost my confidence and silence my doubts. Before I could really go over what to say to him, I was already beside Nevio—and the two girls who gave me their best mean-girl expressions.

"Three is one too many," the girl with dark curls said.

I would have thought two girls was already one too many, but Nevio probably didn't agree. I wasn't naive enough to think he hadn't done pretty much everything you could do sexually, even a threesome with two girls. I shoved the idea out of my head.

Nevio wrapped an arm around my shoulders, one corner of his mouth pulling up. "Rory is always welcome, and there's no reason to be jealous, girls. She's only here to chat with a good friend. Right, Rory?"

I wasn't here for a good-friend chat. I was here to get out of the friend-zone. Three sets of eyes regarded me expectantly.

I swallowed, trying to say what I'd come here to say. Instead, I muttered, "Right," and gave them a tight smile. I doubted the girls believed it, and I wasn't sure if Nevio did either. I took a sip from my beverage, then reached for Nevio's vodka bottle. He regarded me closely as I brought it to my lips and took the tiniest sip. And holy shit, did it burn. I tried to suppress my coughing, but it was useless. My eyes watered, and a few coughs burst out of me.

Nevio took the bottle from me. "You should stay away from the hard stuff." The way he said it made me believe he wasn't only referring to the vodka. Annoyed at myself and Nevio, I retreated. By now, Massimo and Carlotta had found a place on a sofa in the corner. I didn't want to go over to them.

Instead, I headed outside into the garden, which wasn't as crowded as the inside but not as deserted as I would have liked in my current mood. I took a deep breath but only got a whiff of smoke and something sweeter, probably marijuana. My belly tightened. Having seen what drugs did to my grandmother, I'd never been tempted by joints, much less any harder stuff. Dad would have probably locked me into my room until I was thirty if he ever suspected me of doing drugs.

"I warned you," Alessio said, almost giving me a heart attack as he appeared right behind me. He held a joint in his hand.

I gave him a hard look. "You shouldn't smoke that."

"I'm working on my self-fulfilling prophecy. It's all part of the plan."

"That made no sense," I said.

He gave me a dark smile and took a brief pull from his joint. "I know. I guess I'm trying to channel the past."

I hoped he realized that he sounded crazy. He chuckled and tossed the joint away, then squashed it with his boot. "Self-destruction comes in different forms. You have your Nevio. I have my joint."

"Oh, shut up."

He became serious. "Listen, Rory, this emotional bullshit isn't my thing, but if you really feel like you need to ruin yourself with Nevio, then at least pick a different place and time. Nevio at parties is like a crack pipe. The rush is short and not worth the utter havoc it'll wreak on you."

"Why do you insist on protecting me? I don't see you warning Carlotta from Massimo?"

Alessio scoffed. "Carlotta has God, and Massimo has logic. They'll be fine."

I took a deep breath. "I'll be fine, okay? Nevio doesn't want anything from me. We're just good friends, so you can chill."

Alessio's expression piqued my curiosity.

"Right?" I asked.

Alessio backed away. "Let him do the noble thing for once, Rory. Don't be stupid. Don't tempt something you can't control."

He turned on his heel and vanished inside the house. If he'd planned on keeping me away from Nevio, his tactic had backfired.

I went inside, even more determined than before. If Nevio pushed me away because he thought he was being noble, I would show him that I didn't need protection, least of all from him.

I was a Scuderi. I wasn't an outsider who'd cry herself to sleep over all the horrors in his past *and present*. Dad was an Enforcer, and even if I didn't like to dwell on the details of his daily work, I knew it was cruel and brutal. I still loved him, and so did Mom.

Nevio wasn't in the living room when I entered. Massimo and Carlotta were still in the spot I'd last seen them, though. She gave me a questioning look and made a move as if she wanted to come over to me. I shook my head. I was fine. She looked doubtful, but I shook my head again.

I headed for the kitchen, but Nevio wasn't there either, so I moved to the wide staircase that led up to the second floor. What if he was up there with the girls? I really didn't want to catch him in the act. It was one thing to know what he was up to. It was a very different matter to see him.

I hesitated at the bottom of the stairs. What would I even do if I found him with the two girls? Jump between them? Drag him away?

"Are you lost?" asked a guy with dark blond hair, a polo shirt with a turned-up collar, and a scar on his cheek that suggested he was in one of the old-fashioned fraternities.

I felt it sometimes. I gave him a firm smile. "No, I'm fine."

He hovered. "Are you alone?"

"No, here with friends," I said. "Umm, is there anything else you need?" I hoped he'd get the memo. I wasn't interested in his flirting. Maybe making Nevio jealous would have been an option, but I didn't want to start playing these kinds of games, and if Nevio wasn't interested in me, jealousy was hardly on the menu.

I spotted Alessio in the doorway to the kitchen, watching with mild interest. I didn't want to cause a scene, for which the Unholy Trinity was notorious, and narrowed my eyes at him. He stayed where he was and didn't intervene.

The guy followed my gaze, then made a face and left without saying another word.

Alessio strolled past me, looking pleased with himself. "Nevio doesn't get jealous…"

I sighed and went upstairs before he involved me in another of his ominous warnings.

My heart sped up as I reached the first-floor landing. No one was in the hall, but I could hear voices and giggles from a couple of rooms and around the corner at the end of the hallway. I slowly walked through the corridor toward the corner.

A girl's voice rose in anger, and a deep male voice said something in turn. I couldn't hear what was being said, but I could tell it wasn't nice just from the tone. It was definitely Nevio's voice.

I stopped right before the corner, worried about what I'd walk in on. A slap sounded, making me jump. I rounded the corner as Nevio grabbed a girl by the throat and pushed her against the wall, his chin and left lower cheek turning red, and his eyes terrifying enough that even I was a little scared of him. The girl looked positively out of her mind from fear.

"Never again," Nevio snarled, then his eyes slanted to me, standing frozen in the corridor. He released the girl immediately and stepped back. With a harsh smile, he backed up to the wall and leaned against it. His fly was open and his boxers below askew. He wasn't even wearing a shirt, only his leather jacket.

The girl shoved away from the wall and rushed past me. As she did, she hissed at me. "You can have him. Have fun sucking his dick."

I watched her leave with parted lips. I wasn't sure what had happened. From the corner of my eye, I saw Nevio right his boxers and pull up his fly. He obviously didn't expect me to do what the girl had suggested, though he must have heard her. He pulled a cigarette from his pants pocket and lit it up, then took a deep pull.

For a while, we just stood like that, not saying anything.

He was leaning against the wall, his head bowed down, his hair falling into his face, and he was hiding his expression from me. The half-empty vodka bottle stood beside him on the ground. I couldn't believe he'd already drunk half of it. The cigarette dangled from his mouth, the tip glowing ominously. My eyes traced his muscled arms, pronounced six-pack, and the narrow swing of his hips, hating the idea that the girl had felt this part of him, that she'd run her hands over him how I wanted to do. I'd known Nevio all my life, had seen him shirtless countless times, but in the past few years, the sight had had a different impact on me. I wanted to touch him, to feel his body against mine, to lean my nose into his neck and smell him—sandalwood and musk, sometimes the hint of copper, which I never allowed my mind to dwell on.

My skin became hot, then hotter when I followed the hint of dark hairs into his black jeans. His leather belt was already half unbuckled. My chest ached thinking of what I'd almost overheard. It didn't make me want him any less. Every part of me desired Nevio.

It wasn't healthy or advisable, but it was fact, how Massimo loved to say, and in consequence, Carlotta too. I should be with her now, not up here, especially not up here with Nevio. But Carlotta was safe. Much safer than me in every sense of the word.

I had a feeling this was my chance. Maybe my only one. Nevio's guard was down. I could…what could I really do? Talking to him was out of the question in the state he was in. I'd seen how much he'd drunk, not to mention the marijuana he'd smoked, which I could smell even from a distance. Maybe I could… kiss him. Show him that I wasn't one of the guys. He hadn't glanced my way in the way I'd hoped tonight despite my outfit, not in a way that other guys looked at me, even if it was so unlike anything I usually wore. I was air to him. I wasn't sure what else to do to catch his attention.

"You shouldn't be here," he gritted out with the cigarette between his teeth, still not looking up.

"I needed a break from the party and thought it would be quiet up here."

"You shouldn't be at this party," he clarified and raised his face, his dark eyes hitting me.

So that was what he thought.

Chapter Eleven

Aurora

I FLUSHED, FIRST FROM HIS HARD WORDS, THEN BECAUSE OF HIS angry expression. Something in his eyes, however, lit up my insides in a way that had nothing to do with embarrassment over his words. My gaze slid lower. The left side of his jaw and lower cheek were red.

I moved toward him and touched the spot. "It's swelling."

His hand soared up, clamping his fingers around my wrist. I froze and swallowed hard because his eyes were like embers, and my body became aflame. His grip around my wrist hurt a lot. "Nevio," I whispered, and he loosened his hold, dropping my wrist as if it burned him.

He straightened, bringing us closer. I tilted my head back to look at him. The way he still looked down at me made me want to run. I could tell this might end in a very bad way. How could it not? He smelled of weed, cigarettes, and alcohol, not smells I liked, but beneath it was Nevio's very own musky, herby scent caught me in its trap. I licked my lips. Nevio took a step closer and gripped my chin but not in a gentle way. "Did you dress up like that for someone special?"

His voice made me want to run from him and get closer to him at the same time. Something was entirely wrong with me. "Don't you know?" I whispered. He must know.

"What I know is that this house is full of bad people, Rory, and I'm the worst." He bent down so our eyes met. "Stay away from our parties. Stay away from me." He reached for my blouse and buttoned up the top buttons, then he undid the knot above my navel and tugged the hem down so it covered my belly. "That's you."

I winced, my cheeks burning fiercely from acute mortification. I didn't say anything because I was at a loss for words, like I often was around Nevio.

"Now go downstairs, grab Lotti, and get the fuck outta here and back into your comfy bed. Tell Massimo to drive you, and if I see you around when I go back downstairs, there will be hell to pay."

My lips parted, and I felt the treacherous sting of tears in my eyes. I breathed through my nose, determined not to cry in front of Nevio.

He scanned my eyes, too observant yet cruel, bared his teeth, and stepped back. "Get back home, Rory. You're in my way. I need to find a bitch to suck me off."

I wanted to scream and rage, to give him a really nasty piece of my mind, but as usual, nothing passed my lips. I whirled around and stumbled down the staircase. A few tears trailed down my cheeks, but I wiped them off before someone could see them. Carlotta perched on the couch's armrest, Massimo was beside her, and one of her legs was pressed against one of his. I could tell they were caught up in one of their very common discussions about what they believed or, in Massimo's case, didn't.

I didn't want to interrupt them. I slinked over to the kitchen, hoping to find an alcoholic beverage I could tolerate. I hated the taste of most of them. But I wanted to get drunk or at least tipsy right now to forget my conversation with Nevio. Part of me wanted to go back upstairs to confront him and give him a piece of my mind for the first time ever, but that would have required a level of inebriation I definitely wouldn't acquire tonight. I hated my Goody Two-shoes ass sometimes. I froze in the doorway to the kitchen. Alessio was kissing a girl. He immediately pulled away from her, alert as always, and met my gaze. I blushed furiously and stuttered an apology, then fled the room as if I'd caught them naked doing the rodeo. If I couldn't even handle seeing someone kissing, how was I supposed to ever make a move toward Nevio? Though after tonight, that was a distant dream anyway.

Maybe my reaction to public displays of affection was why Nevio didn't see me as a woman but a little girl. If I couldn't handle seeing something as harmless as a kiss, how would I be a part of the dirty deeds Nevio was undoubtedly up to? I wasn't sure I was ready for Nevio's level, but I wanted to be.

Eventually, I settled for a vodka-O, though the orange juice hardly masked the taste of the alcohol. After a few sips, my gaze caught Carlotta's. She got up from the armrest and quickly made her way over to me. Massimo's intent gaze followed her the entire way as if it had been glued to her back. I wished Nevio would regard me with that level of interest, though Massimo always freaked me out a little.

Carlotta pursed her lips as she regarded my drink. "Last time you tried vodka, you threw up behind a bush."

I grimaced, remembering Nevio's amusement over the incident. That had been one of my many embarrassing moments around him. I was a mess. "How do you know it's not just orange juice?"

Carlotta gave me a pointed look. "Because your expression tells me you need something stronger."

I let out a laugh. She knew me too well. I gave a small shrug.

"You and Massimo seemed quite cozy."

"We were just talking." Carlotta's dark brows pulled together, and her eyes moved back to where Massimo sat on the sofa, now in conversation with a guy I didn't know. But he looked straight at her as if he could feel her gaze. She smiled and gave a small wave. He nodded.

I scoffed. "He wants to do more than talking."

Carlotta shook her head slowly and turned back to me. "What about you and Nevio? I thought you wanted to talk to him."

I took another sip from my drink and almost gagged.

"Maybe it's for the best that it's not working out between Nevio and you. He's the monster under your bed," Carlotta said as if I didn't know.

"He has no intention of going anywhere near my bed, so you don't have to worry. You're closer to having a monster under your bed than I am."

Carlotta's gaze moved back to Massimo, and her cheeks turned pink.

I sighed. "Go back to your monster."

"He's not…"

I wasn't sure what she wanted to deny. That he was a monster. Or that he was hers. Neither would have been convincing, so it was good she'd stopped herself.

"I should stay with you. Or better yet, we should go home and watch a movie instead of staying here. I'm sure Massimo would take us home if I asked him."

I remembered how Nevio had ordered the same thing, and my body bristled against the notion. "No," I said firmly. "Go to Massimo, and I'll talk to Alessio. I saw him in the kitchen."

Carlotta gripped my hand. "You come with me. Massimo likes you. He'll be happy to talk to us both."

"I don't want to be the fifth wheel," I muttered. I had too much practice with the role. Most of our lives Carlotta and I had been kind of fifth wheels when we hung around the Falcone mansion. Nevio, Massimo and Alessio had always had an inseparable bond, and even Greta had somehow been part of it.

"You won't," she said firmly.

"Aurora," Massimo greeted me neutrally as I stopped at the sofa.

I gave him an apologetic smile, but his brows snapped together as if he didn't understand why, so I took a gulp from my drink instead. I allowed my gaze to flit around the massive living room. I wasn't even sure whom it belonged to. Many faces were familiar, such as the sons and daughters of Camorrista or people I knew from school. Most were older, college-age like Alessio, Nevio, and Massimo.

It still felt strange to consider that I would be in college this fall. *If* Nevada State accepted me for their nursing program, which was very likely considering who my father was. A part of me wasn't sure it was the right move. I would take the place of someone who needed a degree to work. I could work as a nurse or doctor if I let the Camorra doctors and nurses teach me what they knew. I'd never be allowed to work in a non-mob hospital anyway.

"Why aren't you in college? You're a genius," I said to Massimo when I realized I'd stood there like a salt pillar for too long.

Massimo tilted his head and gave a shrug. "I can't see that it'd make a difference. What I want to learn can be found in online resources."

I supposed he had a point. A degree wouldn't make sense for him either.

"Why nursing school?" Massimo asked.

I jumped. "I like taking care of people. I want to help them heal."

"You could have become a doctor."

I'd considered it, but I wanted to be even closer to the patients. For now, the nursing program seemed like the perfect way to pursue my interests.

Carlotta smiled gently. "I still remember the kind nurses who took care of me when I was in the hospital during the long recovery after my heart surgery. They made the hard times bearable. I don't really remember the names of the doctors."

"The Camorra always needs people who know how to treat wounds, so it's a useful degree," Massimo said.

I nodded. I would prefer to work in the NICU for premature babies later, but I knew that might not be in the cards.

Carlotta said something else, but my attention was on Nevio, who came out of the kitchen with a bottle of tequila. Alessio was right behind him, shaking his head with a look of exasperation.

Massimo rose to his feet, eyes narrowed when Nevio stopped in the center of the room. A group of college-age guys, all of them shit-faced, built a half circle around Nevio.

Nevio pointed with the bottle at one of the guys, the tallest and, from the dynamic of the group, their leader. It was also the guy who'd talked to me in the lobby. "This gentleman likes bets," Nevio shouted.

Massimo released a sigh.

"He thinks I'm full of it and wouldn't cut open my own wrist." Nevio's grin became wider, all teeth. "If I win, he'll shoot fireworks from his ass."

I froze. "He won't, right?"

Massimo's look gave me little hope. Nevio pulled a long knife from a holster at his calf.

The guy's eyes widened. Was it really coincidence that Nevio and the guy who'd tried to flirt with me were at it?

Nevio turned to a girl to his right. "Hold my bottle for me." She took it with a giggle.

A sour taste spread in my mouth.

A hush fell over the crowd when Nevio ran the blade across his wrist.

"Fuck, you're sick! What kind of sicko are you?" the guy shouted, looking close to panic.

My belly constricted at seeing the blood dripping from Nevio's cut. I put my drink down on a table and rushed over to him. When I arrived by his side, he just accepted the bottle from the girl who looked ready to be sick on his shoes and took a sip before he dumped half the bottle over his knife and wound.

Then Nevio toasted at the group of college guys. "Time to shoot fireworks."

"Someone needs to call an ambulance!" came a shout from the crowd.

"Nonsense," Massimo said sharply as he pushed through the crowd to reach Nevio and me. "Get your facts straight. I'll deal with it."

I reached for Nevio's wrist, though my medical knowledge was still limited to putting Band-Aids on Roman's knees or elbows when I babysat him. Massimo pushed me aside. "This is my job."

Alessio tossed a medical kit at Massimo.

I stepped back as I watched Massimo wrap Nevio's wrist while Nevio's intent gaze followed the college guys who tried to leave the party. "Time to collect betting debts," he growled, ripping his arm from Massimo's hold. The end of the bandage fluttered behind him as he chased the guys.

Soon, a brawl broke out, which ended in two of the guys being passed out on the floor and their leader being held between Alessio and Massimo while Nevio put the stick of a rocket between the ass cheeks as he kept shouting obscenities. "You better shut up and be glad I just wedged the stick between your ass cheeks and didn't fuck you with it," Nevio muttered.

When he lit up his lighter, I turned around in search of Carlotta, who had remained in the house. I didn't want to see how Nevio lit the fuse.

Fifteen minutes later, the crowd filtered back in, and Massimo sat down beside Carlotta and me on the sofa.

"He only suffered minor burns on his ass cheeks, in case you're worried about the idiot."

"Why does he do these things?"

"It's Nevio's form of entertainment. And it's far tamer than what he's usually up to," Alessio said as he perched on the armrest on my left.

"He's been a mess since Greta left for New York in March."

Of course I knew that.

Nevio came toward us with a new bottle of tequila and what looked like a joint dangling from his lips. His bandage had soaked through, and blood dripped down his hand. He stopped right in front of us, his brows dipping as he looked at me, and for a moment, he looked more sober than he had all evening. "You should be home." He looked at Massimo. "Take her home."

"And who will fix you when you cut yourself again?" Massimo asked dryly. He grabbed Nevio's arm and tightened the bandage once more.

Nevio handed the joint to Alessio, who also took a pull, then offered it to Massimo. He shook his head, which made relief pass over Carlotta's face. "I like the number of brain cells I have."

"You have too many. It can't hurt if you lose a few to get down to our level," Alessio said.

"That would require you and Nevio to stop consuming."

Nevio fixed me with a hard look. "Get home." Then he bent down, bringing us close. "It'll only get worse from here on out." The look in his eyes made a hole open up in my chest.

"I can take care of myself," I said quietly.

Nevio straightened, took the joint from Alessio, and motioned at Massimo. "Take her home." Then he turned without another look at me and stalked into the kitchen.

"He'll have emptied the bottle in an hour," Alessio predicted.

"It's a new one!" I said indignantly.

Alessio and Massimo exchanged a look that made me feel stupid.

"Maybe we should really go home," Carlotta whispered.

"You should," Massimo said, shoving to his feet. "I'm taking you."

"No," I gritted out. "I'm not leaving only because Nevio ordered it. He's not my boss."

"Maybe you should consider talking like that to his face," Alessio said, then he too sauntered off.

I glared. "He couldn't do anything even if I did."

"That's not the point he was trying to make," Massimo said. "You have another hour, then I'm taking you home. Don't get in trouble." He stalked after his friends.

Carlotta shrugged. Someone turned up the music louder.

"Let's dance, okay?" I asked.

Carlotta hesitated, but when I got up and held out my hand, she took it and let me lead her to the center of the room, where dozens of soles from dancing feet had smeared Nevio's blood everywhere. It said a lot about the party guests that hardly anybody seemed to care.

Carlotta and I danced, and I managed to forget about Nevio for long stretches of time. But about five minutes before our Massimo-imposed curfew, Nevio dragged himself up the staircase. He was alone. No girls clung to him.

I froze.

"It's not a good idea," Carlotta warned.

"Let me talk to him. I'm really worried about him. He should go home with us."

Massimo appeared in the doorway of the kitchen.

"Distract him, okay? I need to use my chance to talk to Nevio when his guard is down."

Carlotta nodded, but it was obvious she didn't like the idea. "Just make sure you don't get hurt in the process. Not everyone can be saved."

I gave her a reassuring smile, and she moved toward Massimo, who looked suspicious.

I used my chance and followed Nevio upstairs. Unfortunately, all the doors were closed when I got up there, so I had to check one room after the other. I found him in the third bedroom I checked. He was stretched out across the bed, his legs dangling off the side, and he was simply staring up at the ceiling as if it held the answers to all the questions. His expression seemed lost, forlorn, more vulnerable than I'd ever seen it. His leather jacket was on the floor, leaving his upper body bare.

His face became hard as if a switch had been turned. He didn't stop staring at the ceiling as he gritted out, "Leave. If you stay, you better fuck or suck me."

My lips parted in utter shock. I hadn't drunk enough for hallucinations, but I couldn't believe Nevio had really spoken to me like this. "I'm here to talk to you."

He chuckled, and the sound tore at my belly. It was raw but also dark and cruel.

My pulse sped, my mind telling me to leave, but I couldn't. I just couldn't leave him here like this. The bottle of tequila that had been full an hour ago lay beside him on the bed, empty. I hoped he'd spilled most of it. I swallowed and closed the door.

With every step I took closer to the bed, my pulse raced faster. I stopped right beside his head and looked down at his stretched-out form. Even stinking-drunk Nevio was magnificent, and I wished I hadn't noticed. His outstretched arms were muscled from Parcour and cage fights. Scars littered his strong body. My eyes lingered on the tattoo of the Camorra on his forearm. The Camorra required a lot from their soldiers, and even more from its future Capo. His belt was unbuckled, the button of his jeans open.

Nevio's head swiveled around, his eyes now at eye level with my thighs. His fingers gripped the back of my thigh and tugged me closer until my knees bumped against the bed. "I wasn't joking," he snarled.

I wasn't sure why, but I reached out and lightly ran my fingers through his black hair, wanting a connection. He hoisted me off my feet, and suddenly, I straddled his naked belly.

I let out a startled cry, then swallowed when I realized how little fabric was between my most private area and Nevio's skin. I flushed with heat, and my core developed a pulse of its own. I'd had countless dreams about Nevio and me in a bed together, but this wasn't exactly how I'd imagined it.

Nevio's gaze hit me. It was unfocused and never reached my eyes, always wandering around as if he couldn't focus on one spot. Then his gaze dipped to my breasts, and his fingers dug into my hips as he pushed me farther back until something hard pressed against me through my panties. I looked down, stunned by the bulge in his pants. I touched his six-pack, my fingers loving the feel of the hard ridges. I bit my lip as the heat between my legs intensified. I rocked my hips and swallowed a moan from the sensation.

"Stop dry-humping me."

I blushed, my hands still against his skin. Nevio shoved up and gripped my neck, his tongue trailing over my pulse point up to my ear. My body went into overdrive from sensation, completely overwhelmed.

Nevio's breath hit my ear. "Last warning, pretty girl. You stay here, I'll fuck you, and it won't be pretty."

I ran my hand over his back, my mind screaming at me to pull back and leave. "I've been waiting so long for you to notice me," I whispered against his collarbone and pressed a kiss to it.

"I noticed you right when you walked in. Now, stop talking, girl," he said, a hint of a slur breaking through the words.

I closed my eyes against his skin, realizing he didn't know who I was. He was too drunk, too stoned. I was just a random skirt he was chasing—a quick pussy fix, as he always called it.

He lifted me, and I knelt above him as he shoved down his pants. I didn't look down at his erection. I only looked at his face, but it was closed off and distant as if he was only half there.

"Ready?"

Sarcasm dripped from his words. I stared down at him and nodded. I wasn't even sure why. Maybe because I was sick of my feelings for him. Perhaps because I hoped this would end them. Maybe because I hoped Nevio would later hate himself for doing this, like I often hated myself because I simply couldn't stop my infatuation. Nevio flipped us over, shoving my legs apart and lifting my ankles on his shoulders. I glared at him. I prayed I could hold on to my anger for this and face him with squared shoulders when realization set in. He spat into his palm and slicked himself up, then swayed briefly as if he was going to topple off the bed—and me—before his entire body tensed, and he regained his balance.

I felt as if I wasn't even in my body, as if I was watching things unfold from above. Blood had soaked his entire bandage by now, and his skin was paler than usual.

Worry filled me. Then Nevio shoved my panties aside and sank into me in one hard thrust. I would have screamed in agony if the vodka-O hadn't been quicker. I turned my head and threw up my dinner and drink.

"Fuck!" Nevio shouted.

I didn't say anything. Tears pressed against my eyes, and mortification and hurt bloomed in my chest, not anger, not hate. Nevio shoved away and out of me, making me tremble.

Silence filled the room. I didn't move for a while, hoping Nevio would leave or say something. Anything. I swallowed and almost threw up again, this time from the taste of bile in my mouth. After a while, I inched my hand toward my skirt and pushed it down to conserve whatever dignity I had left, which was close to none. Gathering my courage, I turned my head to face Nevio. But he lay spread-eagle beside me, passed out. For some reason, this made me cry harder, though I was glad I didn't have to face him or talk to him. I wasn't sure I could *or wanted* to face him ever again.

I pushed into a sitting position despite the ache between my legs. I ran the back of my hand over my eyes, wiping away the tears I couldn't hold back. The door swung open, and I froze.

Chapter Twelve

Nevio

A HEADACHE HAMMERED IN MY SKULL, AND A ROTTEN COTTON candy taste filled my mouth. I shifted. Cold steel engulfed my wrists. My arms were stretched backward over a wooden chair. Any sense of drunkenness dropped away, and my body sprang into high alert as my eyes shot open with blinding pain as light hit my sensitive irises. A wooden chair wouldn't stop me, especially because my legs weren't bound. I could use the broken chair legs to spear the fuckers who'd captured me.

How the fuck was that even possible?

I tried to remember last night but came up with a lot of nothing.

"Got your beauty sleep?" Alessio's voice filtered into my brain. My head swiveled around, finding Alessio and Massimo leaning against the wall of a decrepit basement. A new wave of pain shot through my head and down my spine. Fuck. I didn't particularly mind pain, but in combination with the remaining dizziness from alcohol and the queasy feeling in my stomach, it was a shit show.

My friends were still in yesterday's clothes. Glancing down my body, I realized I was only in boxers. I tilted my head up with a grin. "What is going on? Is this a new sick challenge you want to put me through? I would have thought you'd take away my boxers too."

"They were clean. No need to get rid of them," Massimo clipped. Something in his body language told me this wasn't for fun, and Alessio's eyes didn't reflect his usual mirth either.

I leaned back, fucking confused. "What the fuck is going on?"

"You had vomit all over your pants, and your shirt was gone."

I couldn't imagine that I'd thrown up. I'd never thrown up, no matter how much I'd consumed. I preferred to stay in control of my body, even if yesterday had been a huge exception. Well, not an exception, but a rare occurrence.

I tugged at the metal cuffs. "Unlock them. I'm not in the mood for this humorless game."

Massimo shoved away from the wall. "The girl you were with threw up, and some of it landed on you."

I grimaced. I needed to up my standards when it was time for my next pussy fix.

"You passed out beside her."

I shook my head. "Impossible. I would never lose consciousness beside a stranger."

Alessio shook his head, a look of annoyance passing his face. "I'm outside for a smoke. I'm not in the mood for him right now."

Massimo stopped right before me and his expression pissed me off. "She wasn't a stranger."

I didn't understand what the fuck he meant. I considered everyone outside of our inner circle as strangers. "You're full of bullsh—"

An image of a familiar tearstained face flashed before my eyes. I blinked, sure my drunk and stoned brain was messing with me. Nino and Massimo had often warned me of the risks of marijuana. Maybe this was it. As quickly as the face had come, it was gone until I wasn't sure it had been there in the first place.

I narrowed my eyes at Massimo. "I don't remember."

Massimo shook his head as if I'd disappointed him greatly. "You usually own up to your mistakes."

"What mistake?" I growled, my insides boiling dangerously. Despite the awkward angle my arms were forced into by the chair, I shoved to my feet. Why was he playing righteous now? We both knew he wasn't a knight in shining armor either, even if he liked to play one around Carlotta. "I fucked a girl who wanted to be fucked."

Again, the face flashed before me. I chose to ignore it. My mind was fucking with me. End of story.

"We both know Aurora wants many things from you. A disappointing, quick fuck is not it."

I raced backward, smashing the chair against the wall. My arms and wrists ached from the impact. Massimo watched, unimpressed. "I wouldn't have—" I shut up. "Unlock these fucking cuffs. Now."

Massimo pulled the keys from his pocket and unlocked the cuffs without a word.

"Did she tell you I fucked her?"

"No."

"Did you see me fucking her?"

"No."

I rolled my eyes. "Asshole. Being a genius doesn't mean you know everything."

"I know what happened because I wasn't shit-faced and can read a situation."

I flipped him off, done with his bullshit. "Where is she? I need to talk to her."

"She spent the night at Carlotta's, which was probably for the best, considering her state. If Fabiano had seen her, things would have gotten very unpleasant."

"Take me there."

"No. You need a shower. And Diego won't let you in half naked. He'll call your dad, and we don't want that."

I really didn't care about Diego or Dad right now. I wanted to hear last night's story from Rory. She wouldn't exaggerate things or make things up. I could trust her recount, as long as my memory was a fucking elusive diva.

"I'm getting you home now, and then you can try to talk to her later if she lets you."

I gave him a look. Aurora had never refused to talk to me. She wouldn't now. Whatever Massimo had thought he'd seen was wrong.

So what if Aurora had lain beside me in bed? She had been dressed, and I was probably naked because I'd fucked someone else. No fucking clue why she'd cried. Maybe because she'd embarrassed herself by throwing up. She had a tendency to be a klutz around me.

I followed Massimo out to his car and got in. Alessio wasn't around anymore. Massimo didn't elaborate and just revved the engine and hit the gas.

The mansion was still quiet when we walked in. That didn't mean no one was up, though. It was past eight, so Nino was definitely up for his morning swim. Massimo disappeared into his family's wing, and I dashed toward my room. I wasn't in the mood for a confrontation with Dad now. Though I doubted he'd ask questions only because I was half naked and stinking of vomit. He was used to a lot from me. Nothing probably fazed him anymore when it came to me.

I stumbled into my bathroom and shoved down my boxers. A familiar scent hit me. I'd always been sensitive to certain scents. They caught my attention and spoke to some part of me that scared many. Alessio joked I was probably a freak of nature with shark DNA. But I simply loved the scent of blood. Not just the scent. It's texture, it's warmth when it came out of a body. It's color, both fresh and oxidized.

And now I smelled blood. I stared down my body and found my cock covered in a fine sheen of oxidized blood. My nostrils flared, and beneath the two dominating scents of vomit and blood, another scent caught my attention. I sank down on the edge of the tub, glaring down my body.

Aurora.

She always smelled of light. I almost gagged at my assessment, but that was the only thing I could think of when remembering Aurora's scent. It was light, pure, good, innocent.

I ran a hand through my hair, then tugged hard at it. I needed my fucking memory back. What the fuck had happened last night? Fuck.

I showered for a long time, but my memory remained a black hole. That thought only reminded me of Alessio's favorite comparison, and that

By Frenzy I *Pain*

dampened my mood further. Eventually, I stumbled toward my bed and fell face-first on top of it. Then everything turned black again.

When I woke next, it was afternoon. My headache was still there and so was the loss of my memory.

I stared up at the ceiling. Maybe I should call Greta. Every other woman in this house would guilt-trip me, but Greta never did. I also needed to talk to Aurora. I closed my eyes again. I wasn't a runner. I didn't run from anything, not even problems. I was the hunter, and I preferred it that way, but this damn thing with Aurora was something I wanted to run from. The problem was things like that didn't just vanish into thin air. They festered.

My door creaked. Before I could sit up and open my eyes—I'd never drink and smoke that much again—something smashed against my face, and cold water spilled all over me.

I was wide awake immediately and catapulted myself out of bed. Giulio snickered, his fuck-face alight with mirth. Fuck, I hated kids, and he wasn't even a small kid anymore. I ripped a shuriken from the wall beside me—dozens of the spiked throw stars decorated my room, some of them several hundred years old—and hurled it at my brother. His eyes widened as he dashed away. The spikes impaled themselves in the doorframe after nicking the skin of his upper arm. Grabbing three more shurikens, I chased Giulio.

"You can run, but you can't hide!" I shouted when he stormed down the staircase. He wasn't a little chicken, so he wouldn't run to Mom or Dad for help. That was one of the little shit's few positive traits.

When I caught sight of him again—he was fucking fast, and I was still incapacitated—I hurled two more stars at him in quick succession.

My aim was a little off too, considering my vision wasn't 100 percent yet, but one star left another cut on his upper arm, and the second ripped a hole into his pants and cut one of his ass cheeks. He cried out but didn't stop running. Blood drops littered the floor, leaving a trail like breadcrumbs.

"If you kill me, Mom and Dad will be pissed!" Giulio shouted.

"They'll get over it."

He rushed out of our part of the wing and through the common room where Kiara, Mom, and Gemma sat on the couches with Luna and Caterina, Savio and Gemma's daughters.

"Giulio's bleeding!" Caterina piped.

"Nevio! Stop it right this moment!" Mom shrieked.

I jerked to a halt and catapulted my last shuriken at Giulio, cutting his other arm too.

The star ended up in the wooden cabinet behind my brother. He came to a stop too. Both his sleeves were ripped and ruined with blood, and his pants didn't look much better either. I dripped water all over the floor.

Mom's face was purple with fury. She staggered toward me with a look of utter disbelief. "Have you lost your mind? You could have killed your brother with those stars. What if you'd hit his throat? Or an artery in his leg?"

"I didn't aim at his thigh but at his ass, and his arms are far enough from his throat. I simply taught him a little lesson."

"And what would that be?" Mom seethed.

Kiara and Gemma were checking Giulio's wounds, who squirmed under their insistent care.

"That he shouldn't throw things at me if he doesn't want to have things thrown at him."

Mom scanned my soaked state. "What he did was a stupid prank. What you did was risky stupidity."

I flashed her a smile even as the engagement of so many facial muscles sent a new stab of pain through my skull.

"I'm fine," Giulio whined when Kiara called Nino with her cell.

"What did I do to deserve this?" Mom sighed.

"You fell in love with your kidnapper, which is never advisable," I offered.

Mom gave me a look that suggested she wasn't as opposed to violence as she liked to pretend. She'd never raised her hand against Giulio or me, even if we'd given her plenty of reason to give us a thrashing. I admired her for it. I couldn't even fathom how much self-control that required. Dad at least got to kick my ass during fight training.

Nino entered the room, followed by Massimo. They looked from Giulio to me, to the star in the cabinet, then back to Giulio.

Nino didn't comment, but the tight set of his lips suggested he had no interest in knowing the details.

Massimo went over to the cabinet and pulled out my shuriken after some jolting. He inspected it closely and shook his head. "This masterpiece survived five-hundred years without a scratch, and you have it less than a year, and now it needs restoration."

"He cut me with it," Giulio said indignantly.

"What a waste of a beautiful art piece," Massimo said dryly.

"Is it too early for wine?" Mom asked as she sank on the armrest.

Nino prodded at my brother's cuts and shook his head. "If your intention was to cause your brother lasting pain, your aim is miserable. None of these need stitches."

"Look at his butt. I put more effort into that one," I said.

Giulio backed away. "I'm not showing my butt in front of everyone."

"You moon people all the time. Since when do you possess any shame?" Gemma muttered. She and Caterina still played some ludicrous board game with plenty of pink and unicorns.

"Come to the infirmary, and I'll take a closer look," Nino said in a clipped voice that made Giulio follow him without protest.

"Keep me updated," I called, then headed for the kitchen. I needed a coffee with a double espresso shot and maybe a few energy drinks for breakfast.

Steps followed me. I didn't have to turn around to know it was Massimo. Mom didn't have the patience to deal with me now. And Kiara had long given up her lovey-dovey approach with me.

"Wait with your lecture until I'm caffeinated," I growled and pulled myself a coffee, then two shots from our automatic coffee machine.

"Did you set my brother up to this?" I asked after finishing the cup, motioning at my wet state.

Massimo raised one eyebrow. "Alessio told him you needed a rude wake-up call."

"How about you and Alessio stay out of my fucking business?"

"Not if your business jeopardizes the solidarity of the Scuderi-Falcone families."

I rolled my eyes and regretted it immediately. "Don't exaggerate."

Massimo narrowed his eyes. "This is serious, Nevio. This could spiral out of control. Fabiano and Leona won't take it kindly if they find out what you did."

"I don't remember a fucking thing," I muttered. "I was stinking drunk."

"I doubt that's an excuse anyone's going to listen to. Try to clear things up with Aurora."

"How am I supposed to do that?" He knew everything. Maybe he had a fucking solution to this problem too.

"Don't be an asshole," Massimo said.

I pulled myself another coffee. "Aurora wants something I can't give her. Maybe now she realizes how much of a messed-up asshole I am. Maybe it's the solution to everything."

Massimo didn't comment, and I was glad he kept his opinion to himself for once.

I rarely had trouble falling asleep. My conscience didn't plague me, and many of my nightly activities worked off enough energy to let me sleep like a fucking rock. Tonight, however, I found myself staring up at my ceiling. Only the sliver of moonlight peeking through the curtains allowed me to see schemes in my room. I tried to remember details from last night. Pressing my palms against my temples, I went over what I remembered. My conversation with Aurora where I told her to stay away from me and go home. That obviously hadn't worked.

A new image barreled through the blackness. An image of long legs beside my head. Of golden blond strands on a gray pillowcase. Then another flash and blue eyes locked on mine. Fuck, the look in them. Had she looked at me that way? And I hadn't even realized it was her.

Or maybe I had, and the alcohol had only let the rotten part of me act. Another flash, still those blue eyes, but this time filled with tears and pain. My memory became black. That was probably when I'd passed out.

Remembering her eyes was the worst.

Aurora

"How do you feel?" Carlotta asked when I entered the kitchen in the morning. We were alone. Diego had probably already left for some Camorra duty, for which I was infinitely glad. He would ask questions that I had no intention of answering.

Carlotta and I had been best friends all of our lives. I couldn't imagine I'd ever feel I couldn't face or share my feelings with her. This was probably a low in my life so far, so it was only fitting that she was by my side in the aftermath.

"I don't know," I said honestly as I trudged toward her. She was preparing scrambled eggs in a big pan. Enough for ten people, not just the two of us. She turned down the heat and put aside the spatula, then angled her body toward me, her expression compassionate. "I'm sorry this happened."

I nodded because I was too. I should have left the party sooner and stayed away from Nevio. My belly plummeted just thinking of him. Heartache, embarrassment, and anger rushed through me. Last night had been the worst night of my life. I swallowed hard and wrapped my arms around my chest. The deep hollowness I felt there was worse than the burn between my legs.

The latter would probably remind me of my bad decisions for days to come every time I had to pee.

"Massimo won't tell a living soul." It was very fitting that she limited her statement in that regard because, in Massimo's case, it wasn't unlikely he shared information during an autopsy. The Unholy Trinitiy's and especially his fascination with dead bodies and the morgue was infamous.

My cheeks still burned, thinking of how Massimo had found me.

I wasn't sure how much time had passed, but I was starting to feel sick again. Maybe because the room stank of my vomit, or because my vagina ached fiercely, or because I felt like the biggest idiot on this planet. Nevio still hadn't stirred from where he was sprawled out beside me, breathing evenly, blissfully passed out. I wished I'd pass out too.

Though I really didn't want to be found in my current situation. Our circle was a cesspool of gossip, and this piece of chatter would equal an atomic bomb.

The door opened, and Massimo appeared before I could push myself into a sitting position or figure out what was happening. I was glad I'd covered myself with my skirt, but the situation was still compromising, and Massimo was too intelligent.

His keen eyes took in the scene and probably figured out every little detail of my mortification.

Carlotta's face framed in her dark curls peeked past Massimo's broad frame. Her eyes grew wide, and she squeezed past Massimo and rushed into the room. Massimo closed the door, for which I was grateful. I didn't need anyone else to see me like this.

"Rory, what happened?" Carlotta asked after a disparaging look at Nevio, who still hadn't stirred. I'd never seen him this out of it. He probably wouldn't remember a thing tomorrow. I almost choked on laughter. Had I really thought tonight would end with an epiphany for him?

I sat up, curling my lips when I realized I had splatters of vomit on my arm and leg. My shirt wasn't unscathed either. I cringed.

"I'll see if the bathroom is clear so you can help Aurora clean up. Once you're done, go down to my car. I'll be there in a bit," Massimo said. He barely looked at me as he headed for Nevio, already picking up his phone, probably to call Alessio for backup. "You have to come upstairs, the second bedroom on the left."

He hung up and moved past us into the corridor. He hammered against the bathroom door and scared away a couple of girls I didn't know.

"Thank you," Carlotta said as she led me inside.

He gave a curt nod, then closed the bathroom door, and Carlotta locked it. I sank down on the edge of the tub, and the tears started flowing freely again.

Carlotta dipped a washcloth under water, then sank down beside me and began to clean my face, arms, and legs. "Rory, what did he do?"

The undercurrent of fear and anger in her voice told me she was thinking the wrong thing. "It's not what you think. He didn't force me."

I stopped because even I couldn't describe what had happened between us.

"You slept together?"

I closed my eyes. "He passed out the moment he was in me." I cringed when the words left me. I'd fantasized about having my first time with Nevio. This wasn't even in the same hemisphere as my fantasy. I opened my eyes to see embarrassment and compassion reflected on Carlotta's face. We rarely talked about sex since neither of us was really comfortable with the topic, but I needed to get it off my chest, and she was the only one I could talk to about this.

"You can now say I told you so."

Carlotta shook her head with a look of annoyance. "Not like this, not now." She rubbed my back. "Will you tell someone?"

I shook my head because it wouldn't change a thing. It'd only make the situation ten times worse. "I want to pretend this never happened and just move on." After a look at Carlotta's doubtful face, I added, "I know it'll be hard to move on."

"You see Nevio every day. Your feelings won't magically disappear because he acted like an asshole. He's been doing that for years, and you still fell for it."

"Ouch," I whispered.

"Rory, you really look like a mess."

"Can I stay at your place tonight?" I asked, worried Dad or Mom would pick up on something, and then there would be hell to pay. Dad loved the Falcones, but this would ruin everything. I wouldn't be responsible for a fallout.

"Of course," Carlotta said softly. "But your dad won't be happy if you don't come home tonight."

"Massimo can tell him a lie, and if he wants confirmation that I'm with you, Dad can call your brother."

Carlotta nodded. When we headed downstairs, nobody really paid us much attention. A friend accompanying another friend who had had too much to drink and looked like shit wasn't worth a story.

On our way to Massimo's car, I spotted Alessio and Massimo with Nevio between them, dragging him down the sidewalk. They opened the trunk of the pickup and shoved Nevio inside.

I was glad I wouldn't have to see Nevio's face while Massimo took us to Carlotta's home. I wasn't sure I could ever face him again.

"Do you think Nevio remembers?" I asked miserably. I wasn't sure which option I preferred.

Carlotta let out a huff. "I'm sure Massimo will talk to him. Massimo was furious."

I wasn't the only one being delusional when it came to the other sex. If Massimo was pissed, then because Nevio wasn't in control of himself. Not because of me.

"What are you going to do now?" Carlotta asked as we settled at the table, each with a giant portion of scrambled eggs. I wasn't really hungry, especially when I remembered the taste of my burger as I threw it up, but I didn't want to let Carlotta's efforts go to waste. I shoved a bite of eggs into my mouth.

"You need to get over him."

I gave her a sardonic smile. "I know, trust me, and I'm on my way." Then I amended. "I'm at the very beginning of a long way." I sighed and speared another piece of egg, wishing it were Nevio's privates. "I think I need some space. I can't stay here."

Carlotta nodded. "You want to babysit Roman again?"

I had arranged to travel with the racing circus again for two weeks this summer to babysit Roman. I loved the sense of freedom offered by that lifestyle. "That had been the plan, but two weeks aren't enough. I need more time, more space. I was thinking of asking Aunt Aria if I can spend the summer with them and maybe do an internship with the Famiglia doctor."

Even if I had originally planned to go to college for a nursing degree, my backup plan had been to intern with our Camorra doc, but the Famiglia doc was a valid option too.

Carlotta's eyes grew wide. "Do you really think your dad will allow it?"

Dad was protective of me, but Mom wasn't as strict. And Dad trusted me. He knew I wasn't a troublemaker, which was another reason he couldn't find out about last night. I'd be grounded for eternity. Nobody in the Camorra would care that I was practically an adult.

"If I say the right thing…"

"Aren't you worried he'll get suspicious?"

"He can't ever find out. No one can."

Carlotta bit her lip. "If you ever marry…"

Of course Carlotta's thought would go in that direction. For her, entering marriage as a virgin was of utmost importance. I flushed. "I don't have any plans to marry any time soon." I still couldn't imagine being with anyone but Nevio, which was exactly why I needed to get as far away as possible as soon as possible.

"Rory, did he use protection?"

I froze. "No. I mean…I don't think so. I didn't really pay attention." I swallowed. "But like I said he passed out…"

Carlotta still looked concerned, and I was too. Even if the chances were very slim, they were there. I knew enough about conception and contraception to realize that pregnancy could occur without the man having an actual orgasm.

"When is your period due?"

"In around ten to twelve days."

My stomach tightened. I didn't even want to consider that by some stroke of bad luck, my miserable first time—if it even qualified as that—would lead to lifelong consequences in the form of a child. Nevio's child.

This would definitely end Dad's close bond with the Falcones.

Scratch that. It would end in several deaths…

Chapter Thirteen

Aurora

Mom picked me up at Carlotta's in the early afternoon after a meeting with a client, a Camorra soldier, who was in trouble at the local police station.

Her eyes were practically X-raying me as I got into the car, but I'd showered for almost an hour, put on plenty of makeup to cover my sickly skin tone, and decided on a colorful dress from Carlotta's wardrobe. I looked positively peachy.

"You look nice," I said, not just to appease her but because I liked Mom's business looks of fitted dresses and blazers with matching pumps. She looked so different from the easygoing Mom I knew from home.

Mom smiled slightly and waited for me to buckle up before she pulled away. "Your father isn't happy that you spent the night at Carlotta's without a warning."

"I called last night."

By Frenzy I *Rain*

Mom nodded. "You did, and we appreciate that, but it still would have been nice if you decided your sleepovers in advance so Dad can make sure security is in place."

I couldn't help but roll my eyes. "Mom, I was at Carlotta's, and her brother was there. Dad knows Diego can protect us."

Mom nodded again, focused on traffic as she steered the BMW SUV. "Still, the sudden change of plans made him wonder if something occurred that led to the decision." Mom stopped at a red light and slanted me a look she probably used on her clients too. Stern and X-raying. "Did anything happen at the party that I should know about?"

I didn't miss that she didn't include Dad. Mom knew that Dad, like many Made Men, could be overprotective. "What could have possibly happened? Everyone knows who I am, and the Unholy Trinity would have kicked anyone's ass."

"Language," Mom scolded gently, which I always found funny because sometimes she forgot herself and cursed badly when she drove.

"My life's horrifically uneventful, just how Dad likes it," I said. My skin felt warm and itchy even as the lies slipped easily from my lips. I could still sense Mom's suspicion and decided to sprinkle my lie with some truth to get her off my back. "I had a couple of beers and threw up. It was really embarrassing. Carlotta had to hold my hair back, and I got some vomit on myself and her dress. I didn't want to go home like that. You know what Dad would have said."

Mom pursed her lips. "You shouldn't drink."

"Everyone does, and it was just two bottles of beer, but my body simply doesn't tolerate it. Don't tell Dad about it. He'll make a big deal of it and somehow compare the situation to what happened with Grandma as if me having a drink at a party like every teenager will lead to me becoming a drug addict."

Grandma was Mom's weak spot. I knew she and Dad had fought because of her in the past, so I felt a tad guilty that I was using it to save my ass, but the situation was too dire.

"We won't tell your dad. But you have to promise me not to drink again."

"Never again?" I joked, almost feeling like myself for a moment. Mom always made me feel better simply by being there and understanding.

"Not at parties, and not any time soon," she said firmly.

"Thanks, Mom. I'm glad this stays a secret between us."

A hint of guilt crossed Mom's face. "Your dad wants to protect you, so we shouldn't make it a habit to keep things from him. It's ingrained into every man in this world from birth." As if I didn't know it. Even Davide was already obnoxiously protective, acting as if he were actually the older sibling.

"I've been meaning to talk to you about something else for a while now…"

Mom pulled up our driveway. "Okay…"

I waited for her to park beside Dad's BMW limousine before I spoke again. "You know I want to gain some experience before committing to a college degree in nursing or medicine."

"Yes, you mentioned interning with the doc," Mom said, angling her body to give me her full attention.

I bit my lower lip and gave her a hesitant smile. "I really want to spend the summer in New York and intern with the Famiglia doc."

Mom's face became instantly worried. "That's far away, Aurora, and you know peace isn't even a year old."

"There was peace for a long time before then, Mom, and now that Amo and Greta are married, neither Luca nor Remo will risk another war. I really want to spend some time with our family in New York. I really miss seeing my aunts and cousins. We don't have any family here, which makes me sad. I know I can't ever see Dad's family in Chicago, but I want to be with the family we're not at war with."

Mom sighed. "This is a lot to stomach. It's May, so you're springing this on us late. I just worry that this decision is based on something I should know about."

"I just feel like I need to spend some time with other people. Carlotta will visit family in Los Angeles, and I don't want to spend my summer with the Unholy Trinity or my little brother."

Mom nodded slowly. "I'd rather you don't spend your summer with the trio either."

If you only knew…

Memories from last night popped up uninvited.

"Will you say yes to me spending the summer in New York?" I could

By Frenzy I *Pain*

see the hesitation in Mom's face. "I need you on my side for this. Dad won't agree if you're hesitant."

"I'll give Aria a call tonight. Let me iron out things with her first. If I have a good feeling after my chat with her, you'll have to work your charm on him, and then I'll talk to him to break down his last defenses."

I hugged her. "Thanks, Mom."

"I have to chat with Aria first. I haven't made up my mind yet."

I doubted Aria would say anything that would intensify Mom's hesitation. Aria wanted our family to be together. She missed Dad, and she'd be delighted to have me with them. Now I just had to survive the weeks until I could leave. Even Mom wouldn't allow me to go to New York before my birthday in ten days.

Once home, I went to my room and didn't leave it except for dinner that evening. I could hear the sounds of laughter coming from the pool on the Falcone premises. I couldn't see it from my window, but I could imagine the trio having fun.

I pressed my lips together. Nevio probably went about his day as if nothing had happened. I sucked in a deep breath as a wave of anger mixed with deep hurt welled up in me. If this wasn't proof that Nevio didn't care about me, I didn't know.

I squared my shoulders. I was done. Once and for all. I'd had my pity party last night and this morning. I'd embarrassed myself enough for a life time. I would simply move on from this like Nevio had done. I wasn't going to mope around and cry my eyes out again.

I perched on the windowsill and took out my cell. Since the wedding, I had Isa's number again so I texted her.

> **What are you up to this summer?**
>
> **Write a few essays in preparation for my courses. And hopefully escape New York's heat and spend a few weeks in the Hamptons.**
>
> **The Hamptons sound perfect. I wish I could spend the summer with you.**

Do it.

I grinned. **I need approval from my parents. Mom is having a chat with Aria tonight.**

Will you be coming alone?

Just me.

Good. Keep me updated. If you want, I can chat with my mother.

That would be great. I need all the support I can get.

Done. We'll have the summer of our lives.

I blew out a breath. Being this over-the-top positive was a bit un-Isa-like, but maybe she needed a great summer as much as I did. She'd gone through some shit herself, so we could both kick each other's ass if we moped around.

I felt better, lighter, as if, for the first time in a while, I was the master of my own life, my happiness. I'd been so dependent on Nevio's emotions that I'd felt helpless. Now that he'd broken my heart and I'd fallen as deep as I possibly could, I could start over.

The next day, I felt marginally better. My thoughts revolved around Mom's conversation with Aria, which she'd had after dinner last night, but she and Dad had to work early today, so they hadn't been at the breakfast table.

After a rushed breakfast to avoid Davide's annoying questions about the party, I returned to my room to watch a few of my favorite skateboard YouTubers.

Someone knocked on my door, and my positive attitude went out the window. What if this was Nevio? I was so ready to move on, but I hadn't yet, and a confrontation with him would take a lot out of me. I didn't want to cry. I didn't want to be vulnerable in front of him.

I wanted to give him the middle finger, kick his balls, and send him away. I tried to channel this version of Aurora as I went to my door and opened it with force.

Davide raised his eyebrows. "Why are you scowling like that?"

"Because I want some peace and quiet, and I'm not getting it."

He made a face as if he couldn't be bothered with my emotions. "Whatever. I'm heading over to the pool. Do you want to come too?"

It was sweltering, and I would have loved a splash in the pool, but there was no way I would go over to the Falcone's today. With a little luck, I'd avoid Nevio until I'd hopefully leave for New York.

The splashing and laughter echoed through my window again as if to mock me.

"No, thanks. I'll stay in."

"It's 110 degrees. You'll melt."

"I'll turn the AC up, then."

He shrugged and turned. "Nevio asked when you'd come over, just so you know."

My throat tightened. "You can tell him I'm not."

I closed my door.

Ten minutes later, there was another knock. Gosh, what now? I stomped toward the door and ripped it open.

The floor seemed to drop out from under my feet when I spotted Nevio.

I stared up at him. I couldn't remember the last time he'd bothered coming over. Suddenly, as if reminded of what happened, I felt the soreness between my legs that I'd successfully ignored all day. Every feeling of mortification and hurt was back.

"Go away," I pressed out. I began to shut the door, but Nevio shoved it open with his shoulder, slipped into my room, and closed the door.

"Get out," I said in an even tighter voice. I could feel heat behind my eyeballs, dammit. I would not cry in front of him.

Nevio was in swim trunks, but at least he had the decency to wear a T-shirt over them. If he'd showed up in my room half naked, I would have completely lost it.

"We need to talk, Rory."

Rory.

Rory.

I didn't want him to call me Rory anymore. It had always meant something to me. Now, it meant I'd been stupid.

"No, we don't."

Nevio regarded me as if he didn't understand me but wanted to. Dark shadows played under his eyes. I hoped he'd had the hangover of his life.

"I'm not leaving before we've talked about this."

This.

"Do you even remember what happened?" I whispered harshly.

His expression told me he didn't. Massimo must have told him whatever he'd gathered, and this realization made everything ten times worse.

I turned around and stalked toward my window. I couldn't even look at him. He looked almost uninvolved. Maybe I should just call Dad and have him throw Nevio out. Things would be over then, but at least I'd be spared this painful conversation.

"I don't," he said. "Listen, Rory."

Again, Rory.

I sank my teeth into my lower lip.

"Massimo thinks we slept together. Things didn't look good when he found you and me in a room."

This was the whole essence of our story?

"I want your version."

I swallowed, and then it burst out of me. Everything that had happened just spewed out of me, even the part where I vomited all over the floor. I wanted him to know, and I didn't care.

He was silent for a moment, and I was glad I didn't have to see his face. His hand came down on my shoulder.

I flinched away and stumbled toward my desk. "Don't touch me!"

Not that he'd done much of that last night. What kind of pitiful first time have I had? Maybe Carlotta had a point when she wanted to wait until marriage.

"Aren't you overreacting?" he asked. "It sounds like hardly anything happened. Maybe even your hymen is still intact because I doubt I was really in all the way."

I whirled on him.

Overreacting?

I couldn't believe he really said that. Could he even imagine how hard it was for me to face him right now?

"Hardly anything happened?" I uttered in a shaky voice. "Do you really think this is about my…my stupid hymen?"

His dark eyes searched mine. He ran a hand through his hair, obviously already tired of this conversation.

"Listen—"

"No, you listen!" I hissed, so fucking done with him and his inability to see the problem. "I don't want to see you again. I'm done with you. Leave me alone, or I'll tell my father about this."

Nevio's expression flickered with harshness at my threat. He nodded once, glanced down at his hands, and then his shoulders moved as if he took a deep breath. The harshness was gone when he looked back up, and the nonchalant attitude was back.

"I was the one who was non compos mentis, as Massimo would call it, and couldn't consent to anything. So I reckon I should be angry with you. I bet your dad will see it that way too." He grinned as if this was funny. He actually *grinned*. Was he this oblivious to other people's emotions, this callous? Why was I even surprised?

I turned back to my desk, away from him.

For the first time in my life, rage toward Nevio blacked out my potent infatuation. I could hardly breathe from it, could feel it in the throbbing of my veins, in the hammering of my heart, in the whooshing of my ears.

I gripped the first thing I could from my desk, a heavy hole punch, whirled back around, and hurled it at Nevio. He was closer than expected. As usual, I hadn't heard him move. It flew toward his head, right at his temple. I froze, my eyes widening. His arm popped up, blocking the heavy object. It hit the underside of his arm, right below his wrist.

His face flashed with pain for a bare second, soon replaced by terrifying fury and something I'd never seen in his eyes. Murder. Pure hunger for blood and carnage.

He took a step back, closed his eyes, and sucked in a deep breath. When he opened his eyes again, he was in control, and his ability to do so so easily when I could hardly maintain a subpar level of control around him made me even angrier.

I grabbed a book and flung it at him, then another. Dad's warnings about Nevio's lack of control flew right past me.

Nevio moved toward me, grabbed my wrist, and jerked me toward him so our chests collided.

I scowled up at him. "You are everything bad and rotten that people warned me about. I hate you. I don't think I've ever hated anyone as much as I hate you," I hissed, even as my eyes blurred with tears.

Through them, I could see Nevio's hard face and the bitter smile. "As you should. Finally, some common sense, Rory."

"Let me go. I never want to talk to you again. I'm going to New York for the summer, maybe longer. I don't want to see you."

A hint of confusion in his eyes changed. Nevio touched my chin with his already swelling hand. I recoiled, but he didn't retreat. "You belong in Las Vegas, and you know it."

He released me and stepped back, then walked out of the room. I swallowed hard, fighting for composure, but then the tears burst forth and I couldn't hold them back.

I needed to leave. I'd beg Dad on my knees if I had to, but I wouldn't stay here.

Nevio

Massimo inspected my arm with intense curiosity. "The bruising suggests a defensive injury against an object, not a limb."

Alessio regarded me without pause. "You let Aurora break your arm."

"His ulna," Massimo corrected, still prodding my arm mercilessly.

"Whatever the fuck it's called. The interesting facts aren't your Latin skills, but the fact that Nevio let Aurora break a bone in his body, very likely on purpose, and I bet she still looks pretty unscathed, and he doesn't even seem to be angry."

Massimo slanted a look up at my face. "I wouldn't retaliate if a female from our family or Fabi's family injured me for understandable reasons."

"What exactly happened between you and Aurora that night? And what did you tell her today to bring out her nonexistent violent side?" Alessio asked, narrowing his eyes in that mind-reading way he sometimes had.

I bared my teeth. "Nothing you need to know. We had a little argument about the details of the night."

Alessio scoffed. "We all know Aurora is too in love with you to speak her mind."

By Frenzy I *Pain*

I pushed to my feet. "Get off my fucking back, or I'll unleash some of my rage on you. Aurora's none of your business."

"She isn't yours either," Massimo said.

I stalked out. I really wasn't in the mood to have them analyze me. Their track record with girls wasn't very impressive either.

I headed downstairs in search of Nino. He was more experienced when it came to treating injuries, and more importantly, he was less likely to grate on my nerves. He knew less about Aurora.

Of course, Nino repeated the same boring monologue as Massimo about my injury.

"Three weeks with a cast, and you need to rest your arm for four to six weeks."

"It'll heal faster."

Nino gave me a condescending look. Nobody could pull it off quite like him. "Your body is still bound to the rules of biology, even if your mind breaks the confines on occasion."

I laughed. Nino still landed the best punches, and I didn't mean with his fists.

Chapter Fourteen

Aurora

My confrontation with Nevio had only hardened my resolve to leave Las Vegas as soon as possible. I didn't even care about missing my prom. I'd never been excited to go in the first place. Nobody had dared to ask me or Carlotta to the dance. A foolish part of me had waited for Nevio to do it. Now that dream had gone out the window. Even if he did ask, I'd say no and perhaps throw another heavy object at him. Hurting him had been oddly satisfying.

I searched for Mom and found her in her office, bent over some folders. She looked up when I stepped in. "Did you talk to Aria?"

I knew she said she'd do it, and Mom usually kept her word.

Mom gave me an amused look. "Of course I did. I was actually about to come to your room and talk to you about it before you barged in without knocking."

"Sorry," I said, walking over to Mom's desk. "And? What did she say?"

Mom leaned back in her chair. A few strands had fallen from her ponytail and messily framed her freckled face. She must have run her fingers through it in agitation. I hoped that wasn't about the call. "She was very positive about it. Aria thinks it would be great to become closer as a family, and she'd love to have a girl under her roof again. If this works out, I see plenty of shopping trips in your future."

Neither Mom nor I were big shopping queens. We only went shopping when we needed something and were always quick about it. But I'd bear hours of shopping if this meant going to New York. "So she said yes?"

"Aria said yes."

"And what do you say?" I asked as I perched on the edge of Mom's desk with a small pleading smile.

"I'm still worried about why you want to go, but I also feel like you're old enough to spread your wings a little. It'll do you good to be away from Las Vegas, even if New York's rules won't allow you much freedom either."

I wasn't concerned about my level of freedom. I was used to being guarded at all times. "Thanks, Mom."

Mom made a move with her hand that suggested I needed to slow down. "Aria still needs to talk to Luca about this. She was confident that he'd agree as you aren't a safety concern even by his strict views."

I huffed, but of course, he had a point. If one of the guys had asked to spend a few months in New York like Adamo had done many years ago, the answer would probably be no right now.

"And then there's Dad," Mom said, pursing her lips. She pushed off her chair and touched my shoulder. "I think we can agree that he'll be the hardest nut to crack. But we should have a good chance if we both talk to him. You should talk to him first, and then I'll join in and share my opinion."

"What should I say?"

"Don't say you want to spread your wings or enjoy freedom or anything of the sort. And don't say anything about wanting to leave Vegas either. He'll try to find the source for why you want to leave rather than let you go, and I assume that's not something you want."

"No," I said quickly. Even if I'd threatened Nevio with telling Dad, that was the absolute last thing I would do.

"How about you talk to him now, and during dinner it's my turn?"

I gave Mom a peck and walked out. Since Dad wasn't away for work, that meant he was usually working out.

I found Dad downstairs in our gym, doing stretches. "Dad, I need to talk to you."

Dad looked up from the mat, his eyes narrowing in instant concern. I had made sure to make my voice light and my face matter-of-fact, but Dad had a nerve-racking ability to read people. It made keeping secrets in this house an arduous task. "All right." He pushed to his feet and walked over to the bench. "This sounds serious."

It was, on many levels. I sank down beside him and gave him a hesitant smile. Seeing his worried expression, my hopes for an easy "yes" dwindled.

I cleared my throat. "I want to spend the summer in New York with Aunt Aria."

His expression fell. "What happened?" The hard edge of his voice told me he was ready to go on a vendetta.

I crossed my legs casually and rolled my eyes. If I gave anything away, this would take a really bad turn. "Nothing. I just need a change of scenery."

Dad squeezed my shoulder, his blue eyes practically X-raying me. "Aurora, I need to know if anything happened. Whenever you talked about this summer, you planned to spend it with Carlotta and babysit Roman for a couple of weeks. You never mentioned New York. What about the summer courses you need in preparation for your nursing program?"

My pulse sped up like it always did when I was put on the spot. I gave a shrug. "I changed my mind. I want to spend some time with the other part of our family. I'll have to spend the rest of my life in Vegas, so I want to use this chance to see something new. I also want to do longer internships before I commit to the nursing program. It's a responsible job, and I want to ensure I'm up for it before taking someone else's spot in the program. I could intern with the Famiglia doc while living in New York."

"You sound like living in Las Vegas is punishment."

It had never felt like that, but now, with the prospect of having to be around Nevio and his future conquests, Las Vegas *seemed* like a punishment.

"What happened at the party you attended? Is your sudden change of mind regarding the summer related to your spontaneous wish to spend the night at Carlotta's?"

Dad's eyes seemed to dig into my brain, trying to extract the information

By Frenzy I *Pain*

he wanted. Even if I hated lying to him, this truth was too destructible to share. Dad would try to kill Nevio. They would both end up seriously injured, and his connection to the Falcone brothers would be irrevocably damaged. I wouldn't be responsible for that.

"Dad," I said with a hint of annoyance. "Have you ever considered that my asking you at the last minute is a tactic so you don't overanalyze everything?"

Dad scowled. "I'm responsible for your safety, and I'm taking that job very seriously."

"I know," I said with a huff. "But with Greta in New York, I'm perfectly safe. I really missed my aunts and cousins during the war and want to spend more time with them. Don't you miss them?"

Dad's expression remained stoic. He didn't like to talk about this. Maybe because he really missed them a lot. "I'll have to talk to your mother first, but I have a feeling you already did, and you two are going to gang up on me."

I made an innocent face. "You know Mom is really good at seeing the pros and cons of a situation. She'd never just side with me unless it was really the best option."

Dad chuckled and tousled my hair as if I were a toddler. "Right. I won't make a decision before I've talked to Luca and then Remo. You being in New York is a potential safety risk that needs to be discussed with the Capo."

"His own daughter is over there. If she's safe, I doubt he'll deem the situation as too risky for me."

I could tell that Dad seemed to think the same thing and didn't really like it very much.

Nevio

I stared at the bandage around my wrist. The broken bone limited my range of motion and reminded me of my confrontation with Rory. Not that I needed one.

Ever since our conversation yesterday, my thoughts had revolved around her.

Hearing her recount of what had happened between us at the party left a foul taste in my mouth. I'd really tried to keep my distance from her in the last year. Of course it had to end like this. I was losing control and messing up worse than anticipated.

I wasn't sure how I felt about what had happened. Was the tight sensation in my chest guilt? I wasn't familiar enough with the emotion to be one hundred percent sure. What I definitely felt was regret. Though not exactly in the way that I should feel. I regretted that I couldn't remember anything. Considering how miserable of a fuck I'd delivered, it was probably for the best, but I couldn't help but want a repeat performance that I would remember and would serve as a better first time for her than the shit show at the party.

Fuck, these thoughts weren't good. Not good in the slightest. The devil was on my shoulder, giving me ideas I shouldn't entertain. Aurora wanted space, and I should give it to her. Letting her go to New York? I didn't think I could accept that.

The door to the former ballet studio ripped open. Dad, followed by Nino, walked in, looking as if I was a traitor he had to deal with.

Nino narrowed his eyes at me as he closed the door.

I leaned back in the chair I'd been occupying for almost an hour while pondering my next move. "What's wrong?"

Dad pulled up a chair in front of me. "Fabi informed me that Aurora has asked to spend the summer in New York, possibly even longer. My instincts tell me this has something to do with you. Tell me I'm wrong."

I forced down the flood of emotion his words caused in me. Dad was watching me closely, fury swirling in his eyes. I'd thought Aurora's mention of New York had been an empty threat to get my attention, but apparently, I was wrong.

"Are you listening to a fucking word I just said? Tell me I'm wrong, and this has nothing to do with you."

"Why does it have to be me?"

"Because Alessio and Massimo have too much common sense to mess with Fabi's daughter."

I almost mentioned Massimo's interest in Carlotta but gritted my teeth instead. I simply returned Dad's gaze. Anything I said would only make the situation worse, and it was already fucking bad.

By Frenzy I *Pain*

Dad grabbed my shirt and jerked me closer to him, causing my bandaged arm to bang against the armrest. I hissed through my teeth.

Nino cleared his throat. "His ulna is broken."

"He can stand the pain," Dad said. He was pissed, really pissed, and I doubted he really knew what had happened, or he would have broken my wrist and every finger too.

I grinned. "I get off on it like you, Dad."

"Careful."

"Did Aurora break your ulna?" Nino asked calmly as if the situation wasn't about to detonate. Considering how pissed both Alessio and Massimo were, I was surprised they hadn't run to their dad and snitched on me.

"You think she could?"

"If you mean mentally? Most people are capable of violence if given the right incentive, and you're very adept at bringing people to the brink. From a physical standpoint, she obviously wouldn't stand a chance against you, but in the right situation, Kiara could injure me."

I didn't like the comparison. It lacked a comparable basis, which was really not Nino's style.

"You would die before you'd ever hurt Kiara."

Nino motioned to my bandage. "How's the arm?"

Dad, who'd been listening closely, tugged at my shirt, bringing my attention back to him. "You wouldn't hurt a member of this family, and I count Fabiano's family in it."

Good thing that we weren't related by blood…

I didn't miss the slightest hint of uncertainty in his voice, and I had to admit it stung.

Though I had no reason to get my fucking boxers in a bunch. After all, I *had* hurt Aurora.

"Not on purpose," I admitted, as honest as I rarely was.

Dad released me and jerked to his feet. He drew in a deep breath through his nose. His rage filled the room. Many people thought I was a carbon copy of Dad, and while physically that might be close to the truth, I was far more unhinged than he was.

"You'll tell me what you did, or I swear on this family that I'll get it out of you by whatever means necessary," he snarled. My gaze dropped to the curved knife at his waist. I'd often wondered how its blade would feel, how I would measure up against Dad's or Nino's talent. How would it feel to bathe in my own blood for once?

"I always feared how my genes would come to play in a child, and you surpassed every fear I had."

My heart briefly throbbed harder, but I simply shrugged in reaction to Dad's words. I didn't need reminding that I had inherited every ounce of darkness he harbored.

"Remo," Nino said.

"You don't have to side with me. His words don't hurt me. Nothing does."

"For you, I hope that one day you'll see that's not the case." Dad turned to the door. "I can't force the words out of you, but I can talk to Aurora. Her respect for me is too great. She'll spill your secrets."

I shoved to my feet. "You'll stay the fuck away from her."

"I'm Capo, and you'll watch your mouth," he growled.

I tried to stalk to Dad, ready for the next step. Nino gripped my injured arm tightly, and I ground to a halt with a snarl.

"You can spare Aurora a conversation if you tell your father what he wants to know."

I ripped away from his hold. "It's not in my nature to spare someone. Right, Dad?" I took a deep breath, my chest heaving. Silence filled the room. Dad and Nino simply looked at me. Fuck. I hated them sometimes. "I fucked Aurora at the last party, all right?"

Neither Nino nor Dad could hide their shock. I wasn't sure why they were being preachy, especially Dad. He'd kidnapped Mom. My transgression was nowhere near as bad.

I could see a question in Dad's eyes that stung worse than his knife ever could. I was a monster, and atrocities were dear to my heart, but when it came to Aurora, most of them weren't on the menu. "I was stinking drunk. I could hardly walk, and I remember only bits and pieces from the night, but Aurora came to me. I didn't force myself on her."

"Then why the fuck is she fleeing Las Vegas as if the devil were after her?"

I hadn't dwelled on the question so far. It was uncomfortable in a way I wasn't familiar with. "She wanted something else from me, something I can't give her or anyone."

"You just wanted to fuck her, and she thought it was more."

"I didn't even realize it was her." I didn't mention the disgraceful way I ended the night. That was a part of my memories I hadn't wanted back.

Dad's lip curled. "This is unacceptable, even for you, son. Do you even realize how bad you fucked up this time?"

"If Fabiano finds out, things are going to get very unpleasant," Nino said.

I smiled sardonically. That was the understatement of the year. "I guess I have this talent of treating the ladies right from you, Dad. Kidnapping Mom set a very good example for me."

Dad curled his hands to fists. I could imagine how hard it was for him to control his rage right now. "I should send you away. Aurora shouldn't have to run from your idiocy."

"If you send me to New York, you can kiss peace goodbye."

Dad shook his head, his body stiff with fury. "I don't have the patience to deal with him today. For what he did, the only punishment that comes to mind…" He turned back to the door and kicked it in. It landed with an earsplitting bang on the small terrace, sending splinters flying everywhere. He stalked away without another word.

Nino released a small sigh.

A couple of minutes later, Kiara poked her head in, her brows drawn together in concern. "What's the matter?"

"You don't want to know, trust me," I muttered.

"He's right."

Kiara glanced from Nino to me with pursed lips. "Things have been tense recently."

"And they have the potential to get far worse, so please don't try to find out more," Nino said.

Kiara nodded slowly. But I knew her caring, motherly nature would send her to my room soon. The hopeless optimist in her still thought I needed mental support.

"I assume Dad won't talk to Fabiano about this?" I asked when Kiara was gone.

Nino shook his head. "Keeping a secret of this proportion might look like betrayal to Fabiano, but telling him might have consequences we don't even want to consider. We can only hope that Aurora won't tell him and that the dust settles on the matter."

I doubted Aurora would spill the beans. She wasn't like that, even if she'd threatened me with telling her father.

"I assume you know to keep your distance from Aurora until further notice," Nino said quietly.

"Sure."

Chapter
Fifteen

Aurora

It wasn't the first time I spent time away from home. The previous two summers, I'd spent a couple of weeks with Adamo and Dinara at the racing track to watch their son Roman while they dealt with business.

But I'd be gone longer this time. Maybe just for two months during the summer, or maybe beyond that. I wasn't sure how long my heart would need to heal, how long it would take to come to terms with the fact that Nevio and I were a bad idea that would never happen. I wanted to turn love to hate, wanted to shield my heart with pure contempt for the man who'd ignored me most of my life and then taken my virginity without even realizing it was me, as if I were so inconsequential to him that even then my presence hadn't registered.

When I landed in New York, I was nervous. I wasn't even alone. Dad had insisted on accompanying me. I supposed he wanted to make sure I was really well protected. Things between the Camorra and the Famiglia were still somewhat shaky despite Greta's marriage to Amo.

I'd briefly considered living with them, but they were newlyweds, so my presence would probably bother them. Not to mention, Greta was too close to Nevio. That seemed like an awfully bad idea.

Dad and I took a cab to the townhouse where my aunt Aria lived with her family. My cousin Valerio was around my age, but I hadn't seen him very often due to the physical distance between us and the war.

Dad was mainly concerned about me being under Luca's roof and rule for the time of my stay. Luca was the Capo of the Famiglia and, according to Dad's frequent rants, an overconfident madman.

I never mentioned that Remo didn't have the best reputation either.

When we pulled up in front of their townhouse, I felt a hint of nervousness. The door opened when Dad and I approached the staircase leading up to the entrance.

Aria, closely shadowed by Luca, stood in the doorway. Her beaming expression calmed my anxiety. Luca looked less enthused, though I attributed that to seeing Dad. Those two had butted heads in the past, and the look that passed between them had me worried that Dad might change his mind. After the utter relief I felt upon leaving Las Vegas, I couldn't imagine returning right away.

Aria must have seen the worry in my expression because she hugged me in greeting and whispered, "It'll be all right."

I gave her a grateful smile and followed her into the living room. It was pure Aria—light, bright colors and an air of warmth. I felt instantly welcome, almost at home.

We settled at the dining table, and soon after, a maid carried pots and bowls with food into the room. Enough to feed an army.

"Who else is coming over? Have you planned another surprise ambush?" Dad asked in a sarcastic tone that made me choke on my water.

Aria cleared her throat after a look at Luca, then she said sternly, "Greta and Amo are late, and so is Valerio."

"He always is," Luca said, but his eyes were on Dad.

The tension seemed to rise to crushing dimensions when the front door opened. Valerio, Greta, and Amo appeared in the living room soon after. I was strangely nervous to meet Greta, which was ridiculous. Amo hovered close to Greta, one arm slung around her waist in a protective gesture. She appeared fragile, like a doll, but she'd survived things few other people had. I admired her for her strength.

"You're late," Aria said with narrowed eyes at Amo and Valerio before she sent Greta a smile and pulled her into a hug. Greta settled on my other side and gave me a small smile. I tried not to overanalyze every gesture. Greta had always been a restrained person.

Amo gave me a nod, and Valerio sent me a grin that let some of the tension slip away.

Greta acted at ease during dinner, her expression not suggesting that she knew anything about what went down between Nevio and me.

I wasn't sure if that was because they weren't as close as they used to be or if Nevio realized this was something he couldn't share with anyone. Thanks to Aria and Valerio, the conversations stayed on safe ground.

After dinner, Greta asked me to join her in the garden, which could only mean she knew. Dad didn't mind, so she led me away from the dining table.

The moment we were outside alone, Greta gave me a small, sad smile that made my stomach drop. "I'm sorry Nevio hurt you."

I didn't say anything and hoped my face wasn't giving away anything either. Her words left room for plenty of interpretation, and I didn't want to reveal more than necessary. I'd sworn I would be more careful.

She nodded slowly as if my reaction made sense and peered at the night sky. "Before Amo, I never really wasted time thinking about love or soulmates, and I'm still not entirely sure I believe in the latter. Now that I have Amo, I want the same for Nevio. I want someone who speaks to his soul and balances his dark."

I laughed. "Nevio doesn't have a soul, and if you know what happened, then you also know I'm not that person you want for him. I doubt someone like that exists. At least not on earth."

Perhaps in hell.

Greta clasped her hands in front of her belly. "Nevio called me. I think he's really upset that you left because of what he did. He cares about you, Aurora, and very few people can say that about themselves."

Nevio certainly had a strange way of showing me how much he cared about me.

"You're getting something wrong. Nevio doesn't care about me, not like that. He's probably just angry because I didn't obey his command to stay in Vegas. He acts like a Capo, even when he's not."

Greta tilted her head, her eyes narrowed in thought. "I don't think you're right. For some of us, it isn't easy to understand and act upon our feelings."

"That would require Nevio to have feelings beyond anger and hatred," I muttered.

Greta gave me a small smile, but I could tell she did it because she didn't want to argue with me, not because she agreed. Maybe Nevio could feel more for someone, but I wouldn't be the one who'd wade through layer after layer of whatever messed-up darkness covered it to uncover it. I was done with him. I'd made a fool out of myself, and I wouldn't keep doing it.

When we returned to the dining room, only Aria was there. My belly tightened. "Where's Dad?"

"He's talking to Luca, Valerio, and Amo in the office."

I cringed, considering what Dad would tell them. I bet he had a long list of rules. Before my worry could drive me crazy, the three emerged from the office. One look at Dad's face told me he was ready to leave. He came toward me and grabbed my shoulders.

"I should return to the hotel to grab some sleep before my early flight. All right?"

I nodded with a reassuring smile. I could tell he was still wary of leaving me.

"If you need anything, call me. And if you change your mind, you can come home any time."

"I'll be fine."

Dad stepped back with a nod, but his eyes remained worried.

Aria wrapped an arm around my shoulders. "You don't have any reason to worry, Fabiano. Aurora will be perfectly safe here."

The three of us moved toward the front door. I stepped forward once more and hugged Dad tightly.

"You'll write each day and call your mother every other day, understood?"

"Yes, Dad," I said in exasperation. He'd told me the same about a dozen times. Dad pulled back, then took a step back before turning and heading to the waiting car.

I wondered what kind of instructions Dad had given them. Probably all of them about boys. I waved as Dad drove away, then released a deep sigh. I felt relieved to be away from Vegas and my family's watchful eyes, but at the same time, I was also very nervous. While I was excited about spending time with Isa and my other cousins, I'd miss my talks with Mom and Carlotta. Phone calls just weren't the same.

"I'd like a word with you, Aurora," Luca said.

I froze, not having expected that.

"Uhh, sure."

Aria frowned at her husband, obviously as surprised by this as I was. "I'm sure this can be done right here. Aurora must be tired."

Luca gave a terse nod before he met my gaze once more. "I don't care how things are run in Vegas, but in my territory, I won't allow you to see any boys."

"I'm not here to see boys," I said with an embarrassed smile. I was here to run from one. Though calling Nevio a boy seemed awfully wrong. Nothing about him conveyed the necessary innocence to justify that label. Greta's curious gaze made me even more nervous than Luca.

Luca gave a satisfied nod, but his expression remained stern. "Valerio is going to take over most of your protection and accompany you wherever you go. If he's not available, your cousin Flavio will take his place."

I nodded because that was what Luca obviously expected. I wasn't concerned about any of this. Boys were the last thing on my mind right now.

"I'll keep a close eye on her," Valerio said, winking at me. I wasn't sure if this meant he wouldn't or if he simply wanted to put me at ease. I gave him a smile. His easygoing nature helped to set me at ease. Amo was more closed off, at least in recent years. I remembered him more relaxed.

"We'll return home now. There's plenty of time for Greta and Aurora to spend together in the next few weeks," Amo said to his father before turning to Greta and holding out his hand. She gave me a tight but reassuring smile, which I returned before they left.

"Come on. I'll show you your room," Valerio said and grabbed my suitcase, which Dad had set down beside the door to the coatroom.

When neither Aria nor Luca protested, I followed my cousin upstairs. His blond hair was the same shade as Davide's, lighter than Dad's, but according to Mom, his had been that way too when he was a child. Mom always said it was the Scuderi blond.

Valerio opened the second door on the right. "My room is on this floor as well, but my parents have their rooms on the floor above us. The library is on the ground floor. We don't have a gym room because Mom always goes to Gianna's gym, and Dad and I go to the Famiglia training complex."

"I'll go to Gianna's gym if I feel like working out," I said, though I doubted that time would come. I loved skateboarding, skiing, and snowboarding, but every other sport wasn't for me. Yoga seemed positively sleep-inducing, but I'd do it if Aria or Gianna invited me to join them.

Valerio motioned me to go inside. The room was bright, with a soft gray and mint color palette. The window looked out to the yard. Most townhouses had narrow courtyards without any green, but this was the biggest house on the street, and the yard was accordingly sized, not just a square space of concrete but with actual grass and trees.

"Isa suggested that we'll have breakfast tomorrow morning," Valerio said, leaning in the doorway with crossed arms. Through his white tee, I could see the outline of the Famiglia tattoo over his heart. It was strange to think that while I was visiting family, I was in another mob family, which had always and would always make things a little tense, though Valerio certainly wasn't the reason for it.

I smiled. "Sounds great."

"I hate getting up early, so I won't agree to any dates before ten."

"What do you do when you have Famiglia duties before ten?" I asked, amused.

He grinned. "I drink insane amounts of coffee and am grumpy as fuck."

"I can't imagine you ever being grumpy."

"See, this family bonding time will give you new insights." He glanced down at his watch. "I have a date. Will you be okay?" His blue eyes showed honest interest.

"Sure. I'm exhausted, so I'll go to sleep. Have fun with your date." I wondered what date started at ten o'clock but didn't voice my thoughts. Valerio turned and closed the door.

One thing was the same in the Camorra and Famiglia. Guys could go on dates as they pleased, but girls could not.

I unpacked my clothes into the wardrobe, then undressed for a shower. After a flight, I always felt a little icky and needed to wash off the day. When I was about to enter the shower stall in my en suite bathroom, my phone beeped. I'd already answered texts from Mom, Carlotta, Kiara, Dad, and even Davide, but this message wasn't from any of them.

When I saw the name on the screen, my belly plummeted.

Nevio.

The relaxation that had started to set in evaporated. I hated that I allowed someone to have this power over me. Without looking at the message, I blocked the contact so Nevio couldn't reach me again. I knew he'd probably figure out other ways to message me, but for now, this gesture felt like I was seizing power and taking control of my happiness.

I enjoyed time with Isa, Flavio, and Valerio the following day. Despite their presence, something kept my thoughts rooted in the past. Two weeks after my night with Nevio, I started getting antsy. My period had been due two days ago. My cycle was pretty irregular, so this wasn't anything unusual. But given what had happened, my being overdue made me nervous. If my cycle was particularly long this time, it could still be up to four days before my period came—if it came at all. I couldn't wait that long. The problem was how to get my hands on a pregnancy test. I didn't get a moment to ask Isa while we were with the boys, so I postponed the question until the next day when I met Isa at her mom's yoga studio. We wanted to spend the day together without the guys, who had to work anyway.

Valerio took me there and dropped me off at the reception where Cara worked. She was in her forties but didn't look it, a real MILF how Nevio had once said, and was the wife of Growl, Remo's half brother whom he hated furiously. She was in workout clothes, which revealed how in shape she was and her brown hair was up in a neat bun.

Isa's bodyguard would take over for the rest of the day, so Valerio left right away. "Isa's in Gianna's office," Cara said, motioning to the door at her back, which opened then.

"Office? More like a dump." I glimpsed the chaos of workout material, clothes, and paperwork behind Isa and had to agree with her assessment of the room. She smiled at me, walked around the reception desk, and hugged me. "You look like you didn't get much sleep. Homesick?"

I scoffed. "Not really. But I didn't sleep much, that's true." I slanted a look at Cara, who was on the phone with someone and checking something on the laptop. Isa took my hand and led me into a vacant yoga studio.

"What's up?" she asked, righting her glasses as if that would allow her a deeper look into my soul.

Confiding in her was a risk. I didn't think she would ever share my secrets, but I was still worried. On the other hand, I desperately needed help if I wanted to buy a test, and Isa was still my best bet. I couldn't ask my aunts Aria or Liliana. They were both overly motherly types and might feel like it was their responsibility to tell my mom about it.

Gianna was a rebel, so she probably wouldn't tell anyone about it.

"I need a pregnancy test," I whispered so she had to lean closer to hear me.

Isa pulled back slightly, with a hint of surprise on her face but definitely not the amount of shock many would have shown at the request. She nodded simply as if this was no big deal. "Sure. I have a few in my bag in my locker here."

"You do?" I asked, utterly stunned.

Isa shrugged and led me to a locker in the dressing room. She took out her gym bag and motioned for me to enter one of the changing rooms. I went in, and she followed, then she opened her bag. There were indeed three pregnancy tests inside. "My mom got a bunch for me a while back," Isa said and held one out to me. "I'm keeping them here so Dad won't find them by accident."

I laughed. "My dad wouldn't be too happy about finding a pregnancy test in my bag either."

Isa searched my eyes. "If you want to talk about it, I'm here, okay? And if you're pregnant and you need to find a solution, my mother can tell you all about it."

I paused, wondering what she meant by that, but the hint of bitterness in her tone stopped me from asking. "Thanks, Isa. I really appreciate it. I don't expect this to be positive but..." I trailed off. It was difficult to explain the situation and the slim chances of me being pregnant without revealing more about the embarrassing night that I wanted to forget.

"It's a very sensitive test, so it's almost 100 percent safe if your period is due."

I nodded again and stuffed the test into my bag. "I'll use it tomorrow morning." It would take immeasurable control to wait that long, but I wanted this test to be as accurate as possible.

"Don't let Luca find it," Isa said with comically widened eyes.

I giggled. "I'll be careful."

We spend the day together at a skate park. Isa wasn't a skater, but her current novel was about a drug-addicted skater with all kinds of issues. She wanted me to show her a few tricks in detail so she could understand better when writing from his perspective. Thanks to the embarrassing scowls our bodyguards sent everyone else, we had the half-pipe to ourselves.

It was really fun to show Isa what I could do and let me forget the test in my bag until I sat at the dining table with Luca, Aria, and Valerio, and Isa, Matteo, and Gianna. Liliana and her family would be coming for dinner tomorrow, and all of us would leave for the Hamptons in a week.

Isa and I went to my room after dinner, followed by Valerio. He, Isa, and Flavio were close friends, a bit like the Unholy Trio, but minus the brutality and raids at night. I liked Valerio, especially his brand of humor, but I preferred to chat with Isa alone as I was seriously considering doing the test now.

We talked about our day in the skate park for a while, but Isa and I kept exchanging looks, and eventually, Valerio caught on. He got up and raised his arms in surrender. "I know when I'm not welcome."

"It's not about you. It's your Y chromosome." Isa smirked.

"Many girls would cry bitterly if I didn't have an Y chromosome."

"God's gift to womanhood," Isa said with a roll of her eyes.

"It's a pity we don't appreciate the gift because we're related."

Valerio nodded sagely, but then he slipped out and left us alone.

"He's one of the most easygoing Made Men I know. I can't believe he's related to Luca."

"Trust me, he is like his father when it matters, but he's good at hiding it," Isa said. Then she narrowed her eyes in thought. "You want to do the test now?"

I sighed. "Yeah. I should probably wait until morning, but I don't think I can."

"Just do it. I have more tests, and Mom will buy more if you need them."

Time crawled at a snail's pace as I waited for the result. When the test finally stopped blinking, I held my breath, then released it in a whoosh.

Not pregnant.

I held my chest and squeezed my eyes shut, relief flooding me.

Now I could really move on.

Nevio

I closed my fingers around the skateboard necklace in my jeans pocket. Aurora had asked Carlotta to return it to me after she left for New York. She'd also given me back her unopened birthday gift, which now waited in my fucking nightstand drawer. For the past few years, Alessio, Massimo, Greta, and I had always given Aurora a birthday present as a group, but this year, after the party fuckup, I'd also bought her skateboard earrings to match the necklace. According to Carlotta's words, Aurora's forgiveness couldn't be bought. Maybe that had been the plan. I wasn't fucking sure why I'd thought buying her jewelry was a good idea. The only thing I knew was that Aurora had made herself comfortable in my head. It was maddening.

She'd really fled Las Vegas as fast as she could and left what could remind her of me here.

"You've been out of it since Aurora left," Alessio commented as we sat in the dark of Greta's former ballet studio after a night with a few drug dealers who'd gone behind the Camorra's back.

I didn't say anything as I pulled my hand from the pocket without the necklace and turned my arm in thought. It still occasionally felt a bit stiff from the fracture. I actually liked the dull pain, liked how it reminded me of Aurora, of her rage. It had been beautiful to see this side of her, and because of this crazy as fuck thought, I shouldn't be anywhere near her. Aurora wasn't a vengeful, angry person, but I made her that way.

"It's for the best. Distance will allow Aurora to get you out of her mind. That'll reduce the risk of future drama," Massimo said.

Distance would maybe allow Aurora to get me out of her mind, but she was a constant pounding in my skull. I couldn't shake her off. "If I wanted therapy, I'd go to a shrink."

"The shrink that can stomach your kind of crazy doesn't exist," Alessio muttered, then let out a laugh as if he'd made the greatest joke of all time.

Massimo regarded me closely, though I really didn't know how he could make out much in the dark of the studio. "You're up to something, and I get the feeling it will cause more trouble. You should be glad Aurora is gone for a few weeks so things can calm down. You realize that, right?"

I did realize that her absence would minimize the risk of Fabiano finding out about our night together. I also realized that her absence didn't sit well with me. I didn't like that she was out of our territory, which meant out of my reach and sight.

"Nevio," Massimo warned in a low voice.

I raised my palms. "I'm here and behaving, what do you want?"

"For you not to follow your first impulse for once."

I felt naked traveling without any weapons, but considering that this was a standard charter flight and not our Camorra jet, I had to leave everything at home. I'd just have to buy a few things once I was in New York.

Massimo would probably insist his warning had triggered me like a two-year-old going through the terrible twos, but my decision to fly to New York to check on Aurora and make my standpoint clear had been made pretty much the moment I'd heard that she'd left.

After landing in New York, I went to one of the gun sellers I'd found on the darknet and got the necessities like two knives and two guns. Knowing Luca's overbearing protectiveness, I had to stay on my toes as I walked the neighborhood of the Vitiello townhouse. I didn't know Aurora's schedule yet, so that posed a problem. When I eventually, after many hours of waiting, caught sight of Aurora's face in a car, she was accompanied by Valerio. It was difficult to rate the Vitiello men on my personal dislike chart, but he was probably at the top with Amo merely because of his annoyingly sunny persona that seemed to trick some people into believing he wasn't Luca's bloodthirsty spawn. That guy was a wolf in sheep's clothing.

I knew a mess-up when I saw one.

I followed the car in a cheap Prius that I'd bought for the occasion. Rental cars always attracted more attention. Valerio's car disappeared in the guarded underground garage of the building complex that harbored the Famiglia gym, including Gianna's yoga studio.

My phone vibrated in my pocket with incoming texts. I supposed Massimo and Alessio had noticed my absence by now.

I took my phone out while keeping a side-eye on the building.

The first few texts were indeed from the guys, but then there was one from Greta. She messaged me every day, mostly mundane stuff, but without having opened her message, I had a feeling this wasn't simply one of these life-update texts.

Where are you? Alessio and Massimo are worried.

Of course, those two had to blab to Greta about my disappearance. They knew me too well. That was why real serial killers never had close friends.

I talked to Aurora.

That caught my interest. I dialed my sister's number, and she picked up after the second ring.

"We should meet. I don't want to discuss this over the phone."

Greta released a small sigh that reminded me of Nino. It held a quiet but firm message full of disapproval. "You're here?"

"Where can we meet, without your husband? I hope you won't tell him anything."

"I'm alone at home right now. I can leave, and we can meet in a park or café."

"I'll pick you up. I don't want you running around alone."

"I'm safe."

By Frenzy I *Rain*

It was strange to think that her safety wasn't supposed to be my concern anymore. And now I was supposed to swallow the bitter pill of Aurora finding a new home in New York as well? Fuck it.

I hung up after we'd ironed out a park close to Greta's apartment where we could meet. Of course, I didn't head there. Instead I drove directly to the apartment. She left the building when I pulled up. Her eyes immediately went to my car. She ignored it and walked down the sidewalk, away from the surveillance cameras of the building. The smallest hitch in her walk from the injuries she'd suffered let new rage boil up inside me, but I wasn't here to revisit my failures from the past. Well, not how I failed my sister. I smiled sardonically. I followed slowly until she eventually stopped and got into my car. She hugged me tightly. "I worry about you."

"I'm not the one married to a madman and far away from my family."

Greta pulled back with a frown. The concern in her dark eyes didn't sit well with me.

She released another quiet sigh, then leaned back. I started the car to take us farther away from her home and possible prying eyes. I could just imagine how Amo would react if he knew I was in New York.

The drive to the park didn't take long. Greta was quiet in the meantime, which wasn't overly unusual for her but she was watching me in a way that suggested her silence had a deeper meaning.

The moment I parked and turned to her, Greta shook her head. "I don't think you should be here."

"Because your husband doesn't trust me in his city?" Amo and I still weren't friends, certainly not family. We tolerated each other because of Greta, and even that only barely. Maybe he thought I was here to cause havoc in his city. Or maybe Greta hadn't told him yet.

"Amo doesn't know about this yet. He's at work."

"You could have messaged him the moment you found out I was in the city." I wasn't sure why I still thought it was clever to test Greta's loyalties. She had married Amo and left Las Vegas, the answer was clear.

"This isn't about Amo. It's about Aurora. She doesn't want to see you. She came to New York because of that."

"Who says I'm here to see Aurora?"

Greta let out a small sigh and curled her legs under her body. "You hurt her, Nevio. Physically and emotionally."

The disappointment in Greta's eyes was a knife in my chest. "What did she tell you?"

I wasn't sure I wanted to know how much Greta knew.

"We met at Aria's and Luca's house a couple of days ago, and she told me a few things, more than you did anyway. Still not everything I believe but enough to make me really worry about you. How could you lose control like that?"

"I'm a mess. I don't know why you're surprised," I said with a twisted smile. My smile died down after a moment. "What am I supposed to do now?"

"I don't know. I think Aurora is heartbroken, and unless you want to be with her, I don't think there's anything you can do. I'm not even sure that would be enough. Aurora is trying to get over you, and I think it might be for the best."

"I never saw her like that. She's like one of us boys, not someone I'd fuck." She wasn't even my type. She was too good, too kind, too everything I was not.

"But you did, Nevio, and you took her first without care or consideration." Greta opened the door and got out and left me sitting in the car. Girls and their firsts, bullshit. I didn't even realize it was Aurora.

I got out too and followed her into the park. My eyes scanned our surroundings for any threats, but I didn't detect anything. Still I never fully relaxed. Being in a different territory always felt wrong.

Greta sat down on a bench and I sank down beside her. "How do you feel about what happened?"

Feelings. My favorite topic. In the past, Greta was as wary of emotions as I was, but Amo had to come and ruin it.

I rarely felt guilty unless it involved Greta or Mom, but now an uncomfortable sensation filled my chest. I didn't want to hurt Aurora, even if I got off on hurting people. The right people, not my people. And Aurora was my people.

"You think she's on her way to get over me?" I asked, mulling over my sister's words from the car.

Greta turned her head to me, her eyes searching mine. "Not yet but soon."

By Frenzy I *Pain*

I pulled down her sunglasses perched on her head and covered her piercing gaze with them.

Greta didn't comment but her lips tightened.

I shoved my hands into my pockets and looked out over New York's skyline. I didn't like the idea of Aurora getting over me. If that didn't make me an asshole after everything that had happened, I didn't know. "Then whatever she thought she felt for me can't be that serious."

"How would you know?" Greta asked curiously. "Have you ever been in love?"

I grimaced, and in the reflection of Greta's glasses my face took on a grotesquely monstrous appearance, which was very fitting I supposed. I didn't think Aurora was in love with me. She saw something in me and was attracted to the projection. "You know the answer."

"I didn't think I could fall in love before I met Amo."

I stifled a snide comment about him. Every time Greta mentioned her feelings for Amo, her fucking husband, I wanted to scrub my body with a steel brush. "There's a difference. I've known Aurora forever."

"Not every love is love at first sight."

"I'm not in love and won't be. It's not in my nature."

"Then you should allow Aurora to get over you. Return home and give her a chance to move on, to find that love you don't believe in. It's the right thing to do."

I stared up at the sky. If I tilted my head all the way back, it appeared as if not a single skyscraper surrounded us. "The right thing to do…"

It was typically Greta to think doing the right thing was something that was part of my program.

A small part of me wanted to do the right thing, for Aurora, but the far bigger and darker part couldn't let go of Aurora yet.

Stalking Aurora was a full-time job and required far more stealth than I'd anticipated because Valerio had taken up the job of her personal bodyguard. I followed their car to a coffee shop and watched them enter. To get a better view, I got out of my car and approached the shop until I spotted Rory behind the counter. Her face lit up with a smile, but it wasn't a joke from Valerio that made her face glow like Christmas decor. What the fuck?

The guy behind the counter smiled broadly at her and leaned toward her as if he wanted to jump over the counter to get even closer to her.

My chest constricted, and I curled my hands to fists. I wasn't sure why the sight made me so livid. Fuck, I'd never felt so much rage come up so quickly, and that meant a lot coming from *me*. I'd felt murderous for plenty of reasons in my life, but this time, a feeling I was entirely unfamiliar with had been the trigger. It took me several heartbeats before I could define the sensation and then even longer to really come to terms with it:

I was jealous.

Chapter Sixteen

Aurora

"Let's grab a coffee first." Valerio parked in front of a small coffee shop at the corner. "This is my favorite place to grab caffeine on the go. Isa loves to write here too."

"Cool," I said as I followed him inside the cozy place. Potted plants hung from the ceilings, and fluffy, colorful cushions lay on the low windowsills, which could be used to sit. The furniture was of the mix-and-match type. It gave off a very boho/hippie vibe, which definitely fit Isa, yet not Valerio. However, I supposed he didn't care as much about the design.

Valerio nodded at a pretty brunette who waved at him from her place at one of the high tables. "Can you order an Americano for me?"

"Sure," I said curiously, but Valerio didn't elaborate as he made his way over to the girl.

It wasn't my business really. I wasn't even sure if Valerio was promised to anyone. I waited patiently in line for my turn, trying not to pay attention to Valerio and the girl.

"When I saw you enter with Valerio, I thought you two were an item, but I suppose I was wrong," the male barista said before I could say anything.

I laughed, a little startled. "He's my cousin."

"Ahhh," he said, smiling. "I'm Marcos. Nice to meet you, cousin of Valerio."

He was kind of cute in a normal guy way. Kind brown eyes, wavy brown hair, no visible scars or tattoos. "I'm Aurora. I'm here to visit family. I'm from Las Vegas."

He made a shocked face. "You don't look like a girl from Vegas."

I raised my eyebrows. "How does a girl from Vegas look?"

"I don't know. I've never been. More flashy and with more makeup and glittery clothes?"

I huffed. "That's not true."

He looked a bit embarrassed. "I prefer your looks. You're really cute."

"Uhhh, thanks?" I'd never gotten a compliment from a guy before.

He laughed and rubbed the back of his head. "Okay, this is awkward. Next time you come here, I'll be smoother, all right?"

"All right?" I said, still a little unsure what to make of this.

"Your cousin is watching us, so I should probably take your order now."

I glanced over my shoulder at Valerio, who had indeed ceased his conversation with the girl and was watching us intently.

I sighed. "An Americano for my cousin and an iced latte for me."

"Are you sure you don't want something with foam on top?"

"Why, do you want to add a message?" I teased.

He blushed. "Touché. Next time, I'll be smoother, promise."

"You said that before." I laughed.

He turned and began to prepare our orders, and Valerio appeared by my side. "Everything okay?"

"Sure," I said.

He nodded but didn't leave again. Marcos only smiled when he handed us our order, probably because of Valerio's presence.

Valerio and I left together.

Marcos's awkward flirting had lifted my mood considerably, even if I wasn't interested at all. He wasn't even remotely my type, even if I didn't want to ponder why that was. He'd probably run away screaming if he knew my family background. Though he must know who Valerio was.

"We can walk to the hospital from here. It's not far. That way, we can drink our coffee."

"Great." With a smile, I really felt better than I had in a long time.

We turned a corner, and our surroundings became a little less boho and more… sketchy. The hairs on my neck rose. I slanted a look over my shoulder, searching the street.

Valerio followed my example, then raised an eyebrow. "What's the matter?"

I quickly looked back to the front. "Nothing. I just thought there was someone…" I trailed off. It wasn't a simple assumption or paranoia, even if Valerio's expression suggested the latter. It was a gut feeling, one I ever only got around one person. It was a mix of anxiety, very similar to the sensation of being too close to a predator that could kill you with a swipe of their massive paw, and excitement.

Only one person made my body react like this. Valerio strode along completely at ease. I licked my lips, unsure what to do now. Could Nevio really be here? Nobody had mentioned anything to me. I had been in New York for five days now, and so far, my daily routine had been filled with meeting my cousins and aunts, going shopping, and just relaxing. But today would be my first day with the medical team of the Famiglia.

I looked over my shoulder again. And for a split second, a familiar face peeked out from behind a car across the street. My heart stopped a beat. I blinked, and he was gone as if he'd never been there in the first place. I quickly looked back to the front before I stumbled over my own feet. My instincts had been right. I so wished they weren't.

Or was this my subconscious playing tricks on me?

And even if Nevio was here, maybe it was as a part of a Camorra job to make sure I was safe. However, I couldn't imagine that Dad or Remo had picked Nevio for the task, considering the potential for havoc. None of this made sense.

Valerio stepped in my way and crossed his arms in front of his chest. "Okay. What's going on?" His blue eyes searched the street, but I doubted he'd see Nevio as long as Nevio didn't want to be seen. Still, I didn't want to risk anything. Valerio was a Made Man and Luca Vitiello's son. Many underestimated him because of his sunny display, but I wouldn't be among them. His vigilant eyes scanned our surroundings meticulously.

I grabbed his arm. "Come on. I don't want to be late on my first day. I hear the doc is a tough one."

Valerio allowed me to drag him along. "He's a misogynist and grump. No matter what you do, he'll probably find fault in it." His eyes still strayed back to where Nevio had been. "Do you think someone's after you?"

I shook my head with a laugh that sounded a little fake in my ears, but Valerio didn't know me that well, so I hoped it passed his scrutiny.

"I had a nightmare last night of someone stalking me, so I'm a bit jumpy today."

Valerio gave me a searching look as if he could tell I was lying, but he didn't push the matter. Maybe because we arrived at the warehouse where the Famiglia hospital was situated.

Valerio entered a code into a keypad beside the steel door, which unlocked with a soft buzz. He pulled it open and gestured for me to go inside. His eyes scanned our surroundings once more before he followed me into the building.

Valerio had been right about his assessment of the Famiglia's doctor. He was in his mid-sixties, and his comments throughout the day made it clear he thought women less capable than men. Maybe that was the reason the two other doctors who worked under him were men.

I was used to the male-dominated nature of the mafia world and kept my mouth shut when he spewed his old-fashioned opinions. The day wasn't busy, with only two patients who'd suffered third-degree burns on their arms and chest in a recent fire. But the nurses showed me around the place and kept me busy enough that I managed to forget about this morning's spotting of Nevio.

For my lunch break, Valerio surprised me by bringing Isa and Flavio along.

Flavio wasn't as outgoing as Valerio. He was more thoughtful and observant, but like Valerio, he always made me feel welcome. We went to a small Italian place around the corner from the hospital. Valerio and

Flavio nodded greetings at the owners as well as several customers, so I assumed the mob frequented it.

We picked a booth close to the window, and my eyes scanned the sidewalk in front of the restaurant to see a sign for Nevio. I couldn't imagine him being unreasonable enough to follow me to a mob restaurant.

Isa jabbed her elbow into my side, making me jump. "What's wrong?" She followed my gaze, and so did the guys.

I smiled awkwardly. They probably thought I was paranoid.

"Aurora thinks she's got a stalker," Valerio said with a teasing smile.

I pursed my lips. "Do not."

"Do you want me to walk around the area and take a look?" Flavio asked, already scooting to the edge of the bench.

"No, it's nothing. Valerio misinterpreted my words on purpose."

Flavio's brown eyes moved back and forth between Valerio and me.

"Let's eat, okay? There's always a potential danger lurking around the corner waiting to kill us all, but I'm starving and would rather die with a full stomach," Isa muttered.

My eyes widened, and I pressed my lips together, torn between wanting to laugh and concern because of Isa's bitter words.

"Spoken like a true pessimist," Valerio announced.

"I'm not a pessimist."

"Flavio and I are around to make sure you can torture us with your hangry attitude for years to come."

"I've been well protected all my life. It doesn't mean I'm safe, and that's realism, not pessimism."

Flavio and Valerio exchanged a look that spoke of buried guilt. I knew what incident they were all thinking about, which was why it was important that Nevio left New York as soon as possible.

An hour later, Valerio returned me to the hospital while Flavio took Isa back to Gianna's gym. Again, I thought I had seen a brief glance of Nevio's reflection in a shop window across the street, but I was starting to doubt my own perception.

"I'll pick you up in about two hours, okay? There are three guards on the premises, so don't worry."

"I'm not," I insisted, at least not for my safety.

My sanity. Peace. My heart. For those, definitely yes.

As expected, my paranoia festered overnight, and when Valerio and I walked into the coffee shop to get our caffeine fix, I couldn't stop looking over my shoulder. But I didn't spot anyone following me until he dropped me off at the clinic, where I spotted Nevio again right before I walked inside.

This had to stop. The problem was I didn't know how to get him off my back before this ended in a major disaster. Plus, I needed him gone for my own sake. I wanted to forget him, and his stalking wasn't giving me the chance to do so.

I was jumpy all morning, trying to come up with a plan to confront Nevio, even if it was the absolute last thing I wanted. Unfortunately, the hospital was closely monitored by security cameras, so my every move was recorded and seen by the guards. I couldn't leave the place without someone noticing, and then they'd stop me. Luca definitely wouldn't be impressed if I ran off from his protection.

I was helping one of the nurses change the dressings of one of the patients when a shrill alarm filled the vast inside of the building. I clamped my ears shut, my eyes scrunching up in pain and my pulse pounding madly in my veins.

"What is it?" I screamed at the nurse.

"Fire alarm," she screamed back, but her words were drowned out by the unbearable noise. It finally turned off.

"We need to leave the building," she told me.

The patients, nurses, and doctors as well as the guards gathered in front of the building.

"We need to find the source of the fire," one of the guards explained. A second was on the phone. I glanced around. This was a big coincidence. One day after I started interning at this place, a fire broke out.

In the general confusion and commotion, nobody really paid attention to me. I knew I didn't have long before more guards would arrive. I rushed away, out of the back alley where the hospital's entrance was. This area wasn't one I'd usually like to spend time on my own. Many strange-looking people walked around, but I was confident I wasn't

By Frenzy I *Pain*

alone as I hurried along the sidewalk. An arm shot out and grabbed me, pulling me into a narrow dead end.

My pulse spiked. I was pressed against a rough wall and found myself face-to-face with Nevio.

I wasn't shocked, yet I felt disbelief and indignance over his presence.

I glared up at his overly pleased face. As usual, he was dressed in all black—T-shirt, cargo jacket, cargo pants, and boots—but he had a baseball cap on his head, which was new. Probably to hide his identity.

"I don't know what you think you're doing," I gritted out.

Nevio tilted his head as he regarded me from head to toe, his hands casually stuffed into his pockets. His nonchalant attitude really pissed me off. "I'm disappointed that you're not in a nurse outfit."

I balled my hands to fists, unable to believe his audacity. "Why are you here? I don't want to see you, to talk to you, to even think of you."

"You can't ignore me forever, Rory."

I stared. "I'm not ignoring you, or I wouldn't be here talking to you, which is, in case you didn't realize, the last thing I want to do. And if I remember correctly, you managed to ignore me for eighteen years."

"I never ignored you. And by running to New York, you're ignoring me or trying to. But it's very difficult to ignore me."

I scoffed. I nodded at his wrist, which was no longer bandaged, though my attack had only happened about three weeks ago. "How's your wrist?" It was probably still tender. Maybe I could rebreak it to pay him back for showing up here. I didn't like my new violent tendencies and would have been truly concerned if they didn't only appear around Nevio.

Nevio's smile became darker, and he moved closer. With the wall at my back, I had no way to escape. "I'm used to pain, Rory. In any shape and form. You can't deter me with it."

The way Nevio said "pain" raised goose bumps on my skin. "You shouldn't be here. I doubt your dad knows about this. Luca would throw a fit. It's his territory, and I'm only a guest."

"*You* shouldn't be here," Nevio growled, pressing the palm of his injured arm into the wall beside my head. His scent engulfed me as he did so, but my anger stopped me from falling in its trap. Still, Nevio's dark eyes almost made me buckle from their intensity. There was something in them that had never been there before in all the years. As I had suddenly become his prey. "You belong in Las Vegas."

"Maybe I don't anymore. Maybe my future is here. Away from Las Vegas. Away from *you*."

"It's not."

An indignant laugh burst out of me. "Says who?"

"I'm saying it, and that's the end of the story."

"You can't tell me what to do. Now less than ever. Not after what happened." My voice still wavered when I mentioned that night, and my heart felt too heavy in my rib cage.

Nevio braced his other arm beside me. I sagged against the wall. I was scared of his closeness because of what it still did to my body, to my mind, to every part of me. "I think after what happened, I can tell you that you belong in Vegas."

"Why? Do you need another disappointing drunk one-night stand? I'm not up for the job, in case you're wondering. Find someone else, like you did in the past."

"You're not a one-night stand," he growled.

"I'm not? Please enlighten me how I'm not a one-night stand if you banged me once and then disposed of me like you do with every girl."

"Aurora." The edge in his voice raised the little hairs on my forearm. His dark eyes burned with anger and frustration. "You're not like every girl. If you were, I wouldn't blink twice to kill you, but I can tell you that you're one of the very few people on my 'I doubt I could kill' list."

This would have come as a joke at the wrong time with anyone else, but I knew Nevio wasn't joking. "Is that supposed to give me warm feelings?"

"I don't know what it gives you. It's the truth."

"I'm staying in New York. Right now, nothing in Vegas is drawing me back."

"Don't think you being outside of my territory will stop me from doing what's necessary to protect you."

"It's your father's territory, not yours, and I'm well protected in New York."

Nevio smiled in a way that made a shiver race down my spine.

"Luca won't let you kill in his territory," I whispered. It had to get through Nevio's thick skull. The problem was that Nevio wasn't blind to the truth. He just didn't care about the consequences.

"Then don't get yourself into trouble that forces my hand, Rory."

"What's that supposed to mean?" I asked.

He shifted, bringing us closer but not touching me, maybe because I tensed or because he didn't ache for a touch like I did. "I don't trust other guys around you. Stay away from them."

I blinked. Before I could say something in turn, though I wasn't sure it would have conveyed the necessary spite, Nevio stepped back, turned around, and disappeared in the shadows as if that was where he belonged all along. I couldn't believe it. Had he really just warned me away from other guys? What was this? Some strange possessive streak? Jealousy? I almost laughed. Whatever it was, I wouldn't bow down to it. Nevio held no power over me, not anymore. I wouldn't let him ruin this trip for me. If I had to, I'd call his mother, and then Remo would definitely move everything to remove Nevio from New York. If Nevio decided to play dirty, so would I.

I gripped the strap of my purse, took a deep breath, and left the alley. A search party was probably on the way by now. I slowly made my way back to the hospital.

Halfway there, Flavio jogged my way, looking stressed. "Aurora!" he exclaimed. He picked up his phone. "I found her. She's fine." He stuffed the phone into his back pocket and grabbed my shoulders. "Why did you run off? Something could have happened to you."

For a second, I wondered if Nevio already considered Flavio to be one of the guys I wasn't supposed to be around, but considering he was my cousin, I doubted it. I hated that Nevio's comment had the power to steer my actions. He had absolutely no right to tell me what to do.

"Aurora?"

I blinked, then gave Flavio a reassuring smile. "I'm fine. I'm sorry about running off, but the fire alarm and all the commotion gave me anxiety. It brought back bad memories from…you know…" I allowed Flavio to draw his own conclusions.

He nodded grimly. The night of the ambush probably haunted quite a few people in the Famiglia and the Camorra.

"Still, you shouldn't risk anything. This was dangerous. You need to stay with a bodyguard at all times," he said as he guided me back to the hospital. I'd never been in danger. From the moment I'd realized Nevio was in New York and on my trail, I'd been safe. He would protect me in his own twisted way.

Chapter Seventeen

Aurora

Like every morning, Valerio drove me to work. Today, my spirits were particularly high as I hadn't seen Nevio in the past two days. Maybe he'd really listened and returned to Las Vegas. Additionally, my internship with the Famiglia's doctor was a lot of fun, even if I wasn't allowed to be present during everything. Not so much because they worried that I couldn't handle it, but because I could still feel weariness despite the fresh peace treaty between the Camorra and Famiglia.

And like every morning, we stopped at Valerio's favorite coffee shop. I liked coffee, but Valerio was positively addicted to it. I doubted he needed it to wake up in the morning because he was one the most nauseatingly cheerful morning persons I'd ever encountered. His words about being grumpy in the mornings had never proven true. Or maybe he was just grumpy deep inside.

We got out of his red Porsche 911, which he'd parked at the curb right in front of the shop. The moment we entered the shop, I noticed that Marcos wasn't behind the counter. This was the first time he didn't take our orders. Valerio gave our usual orders to the girl behind the counter. Something in her face told me something was up. Her skin was blotchy, and eyes teary as if she'd recently cried.

"Where's Marcos?" I asked casually, not wanting Valerio to draw the wrong conclusions. I wasn't interested in the barista. I simply liked his flirting because it lifted my ego.

Valerio slanted a look at me, blue eyes narrowed in consideration. If I'd thought I would have more freedom away from home, I was thoroughly mistaken. The Famiglia had strict rules that even the easygoing Valerio paid attention to.

The girl blanched. She turned around to where her manager was talking to someone on the phone, looking upset. "He was found dead in an alley last night. That's why he didn't show up to work this morning. The police were here to question us before we even opened the store."

I swallowed hard. Was this a coincidence? What if Nevio was still in New York? Maybe he'd decided Marcos had looked at me the wrong way, and suddenly, he was dead.

I felt sick. Even without any proof, my instincts told me Nevio had been involved in this. Because of me. I didn't understand any of this. What was this for him? A sick game?

"Do they know what happened?" I asked, trying to sound sympathetic but not as freaked out as I was. Considering Valerio's very intent expression, I probably wasn't doing a very good job.

The girl glanced at her manager again, then whispered, "The police think it was a mugging. He was stabbed, and his wallet was on the ground beside him."

"Stabbed? Just once, or did he have any other injuries?"

Knowing Nevio's inability to control himself, a single stab wound seemed odd, but maybe that had been his intent. Maybe this controlled kill showed that he didn't really care about me, wasn't really deeply emotionally involved, but acted out of a sick sense of possessiveness.

The girl looked uncomfortable. It wasn't normal to ask these kinds of questions as a bystander. Tomorrow, the police would probably want to question me because of my suspicious behavior, but I needed to find out more.

"I think he was stabbed once, but I didn't ask for details." The way she said it made it clear I shouldn't have asked either.

"I should probably...uhhh...get your order before my manager notices the long line," she said quickly, then turned on her heel and began to work on our beverages.

Valerio raised one blond brow. "What was that about?"

I gave a shrug. "Just curious. He seemed like such a nice guy. It's horrible that he got killed."

"Horrible," Valerio repeated as if he couldn't care less, which was probably true considering he was Luca Vitiello's child and had killed his own fair share of people in his life.

The barista returned with our orders, and we left. When we got into the Porsche, Valerio didn't start the engine.

I pretended to be busy with my Americano. Since Valerio had introduced me to it, I'd developed my own addiction to the concoction.

"I'll ask again. What was that interrogation about?" His voice lacked his usual cheer and lightness and gave me a glimpse of another more serious and dangerous side of him.

I frowned. "I was just being compassionate. The girl must feel bad after such horrible news."

"Horrible," Valerio repeated with a hint of sarcasm. "Even I could tell the girl was freaked out by your questions. She certainly didn't get compassionate vibes from you."

"Maybe I had a crush on him," I muttered, feeling defensive. My thoughts were a jumbled mess, and it was only a matter of time before I'd let something slip.

"I didn't get the vibe that you had a crush on him. He had the hots for you, no doubt, but you weren't into him. I have a feeling this isn't just you being your caring self."

I sipped my coffee, hoping Valerio would stop prodding. On the other hand, maybe getting him and, in consequence, Luca involved would make Nevio retreat.

Peace was still a fragile construct, though. What if Nevio's actions caused a new rift that led to war? With Greta in New York, things would get even more complicated. Could I really risk this out of an unfounded suspicion?

Valerio angled his body my way, his back against the door and one elbow propped up on his steering wheel. "It's strange. You get lost when a fire breaks out in the hospital, and Flavio finds you completely flustered. You keep checking our surroundings as if you know someone is after you. My instincts tell me someone has been watching us. Someone who's really good at staying in the shadows, someone who's used to creeping up on others, on hunting them. And now a guy who was into you is dead."

"People get mugged and killed all the time."

"Sure, they do," he said. "Still, I find the string of events odd. Are you promised to someone in Las Vegas?"

"You know I'm not."

"Does someone think you belong to him?"

"I'm not a pet. I don't belong to anyone."

Valerio just smiled as if I'd said something funny. I had underestimated him. His funny nature made you forget what he was at the core of his being. A Made Man and Luca Vitiello's son. "Sure. If the lie makes you feel better."

He finally started the car and pulled away from the curb. I really hoped he'd let the matter drop. I couldn't do it. I needed to find out more about Marcos's death. The problem was how to do it without making the police or the Vitiellos suspicious.

Luckily, Greta and Amo were invited over this evening again, and I used my chance to have a private chat with Greta right after dinner.

We settled on the Hollywood swing in the backyard, away from prying eyes and ears.

"Is Nevio still in New York?" I asked in a whisper.

"He hasn't been in contact with me in over twenty-four hours, so I assume he has returned to Las Vegas."

"Or he's laying low in his own way," I muttered, then told Greta what I'd found out today. My pulse spiked just talking about it, and my eyes burned as they had done every time I'd considered my role in an innocent's brutal death.

She didn't say anything, only looked thoughtful. Nobody knew Nevio better than Greta, even if I'd often wished it were me. Now I wasn't so sure anymore. "Greta?"

She ran her elegant fingers over her skirt, dark brows curving in deep contemplation. "I told you he cares about you."

"And that's his way of showing it? He killed an innocent man because he didn't like me talking to him."

I still didn't want to believe it. I wasn't sure my conscience could take it. How could I ever risk talking to a man again if it meant risking his life? Wasn't this fear exactly what Nevio wanted to evoke in me so he could control me? But revolting didn't pose a risk to my safety. I was playing with other peoples' lives, and I couldn't do that.

"Can you please talk to him? He needs to stop this. We're not an item. He's never given me any indication that he wanted to be in a relationship with me. He doesn't get to decide who I hang out with. I want him to return to Las Vegas and stay out of my life. We're not dating. We're nothing, not even friends after everything he did. I don't want anything to do with him ever again."

Greta sighed. "Aurora—"

"Don't try to make me understand him or even feel sympathetic for him. He's out of line. I'm done with him."

Greta bit her lip. "I'll see if I can contact him, and then I'll let him know. But I can't promise he'll listen. Nevio is unpredictable."

The sliding doors made us both go silent. Luca stood in the doorway, and my stomach tightened. Something in his face told me I was in trouble.

"I need to talk to you, Aurora."

I got up from the Hollywood swing. Greta gave me a worried look. Did she worry I'd expose Nevio?

If war weren't on the horizon if I did, I might have done it. He deserved punishment. All his life his actions had never been followed by consequences, and now an innocent had to pay the price.

I followed Luca into his office where Matteo, who'd also been at the dinner with Gianna and Isabella, and Valerio were waiting. I assumed Amo would try to get information out of Greta in the meantime.

I gave them a hesitant smile. "Did I do something?"

"Sit down," Luca said, motioning at the armchair on the left across from them, as if I was facing an inquisition.

Nerves twisted my belly as I sank down. I wasn't concerned for myself. The worst that could happen to me was that Luca would send me back to Las Vegas, and while I wasn't ready for that yet, it wouldn't be horrible.

"Valerio told us about the murder of a man you were in contact with."

I flushed. "I bought my coffee in the coffee shop where he worked, and Valerio or Flavio were always there too."

"I didn't suggest you were involved with this man, but he seemed interested in you. Flavio and Valerio are good at hiding their nature, so it's not surprising that he didn't get the message that you were off-limits. It seems someone else conveyed the message to him in a very obvious way."

"The police think it's a mugging gone wrong."

"Of course, they do," Matteo said with a snort.

"What do you think happened?" I looked Luca in the eyes but quickly lowered my gaze, unable to stand his.

"He was killed with a sawtooth knife."

Matteo cocked an eyebrow at me. "Who do you know who has a pet sawtooth knife?"

It was Nevio's favorite knife. Everyone knew that. "Many people use sawtooth knives, right?" I tried to look as innocent as possible.

"Bullshit. Our favorite psychotic killer has that knife. Fuck, he probably even sleeps in a bed with it and uses it to fuck his own—"

"Matteo—" Luca's voice whipped through the room, making me wince.

Matteo waved him off. "Living under a roof with the Falcones, she's probably seen and heard worse."

"She won't under my roof, though. She's barely of age and innocent. I want you to remember that."

"Blond and blue eyes always make you believe in someone's innocence, Luca."

"I'm the epitome of innocence," Valerio said with a chuckle.

"My point," Matteo said.

I pressed my lips together, not sure what to say or do. If Nevio had really wanted to cover up his tracks, he would have done a better job. This kill probably served two purposes: control me and provoke the Famiglia.

I feared he'd succeed in doing both.

"I accepted that he came to New York to slaughter the people responsible for Greta's attack, I even accepted him being here for the wedding, but I don't want the fucker in our city whenever he damn well pleases. I'd still love to slice his throat open for what he did to Isa and Gianna, and if he crosses my path in the next few days, I sure as fuck will show him my favorite knife," Matteo said.

Aria cleared her throat, and we all turned toward the open door. She looked furious. She was one of the few people I knew who still managed to look gorgeous as she did. Her fists were propped up on her hips. "We promised Fabiano to keep Aurora safe, but now you're questioning her and saying all these inappropriate things to her. This is unacceptable."

Luca sighed. "It's also unacceptable to have Nevio running rampant in my city."

"Do we know it's him?" she asked.

"We suspect it."

"Why would he even be here?"

All eyes turned to me once more.

"Why did you want to leave Las Vegas?" Luca asked.

"Maybe there was someone there who made her feel uncomfortable. I don't want to be the poor woman Nevio puts his sights on," Matteo said.

"Nevio hasn't set his sights on me. Nevio only cares about the Camorra and violence."

Matteo gave me a shark grin. "That's what everyone said about his old man too, and then he kidnapped a poor woman, and now they live their happily ever after."

The story of how Serafina and Remo became a couple still shocked me, though I'd known about it for a while. How could you fall in love with someone who kidnapped you to destroy your family?

"Like father like son. They both like blondes," Matteo said.

I blushed. "We're not—"

"Did he do something? Is he threatening you?" Aria asked in a motherly tone as she crossed the room and gently touched my shoulder. I appreciated her support, but at the same time, it made me feel even guiltier for having brought trouble to their doorstep. "We can protect you from everything, and Fabiano would stop at nothing to protect you too. He was willing to break with the Camorra for your mother."

That was exactly what I feared. If Dad found out, his bond with the Falcones would suffer or even break.

Nevio had hurt me. I wasn't even that concerned about the physical aspect, even if I hated how I'd lost my virginity to him, how he didn't even remember. But Nevio hadn't intended to hurt me, not physically at least, because he hadn't realized it was me.

I still hated him for that night and for everything that came after. But I wouldn't try to get revenge on him through my dad or Luca. I wouldn't risk everyone's safety because I had been stupid enough to fall for someone like Nevio.

I knew what kind of person he was.

"I don't need protection," I said firmly, and it wasn't even a lie. Nevio wasn't out to hurt me, only everyone else.

Valerio or Flavio and, on a few occasions, even Luca played my bodyguard since the latter's presence was a bit disconcerting. It wasn't that I wasn't used to the intensity of a Capo—I'd grown up around Remo, after all—but I had never been alone with him. It felt awkward and also nerve-wracking because I knew why the Capo himself had decided to keep me safe. Though I wasn't even sure this was about my safety. None of them could believe that Nevio was a danger to me. They wanted to capture him in their territory, and I was the bait.

By Frenzy I *Rain*

I really hoped Nevio wasn't cocky enough to risk contacting me again while I was under close watch. Maybe I was worrying for nothing, and he'd actually returned to Vegas. Greta had assured me she'd sent him a message, but she wasn't sure if he'd followed her advice. She'd also mentioned that her dad, Remo, was seething since Luca had told him about the strange events in New York. Maybe he'd find a way to stop his son.

Nevio

"Listen, Nevio, I have no clue what's going on in your head, but your father is ready to explode. Luca called to ask about you and your dad lied that you were here. You need to return," Alessio muttered.

"I'll be back tomorrow," I said, then hung up. After a week in New York, my job here was done. Aurora understood that I was dead serious. I wouldn't let some random asshole flirt with her without consequences.

Not to mention that Luca had upped his protection for Aurora. Tomorrow the whole Vitiello clan would go to the Hamptons for a few weeks.

Returning home would definitely lead to a big conflict with Dad. I'd ignored all of his messages, and the same went for the messages from pretty much everyone else.

When I left the airport the next day, Dad was already waiting for me. His expression made it clear he was ready to kill me. It wasn't the first time, but I had a feeling he was closer to the end of his patience than ever before.

I got into his car without a word. Evading his explosion would only make it worse, though I had a feeling this would be pretty bad. Did I care? Not really.

"What the fuck is wrong with you?" Dad snarled the second my door was closed.

"We both know the list is long."

Dad gripped the steering wheel in a death grip, his knuckles turning whiter than the cocaine the junkies ripped out of our hands. "You were in New York?"

I nodded because Dad knew and only wanted to test me further.

"I lied to Luca and told him you were here. Fuck, the second you went missing, I immediately had a feeling it was because of this nonsense. What the fuck is wrong with you?"

The answer was still the same, but I didn't bother pointing that out. I also didn't mention that he had been notorious for his crazy moves when he was younger, kidnapping a bride, for example, and had only calmed slightly since he had family.

"Did you kill that outsider? Because Luca thinks that was you, and I have to agree with his instinct."

"He picked the wrong girl."

"Aurora left Las Vegas because she wanted to get away from you. What about this message didn't you get?"

"You kidnapped Mom. It's not like you are a shining example of how to treat a woman."

Dad gripped my throat. I was surprised it had taken this long for him to get violent because his anger must have accumulated over the past few days. Hell, the past few weeks. "This isn't about your mother and me. She doesn't know about your mess up, by the way. I lied to her, told her I had sent you away on a special mission, so she doesn't worry. Fuck, and I had to lie to Fabiano too. I'm stacking up too many lies because of your bullshit."

"I pissed Luca off. Isn't that a mission you can get behind?" I asked, grinning despite my lack of oxygen. Dad's fingers flexed, but he released me, turned away, and started the car as if he needed to busy himself with traffic to make sure he didn't choke me to death.

"We need peace for Greta's sake, Nevio. Isn't that something even your brain should be able to understand?" he gritted out, every word shaky with anger.

I leaned back. This was a topic I had no interest in discussing. If I were keen on war with the Famiglia, my week there would have looked different. Luca hardly gave a fuck about that dead Outsider, and he definitely wouldn't start a war over him.

"Just give me one reason for this major fuckup. One sane reason that maybe makes me want to send you away a little less."

"I wanted to show Aurora that I wouldn't give her up just because she ran away."

Dad glanced at me, his lack of understanding as plain as day on his face. "What do you want from her? And if your answer is anything less than marry her, then don't say anything, and for fuck's sake, let that girl be. She's Fabiano's daughter. If you want to mess with a girl's life, pick another. This is my last warning, Nevio. I won't risk losing Fabiano because you got it in your head to give chase simply because she started running."

I kept my mouth shut because fuck if I knew what I wanted with Aurora. I couldn't let her go. I knew that, and the consequences? Fuck, they would hopefully be worth it.

Chapter Eighteen

Aurora

After six weeks in New York, I returned to Camorra territory with trepidation. My short encounter with Nevio in New York hadn't been conducive to forgetting him and what had happened between us.

If Nevio's intention had been to unsettle me, he'd succeeded. Maybe this had turned into a sick game for him. I wouldn't be played. Still, Marcos's death weighed heavily on my conscience. Of course, I couldn't be sure it had been Nevio. Nothing pointed toward him. I wasn't familiar with his killing style. All my life, I'd done my best not to dwell on what he did not only for the Camorra but also for fun at night. Marcos hadn't been tortured. The police still thought it was a mugging gone wrong. But Luca's suspicion had confirmed my own.

Mom, Dad, and Davide had picked me up in New York themselves, and we'd spent two days in the city as a family because I wasn't returning to Las Vegas right away. I'd spend a few more weeks with the racing circus. I was excited about the chance to see Roman, Adamo, and Dinara again and really spend time with them, as their visits in Las Vegas were usually short.

Dinara hugged me when I got out of Adamo's car. Roman flung himself into my arms, and I lifted him with a huff. "You've gotten heavy!"

It felt as if he'd grown several inches since I'd last seen him.

"We're so happy that you're going to join us for a while," Dinara said with a smile.

"You're happy to have me as a babysitter," I joked.

Dinara tossed her red hair back, looking indignant. "You know we love having you. But Roman missed you, so he'll definitely want to spend time with you." She grinned, and I laughed.

"I missed him too." I hugged him even tighter until he started squirming, and I had to set him down.

"We got you your own trailer this time, so you have privacy." Adamo said led me toward a campervan that stood right beside their mobile home, which was huge compared to most trailers, campervans, and VW buses that many of the drivers used as their home during the races. Of course, most of them didn't travel with a family.

"And you really want to help our doc and not join the races?" Dinara asked as we sat down in front of their motorhome a bit later for a dinner of grilled steak and delicious Russian potato salad.

I shook my head. "I don't think racing's really in my blood. I love the wind in my hair when I throw myself down the half-pipe, but barreling through the desert at 150 miles per hour doesn't really seem appealing to me."

"If you change your mind, I'll give you a crash course, and I'm sure we can find a car really quickly for you," she said.

"Dinara has been trying to recruit girls for the races for ages, and you're one of her top choices. She'd love to have you around more often."

I grinned. I really liked the freedom living with Adamo and Dinara gave me, but I'd miss my family and the crazy Falcone clan in the long run.

It was past midnight when Dinara glanced at her watch with a deep-belly sigh. "Tomorrow's a qualification race. We should probably head to bed."

I was ridiculously tired anyway. The moment my head hit the pillow, I was asleep.

The air was ripe with nervous energy when I emerged from my campervan the following morning. People buzzed around, making last-minute repairs on their cars. Adamo and Dinara were set for tomorrow's race, so they didn't have to join the qualification race. As the organizers, their workload was still massive, so I would spend the day with Roman until the actual qualification started.

"Look!" Roman shouted excitedly, pointing at a car that pulled up in the line of participating cars. It was a black Ford Mustang with red headlights. Even before I looked inside, I knew whom I'd be seeing.

My lips still fell open when I spotted him behind the steering wheel, one arm casually draped on the lowered window: Nevio.

Roman let out a holler and waved at his cousin. My belly, however, coiled so tightly, I worried I'd projectile vomit my breakfast. This time, Nevio wasn't alone. Alessio and Massimo were in the car with him. I knew those two would hardly hold Nevio back from whatever madness he had planned now.

"Dad!" Roman shouted at Adamo, who stood only a few steps away and was discussing something with one of the race drivers. He looked up and followed Roman's pointing finger. His dark brows dipped in confusion. I walked over to him while Roman rushed toward the Mustang.

"Has he ever joined a race before?" I asked Adamo when I arrived by his side, doing my best to sound mildly interested and not show how anxious Nevio's appearance actually made me.

Adamo shook his head. "I thought motocross was his thing. Maybe he needs a new hobby to keep him out of trouble. But Massimo, Alessio, and he have visited the races before to hang out with me."

I had a feeling Nevio wasn't here to stay out of trouble. He was here to cause it. For me. When our eyes met and he gave me a sly smile, I knew I was right.

He joined the qualification race that day. As the Capo's son, he didn't have any trouble getting a spot, of course, and knowing Nevio, he probably would have gotten rid of anyone in his way.

Roman and I accompanied the race in one of the camera cars. I knew the driver from my last time at the races. Gigimo gave me a broad smile when I slipped across the back seat with my little cousin. "Any bets on who's going to win the qualification?" he asked.

I shrugged. Nevio would probably play dirty, so his chances weren't too bad, though I seriously doubted his incentive to come here was to win any races.

I tried to enjoy the atmosphere and the thrill of the race, but every time I caught a glimpse of the black Mustang with the eerie red headlights, my belly plummeted again. A small part of me, some really insane part I tried to ignore, felt thrilled about Nevio's sudden interest in me. Though interest seemed a strange word for his deadly obsession.

"He seems eager to catch your attention," Gigimo said about halfway through the race. We raced alongside the leading group of cars, but we kept losing them as their maneuvers got riskier.

I followed his gaze outside. The black Mustang drove close to us. Nevio had his window down, his arm propped up on the door, and was steering his car with one hand despite the mind-boggling speed. I sent him a scowl that he couldn't misinterpret. The corner of his mouth tipped up in a half smile, then he tore his eyes from me to briefly assess Gigimo in a way that worried me before he focused on the track and his opponents.

Nevio came in third place, which was surprisingly good, considering he'd never joined a race before and had been busy annoying me throughout the race.

The moment Gigimo parked the camera car in the camp, I shoved open the door and got out. I wanted to put distance between him and me before Nevio misjudged something. Of course, Roman had other plans and chatted with Gigimo about every detail of today's race.

I waited outside, but right when Nevio pulled into the camp, Gigimo joined me with a friendly smile.

"How did you enjoy today's race?" he asked as he propped up one arm casually against his car, bringing us closer.

"It was cool."

I knew it was rude, but I took Roman's hand, and with a curt bye, I walked away. Gigimo was a nice enough guy. When I first met him at the races, he'd been a driver hiding from the police for robbing a gas station. Most people who were part of the race circus were either part of the mob or had a criminal record for other reasons.

I hid in Adamo's and Dinara's mobile home despite Roman's protests and my annoyance. I didn't want to have to hide. I'd been excited about spending time at the races. I loved the atmosphere, the crazy people, and the sense of freedom. I didn't want Nevio to take this from me. Eventually, Roman's begging and my own annoyance won out.

When many of the racers gathered around the bonfire, which was the tradition after every race, I finally emerged, too. I snatched a seat beside Dinara on a log. Adamo shared another log with the Unholy Trinity, and Roman rushed over there too.

My eyes briefly met Alessio's. He looked almost sympathetic, but there was a hint of *I told you so* in his expression too. And he had warned me about Nevio. I'd like to think that I would have pulled away much sooner if I'd known what my infatuation would lead to, but if I was honest, I couldn't be sure.

Dinara gave me a strange smile, her eyes keen. "Everything okay? You've been acting strange since the three showed up."

I gave a small shrug. I didn't want to lie, but I couldn't tell the truth either. I had to call Carlotta again tomorrow, even if I knew what she'd say, the same thing she'd said when I'd shared how Nevio had stalked me in New York, minus the killing part, because I was worried the FBI or someone else was eavesdropping. She wanted me to tell on him, to talk to Remo, and if all else failed, even my father. But I simply couldn't do it.

"I had an argument with them, so I'd rather not see them."

I could tell from Dinara's expression that she didn't believe me. "Hmm."

"Hey, can I join you?" Gigimo asked and sat down cross-legged on the dirty ground in front of us before we could say anything.

Dinara leaned over to me. "Do you want to be alone with him?"

"No," I pressed out quickly. I didn't even want him close.

Gigimo knew who I was and who my father was, but he wasn't part of the mob, so maybe he didn't understand what it meant. Plus, he didn't know anything about my crazy stalker.

I glanced toward the log with the trinity, and of course, Nevio's eyes were on us.

I wasn't sure what to do. I was sick of him telling me what to do. If I wanted to chat with someone from the other sex, that was my business, not his. He probably still banged every girl he wanted.

"Are you and him an item?" Gigimo asked quietly, leaning closer so I could hear him over the blaring country music and the crackling of the fire. His arm bumped my shin.

"No," I said, shocked that he'd think that.

Dinara emptied her beer with a chuckle. Apparently, she found the situation entertaining. I couldn't blame her. I probably looked like a deer in the headlights.

Like the animal, I simply wanted to run away but couldn't.

"I think I'll go to bed," I said eventually and rose to my feet.

"Do you want me to walk you to your trailer?" Gigimo asked and made a move as if to get up from the ground. That was the absolute last thing I needed.

Dinara rose to her feet. "I'll take her. We have girl stuff to discuss anyway."

I gave her a grateful smile when we were out of earshot and sight from Gigimo. Dinara wasn't a woman who did girl talks, but she'd saved me from an awkward situation. "You can talk to me about everything, you know that, right? I'm not obligated to share any information with the Camorra."

I nodded. I often forgot that Dinara sat between the chairs because her father had been the Pakhan of the Russian mob in the Chicago area before her half brothers had taken over.

We reached my campervan, and the motion sensor cast its dim glow on us. "If you don't feel safe for any reason, I'll help you figure something out, all right?"

"Nobody's safer than Rory." Nevio's low voice came from the dark, almost giving me a heart attack.

Dinara and I whirled around to find Nevio a few steps behind us. His stalking talents were disturbing, albeit not surprisingly, outstanding.

"For heaven's sake, Nevio, you almost made me pee my pants!" Dinara hissed.

Nevio stepped closer to us into the light, his hands casually tucked in his pockets. "I need to talk to Aurora."

Dinara frowned at him, then glanced my way. I nodded my okay because I'd have to talk to him eventually. He was here because of me, and he wouldn't leave.

"I'll be over at the bonfire if you change your mind about going to bed." Dinara gave Nevio a stern look, which he ignored before she walked away and disappeared behind another trailer. Now Nevio and I were alone and out of sight from prying eyes, which made my pulse spike. I wasn't scared of Nevio, not in a way many people were scared of him. Maybe that was my main problem.

Nevio reached up for the lamp and turned it in the other direction so we weren't in its direct beam anymore, then he leaned against my campervan. "Gigimo looked quite cozy next to you."

"He knows me from the last two summers when I watched Roman." I was proud of how controlled and cool my voice sounded despite the madness rocking my insides.

"So he thinks you two have history?"

I stared into Nevio's dark eyes, wondering what the hell went on behind them. "If you count that as history, I have history with at least half of the race circuit, okay?"

He smiled strangely, and with the shadows playing on his face, it looked ominous. "You're trying to protect him."

"Are you jealous?" I asked scathingly.

Nevio's smile sent a chill down my back. "I don't get jealous, Rory. I get murderous."

"You can't kill everyone who talks to me."

"Who's going to stop me?"

"Your father will eventually have enough. People will ask questions and even a Capo has to answer to his soldiers at some point."

"Oh, he'll be mad at me. He'll wanna kick my ass. But he's not a saint. He's got his own long list of hardly justified kills. And he'll always have my back in front of others, so you really shouldn't count on him to stop me."

I shook my head. I took a deep breath, asking a question I'd avoided from fear of what it would do to me. "It was you, right? You killed Marcos because of me."

Nevio's eyes didn't hold a hint of regret. He stepped closer, his gaze sliding over me like a cold shower. "He was too invested in your coffee orders."

I took a step away from him, bumping into the side steps. "He was a normal guy. He was just flirting. He didn't do anything, certainly nothing to deserve his death. What's wrong with you?"

"The list is very long. I warned you to stay away from me, Rory. I really tried to keep you out of my head. He wanted the wrong girl, and I don't play games."

I swallowed hard. "He wasn't even part of our world. You could have just scared him. You didn't have to kill him. Do you even realize what this did to me? How the guilt has been eating away at me? Do you want to break me?"

Nevio grabbed my hand and pressed it against his chest. "I don't care about him or pretty much the entire world population with a few exceptions. I don't feel pity, and I fucking love hurting others. Yet you think I would send him off with a little warning like a normal guy?"

Feeling his heart beat calmly against my palm, a wave of anger mixed with despair overcame me because I still wished for his heart to beat for me. Did it? Did murdering someone so he couldn't have me say it did, or did it just show how messed up Nevio was and that he'd turned whatever was between us into a sick game, a new adventure that would fill his nights?

I ripped my hand from his hold and turned away from him, feeling my eyes burn with unshed tears. I didn't even know if Marcos had a family. Maybe I could send them an anonymous apology and some money to alleviate some of the guilt I still felt.

"Don't cry for him, Rory. He wasn't the nice guy you thought he was if it makes you feel any better. His last girlfriend got a restraining order against him because he kept breaking into her apartment and following her after she broke up with him. He even put dead birds on her doorstep."

"You're making that up to make me feel better," I gritted out. I really wished he'd told me before because my conscience had been an absolute mess these past few weeks, but I guessed Nevio simply didn't understand how a person could suffer because someone they barely knew had died. And even if Marcos was kind of messed up himself, did that make him deserving of death? No, but maybe it said a lot about me and made me feel better, just like Nevio intended.

Nevio shook his head slowly, a few strands falling down his forehead. "Didn't I just make it clear that I don't feel pity?"

I slanted him a look. "You also made it clear that you don't care about others. What about me?"

Nevio regarded me in a way that halted my breath in my chest. It was an intimate look that slipped under my skin, warming every inch of my body, "I think that's a question you can answer on your own."

I huffed. "And your justification of why it was okay to kill him doesn't even make sense coming from you since you're also a stalker. I could probably get a restraining order against you if we weren't part of the Mafia world."

Nevio chuckled, obviously amused by my anger. "I don't need justification to kill, Rory. I only told you for your benefit. I'd kill a fucking priest or Nobel Peace Prize winner if he made a move toward you."

Chapter Nineteen

Nevio

"Just stop it," Aurora seethed. Her anger rolled off her in waves, but it wouldn't change a thing. I would not, could not stop this. As long as I wasn't sure what Aurora had done to me, as long as my own emotions and mind were a jumbled mess, I would make sure nobody got close to her. Fuck, I hadn't even intended to follow Aurora to the races when I'd found out about it. I wasn't the jealous type and never even understood the reasoning behind it in the first place. But the night before Aurora's move to the race circuit, I had been unable to fall asleep. I'd thought back to the asshole I'd killed in New York, had thought about how many more assholes would be at the races. Assholes who would dare to make Rory smile, to make her laugh, to fucking touch her. That thought had festered inside me and made my skin itch as if thousands of ants were digging tunnels under it. Usually, this kind of restless craziness only took hold of me when

I hadn't killed in too long. Now the idea of not being near Rory caused it too. What a shit show.

When I returned to the bonfire a little later, I felt the itch under my skin again.

"I don't like the look on your face," said Alessio when I sank down beside them.

I took out my knife, half tempted to cut open my fucking skin to get rid of the itch, but it didn't work that way. I knew only one thing that elevated the sensation…

My eyes were drawn to Gigimo, who drank a beer with a couple of guys. Just looking at his stupid face drove me up the wall. He emptied his beer and excused himself, probably to take a piss. I rose to my feet.

"I can smell trouble," Alessio muttered.

"Adamo won't be happy," Massimo added.

I waved them off and stalked after Gigimo.

The next day, I stepped into the makeshift hospital tent where Aurora helped out.

She looked up from the folding desk. She immediately shook her head and got to her feet, rushing around the table and toward me.

"I don't want you in here," she said as she stopped right in front of me with her fists propped up against her hips and fury in her blue eyes.

One corner of my mouth dragged upward at her feistiness. A few wayward strands had fallen out of her ponytail, accentuating the wild look in her eyes. This wildcat side of her was one I greatly appreciated.

"This hospital is for everyone, right?" I said, looking around. Only one bed was closed off with curtains. I supposed that was where I'd find Gigimo.

"You're not injured."

"I'm sure you can change that," I said, amused.

I shifted my weight but Aurora's hand came up against my chest to stop me from moving to Gigimo's bed. But she quickly dropped it as if she couldn't bear touching me and raised her finger in front of me like a scolding teacher. "Not another step, or—"

My eyes met hers, and my smile broadened. "Or what, Rory?"

It was adorable that she thought she could stop me. Maybe I'd even let her. But we both knew this would only be because I was being unusually charitable.

She pressed her lips together. "You won't hurt me."

I tilted my head. "I thought I already did."

A blush spread on her cheeks that exhilarated my heartbeat almost as much as torture did.

"Stop it. You broke half the bones in his body," she whispered harshly.

That was a major exaggeration. I'd really held back as much as I was capable of. "I didn't kill him." If only she knew how fucking much I'd wanted to cut his throat, how hard it still was to resist. One slash of my knife and the stupid fucker would spill his warm blood over my hands. Instead, it flooded his worthless body, a waste of perfectly fine blood.

"Do you expect me to thank you?"

I walked past her, sidestepping her feeble attempt to bar my way. Her attempts to stop me by grabbing my arm were futile too. "I did it for you. I would have broken the rest of his bones and then slit his throat, but I knew it would upset you, so as a show of goodwill, I left him alive."

I reached the closed-off curtains and ripped them open. Gigimo, covered in bandages, lay in the narrow hospital bed. Aurora was talking to someone on the phone, but I didn't pay attention. I was in hunter mode.

The fear in his eyes gave me a sick kick, and my body called out for more of his blood, a call I would have gladly answered if it weren't for my initial reason to come here.

Aurora squeezed in front of me, her pure scent flooding my nose. "I called Adamo. He'll be here any moment."

He was at least ten minutes away by car, enough time for me to off Gigimo and half the camp. I lowered my gaze from Gigimo's terror-stricken face.

Aurora glared up at me. "Did you hear what I said?"

"Every word. Don't worry, Rory, I didn't come here to kill Gigimo. I'm here to bring my message across."

"I think he got whatever message you had for him when you beat him up," Aurora seethed.

I flashed her a hard smile. "I'm sure he did, but you didn't, and that's why I'm here."

Her brows dipped in confusion and a hint of anxiety. I grabbed her by the waist, lifted her off the ground, and carried her the few steps to the neighboring bed, where I dropped her off.

I jerked the curtains closed. While I wanted Gigimo to get the message too, I didn't want him to see Aurora and me. That was our moment.

"I was the first inside you, and I'll be the last one." Until the words shot from my mouth, they hadn't even been in my mind. I hadn't given much room for thoughts of the future, had lived in the moment, but now I knew these words to be true. I wanted to be Aurora's last, and no matter how brutal I had to be, I'd make sure I was. But fuck how could I be her last when it went against my core belief, when I knew I could never be hers in the way she wanted?

It didn't matter.

Aurora's skin turned even redder. It was hard to say if her anger or her embarrassment were in the lead this time. "Why do you even want me? What is all this about? The stalking, the jealousy, the killing. Why the change of heart?"

I didn't like that phrase. I preferred to see it as a more primal need to claim what already felt like mine. My head was already enough of a mess. I didn't need emotions to get in the way.

I cupped her neck. Trepidation filled her eyes, but there was longing beneath it, an emotion I was well-acquainted with in my victims. Longing for me, the same longing that now pulsated in my veins like a jungle drum. I'd taken her virginity but didn't remember. There were so many more firsts to claim, and I'd never forget any of them again. I leaned over her, bringing us closer. She fell back on the cot with my arm under her lower back, her palms against my chest. I lowered my head and pushed my lips against hers, wanting a taste. Her eyes widened a fraction, her mouth firming up. My tongue traced the hard line of her lips. She parted them but only to nick my lower lip with her teeth, drawing blood.

My grip on her neck tightened as I pulled back an inch. She breathed harshly, her chest heaving beneath me. Copper bloomed on my tongue as droplets of blood fell from the small cut.

"You don't deserve any part of me," she growled.

"Fuck, that's why I always told you to stay away from me, but you wouldn't listen, and now it's too late, Rory. You're in my fucking head, and there's no escaping from there."

Her lips parted, her brows snatching together as her eyes roamed my face. She was trying to understand me, but that was something she'd never do. Even I didn't.

"Now I'll have to hurt everyone who gets too close to you."

She shook her head slowly.

"Because while I still think you should stay the fuck away from me, unfortunately, I can't stay away from you. And even if I don't deserve any part of you, every single part only belongs to me."

I leaned down again so our lips brushed. She didn't move this time, even as I coated her mouth an enticing red with my blood. "And we both know that deep down you still want to belong to me. Every part of you."

I reached between us and tugged her hardened nipple through her shirt, then pressed my flat palm against her jeans-clad pussy, making sure to really increase the pressure with my middle finger so she'd feel it deep in her core.

She tensed but didn't push me away. I could see the fight in her eyes. The fury, not just at me but also at herself. Resolution filled her face, and she grabbed my shoulders as if to push me away.

Steps crunched outside the tent. Aurora's eyes widened. I removed my hand from her crotch but stayed bent over her. "I mean what I said. Every guy who wants a piece of you better be willing to lose at least a piece of himself."

The tent flap moved, and Adamo stepped inside, frowning at the scene we created. I pushed away from Aurora and stepped back.

"Hello, Uncle."

Adamo stalked inside and toward Aurora, who was sitting up with a deep red face and blood-covered lips. "Are you all right?"

She gave a jerky nod. "I'm fine."

Adamo stopped in front of her, obviously not convinced. He glanced over his shoulder at me with suspicion and disapproval. "I need a word with you, Nevio."

I smiled and headed out of the tent. The heat blasted my body, and the sun beat down on me. After I'd found a spot in the shadows, I shoved my hands into my pockets and closed my eyes, soaking up the sounds around me. The hum of engines, laughter, a door being thrown shut, the low murmur of too many voices. Adamo's voice was one of them, but I couldn't pick up what he said, even if the thin tent fabric hardly served as a barrier. A couple of minutes later, steps crunched on the dry ground, and I opened my eyes as Adamo joined me outside. Anger reflected on his face. "If you came here to cause trouble for Aurora or me, or other members of this racing circuit, then you'll get in major trouble with me. Got it? I won't stand by and watch you ruin everything. And I sure as fuck won't stand back if you harass Fabiano's daughter."

"Did she say I'm harassing her?" I asked, not really concerned. Dad knew I was here. I wasn't sure why he'd agreed to let me come. Maybe he thought it was better if I did it under his watch than on my own like in New York. I hadn't killed anyone yet, so he had a point.

"She didn't say much. The strange thing is I don't even think it's because she's scared of you. I don't know what's going on, and I'm really not sure I want to, but maybe you should consider the consequences of your actions for once. This isn't just anyone. This is Aurora Scuderi, and her dad is like our family. Consider what you risk destroying, and ask yourself, is it worth it."

My smile had become harder to maintain. I knew what was on the line. I also knew it wouldn't stop me.

That night, I snuck to Aurora's campervan. It was locked, but it took me only a few seconds to pick the lock and slip inside. The windows were open, letting the cool night air in, but the inside still smelled of Aurora. Sweet and light but also a hint of musk. I moved toward the bed. Even in the dark, I could see that Aurora was wearing headphones and a sleeping mask. She hoped to keep the anxiety at bay that way. It made her more vulnerable. She was lucky she was as safe as she was.

I flipped on my flashlight on the lowest level. Rory's sleep was fitful. She was mumbling under her breath and twisting and turning. A nightmare, maybe about me?

She sank her teeth into her lower lip, her breathing too deep for a nightmare. One of her arms was under the covers. I tugged at them and found her hand between her legs, but she wasn't doing anything except for squeezing it between her thighs.

"Oh Rory, I hope you're not dreaming about poor Gigimo, or I'll have to end his miserable life tonight."

Her legs squeezed her wrist even tighter, obviously seeking friction and chasing the same pleasure she was experiencing in her dream.

I directed the light beam to her chest. Her nipples poked her thin T-shirt. She tossed one arm up above her head, almost frustrated, her lips parted, and then she said one word that saved a life, at least for now. "Nevio."

Hearing her moan my name was my fucking undoing, and it gave me a sick satisfaction to know that she couldn't escape me even in her dreams. I shone the light on her thighs and stroked them, then pushed them slightly apart until my hand was between them. I wedged the flashlight between my teeth and used my now free hand to remove her arm from between her legs. Her breathing changed, but she wasn't awake yet. Her pajama shorts were wedged between her pussy lips, and I pushed my thumb into the crease. Soon, Aurora parted her legs, and I massaged her clit and slit, up and down, until her breathing quickened and the fabric of her bottoms was soaked by her juices.

Feeling her heat and arousal through her pajamas filled my own body with lava-hot desire. My attraction toward Aurora had been growing by the day, and it seemed to reach an almost unbearable peak today. She shuddered in her sleep as I rubbed her little clit, and she succumbed to an orgasm. It ended too soon and was nothing in comparison to the orgasms I wanted to give her when she was awake.

I put down the flashlight and leaned down to her pussy so I could inhale her scent. Fuck. This was pure torture. My dick hardened in my shorts. I darted my tongue out, couldn't fucking resist and wedged it into the crease, tasting her through the fabric. She shuddered again. I pulled back, then slid my hand into the leg of her shorts and rubbed my thumb over her dripping pussy, gathering as much of her juice as I could. I removed my hand and touched my coated finger to her parted lips, then slid it carefully into her mouth, rubbing my pad over her tongue. I wanted to kill my own stupid ass for not remembering how my cock had been engulfed by these pussy walls.

I pulled away and got up. My cock was rock hard, and I wanted nothing more than to fuck Rory senseless. But that would definitely wake her, and I knew her stubbornness would stop her from enjoying my touch as much as she'd just done.

One day every of her firsts would be mine.

Aurora

I woke before my alarm rang. My skin was sweaty, and to my mortification, my dreams had left a visible impact on me. My shorts stuck to my pussy. They were completely wet, almost as if I'd peed myself but I knew it wasn't that. I'd come in my sleep. My dream had been incredibly intense. Of course, Nevio had been in it. He'd stalked me at night and then taken me against a house wall. After everything he'd put me through, you'd think my body would stop lusting after him. Sadly, that was far from the truth.

I was incredibly annoyed and furious even by his stalking, but my subconscious seemed to spin all kinds of erotic fantasies around it. The most disturbing had been one a few nights ago where Nevio had snuck into my bedroom, covered my mouth with his hand so I couldn't scream and then fucked me from behind, his body pressing me into the mattress. He hadn't even asked for permission or made sure I was wet. He'd just thrust into me brutally and it had gotten me off.

I rubbed my eyes, not sure what was wrong with me.

I quickly changed into clean shorts, then put on a bathrobe before I rushed to the motorhome with the washrooms. I needed to clean my body and mind of last night's fantasies. Unfortunately, Nevio was there too. He was only dressed in boxers, and his hair was wet from a shower.

I stomped up the stairs, sending him a scowl.

"Good morning, Rory. How was your night?" The way he smirked made my cheeks go hot.

"I had a nightmare about you," I said, trying to get into the only free shower room, but Nevio stepped my way. "A nightmare, are you sure? I don't smell fear on you, only arousal."

My eyes widened in mortification and indignation as I did a quick scan of our surroundings to make sure nobody had heard Nevio's words. The showers in the occupied shower rooms were running, and the other people mingling around were too far away. "Are you a dog now?"

He grinned. "I'm just very in tune with your scent."

I shook my head with a disgusted look. "Stop it."

He stepped back, and I stormed into the shower stall, then thrust it shut and engaged the lock. I took my time showering, even if the rules limited shower time to five minutes. I needed to wash any thought of Nevio away. When I stepped out, Nevio was gone, but so were my soaked shorts when I returned to my campervan. I knew I'd put them down on the heap of dirty clothes in the basket in the corner, and now they weren't there. I should have locked my door, but I doubted that would have stopped Nevio.

I stormed out of my camper and rushed over to the one that Nevio, Alessio, and Massimo shared. I hammered against the door, then stormed inside. Nevio leaned against the small kitchenette in the trailer with a cup of steaming coffee in his hand. I had half a mind to spill it down his privates.

Alessio slunk on the bench in the corner and got up before I could say anything. He was only in boxers, his many tattoos and a nipple piercing on display. "I don't want to know. I warned you, and now you two have to deal with each other. I'll let Massimo know that the campervan is off-limits for now." He grabbed a T-shirt and left the campervan.

"This won't take long!" I shouted, but the door had already fallen shut.

"Give it back," I growled, turning back to Nevio.

Nevio's dark eyes held mine, mirth dancing on his face. "I fear that's not how it works, Rory. What's gone is gone."

I flushed when I realized he wasn't referring to the shorts. "I hate that you took it," I whispered harshly, on the verge of crying, which made me hate him even more at that moment.

"I didn't take your virginity. You gave it to me. And I only hate that I don't remember every second of it."

I staggered toward him. He held the coffee out of my reach, obviously anticipating my need for violence. I shoved him, and a bit of the hot liquid spilled on his chest. He hissed, then smirked. "This and the scent of your soaked shorts will get me off in no time."

"Have you lost your mind?" What a stupid question. "Give me my pajama shorts. I didn't know you were a creep who steals women's underwear."

"I only steal yours, Rory, and I'm definitely a creep."

I shook my head. Maybe he'd stop this bullshit if I stopped reacting to it like a crazy person. I needed to learn to ignore Nevio, but I was incapable of doing it. I shrugged. "Then keep it. I don't care."

His answering smile was even more infuriating. "I still have your panties from the wedding too. I think they smell of you, but not nearly as intense as the ones from last night."

My eyes widened. "You promised to throw them away."

His dirty grin drove me insane. "I couldn't part with them. I knew it would be a while before I'd get the chance to get closer to your pussy."

I couldn't believe he'd kept them. Part of me was sickeningly elated by the news when I should really just be annoyed and repulsed. Everything Nevio did was a provocation. "Throw them away. They only smell of chlorine anyway. They were wet when you took them."

I regretted my choice of words when I saw Nevio's answering smile. It was dark and daring enough to make my panties wet this time for entirely different reasons, and I hated that my body still reacted to him like that. "Maybe I'll throw them away now that I have the shorts with your lust all over them."

"Your sense of smell is obviously off," I muttered, even as my cheeks burned.

"Don't pretend you don't finger yourself to sleep every night imagining it is me, Rory. I can practically smell your arousal whenever we're close. And last night, I was witness to your wet nightmares."

I froze, swallowed hard. Had he watched me sleep? Had he seen me touch myself? I wasn't sure what I'd done during my very hot dream but judging by the state of my shorts this morning, I might have actually touched myself.

By Frenzy I *Pain*

Part of me wanted to turn on my heel and run away. The need to escape the situation was unbearably strong, but I didn't want to give Nevio the satisfaction. He was the one in the wrong. He should have never been in my camper at night! "I bet you're having wet dreams about me as well."

"I won't deny it. Not just at night. I think about how it'll be to bury my cock inside you all the time."

I shrugged, almost as if it didn't matter, though my heart still beat furiously. "You were inside me."

"That doesn't count. Next time, I'm going to remember every inch of my cock claiming your tight pussy, going to memorize the smell of your arousal, lick it up after I make you come over my hands and face after I licked your pussy and your ass."

I blinked up at him, trying to determine whether he'd really said it. Maybe I was actually asleep again. Because sometimes he said similar things in my sleep, but never when I was actually awake. Silence spread between us, and I could tell that Nevio enjoyed making me speechless again.

I glowered. "You're all words, and I'm sick of them."

Nevio dropped the coffee cup in the sink, grabbed my hips, and jerked me toward him. I breathed harshly, feeling a wave of rage but also desire for the man before me. Before I could choose either, Nevio's lips pressed against mine. They were softer than I'd expected. I sank my nails into his shoulder, determined to shove him away and maybe bite him again, only harder this time, but instead, I pushed into the kiss, letting my rage consume me.

Nevio turned us around so my back pressed against the counter and kissed me even harder. His heat was everywhere, and he tasted and felt so good, like temptation and darkness.

A rage-fueled kiss wasn't what I'd imagined for my first real kiss. It felt good, addicting, but also as if I was being pulled in a direction that wasn't me. I tore my lips away and shoved Nevio's arm until he pulled it back so I could move away from him. I didn't want to be fueled by rage or hatred. Nevio obviously thrived on these destructive emotions, sought them like an addict, and I could see how they could become addicting in situations like this. They were easier to process than emotions like love and affection, which bared your soul and made you vulnerable.

I wanted to be vulnerable with the person I kissed, not driven by instinct like an animal.

"I think you gave me another one of your firsts," Nevio said. I didn't look at him. I wouldn't give him a reaction, not when this was obviously a game that got him higher than any drug could.

"Keep my undies. I don't care. I can't play by your rules. I won't." I left his caravan without a look back. Part of me was satisfied with these highs, even if they were fueled by negativity. I had no intention to let that part win.

Chapter Twenty

Nevio

AURORA IGNORED ME COMPLETELY OVER THE NEXT TWO DAYS. I had sworn to Dad that I wouldn't spend more than a week at the race circus, so my time was coming to an end. I could tell that especially Massimo was growing restless with the lifestyle. He needed a task, and he probably missed his arguments with Carlotta.

I too missed Las Vegas, mainly because of our raids. Not killing anyone in a week really gave me an itch.

Still, I had every intention to stay until the race tomorrow and try to get one more rise, and hopefully orgasm out of Aurora.

In the afternoon before race day, Massimo, Alessio and I sat on folding chairs in front of the trailer we shared. Another thing that grated on Massimo's nerve. He preferred privacy, especially at night.

Adamo came over to our trailer. He gave Massimo and Alessio a smile before he narrowed his eyes at me. He was still pissed because of

Gigimo. It was an open secret in camp that I had attacked him because of Aurora. Nobody had dared to look at her twice since then. Even Adamo's wife Dinara had given me the nasty eye ever since the incident. "Nevio, a woman came to me today. She told me she needs to see you. It's of *utmost* importance."

"What did you do now?" Alessio asked, his black Converse propped up on the folding table in front of us. "We're in the middle of the desert, and trouble still finds you."

"How did she look?" I asked, not really interested in the matter. If she was a groupie wanting to have sex…well, I was out of the business of having sex with random girls. And if she was a girl from the past…hard pass from me.

Adamo gave me a look that made it clear he didn't want to get involved in whatever went on. "Tall, dark hair, with a French accent."

I frowned. "I can't remember a French girl…"

"You had two French girls so far. One last year, one the year before," Massimo said, not even looking up from his phone where he was probably reading the newest *Science Weekly* or whatever tickled his fucking fancy right now.

Adamo let out a long sigh. "Whenever I'm around you three, I realize why Remo was constantly pissed off at me when I was a teenager. You're a nuisance. Any plans to return to Las Vegas. Perhaps tonight?"

Massimo gave a small shake of his head. "Technically, only I'm still a teenager, if you go strictly by the numbers and not by intellect and level of development."

"Uncle Adamo," I said with fake hurt. "We're family. This is our bonding time."

"Your version of bonding causes me too much trouble."

I chuckled. Adamo sighed again. "The girl looked really panicky, and I think it's urgent. So maybe you should talk with her before she disturbs the race tomorrow. I'd be really pissed if that happened. It's an important race. We have halftime so new bets will flood us. Lots of money to be made."

I lowered my feet from where I'd rested them on a vacant chair. "All right. Where is the mystery girl?"

"She wants to meet you at the car cemetery. She seems to share your sense of morbidity."

"And his level of crazy if she meets with Nevio at a place where he could dump her body," Alessio added.

Adamo gave me a hard look. "No bodies. What you did to Gigimo was enough. This is my last warning, Nevio."

"She'll live," I said as I stretched out my arms. "I don't see how she could piss me off enough to make me want to kill her."

"You want to kill pretty much everyone," Alessio said. "Do you need moral support?" I answered his mocking grin with my middle finger.

After a yawn and stretch, I rose from the chair, strode over to my car, and got in. I missed the comfort of my RAM. The hard suspension of the Mustang was a nuisance.

The drive to the cemetery took me thirty minutes. I tried to remember any French girls from my past, but my mind came up blank. It wasn't surprising, though, considering I'd even forgotten my night with Rory, who overshadowed every other girl in my past.

A rental Toyota Yaris waited on the gravel parking lot next to the car graveyard. Over the years, Adamo and other racers had buried the remains of their cars in the dusty ground. Now dozens of cars emerged from the ground like dominos.

I came to a stop with my bumper facing the other car's bumper and got out.

I could see a woman sitting behind the steering wheel. She didn't look happy to see me. Maybe this would end in a tirade. Who knew what I'd done after I'd fucked her. It must have been bad if she hunted me down more than a year later to give me a piece of her mind. This could be fun.

Finally, the driver's door opened and she got out. Adamo was right. She was tall and had good curves, but she definitely wasn't dressed to impress today. She wore simple jeans and tight tee plus flip-flops and no makeup. I hoped she hadn't forgone her face paint because she planned to ugly cry. She'd soon realize that crying didn't work on me.

She hadn't pulled the keys from the ignition so she was preparing for a quick escape. My interest was piqued. Her face didn't conjure up any memories. I couldn't even say if she was my type. I had been a mood fucker. One night, I picked the tall, model type who turned everyone's head, and one night, the wallflower who gave you the blow job of a lifetime, risking lasting damage to her throat in gratitude for picking her.

She stopped in her tracks and looked at me, her expression filled with anxiety. "You don't remember me, right?"

I shoved my hands into my pockets. "No, not at all."

"I figured," she said, her eyes darting to her car. I had a feeling there was someone in there. Did she bring her new lover for support?

Narrowing my eyes, I stalked toward the back door and opened it. She didn't stop me, only watched.

I froze when I spotted a small child in a dirty child seat in the back seat. He was only in a diaper, which was probably enough in the blistering heat outside but not in the AC air inside the car.

I took a step back and glared at the woman. "I want a fucking explanation, and I want it ASAP, or this is going to become a very unpleasant experience for you."

She came toward us and picked up the child, a boy I would guess from his facial features, from the seat. She held him as if he was a dirty mutt she'd found on the street and couldn't wait to drop off at a shelter.

I had a fucking bad feeling about this.

She held him out to me in her outstretched arms. The boy stared at me with wide eyes.

Fuck it.

"He's yours." She tried to hand him over to me again. I took a step back, staring at the kid, then at the woman.

She put him down on the hot desert ground, and he crawled toward her legs, trying to be picked up again. The ground was probably blistering.

"Put that fucking towel under him or pick him up," I snarled.

She reached for the dirty towel on the floorboard, thrust it on the ground, and set him down on it. "Stay," she said impatiently as if he were a disobedient dog.

She met my gaze. "He's your son."

I shook my head. My son? What the fuck? I'd forgotten a condom on occasion in the past. Was this really coming back to bite me in the ass now?

By Frenzy I Pain

"How do I know he's mine?"

She glared. "I usually use a condom. You were the only one where I didn't use protection."

"If you went bareback with me, you might have fucked other guys bare too."

"He's yours! You can do a DNA test if you don't believe me."

I didn't want to believe a fucking word out of her mouth. But I didn't need a DNA test to know he was mine. Fucking mine. He had my eyes, and something about him just screamed Falcone. I couldn't explain it.

"I'm not taking him back with me," she said as if we were discussing a piece of furniture, not a kid. Didn't women usually have motherly feelings for their brood? My mother would have chopped herself to pieces before she would have abandoned us, but of course I knew the stories about my crazy-ass grandmother who tried to kill my father and his brothers. Wasn't it fitting that I had picked a crazy bitch for a fuck?

"I'm not taking him back," she repeated as if I hadn't heard her the first time.

"I don't want him either!" I roared, fucking furious and also fucking overwhelmed for maybe the first time in my life. She'd popped him out of her vagina and taken—more or less—care of him since then. I was seeing him for the first time. If she didn't have feelings for the kid, did she really expect me to have them? Fuck, feelings and I weren't on a first-name basis.

He was a kid, all right, and had part of my DNA, but I didn't feel like a father. I didn't feel anything but utter confusion and rage.

She shrugged. "Then abandon him in the desert or drop him off in front of a hospital, or do what you do at night. Everyone knows what you are."

Was she fucking serious? Was she really suggesting I kill that kid? Fuck, I was a psychotic fucker, no doubt about it, but even I had certain limits.

I grasped her throat so tightly that my fingers dug into her skin and slammed her against the side of the car. Her eyes bulged, face turning red. She wanted to speak but couldn't. I wasn't sure how much the kid had understood of her cruel words, but since he hadn't sought her closeness since she'd dropped him on the towel, I supposed he wasn't used to affection from her.

I would have killed her, most likely, if the kid hadn't started bawling. Fat tears rolled down his chubby cheeks, and his face turned dark red. I released her, and she bolted, losing a flip-flop as she rounded the hood of her rental, then flung herself inside. The car jerked as she reversed it, then steered it to the side and raced away, scraping the side of my bumper with hers in the process. She left a trail of dust behind—and the boy.

Chapter Twenty-One

Nevio

I watched the car disappear on the horizon, whirling up dust. Fuck.

Slowly, I looked back down to the kid sitting on the dirty towel. He was covered in a fine sheen of dirt, which clung to him because he'd broken into a sweat after he'd been moved from the cold inside the car to the heat outside.

He had dark hair that curled above his temples and at the nape of his neck. Only Adamo had curls in our family. But maybe this was her heritage. She'd looked like she didn't originally hail from France but rather North Africa or maybe the Middle East.

I didn't even know how old the kid was. Fuck, I didn't remember much from party nights. He looked really small, definitely under one.

My head felt like it was going to explode, and not just because the kid didn't stop bawling. I wasn't sure if he was crying because his mother had taken off without another glance at him, though I could hardly imagine that she deserved to be missed by him. Or because I scared him.

I glanced back at my own car, half tempted to take off as well. What was I supposed to do with a kid? I sighed and rubbed the back of my head. It seemed to be getting hotter by the minute, and sweat trickled down the nape of my neck. A small body probably had a harder time against the sun.

I stepped closer to the kid, and he cried harder. I got down on my haunches like you were supposed to do with scared animals, but the kid cried still harder. Not that I had expected anything else. Most people cried when I pretended to be sympathetic.

"Shhh," I said. But the boy didn't even react. Usually, I shushed in a very different context, mostly to mock my victims.

I picked up my phone and called the first person who came to my mind to save the day in a situation like this.

"Isn't it enough that you follow me everywhere?" I hadn't been sure if she'd even pick up, but trust Rory to have a too big heart even when she tried to hate me.

"Rory, I really need you to come to the abandoned car yard."

Silence on the other end.

"I'm not meeting you in the middle of nowhere."

I smiled. Maybe she finally understood that she should stay away from me. A little too late. "What's that sound in the background?" she asked, her voice dripping with concern and suspicion.

My crying son. Fuck, I really couldn't believe it.

"I need your help. This is serious. I can't call anyone but you. I'm fucking desperate."

"What—"

I hung up. Maybe if she thought I was lying in the desert bleeding to death, she'd come running. Though she had every reason not to care. Knowing Rory, she would help. She was too good.

I stuffed my phone back into my pants pocket, then glanced down at the still crying boy, though his volume had reduced considerably. His voice was becoming hoarse, and his hiccuped breathing was causing more breaks in his cries.

"Listen, buddy," I began, but the kid only stared at his dirty feet and kept crying.

By Frenzy I *Ruin*

Who was I kidding? Nothing I'd say would calm the kid. I bent down and grabbed him under the arms and lifted him off the hot ground. He froze in my hold like a baby gazelle the second before the lion broke its neck.

Without a word, I carried the kid to my car and put him on the back seat. I turned on the AC but made sure it wasn't too cold, then closed the door. I would have loved to sit in the cool inside too, but his cries were starting to grate on my nerves. I would have thought I was used to human screams by now, but his bothered me. Maybe because I had no way to stop them. Well, I wasn't willing to use the methods I usually employed to shut people up.

I leaned against the side of my car, hoping Rory's helper syndrome would bring her here quickly. If she didn't show up… Fuck, I'd have no choice but to call Alessio and Massimo, but then what? Alessio would probably insist on finding the boy's mother, and Massimo would insist on taking him home to Vegas. There was no way in hell I was doing either.

Rory didn't disappoint. Thirty minutes later, her car pulled up. She hesitated a moment before she got out. The amount of relief I felt when she got out was alarming.

She'd always seemed like a beacon of light, but today, she trumped even the aurora borealis.

Aurora

I wasn't sure why I was here, why after everything, I was on my way to Nevio because he supposedly needed help. Maybe this was a new form of his game. Maybe after weeks of stalking me despite my more or less clear rebuke, he wanted a change of pace. See me run to him again.

I had almost convinced myself to turn around when I pulled up in the car graveyard where trunks and hoods of cars peeked out of the earth as if they were undead and about to rise again. Nevio leaned against his car. Nobody else was around, and again, I wondered whose cries I'd heard before. They had tugged at my heartstrings in a way I couldn't quite explain. If Nevio had called me here to help him dispose of someone, I'd run him over with my car and finally be free. Though knowing Nevio, he'd still find a way to haunt me from the other side.

With a monumental sigh, I got out of the car and put my sunglasses on. It was always easier to battle with Nevio if he couldn't look me in the eyes. I still wasn't immune to his power. Kissing him definitely hadn't helped, though it hadn't changed my feelings, only my level of desire.

His eyes just held a certain amount of power that always grabbed you by the throat. I knew I wasn't the only one who had trouble resisting his eyes, but for most people, their fear and primal flight instinct got in the way of feeling any real draw to him.

I made my way over to him. He straightened, and the relief on his face surprised me. "Why am I here?" I congratulated myself silently for my hard tone. Luckily, I was furious. Running him over with my car was still one of the options I entertained.

"Because you want to help me," Nevio said with a twist to his mouth that only fueled my anger.

"I'm done," I growled, so mad at myself I felt a little sick. I turned on my heel to stalk back to my car. A hand clamped around my wrist.

"Don't go," Nevio said firmly. Then a tad softer. "I really need your help with this, Rory."

I squeezed my eyes shut. Part of this was curiosity, but the other part definitely involved me being unable to say no to Nevio, even now. I let out a sigh and turned back around, then tugged my hand from his grip. "If this is a trick…"

"It's not." He pointed at his car. "I'll show you."

Maybe he really needed help burying someone.

"I won't help you dispose of a body."

Nevio let out a chuckle. "I'd call Massimo or Alessio if I needed help with that."

He led me toward the back door and opened it. I hesitated briefly, still suspicious of his motive, but then a new wave of cries hit me. I peeked inside and took a stunned step back. In the back seat sat a small boy with dark, slightly curly hair, only dressed in a diaper. Snot ran out of his nose from crying, and from the sound of his wails, a little raspy and choked, he had been doing so for a while. My heart clenched.

"Where are his parents?" I demanded. A sinking feeling told me

Nevio had killed them and then noticed the little child. I could only hope the boy didn't have to watch.

"I didn't kill them if that's what you're insinuating."

I moved closer to the boy. "Shhh, it's okay." The boy briefly glanced my way with a look that made it clear he knew I wasn't telling the truth. I froze because something about the boy's eyes and even his features were familiar. They weren't as sharp as those of the man beside me, but there was no doubt in my mind that this kid in front of me was related to Nevio.

I swallowed, then glanced up at Nevio. "He's yours."

"Massimo would say a human being can't legally be anyone's possession."

I glared. "Did you sleep with the mother?"

"It's a possibility."

"You don't remember?" I chuckled and shook my head. He hadn't remembered sleeping with me either, so why was I even surprised. Ignoring the infuriating man beside me, I leaned into the car and picked up the crying boy. He didn't stop crying and barely reacted to my presence, but I kept rocking him, hoping to calm him down eventually. I turned back to Nevio, who was watching me with his hands in his pockets.

"How many more kids have you fathered?"

"Fuck, you think I know? You know how I partied."

"...and fucked," I added, even as the word made my cheeks heat.

He partied hard and fucked even harder, his trademark motto, one I'd never really understood until that night.

"I don't anymore," he said, but I ignored his comment. I didn't want to know what he did when he wasn't trying to make me miserable.

"What about the mother? Where is she?"

"Ran off."

"What's his name?"

"I didn't ask."

"And I don't suppose you have a way to find his mother and ask?"

"She's probably halfway to Mexico by now. I might have tried to kill her a little."

"How can you kill someone a little?"

"She's still alive."

I stifled a nasty comment and drew in a deep breath. "He needs a name."

"Call him Kid, or choose whatever name you think would fit him."

I ran a hand through my hair, torn between wanting to help this boy (and some stupid part of me, even Nevio) and wanting to let Nevio feel the consequences of his actions for once.

I cradled the little boy gently against my chest, my heart aching for him, for what he'd been through and what lay ahead of him. He put his cheek against my chest and let out a shuddery breath as if he'd been waiting for the moment he could let go of his distrust. I stroked his back. His body was dirty and soaked with sweat and, from the smell of it, urine. At least, he looked well-fed, so maybe his unwashed state had more to do with him being out here in the desert than how he'd been treated since birth. I hoped it for him. "He needs to see a doctor to make sure he's okay."

"You want to be a nurse, so can't you check him? I can't see any obvious injuries."

I glared at Nevio. I would have screamed at him if I hadn't held the obviously shell-shocked little child. "I did two internships. I haven't taken any courses, and even if I did, most of them don't cover small children. Their bodies handle many things differently than we do. He needs to see a pediatrician. I don't care if this complicates things for you, Nevio."

Nevio narrowed his eyes, probably because of my tone, which was still tame to the tone I actually wanted to use right now, then he nodded. "I'll take you to a pediatrician. But he can't be linked to the Camorra, so I'll have to do research."

"You want to keep your son a secret?"

Nevio's expression stilled when I said "son" as if he hadn't allowed himself to think of the boy as such. Nevio certainly wasn't the most empathetic person on this planet. It wasn't that he didn't understand other people's emotions. He just didn't care, but this, seeing his own child, must do something to him. At least I hoped it did.

"I don't want my father or the rest of my family to know."

I had figured as much or I wouldn't be here. I'd carried secrets before. "So you call me? You really think I'll help you?"

Nevio looked at the boy, then back up at me. "What am I supposed to do with the kid?"

"How old is he?"

He gave me a blank stare. "I thought you'd know. You used to babysit Adamo's kid."

"From looking at him? He's your kid. When did you sleep with his mother?" I laughed, realizing how ridiculous the question was. "Never mind."

I looked more closely at the boy. He obviously couldn't walk yet but he could sit on his own. Even though I'd watched Roman, I wasn't an expert on little kids. I would have guessed he was between eight months and a year old, but only a doctor would be able to tell. Unless Nevio found the mother and figured out the boy's birthday. "So what's your plan? How do you expect me to help you in this situation? You're not thinking about giving him up for adoption, right?"

"No," he said immediately. "I don't trust strangers."

"Then what?" I asked. If he didn't want help from his family who would definitely gladly raise the boy, then what was there to do? He looked at the boy for a long time, his dark brows puckered, then he looked up at me. I'd never seen him like this, a little lost and almost scared of the small boy who hung limply in my arms.

Then it dawned on me.

"You expect me to take care of him? Like a mother? Have you lost your mind?"

Chapter Twenty-Two

Aurora

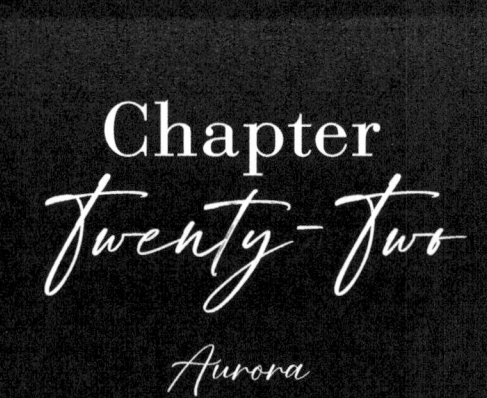

I stared at the man I hoped to spend my adulthood hating, the man I'd spent my childhood and teenage days loving with such abandon that I'd overlooked his many faults, the man I still loved and hated in equal parts.

Nevio had broken my heart with little care, and I doubted he'd ever be willing or ready to mend it. Despite all of this, he wanted me to take care of his child.

He trusts you enough with his child, a small voice amended. But I shushed that voice immediately because it was the same one that had made me fall for him in the first place.

"Not for long, just until I figure something out. You're moving into your own place soon. It'll be easier to hide the kid there than in my room in the mansion."

He stepped closer, too close. I tilted my head back to meet his gaze. His dark eyes captured me like they always did.

I hate him. I hate him.

But part of me loved him, every twisted, psychotic part of him. Nevio was a lost cause. Everyone knew it.

"Rory, I need your help and so does he. Your internship with our doc will give you enough time to take care of him."

"Don't," I growled. "Don't play the emotional card, or the best friends card. You've lost either privilege."

"Then don't help me! I'll drop him off in front of a hospital like I should have done right away. He'll be better off without me."

"You mean you'll be better off without him. Be honest, you don't want the responsibility."

We both breathed harshly. I swallowed, trying to control my emotions. I wasn't sure how much a child that age could understand but he'd definitely pick up on our raised voices. "What about all the times when I'm working in the clinic? He's not a dog. You can't leave him alone for a few hours. He needs constant care."

Why was I even discussing this? I couldn't take care of a little boy. I was eighteen. I wasn't ready for this level of responsibility. This was Nevio's responsibility, not mine.

Nevio shrugged. "I could watch him on occasion."

"On occasion? He's your son!" The boy winced against me, and I cleared my throat. "If I help you, I expect you to step up and really make an effort to take care of him. And this can only be a temporary thing. You'll have to figure out a way to tell your parents. You'll need their help with this."

Nevio briefly glanced at the boy, his reluctance obvious. "If that's what it takes. I can sleep at your place now and then to help you with him. I had every intention to keep a close eye on you anyway."

Fury raced through my veins. "Carlotta will be there. I'll have to tell her. I need her help for this."

God, was I really agreeing to this nonsense? I had to be out of my mind. And having Nevio sleep over was definitely a very bad idea. The boy shuddered against me, and I focused on him. His well-being was top priority right now. Everything else could wait. "We should take him to a doctor now."

Nevio opened the back door of his car. I glanced at Dinara's pickup, which I'd driven here.

"I'll tell Massimo or Alessio to pick it up."

With a nod, I sat down in the back with the boy on my lap while Nevio googled pediatricians. The boy was silent and still against my chest, breathing very low.

"Is he asleep?" I asked when Nevio slipped behind the steering wheel. He glanced over his shoulder. "No, he's just staring straight ahead. But he looks like he might be falling asleep soon."

"Drive carefully. He's not in a child seat."

Nevio did drive more considerately than his usual style but my heart was pounding madly in my chest when we finally came to a stop in front of a pediatric practice. It had been a longer drive than I would have liked, over an hour.

It was two minutes after their closing hours and I could see a nurse closing up the door.

"Let me go in first. I'll give you a sign when it's okay to come in," Nevio said and slipped out of the car before I could argue. There was only one reason he didn't want me inside with him right away. He would be threatening the doctor and nurses, and knowing Nevio, he'd succeed.

Fifteen minutes later, Nevio opened the door again and waved for me to come. Getting out of a car with a child in your hold was harder than I'd thought. Nevio jogged over to me and grabbed my arm to steady me. When I was safely on the ground on my own two feet, I pulled away from his grip and headed into the practice. Nevio stayed close to my side.

Inside, a middle-aged male doctor with salt-and-pepper hair waited for us. Behind him stood an obviously terrified older nurse. The doctor also appeared apprehensive but was better at keeping his composure, for which I had to applaud him, considering Nevio's talent for scare tactics.

The little boy clung to me when we stepped into one of the treatment rooms. "What's his name?" he asked.

I glanced at Nevio. This was a mess. The boy needed a name, preferably his real name, if he even had one. The situation was horrible. Maybe his birth mother had never bothered to actually name him. My eyes burned, considering the possibility.

"Battista," I said the first name that popped up in my head. Nevio raised an eyebrow but didn't argue.

Of course, the boy didn't react when the doctor called him by that name. He took his time weighing and measuring the boy, checking his body for injuries and how many teeth he had. Battista was calm throughout it all. Maybe he'd already cried all his tears before. I stayed right beside him, hoping my presence would calm him even though he didn't know me.

Nevio perched on the edge of the doctor's desk, watching everything with crossed arms.

My anger for him had taken a back seat, not because I wasn't still furious, but because my brain was busy trying to figure out how I was going to take care of a child without anyone finding out the truth. I'd have to come up with a good story. My future would be filled with lies, all for Nevio.

I could already imagine what Carlotta would say. We'd fought so hard to move out from our homes and share an apartment, for this slice of freedom. Caring for a baby would definitely take away from the life we'd imagined.

"His weight is on the lower part of the chart but still okay. He's dehydrated, though. You need to get him formula. He's around nine months, so that's still his best form of hydration."

Nine months. Still a little baby. He probably still woke at night for his bottle. My life would be completely upended in the next few months. I didn't believe in fate, but it was strange that I had decided to postpone college to have more time to figure out what I wanted in the future, and now I had a little human full-time job.

"The rash on his bum will go away if you change his diapers regularly."

I nodded.

"Are you done?" Nevio asked.

The doctor nodded, but I could see that he had a myriad of questions he wasn't asking. Nevio pulled out a wad of cash from his back pocket and handed it to the doctor. He began shaking his head, but Nevio simply shoved it at him.

I put a fresh diaper on Battista. Luckily, they had a stash in the room, but I still didn't have any clothes. Or anything else to take care of a little child. I could have asked Dinara. She'd probably kept a few things, but that would have raised questions I couldn't answer. My early leave of the racing circus would already be met with surprise.

Nevio and I left the practice with Battista in my arms. And for the first time, the question "what now?" really hit me. How could we return to race camp? Even if I had my own small mobile home, everything was close together and people might notice if I tried to sneak in a child. Not to mention that baby cries would definitely alert people.

Roman was the only other kid there, and he wasn't that small anymore.

"This won't work," I said. This was too big for me. "We can't return to the race circus, not even for a night, and I can't move into the apartment yet. Dad has the codes for everything, and I don't have any stuff there yet…" I took a deep breath, overwhelmed.

Nevio's brows pulled together as he stared straight ahead, obviously lost in thought. "We could find a motel for you for the night. And tomorrow, we could make up a lie about why you have to return to Vegas and move into your apartment early."

"People will ask questions," I said. Mom and Dad, in particular, though they were probably glad that I'd return to Vegas. Still, another change in plans. Mom would continue her prodding, insisting emotional distress was a catalyst for my sudden behavioral changes. She wasn't wrong of course. I hated the idea of having to add even more lies to my already long list of recent lies. I loved my parents and didn't want to deceive them.

"I'm supposed to eat dinner with Adamo, Roman, and Dinara. They'll wonder where I am."

"You're with me. Having dinner with a friend."

The way he said friend made it clear he didn't think that was what he thought he was, a friend. And he was right, we hadn't been friends since that night. At times, it had felt as if we were enemies. "Frenemy, then," I said with a shrug as if it didn't matter to me.

Nevio touched the small of my back, surprising me. "We're not enemies, Rory. Not friends either. Friends don't want to do what I want to do to you."

Heat traveled up my neck. "Eat me and make me watch." I meant it in the Hannibal Lecter kind of way, but Nevio's answering smirk said he didn't.

"All night long," he murmured. Goose bumps rose all over my body, and I took a step away from him so his hand dropped from my back.

"We need to buy stuff for Battista. It's getting late, and he needs food and sleep."

He looked at me with an expression that made sweat trickle down the nape of my neck before he gave a nod. "So it's Battista now?"

"It's the only name I came up with on short notice. But it's your choice. He's *your son.*"

Something passed his face, but it was gone too quickly for me to grasp. "Then let's go shopping and find a motel for us."

"Us?"

"I won't let you stay in a fucking motel in the middle of nowhere by yourself, Rory. End of discussion. Now get into the car."

"You realize you're acting as if you're the one helping me when you're not."

"Get in," he said in a softer voice.

I climbed into the car. Battista was sucking his thumb. Now that he wasn't crying, he was awfully quiet.

"If my parents find out we spent the night together, even in a platonic way, there'll be hell to pay."

"Our families think we're too close, like brother and sister, so they won't suspect any dirty deeds."

Not all of them. I was sure Kiara had watched our interactions with worry on occasion. After our shopping trip and another thirty-minute drive, Nevio finally pulled up in front of a motel. By now, I had completely lost my bearings. I wasn't sure if we were in Arizona, Utah, or Nevada.

Battista was asleep. I'd given him a big bottle with formula in the car plus another fresh diaper and dressed him in a cute romper, and he'd fallen asleep right after.

Nevio and I walked into the reception building of the motel. The guy behind the desk glanced from me, to Battista, then to Nevio.

He nodded at me. "She legal?"

I wasn't sure if he meant if I was of age or if I was a prostitute. Nevio flashed his teeth at him. "A room for us."

The man looked at Nevio for several seconds before he nodded slowly, obviously deciding he didn't want trouble. Considering this place wasn't really inviting, he probably had suspicious-looking customers on a daily basis.

"Do you have a bed for the baby?"

The man gave me a look that suggested it was stupid of me to ask. Something in Nevio's eyes told me he wouldn't mind having a private chat with the man, but I didn't want more trouble than we already had. I gripped his arm. "Let's go."

Nevio finally picked up the keys, and we headed toward our room. The moment we stepped inside, my belly tightened with nerves. There was only one bed in the motel room. It wasn't even king sized. The last time I had spent in a bed with Nevio had burned itself into my brain, and I wasn't keen on a repeat performance. Not like that.

Not at all.

"Where are you going to sleep?" I asked when I walked over to the bed. The scent of a strong cleaner hung in the air, which wasn't the worst thing because it gave me hope this place was cleaned regularly.

"In the bed just like you," Nevio said, one eyebrow pulling up in a challenging way. "We're both adults, I think we can handle it."

"Your actions of the past and even today suggest otherwise," I muttered. Nevio was many things but not trustworthy, at least not in that regard.

He perched on the bed and took out his phone. "I'll give Alessio and Massimo a heads-up, so they can fill in Adamo."

I put Battista down in the middle of the bed so he wouldn't accidentally roll off and hurt himself. The bed wasn't very high but if he landed on his head…I didn't want to risk it.

"I assume you won't tell them the truth?"

Nevio's dark brows pulled together. He and his cousins were close. Closer than close. The secrets they shared were more than an average human could stomach. But I had a feeling Nevio didn't want anyone to know about his son, not even his best friends. This made me feel special, even if I knew I had been the convenient choice. Alessio and Massimo were hardly nanny material.

I gritted my teeth, my annoyance for Nevio on the rise once more.

"Not yet. I need to wrap my mind around everything," Nevio said quietly, surprisingly reflected and reasonable.

"What are you telling them? Everyone will wonder why we're both gone." My cheeks heated when I thought about how this would look. "After the scene in the hospital tent, Adamo will definitely be suspicious."

A sly smile pulled at Nevio's mouth. "He won't share his suspicions with our families. There's a reason he prefers to stay at the races. A controlling family is annoying as fuck."

It could be but I didn't mind Dad's protective ways most of the time. Of course there were instances when they were very inconvenient.

"Adamo will ask questions."

"We'll deal with him tomorrow." Nevio rose to his feet and pulled his T-shirt over his head.

"What are you doing?" I asked after my eyes had done a quick scan of Nevio's marvelous body as I always did. It was impossible for me not to check him out, but I made sure to only skim the tattoo on his back because I simply didn't want to see it grow.

"I'm grabbing a quick shower." The way he said it made heat rise into my cheeks.

"You could sleep in the bathroom. Maybe there's room in the tub."

Nevio moved into the bathroom with a low chuckle. "Are you scared of sharing a bed with me, Rory?" He threw me a look over his shoulders, his dark eyes full of challenge.

I held his gaze. "No," I said firmly. "I simply don't want to." It wasn't the truth. Part of me was scared of being in a bed with Nevio, not because of what he might do—no matter what Nevio was, he'd always respect my no—but of what I might want him to do. I didn't want to go down that rabbit hole again. I felt like I was finally making some progress with my emotions and didn't want to ruin it all. Nevio disappeared in the bathroom but left the door about an inch open.

I wasn't sure if he did it because he was vigilant or as another way to unsettle me.

I sank down on the bed, suddenly tired. Battista rolled over on his belly in his sleep but didn't move apart from that. He'd definitely have to sleep between Nevio and me so he wouldn't fall off the bed and also to act as a barrier between us.

I took my phone out of my purse, which I hadn't done in almost two hours. I had gotten eight texts. Three from Carlotta, one from Adamo, one from Alessio, two from Mom and one from Dad.

I replied to Dad first because he was the one who'd send out the cavalry if I didn't. Like Mom, he was just generally checking in like he did every day. Adamo's and Alessio's texts had arrived after Nevio's message to them. And Carlotta was worried Nevio had done something because I hadn't replied to her first text from almost two hours ago.

I wondered how much I should share with her, but a message or even a phone call seemed too risky for the news. She would eventually find out, and I knew she wouldn't be impressed. I simply messaged her that I was okay but needed to talk to her urgently tomorrow regarding our move into our shared apartment, then I put my phone down on the nightstand.

I didn't have any spare clothes to change into. They were all in the campervan, and there was no way I was going to sleep in my underwear next to Nevio, even with a baby between us.

Not going to happen...

Since there was only one cover and Battista was lying on top of it, I'd probably just sleep with today's clothes on top too. It wouldn't be a restful night I supposed. I wasn't sure what Battista's rhythm was but I assumed he'd wake for a bottle at least once at night.

Not to mention that Nevio was in a bed with me.

I slipped off my sneakers, then stretched out beside Battista. This felt surreal in a way I could hardly describe. When I'd thought I might be pregnant, I had been terrified of the responsibility of raising a child. Now I was in the same situation, only it was another woman's child.

I turned my head to Battista who had his chubby cheeks turned to me as he slept on his belly. It was hard to believe that Nevio was a father. He was responsible for this boy. I didn't think he really understood what that meant yet.

I closed my eyes, allowing myself to rest even as my nerves were too frayed to fall asleep right away. The creak of the door told me that Nevio was done showering and had entered the bedroom again.

"I really hope you're decent," I muttered, keeping my eyes closed just in case.

"I'm many things, Rory, but not decent," he said, and from his voice,

By Frenzy I *Pain*

I could tell he was coming closer. My pulse spiked as it always did when he was near.

"There's nothing you haven't already seen."

"For your information, I didn't really pay close attention to that part of you."

"That's a great loss."

"Your drunkenness and obnoxiousness were kind of distracting."

The bed dipped. Definitely on my side and I felt a light pressure against my hip where some part of him touched me. "Then why did you have sex with me?"

My cheeks burned. I had asked myself that question hundreds of times since that night. It wasn't even that it had been my plan to sleep with him. Not that night. I'd always wanted to be in a relationship with Nevio and take one step after the other. I opened my eyes and glared at him. "Because I thought—"

Nevio perched on the edge in his boxers and nothing else. His muscled back was turned my way and he was twisting around to look at me. His dark eyes weren't mocking as his tone had suggested. They were curious.

"You thought?"

"Never mind," I said with a shake of my head.

Nevio braced one arm beside my other hip, leaning half over me. "If you wanted to have a good time, you could have asked."

I pursed my lips. "You would have never touched me if you'd known it was me that night. And what we had was far from a good time, so no thanks."

Nevio chuckled. "You're right. You were off-limits. And I'm usually a hell of a good time."

I wondered if his use of the word "were" meant I was no longer off-limits in his mind, and if he would have sex with me if I asked. What had changed? "Why was I off-limits and am no longer? Is this some sort of the present was already opened so now it doesn't matter anymore?"

I hated the idea that it was like that. I wouldn't have pegged Nevio the old-fashioned type, but maybe I was simply delusional when it came to him.

Nevio's brows snatched together, and his mouth built a hard line.

"What a heap of bullshit." He bent down so his face was right above mine. I froze. "Aside from the fact that I doubt I really opened your present that night, considering I passed out on the first push, you were off-limits for a myriad of reasons that had nothing to do with the state of your hymen."

He had that directness from Massimo, and it still flustered me every time.

I didn't say that considering how much it had hurt, I doubted the present wasn't opened. "Name one," I dared him.

"You are Fabiano's daughter."

I rolled my eyes because it was the obvious one, but for some reason, I doubted it was the main one. "You're not someone who lets social rules or conventions stop him from something he wants. I was just one of the guys for you. That's it."

Nevio didn't contradict me. "I don't think you're one of the guys now."

I swallowed. "It's irrelevant. I never wanted and still don't want anything casual. I want a serious relationship."

"Then you picked the wrong guy."

"So you can stop stalking me now since we both agree there won't ever be anything between us. I should be free to look for someone who wants to be in a serious relationship with me."

The thunderous look in his eyes gave me an answer before his mouth did.

Chapter Twenty-Three

Nevio

Anger surged through me. No way in hell was I allowing anyone to touch Aurora. Maybe I wasn't relationship material. Hell, most days I wasn't even bare-human-interactions material, but I couldn't give Rory free. She felt like mine in some strange way I couldn't explain. Maybe she had always felt a little like mine, but in the past, I'd never had to worry that she'd pull away. She had been a constant in my life, her adoration of me a familiar presence. Until I'd fucked up that night.

For her, that night ended her obsession with me and started mine with her. I wanted to return to how it had been. The kid let out a small cry, destroying the moment. I pulled back so Aurora could roll over to him. She lightly rubbed Battista's back and made a low shushing noise, which seemed to work as his eyes remained closed. I rose to my feet. It was strange seeing Aurora console Battista. Not because I'd never seen her console someone. She had a huge heart, so naturally, she was the consoler in our huge group of friends and family. This was strange because she was consoling my kid—fuck, *my* kid—as if it were her own. Caring and loving as she was born.

My instincts were of a very different nature.

I wouldn't have known what to do with the kid if it started bawling. I still couldn't wrap my head around his being here and mine.

What was I supposed to do with a kid?

I didn't want that kind of responsibility, and no matter who you asked, they would tell you that I wasn't a person who should be handed this sort of responsibility either. Aurora knew it too, which was probably another reason she'd quickly agreed to take care of him. She was probably worried I'd lock him in a basement if he cried too loudly.

I tore my eyes from Rory and my son, hating how confused the sight left me, how it reminded me of my deficits. Deficits I usually used to my advantage, but in a situation like this, they were just that: deficits.

I ran a hand through my hair, trying to refocus. I glanced at Rory's butt to get me in another mindset. She was in high-rise jean shorts, which allowed me to see the dip below her ass globes and thighs the way she was stretched out.

Rory cleared her throat, and I gave her a dirty smile.

"Battista will sleep between us tonight so he can't fall out," she said pointedly.

I rounded the bed and stretched out on the other side. I hadn't expected there to be any action tonight.

She wanted me to redeem myself at the very least. But the road to redemption was closed to me.

Maybe that would change if Rory and I started getting it on, or maybe not. Maybe that kind of emotional bond would always elude me. Rory didn't want to risk it, and a part of me was glad because it protected her from me. But the other part, which was unfortunately growing by day, wanted her no matter the price.

"Can you turn off the lights?"

"Aren't you worried about being in the dark with me?" I was only half joking.

"Does it make a difference?" She sounded tired.

By Frenzy I *Rain*

In the dark, the monster was always closer to the surface, harder to control and cage in. But Rory was right, that monster didn't call out for her.

I hoped it never would.

I didn't sleep at all that night. Not just because the kid woke three times screaming desperately until Aurora fed him a bottle and rocked him in her arms.

She and I didn't speak as she took care of him. She, because she was exhausted and pissed at me, and I because I was in awe of her and still trying to figure out how to handle the next few weeks. Hell, the next few days even.

Aurora and I would need a good excuse for why we didn't stay for the race, why we'd return to Las Vegas and have her move into the apartment early. People expected that kind of erratic behavior from me but not Rory, though she'd been unpredictable ever since our night together.

I got several messages from Massimo and Alessio that night, and especially the latter made it clear what he thought of me being out somewhere with Aurora.

It was before sunrise when I finally got up and dressed. Lying in this moth-eaten bed and staring at the ceiling splattered with fly shit, my pulse seemed to thump in my ears and my heart to hammer a hole into my rib cage.

I felt restless, erratic, like a junkie who needed a fix. If it weren't for Rory and the kid, I would have gone in search for someone to kill, but this seemed like the worst possible moment to do so.

Aurora needed me; they both needed me here. I pulled a chair up next to the bed, sank down in it, and propped my feet up on the mattress. The curtains didn't block out the lamp in front of our room, so I could see Rory's face as she slept.

Tonight, she didn't have any naughty dreams but her sleep was fitful nonetheless. Battista stirred around five in the morning, and Rory's eyes opened slowly, then went wide when she saw me watching them.

She frowned and slowly sat up. Her hair was a tousled mess and her eyes were a bit puffy. She was still the most beautiful girl I'd ever seen, and that thought made me want to get up and run like a fucking coward.

I didn't like the turn my thoughts often took when I looked at Rory, especially in recent weeks, and I felt the last twenty-four hours had worsened the situation.

"How long have you been watching me? It's really unsettling," she said in a sleep-roughened voice as she stroked Battista's head. I doubted he would fall back asleep.

"For two hours perhaps. I couldn't fall back asleep."

Aurora lifted Battista into her arm. "Can you heat his morning oatmeal in the microwave?"

I got up and picked up one of the food jars labeled as breakfast meal, then popped it in the microwave.

Aurora got up. "Can you feed him so I can grab a quick shower?"

She raised her eyebrows expectantly. I really didn't want to be alone with the kid, much less feed him, but I sank down on the chair and let Aurora put him on my lap. Battista tried to cling to Aurora, obviously as opposed to us being alone as I was. She eventually managed to put him down. "You got this."

Battista and I both watched as Aurora disappeared in the bathroom.

With a sigh, I picked up the spoon and dipped it in the food. Battista allowed me to feed him, even if his eyes kept moving to the bathroom door, waiting for Aurora's return.

"You and me both, buddy," I muttered.

Aurora

The next day, after convincing my parents of my early move, I called Carlotta to tell her I would move in to our apartment today and not in two weeks as had been my original plan. She had been suspicious right away, wanting to know why and if Nevio had done something. I lied that I just couldn't bear his obnoxious presence at the race circus anymore and asked her if she could move in early too. Diego had forbidden her from moving into the apartment by herself, even just for a few weeks.

When Nevio and I arrived in Las Vegas in the early afternoon, I warned him again, "You need to spend the day with him until the coast is clear. I'll give you a call when you can bring him to my place tonight."

Nevio stared at the boy who was shaking a rattle with huge eyes and sucking quickly at his new dummy. I doubted he'd ever had a rattle before considering how mesmerized he seemed by the thing.

"What am I supposed to do with him?"

"I don't know. Take him to a park and go on a walk with him in his stroller. I prepared his milk portions for you and put enough bottled baby food into the nursing bag to last for a week."

"I can't take care of him for more than a few hours, Rory, trust me."

I gritted my teeth. "You've said that before, and I'll try to get rid of everyone except for Lotta as soon as possible, but until then, your son is your responsibility. My parents are suspicious anyway. They probably think I'm about to have a mental breakdown soon."

If things kept progressing like this, maybe I would.

He nodded slowly but I could tell he didn't like it. He could deal with it. I hopped out of the car and walked toward the security gate of my family's mansion. It opened when I arrived in front of it, and Nevio pulled away when Dad appeared before me.

"What's that about?" Dad asked as he watched Nevio race away.

I gave a shrug. "I think he wants to return to the race. Or maybe he's in the mood to kill someone. With Nevio, you never know."

Dad narrowed his eyes at me. "What's going on, Aurora?"

I sighed, buying time to come up with a reply. "When I helped in addiction care, I felt reminded of Nevio. He's not addicted to drugs, but to the thrill of the kill, and I thought I could help him with it. But he's untreatable, and I'm just sick of his antics. I want to help people who really want and need my help."

Dad nodded, but his suspicion remained. "I could have told you that before. Nevio's disposition is permanent and will probably make him a feared Capo one day. If he manages to control himself on occasion, maybe even a respected one. But you need to take care of yourself, not him. Your mom and I are worried. Changing plans on short notice isn't your style, Aurora."

"I feel like my life is up in the air. So far, every step ahead was clear, but now that I finished school, uncertainty has entered the picture. It's difficult for me because I want to know what lies ahead, but I don't." It wasn't even a lie. Nothing seemed decided yet. I wasn't sure what I'd do in the future, but at the same time, my options were limited as the daughter of a high-ranking mobster.

Dad nodded, then he cocked an eyebrow. "We could arrange a marriage, then one thing would be certain."

I could tell he wasn't serious. "You would have a harder time giving my hand away in marriage than me."

He chuckled. "True, and I don't know any man who would be worthy of you."

I smiled. "I suppose he would have to be a high-ranking Camorrista."

Dad shook his head. "He would have to be a good man willing to treat you like a queen, and a Camorrista."

"Which means I'll never marry," I muttered. While Nevio fit the latter to a T as future Capo, he definitely wasn't a good man, not even by my dad's standards, and he was worlds away from treating me like a queen.

Dad wrapped an arm around my shoulders and led me toward our house. Mom was already waiting for us in the doorway. "Your mom wants to talk to you about your move again."

After an initial attempt to have me stay with them for a few more weeks, I got them to agree to me moving into my place today. Mostly because I pretended that Carlotta would be heartbroken if I bailed on her now.

I only had to pack my clothes and care products since the apartment was already equipped with everything else we might need. Dad entered the security code into the elevator so it started moving to the floor where Carlotta's and my apartment was. There was only one more apartment on the floor, but it was empty. I had a feeling that wasn't a coincidence because the apartments on all the other floors were occupied. Normalcy was difficult if your father was Enforcer for the Camorra.

Diego and Carlotta were already in the apartment when we arrived. I hugged Carlotta, excited to share the place with her, but at the same time anxiety over having to take care of Battista dimmed my excitement. Carlotta didn't even know yet, and I could only imagine how she'd react.

She regarded me closely, her eyes narrowing. "Everything okay?" she whispered.

"Later," I mouthed back. I didn't want Dad to think my worry was related to living on my own. He'd jump on that wagon without hesitation and insist I live at home instead.

Dad and Diego walked through every room of the apartment—two bedrooms, a shared bathroom and a living room with open kitchen—to check it for any security concerns yet again. Every inch of the entire complex had already been checked by them in the weeks before. The security guards were probably already sick of Dad's criticism and suggestions for improvement.

Mom went into my room with me. She helped me put on sheets and hang up a few photos from our family and Carlotta and me. Once everything was in place, except for my clothes, which I wanted to sort into my closet later, Mom let out a sigh. "Wow, this really hits me harder than I'd thought." Tears glistened in her eyes.

I went over to her and wrapped my arms around her. "I'm only a ten-minute car ride away, and you still have Davide."

Mom nodded, but I could tell that she wasn't really consoled. I felt a bit sad too, but I simply wanted to have my own place with Carlotta. I wanted to be responsible for cooking, for housework… and now a child.

Dad came in. He wrapped an arm around Mom, and she leaned into him. "She's safe, Leona."

"I doubt Mom's crying because of safety concerns," I said with a laugh.

Mom laughed too, but it sounded a bit choked. Dad frowned at her, and she swatted his arm lightly. "I'm fine. Go give her the lecture, you surely have in mind."

"The building is closely guarded, Aurora. Don't give the security codes to anyone."

It was why Nevio would smuggle Battista into the apartment and then the poor kid would probably have to stay inside for a while until he and I came up with a plan how to get him in and out without anyone noticing, or until we found an explanation for a kid visiting me, or better yet, until Nevio told his parents and they'd figure out a final solution for the boy. He needed a forever home, a forever family, and that could only be the Falcones.

"I know, Dad. I know where every single emergency button is in this building. I know the names and faces of every security guard on the premises..."

I trailed off at the look on Dad's face. "I'm going to be okay."

Fifteen minutes later, Carlotta and I had finally managed to usher her brother and my parents out of the apartment. The moment the door closed, Carlotta sighed, grinned, and rushed over to the sofa, where she flung herself down with widely spread arms. "Freedom!"

I grinned. "Not quite but better than nothing." I quickly messaged Nevio that the coast was clear. As the Capo's son, no guards would stop him from entering the premises. I just wondered how he'd get Battista into the apartment.

I sank down beside Carlotta, trying to come up with the gentlest way to break the news of our new house guest to her. "Will you have Massimo over now that your brother isn't breathing down your neck anymore?" I asked instead.

Carlotta pursed her lips. "We're just friends."

I gave her a doubtful look.

She shrugged. "Why would he come over by himself? Maybe the trio comes over for movie night or so, but do you even want Nevio around? I thought you were trying to put some distance between you and him."

That was working splendidly, now that I had agreed to take care of his son. Why was I such a sucker for people who needed help?

My phone beeped with a message from Nevio, in which he informed me that he was already in the elevator. I jumped up from the sofa.

Carlotta still lay spread-eagle on the sofa, her brown curls flung about her, and she made a face that expressed her concern for my sanity. "What's wrong?"

I bit my lip when a knock sounded. "This is Nevio."

"Nevio?" She sat up and swung her legs down. I gave her an apologetic smile then hurried to the door. Nevio must have waited with Battista right around the corner to be here this quickly after everyone left.

I opened the door, and my eyes widened in surprise. Nevio waited in front of it, no surprise there, but instead of Battista, he carried a huge cardboard box. Had he left the boy in the car and decided to carry his stuff up first?

Chapter Twenty-Four

Aurora

"This is getting heavy," he said with a cocked eyebrow. I stepped back, and opened the door wider. He passed by, and I closed the door after finding nothing and no one else in the hallway.

He put the box down slowly and opened the lid. My eyes widened in surprise. Inside was Battista in his carrier, fast asleep. "You put him in a box?" I asked.

Nevio motioned at the holes he'd put into the cardboard as if this was for a cat or bunny. "It was only for a few minutes. I put him in there in the parking lot across the street, then walked over here. I didn't want to risk anything on the premises."

Carlotta approached us with obvious curiosity and peered down into the box like I still did. Her eyes widened comically, and she slowly turned her head toward me. "There's a baby inside the box."

"Thanks for the heads-up," Nevio said, but his voice was less cocky than usual. His hair was tousled, and he was sweaty. It seemed like being alone with a nine-month-old was too much for him.

Carlotta still stared at me, her eyes growing even wider. "There. Is. A. Baby. In. The. Box."

I bent down and carefully picked up Battista. He briefly stirred but never opened his eyes as I pressed him to my chest.

"What's going on?" Carlotta asked, her eyes narrowing on Nevio who shoved his hands into his pockets as if it wasn't his job to explain the situation. If he thought his job was done here, he was very wrong. I would help him and Battista, but he would be part of this. He wouldn't just keep on living as if nothing had changed.

"I have another box with his things in the car. I'll pick them up," he said and left the apartment without another word, leaving me alone with a very upset Carlotta.

She flung her arms up. "Aurora! What is going on? You're my best friend, but if Nevio kidnapped this kid, I won't just stand by and watch."

"He didn't kidnap him, Lotta, I swear." I sighed.

Carlotta stared at the little boy and shook her head.

"You can't tell anyone about this," I told her. "Not even our families. No one."

"He's not yours, that's for sure," she said and her lips thinned. "I know only one person who'd mess up like that and then ask you for help. Fits that he's the one who brings him here in a cardboard box."

I shrugged. Of course, there was only one possible suspect in this case.

She moved closer and looked at Battista, who I cradled in my arms so his peaceful face was on display. "He's Nevio's son, isn't he?"

I nodded because I didn't want to lie to Carlotta. I needed her help with this. "Yeah. He found out about him yesterday. His birth mother dropped him off with Nevio because she doesn't want to take care of him."

Carlotta's expression twisted with contempt. "I'll never understand how a mother can abandon her child."

I shrugged. I didn't know the exact circumstances. What made me angrier than the fact that the woman had decided to give away her son was the fact that she hadn't taken very good care of him before then.

"And to hand him over to a madman like Nevio?" Carlotta shook her head and scoffed. "He's the last person I would put up with the task of watching a helpless child."

"He's not that bad."

"He is. And he's irresponsible."

That was true. Nevio lived for the thrill. Of course, he took responsibility when it came to the Camorra, but many of his tasks were directly linked to activities he loved: torture and killing.

Carlotta lightly touched Battista's small hand and her expression softened. She loved kids and would definitely help me with him. When she looked back up at me, her expression was less gentle. "Why is he here?"

I grimaced.

Carlotta threw up her arms again. "Rory!"

"Nevio doesn't want his family to know about this. He didn't even tell Massimo and Alessio yet. He has nowhere else to take him. And he knows he'll be safe with me. It's just until he's figured out another solution."

Carlotta pressed her palm against her forehead, slowly shaking her head. "You should tell on him, Rory. I know you think you need to help him to unleash his humanity, but we both know that won't work. He's a mess, and you should stay away from him."

"You never said it like that before."

"Because I didn't want to hurt your feelings, but this is about more than just your feelings, Rory. This boy needs a family."

"I know," I said. "But he lost his mother already. I don't want to rob him of any chance to have a father. If I tell the Falcones about this, Nino and Kiara, or Remo and Serafina are going to adopt him. It'll be easy for Nevio to pretend this isn't his problem, to just let others become caregivers for his son, but if I care for the kid for a while, Nevio will always know it's only a temporary solution, and he'll eventually have to step up and own up to his responsibilities."

Carlotta shook her head. She couldn't seem to stop. My own disbelief over the situation was still strong so I understood her only too well. "You know Nevio, do you really think that'll happen? How is this going to work? You're starting your internship with the doc in a few days, but a baby needs twenty-four-hour supervision. If you don't want to tell anyone, that leaves only us. I'm not even going to take Nevio into calculation."

I bit my lip. "My work at the Camorra's clinic allows my schedule to be flexible. I'll try to work shifts at night or in the evening. And I still have two weeks before I'm even supposed to start working there."

"But he can't be alone."

"I know," I said. "Nevio can watch him on occasion, and…" I gave her a sheepish smile.

Carlotta pursed her lips. "And I can take care of him when Nevio can't, so always?"

I sent her an apologetic smile. I knew I was asking a lot. "I'll try to do all the work, and it's only going to be for a few weeks. I'll kick Nevio's ass as often as possible."

She closed her eyes and took a deep breath. "I can keep an eye on him some nights when you work."

I hugged her. Another knock sounded and Carlotta pulled away and stalked toward the door. She opened it with a little more force than necessary and gave Nevio one of the darkest looks I'd ever seen on her face. It didn't faze him in the slightest, judging from his unimpressed expression.

"Do you have a room where I can put his stuff?" Nevio asked, directed at me.

"I suppose my room. We don't have a nursery since we didn't plan on having children over," I said, letting my own annoyance shine through. I motioned him to follow me as I headed for my room. It was moderately sized. Carlotta and I had wanted a small apartment, but it was still bigger than most rooms on campus.

Nevio began unpacking everything, then put together the crib. He positioned it beside my bed once it was done. I released a low breath, reality sinking in. While I had experience babysitting Roman, I'd never been solely responsible for a baby. His parents had always been a call away if I had questions or needed help. This was different.

Nevio ran a hand through his dark hair, his eyes settling on the baby still asleep in my arms. I was rocking on my heels lightly because it was a move that Roman had always loved, and it seemed to soothe Battista too.

"You're good at this," he murmured. "Good with him." Nevio's gaze hit me, warm and appreciative in a way I'd rarely seen.

"You can be too if you want," I said firmly. I didn't want him to turn this into a natural motherly instinct thing and use that as his way out of responsibility.

Nevio's lips pulled into a sardonic smile, but he didn't reply. "Where do you want the rest of his stuff?"

"Everything for his bottles in the kitchen and the changing station in the bathroom."

I slowly walked into the kitchen and found Carlotta. My parents had stocked our fridge with everything we might need in the next few days. She stared into the fridge but didn't take anything out. Her scowl suggested the inside of the device had personally insulted her. Her fingers twisted the ancient cross around her neck, which had been her grandmother's.

Battista stirred in my hold and let out a short cry as his eyes peeled open. Then his gentle protest turned to high-pitched wails. Nevio came in from the bathroom where he'd set up the changing station, looking alarmed. "What's up?"

"Maybe he's hungry," I said, intensifying my rocking, which only made Battista squirm and cry harder.

"You could make him a bottle. Aurora's arms are full," Carlotta said with a very tight smile, the cross in her hand turned toward Nevio as if she was trying to keep his evil from her. I doubted she noticed. Nevio shrugged and moved over to the formula we'd bought. He picked up the box and read over the description while the noise level in the kitchen reached headache-inducing volumes.

He cursed when he spilled hot water over the counter, then knocked over the formula and spread powder over himself and the floor. I sent Carlotta a pleading look. I knew Nevio needed to learn how to do this. He needed to step up, but I'd had a long day, and Battista's cries were too much. She moved to Nevio's side and took the box from him. After a quick scan of the instructions, she'd assembled the milk bottle within a minute, and I gave it to Battista, who immediately quieted.

Nevio leaned against the counter with a dark look and gave me an I-told-you-so look. I shook my head. "This doesn't mean anything. Most fathers have to learn how to take care of a baby. It doesn't come naturally. In a few weeks, you'll prepare a bottle with your eyes closed."

I really hoped that his parents were involved by then.

"Shouldn't he eat solids at some point?" Nevio asked, only briefly glancing at Battista, who still happily sucked at his bottle.

"You can't feed him pizza if that's what you think," I said, then yawned.

Nevio glanced at his watch. It was seven-thirty, and my rumbling stomach told me Battista wasn't the only one who needed to fuel up on food.

"I'm going to order pizza for us," Nevio said. "Not Battista, though."

I just nodded, and Carlotta came over to me, not uttering a protest either.

When we sat at the dining table, she turned to Nevio. "Do you really think you can keep this a secret from everyone? Especially Massimo and Alessio, who are practically attached to your hip. They'll get suspicious at some point."

"If you don't let something slip to Massimo, we should be fine. It won't be the first time I'm gone for a few hours or overnight."

Battista watched me eat the pizza with interest, reaching for it several times. Eventually, I put him down on the floor because he seemed eager to move, but once there, he just sat on his bum and watched everything with curious eyes.

Nevio's phone lit up with a call. Massimo. He pushed the call away. Seconds later, a message popped up.

"What's up?" I asked, half hoping they'd somehow found out about Battista.

"They're back in Las Vegas and want to know where I am."

"It's on security camera, so eventually someone will know you're here," I reminded him, though I was sure he'd taken that into consideration. If Nevio visited us frequently in the next few weeks, Dad would definitely ask why. He'd draw the wrong conclusions.

Nevio shrugged. "They definitely won't think I'm here because I have a son."

"Because it's crazy," Carlotta said.

Nevio's phone beeped again. He rolled his eyes. "They can't be without me."

"Well, they'll have to learn to get by now that you have more responsibilities away from them," I said.

Battista began to squirm again and to rub his eyes.

"I think he needs to go to bed," I said.

Nevio rose to his feet. "I'll let you handle it. Better I go to Alessio and Massimo before they start looking for me here."

"Aren't you going to help me put him in bed?" I asked pointedly.

"I doubt he wants that. He still looks at me like I'm going to eat him."

Battista indeed watched Nevio warily. "Most children are wary of unknown men. If you spend more time with him, that'll change."

Nevio stayed, but he looked more uncomfortable than I'd ever seen him. Unfortunately, Battista proved his point and kept rousing from slumber to eye Nevio wearily. Eventually, I told Nevio to go, and he did so without hesitation.

Battista fell asleep soon after Nevio had left. I stayed beside him for a few more minutes before I left the room. With Roman, it had sometimes taken more than an hour to get him to fall asleep, but Battista was obviously used to falling asleep alone.

To my surprise, Nevio was still in front of the door. I'd have thought he had already left to meet with Alessio and Massimo. I wasn't, however, surprised that he hadn't gone back into the kitchen to spend time with Carlotta. Her Nevio tolerance was very low today.

He simply leaned against the wall, his face tipped forward, dark strands falling over his eyes. I'd often wondered how it would feel to run my fingers through them, to tug him toward me and feel his own fingers raking through my hair. I paused with my hand still on the doorknob, but now the sight reminded me of the night when everything had changed. My belly clenched as it always did when I thought about it, but the emotions weren't quite as raw as they used to be. Maybe this was a sign.

"He's asleep," I said in a quiet voice.

Nevio looked up, his eyes narrowing as they settled on mine. He nodded slowly, still with the same confused and thoughtful expression on his face. Nevio pushed away from the wall and approached me. I held my breath, not even sure why.

Nevio stopped in front of me, raked a hand through his hair, then gripped the dark strands. His face twisted with conflicting emotions. "Listen, Rory. I know I can be an asshole."

I gave him a go-on look because I certainly wouldn't contradict him on that point. His fingers curled deeper into his hair, and his expression became even more pained. "I won't ever forget what you're doing for me and for him." He nodded at the door. "You're the kindest person I know, way too fucking kind for this world." He smiled strangely. "You have every reason to hate me, and I know you're really trying, but still you're here. Thank you." The last two words sounded as if he had to press them past shrapnel. I supposed saying thank you wasn't in his standard repertoire.

He cupped my head, and I tensed, my fingers around the doorknob becoming numb from my tight grip. For a moment, we remained like this. I didn't want to be kissed by Nevio, not today, not as long as my emotions and thoughts were a jumbled mess. Nevio briefly touched his forehead to mine, which felt even more intimate than a simple kiss and took me wholly by surprise.

He stepped back and let go of my head with a strange smile. "I'll go now. Sleep tight, Rory." He headed toward our front door, opened it, and then stopped in the doorway. "I'll be back tomorrow." The long pause before he uttered those words told me they weren't what he'd had in mind. He disappeared from my view, and the door clicked shut softly.

I released the doorknob, my fingers prickling as blood flooded back into them.

Carlotta appeared in the kitchen doorway. I wasn't sure how long I'd already stood like that. "Our first night in our own apartment," I said. I didn't want to talk about Nevio. I tore my eyes from where Nevio had been moments before and headed toward Carlotta, who was still hovering in the entry to the kitchen. "How often has Diego messaged you so far?"

Carlotta's phone binged as if on cue, and she checked it after rolling her eyes. "Now six times since he left, and Antonia twice. Even Massimo messaged."

"You'd think we moved to the other end of the world," I said with a laugh. I wanted the tension gone. I wanted tonight to be about us girls and our silly dreams of freedom. "Let's chill on the couch and watch some TV."

"You should check your phone first. While you put Battista to sleep, you got about a dozen messages. Your dad will be back in no time if you don't reply soon, and then we'll have a hard time explaining the Battista situation to him."

I giggled. "A nine-month-old is definitely not something he expects to find in my room." I grabbed my phone from the kitchen table. Carlotta was right. We couldn't risk someone coming over unannounced. Carlotta followed me into the living room, and we settled on the couch. I began answering all texts.

Carlotta was quiet, probably still mulling over our situation. I felt guilty for dragging her into this.

"What about Battista? Will we hear him?" Carlotta asked after she'd turned on the TV.

Our apartment wasn't very big, so I thought his cries would carry over to us.

We both listened for a moment, but it was absolutely silent. We leaned against each other and watched for a bit. I had trouble focusing on anything, so we chose some trash TV that didn't require any form of concentration.

Maybe forty minutes later, Battista's cry made me jump. I got up and hurried into my bedroom. He was sitting in his bed, crying. His pacifier had fallen out and landed on the floor. I picked it up and put it back in his mouth, making shushing noises all the while. But he didn't stop crying. I picked him up and began rocking him when Carlotta came in with a bottle of milk. I gave her a grateful smile. Battista only took a few gulps from the bottle before he began crying again. I wasn't sure what he wanted. Not food or his pacifier, and his diaper wasn't full either.

"Maybe he's just confused because he's in new surroundings."

I nodded. "I wish I knew more about his past."

"I hope his future will be less dramatic than his past has been," Carlotta said.

I released a small sigh and stroked Battista's soft hair. He quieted a bit but still sounded distressed.

"Maybe I should go to bed so he's not alone. I'm tired anyway."

"I can hold him while you get ready for bed," Carlotta said. I gave her a grateful smile and handed Battista over to her. She began singing to him in her beautiful voice, but even that only briefly stunned him into silence.

I grabbed my pj's and rushed into the bathroom. After ten minutes, I returned. I stretched out on my bed with Battista by my side. Carlotta moved his bed against the mattress so he couldn't accidentally fall out of bed in the night.

"I still think you're crazy for doing this, but I'm glad to know that you'd be by my side if I ever got pregnant by accident," Carlotta said with a hint of irony.

"I would definitely help you if you ever accidentally slept with Massimo and got pregnant," I said with a small laugh.

Carlotta made a face and closed the door, cloaking Battista and me in darkness. I rubbed his back for a long time, and eventually, he fell silent. I was no longer tired. I felt too anxious. What qualified me to become the main caretaker of a possibly traumatized child?

"Why am I doing this?" I muttered, then glanced at the helpless kid beside me. His soft breathing was reassuring. He needed me to do my best for as long as there was no better solution. I hoped Nevio would figure out something fast. The longer Battista stayed with me, the more he'd get used to my presence and then be ripped away again.

My phone lit up with a message. I was glad I'd muted it.

Of course, it was Nevio. Nobody else would message me this late.

Thinking of you. I'll bring breakfast in the morning. Sleep tight.

I would have found his message sweet under different circumstances. I was pretty sure some of my fantasies from the past included late-night texting with similar messages.

I can't sleep. Angry with you.

I turned off my phone. I didn't want to chat with him now. He was probably driving around with Massimo and Alessio, looking for new victims so he could extend his back tattoo, and I was here with his son.

Chapter Twenty-Five

Aurora

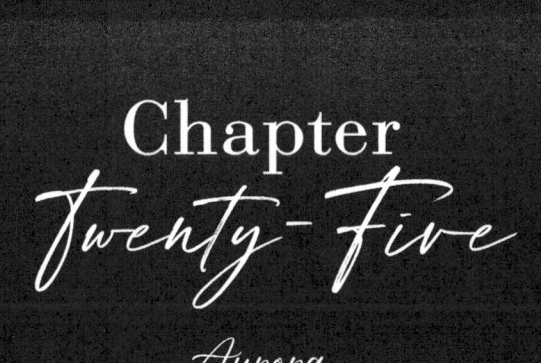

I'd barely slept and hadn't had time to get dressed yet when Nevio showed up at the apartment the following morning. I was too exhausted to care that I was only in panties and a tank, the clothes I'd changed into in the middle of the night after Battista had spit up on me. Battista had fallen back asleep around six thirty, three hours after waking me with his spit up. Unfortunately, my body refused to do the same and catch up on sleep.

I was on my second coffee but felt no closer to being ready for the day. A direct caffeine infusion was probably my only chance to survive the day at this point. Carlotta had already left for a doctor's appointment. Because of her heart, she had them regularly.

After making sure Nevio was in front of the door, I opened it for him but stayed hidden behind the door, not wanting to be caught on camera in my half-dressed state.

Nevio scanned me from head to toe when he entered the apartment. I was too tired to feel embarrassed. Nevio looked as if he hadn't had much sleep that night either, though I suspected for very different reasons. Annoyance filled me when I imagined how he'd probably enjoyed himself with Massimo and Alessio.

Nevio raised a paper bag with the name of one of my favorite donut shops on it. "I got breakfast."

The donut shop wasn't on the way from the mansion to the apartment. I wondered if that meant Nevio had slept somewhere else or if he'd gone out of his way to get me breakfast. I didn't ask. Maybe it was for the best if I didn't know. I didn't have enough energy for a possible argument.

I nodded and trudged back into the kitchen, where I'd left my coffee. I sank down at the kitchen table, cradled my coffee cup, and tried not to let my anger suck what little energy I still had from my body.

"Rough night?" Nevio asked as he set the bag down on the table in front of me.

I glared. "What about you?"

Nevio opened the paper bag and showed me the selection of six donuts he'd brought, then sank down across from me. "I had to let off some steam."

I slammed my coffee cup down on the tabletop. "So that's how it's going to be? I'll watch your son so you don't have to, and I'll stay single for the rest of my life so you won't feel the need to kill anyone, and you keep living your best life sleeping around with girls and killing people for fun."

Nevio stared at the spilled coffee, then up at my face. "I haven't slept with a girl since I visited you in New York. I tried after our night at the party, but like I said, you are stuck in my head, and I have a feeling it'll be impossible to get you out."

Surprise shot through me, but I didn't allow my initial response to show. I was still suspicious, and Nevio needed to know that. "You haven't been with any girls for three months?"

"It's only me and my hand."

I stared at his hand and of course flushed thinking about how he was touching himself. Was he thinking of me when he did? He'd mentioned it once, but it was still hard to believe. After years of yearning, he was suddenly into me.

I got up, trying not to let my tired mind run rampant. I needed to stay calm and in control. Grabbing a dish towel, I wiped up the coffee stain to buy some time.

When I sat back down, I felt calmer. "Why? What do you want from me? A relationship obviously not."

Nevio tilted his head, letting his gaze wander over my face. I couldn't imagine that I was an enticing sight right now. "Fuck if I knew. Maybe even a relationship. But I'm not relationship material."

I shook my head. "So you think stalking me for months and threatening everyone who looks at me is a good way to win me over?"

"Do I need to win you over?"

I glared. "Maybe I had a crush on you, but what happened between us was a major eye-opener. Not to mention that you having a kid and not wanting to own up to it is another sign that you're just not ready to commit to anything."

"My brain's a train wreck, Rory. Sometimes I feel like you might be the only one who can stop me from going off the rails. Sometimes I'm sure it's inevitable, and I'll just overrun you in the process."

My throat clogged up. He thought I had this power over him? I didn't want to let his words lure me in. I sighed. "Maybe you took too many drugs at the parties, and now your brain's not functioning properly."

"Trust me, my brain wasn't an orderly place long before I had my first glass of alcohol or smoked marijuana."

"I don't want to be your stopgap, the one you run to when you're desperate. I want to be in a real relationship, with commitment and honest emotions, with someone who's reliable and responsible."

Nevio shook his head. "Those are not attributes anyone in their right mind would associate with me."

I glared down at my coffee. "But it's what I want."

"Then you really chose the wrong guy, Rory. You've known me all my life."

"Yeah." He had a valid point. I'd fallen in love with the Nevio I knew, but was he someone I could really see myself dating the way he acted now? "It's called growing up," I said eventually.

"What do you want, Rory?"

That was a loaded question. I got up and refilled my cup to gather my thoughts.

"I want you to take care of Battista like a father and stop playing games with me. I want you to be serious about us. I want you to spend time with me without trying to get into my pants constantly and without the crazy stalking."

I heard the scratching of Nevio's chair as he got up and moved toward me. He grabbed the counter on either side of my hips. "I'm serious about you. But I still want to get in your pants, and I sure as fuck won't stop the stalking if it means keeping other guys away from you." His smile was twisted. "I'm still me, still a Made Man and a bloodthirsty killer, Rory, and that won't change. Falling for someone like that comes with a price, and you should know that."

He brought our faces closer. "And stop pretending it's only me who wants to get in your pants. What's so wrong about enjoying each other while we get serious?"

Nevio's hand stroked over my shoulder and collarbone, then lower until his fingers slipped under the hem of my tank, shoving it down in the process. My skin heated when my breast popped out, and his fingers cupped my nipple. A heavy feeling settled in my core, warm and wet. Nevio kept tugging my nipple, and I just looked at him as my breath became faster. He leaned down, his lips sliding over mine as his hand trailed over my belly. My pussy clenched as he got closer, eager for a touch I'd dreamed about countless times.

Battista's cry burst through my bubble. I tensed and quickly set down my cup, then pushed Nevio's chest. He stepped back with a look of frustration on his face.

I was relieved for this dose of reality and rushed over to my bedroom where Battista's crying only grew in volume.

Nevio

"Fuck," I gritted out. I grabbed the counter tightly. Aurora had fled as if the devil were after her. She wanted emotions. I wanted her to realize that I could not give her the emotions she desired. Or maybe I hoped to hide this fact from her because I fucking couldn't imagine losing her right now. She was trying to pull away, and I wasn't letting her. An asshole move. And exactly my style.

I drew in a deep breath and pushed away from the counter, trying to eliminate the lingering tension in my body.

Aurora returned to the kitchen with Battista. I still couldn't process that he was mine. I barely had control over my own life, so I definitely wasn't equipped to take care of a helpless kid.

Aurora walked over to me, but she pointedly avoided my eyes. From the firm set of her mouth, I could tell she was annoyed, and I doubted it was at Battista.

"Here, how about you hold him for a bit?" she asked, holding the kid out to me.

Battista didn't look convinced, and neither was I.

"Nevio," she said in exasperation when I made no move to take him from her. "I agreed to help you, but that means you have to do something too." I finally took him and held him in my arms. Of course, he started crying. What a fucking surprise. I immediately held him out to Aurora, but she shook her head. "Talk to him. Try to show him that you aren't a danger, that you care about him."

How was I supposed to do that, when neither was true? I was a danger to everyone and I didn't know the kid. I hadn't magically developed any fatherly emotions only because he shared blood with me.

Aurora let out a sigh and took him from me. She frowned at me. She didn't look angry, only disappointed. I would have preferred her anger. "If this is you trying, then we really have a problem, and you need to talk to your parents sooner than later. And I really think you should only come over when Carlotta is here in the future."

Ouch. I nodded slowly. "I told you so."

"I think the problem is that you're telling yourself that you can't do it, when you simply don't want to."

I could see and feel Aurora pull back from me, but it was like we were connected by an invisible rope, and the more she tried to pull away, the more I wanted to drag her back to me. "Fuck, I'm trying, Rory. This isn't easy for me either. I haven't slept with anyone in months. I'm here with you and Battista when I should probably grab some sleep. Give me some time."

She sighed. "Okay. Then let's all have breakfast together."

I nodded and sank back down at the table. Aurora put Battista in his high chair before preparing his morning meal. Battista eyed the colorful donuts with interest. I pushed them over to him. His eyes widened, and he snatched up the pink one closest to him and squeezed it tightly until the filling shot out. He slammed his palm down on the white cream with a giggle and brought it to his mouth. His eyes grew even wider when he tasted the sugary filling, and he began to lick it off his hands eagerly.

Aurora raised her eyebrows. "I suppose keeping sugar off his meal plan is a fail."

Aurora's phone beeped. My eyes immediately checked who had messaged her. Of course, Aurora noticed and sent me a glare. It was from her mother.

Aurora scanned the message with a frown. "Mom asks me to come over for dinner tonight. Apparently, a big Falcone-Scuderi feast is planned. Kiara went all out."

She and I both glanced at Battista. "Carlotta can watch him, right?"

Aurora nodded, but her hesitation was plain on her face. "I have to ask her. I can't just expect her to babysit whenever something comes up." She bit her lip. "Tonight would be a good chance to tell your family."

"No," I said immediately. "I'm not going to tell them before I have figured it out myself. This isn't just any news. It's a huge mindfuck of news."

When I returned to the mansion afterward, I felt erratic, as if last night's raid hadn't happened. Maybe I could convince Massimo and Alessio to go on another hunt with me tonight.

Mom sat on the couch, reading a magazine when I entered the common area. I headed over to her and plopped down. She put away her magazine. That was Mom. She always made time for us, no matter how annoying we were. Her blue eyes scanned my face, and her brows crinkled in concern. "Are you okay?"

"Sure," I lied casually. "Not enough sleep, that's all."

Mom never asked about the details of my nightly hunts. The only time she'd been witness to my depravity had been on my twelfth birthday when she'd walked in on me torturing a guy who Dad had given me as a present. She knew what I was. She tried to pretend I wasn't.

"I love you no matter what. You know that, don't you?"

I gave a terse nod. Mom made a habit out of loving monsters. "It's because I'm your child. You have no choice."

Mom's frown deepened. "That's nonsense. I love you for who you are, for the man I know you'll become."

"Mom, you should lower your expectations if you don't want to be disappointed." I could tell she was going to argue with me, so I changed the topic. "Did you think Dad would be a good father? Or did you worry he'd mess up because of what he is?"

"I worried, but I shouldn't have. He's a good father."

I nodded. He was. Maybe not in the conventional sense. My twelfth birthday present would probably be frowned upon by most people.

Mom watched me closely, worry clear on her face. She often worried about me.

"I can tell something is up."

I considered telling her for a second, but instead, I patted her hand and rose to my feet.

Savio sauntered toward me. "My favorite psychopath." He clapped my shoulder. "And the reason I'm happy being a girl dad."

"I'm sure you'll change your mind once they start dating."

"They won't. I'll shoot whoever goes near them. I hear you're trying to get Fabiano to do the same to you?" Mirth and curiosity danced in his brown eyes.

"Aurora and I are friends."

"So were Gemma and I."

"I don't have a bull in my pants," I said with a smirk.

"Only a tally list on your back."

"And it's growing."

Savio rolled his eyes. "Your dad wants to talk to you in his office."

I grinned. "Am I in trouble?"

"Were you ever not?" He clapped my shoulder, then sauntered off again.

Dad and I had been avoiding each other as well as possible. He was probably worried he'd strangle me if we spent too much time together. And me? Maybe I avoided him because seeing his disappointment reminded me that I was crossing lines that even I shouldn't cross.

That he wanted to talk to me could only mean I had messed up again. What if Battista's mother had informed my family about his existence?

I knew Rory wouldn't have done it. She was pissed, disappointed, and desperate to hate me, but she was also loyal to a fault. I trusted her.

Dad was pummeling his boxing sack when I stepped into his office. Fabiano and Nino were there too. The wary look on Fabiano's face told me he didn't know what had happened between his daughter and me.

"Fabiano checked the security footage of the apartment complex and saw you visiting last night and again this morning."

I shrugged. "I would have understood a meeting if I'd stayed the night, but as you said, I left last night and came back this morning."

Dad sent me a warning look. "This isn't funny."

"What were you doing at Aurora's place?" Fabiano asked tightly.

"We had pizza together, Aurora, *Carlotta*, and me. That's what friends do."

Fabiano narrowed his eyes. "That's what normal people do. That's not something you usually do. Where were Alessio and Massimo?"

"We eat pizza all the time. I wasn't made aware that psychopaths are banned from enjoying pepperoni and cheese on a carb base."

Fabiano pushed to his feet. I could tell he wanted to hit me.

"And Alessio, Massimo, and I don't spend every second of the day together. We went on a raid last night, so we had enough *boys time*."

"This is all bullshit," Fabiano muttered. "When I called Aurora this morning, she confirmed the pizza-friends story."

I cocked an eyebrow. "Then I don't see the problem."

"Because Aurora wouldn't tell on you. I know you followed her to New York and to the race circuit. I don't know what you want from her.

What I know is that Aurora is a good girl with a big heart, and you should stay away from her. Destroy someone else's life, not my daughter's."

Neither Dad nor Nino came to my defense, and honestly they had no reason to do so.

"Why do I have to be the villain in this? Maybe I'm the good guy for once. Maybe I try to protect Aurora to prevent a repeat performance of what happened to Greta."

Regret passed Dad's expression. I got it. I too blamed myself for the night of Greta's attack. She should have been protected. If either Dad or I had been present, this wouldn't have happened.

"I'm responsible for her protection, and rest assured that when I think you're a danger, I won't hesitate to protect her from you no matter the cost."

"Nevio only wants to be a good friend for Aurora. She's like family for him," Dad said firmly, his eyes on me.

Fabiano released a long breath and nodded slowly. With a last warning look, he left. Dad shook his head, the harsh lines around his mouth telling me this conversation was far from over.

"Because of you, I have to lie to Fabiano," Dad finally gritted out.

"I never asked you to. You're not doing it for me. You're doing it to keep peace between Fabiano and our family."

"He would kill you if he knew the truth," Nino said. Dad seemed to struggle with his rage.

"He would try and not succeed."

Dad shoved to his feet. "There was a death fight between our families once, dammit. I swore to never let it come this far again. Don't you have any lines you wouldn't cross?"

"I wouldn't attack him. I'd only defend myself."

Dad stalked toward me. "You need to learn control. You're going to put everything to ruins if you don't. Is that what you want?"

I didn't say anything. Ruins were more fun to play in, but I didn't want to hurt our family.

"I'm like you, Dad. I don't know why you're surprised."

"When I was your age, I had been to war for our territory."

"You make it sound as if that's a bad thing. You could unleash your inner demons for years. I would have loved to be in your stead. Kill or die. Every day a battle of wills."

"It wasn't for fun."

"But I bet you enjoyed many aspects of it."

"I did, but I also knew when it was enough, when I had to restrain myself for the sake of my family. Would you have managed to take care of Adamo and Savio like I did?"

I couldn't even take care of Battista, and I wasn't in a war to become Capo.

"You would have lost yourself to the frenzy of killing and forgotten all else," Dad growled. I feared he wasn't wrong.

"I'm restless," I said simply because it was true. "A war like that would have finally sated my blood lust."

"Or it would have made you addicted," Nino said.

"It's not in our nature to sit around like a domesticated house cat and wait to be fed. We need to hunt."

"You're going on raids with Alessio and Massimo all the time, and you have jobs for the Camorra. You don't have to restrain yourself very often," Nino said.

Dad glowered. "If you're so desperate for war, go to Italy and help the Camorra there."

That piqued my interest. I knew the Camorra was attacked from all sides in Italy. The police and the other Italian mob families and clans from other countries like Albania or Serbia.

"Your father didn't mean it," Nino said. "And your mother would never forgive him if he sent you there."

Dad grasped my shoulder, his expression hard, but his eyes were imploring, almost gentle. "Just get a fucking grip, Nevio. For the sake of our family, and if that's not enough, for Aurora's sake."

Chapter Twenty-Six

Nevio

After a tense dinner, I tried to talk to Aurora alone, which proved difficult, with Fabiano and Dad watching us like hawks. But she had been nervous all through dinner, and someone would catch on if she kept it up.

Eventually, Massimo, Alessio, Aurora, and I headed for the garden, and I used my chance to corner Rory. "You need to stop acting suspicious," I murmured.

She narrowed her eyes. "I don't like lying to everyone. I'm stacking up lies for you, and I hate it. Not to mention that Carlotta is angry with me because she has to babysit your kid now too. This house of lies will collapse on us."

"Not if we're careful."

She shook her head with a sigh. "Everyone's going to be angry when they find out because we lied to them."

I ran a hand through my hair. "I'll figure it out."

"What are you two talking about?" Alessio asked from where he and Massimo chilled on the couch. He couldn't have overheard anything. "Maybe Nevio's desire is to fly to Italy to play war for the Camorra there?"

I sent him a scowl. Asshole. Aurora's shocked gaze slammed into me. "What?"

"He's full of shit."

"Is he?" she muttered.

"Dad suggested I could go there to let off some steam, but I never agreed."

"You can't agree because you have a fucking son to take care of!"

It was the first time I heard Rory curse like that.

"If you leave me here with him, without telling your family about him, you're dead to me."

"And if I told them and then left, would you be happy to be free of me?"

Aurora swallowed and looked away. "You have to tell them. Take responsibility."

She turned on her heel and walked toward the house. "I should return to the apartment. I don't want to leave Carlotta alone with this."

I headed over to Alessio and Massimo.

"If you leave for Italy, Aurora will move on. She'll find someone new, and if she's clever, it'll be someone from the Camorra."

Dad wouldn't allow me to kill one of our men because of this. It would set a bad example, especially since Rory wasn't mine officially. She was absolutely mine in my head, but I had never claimed her as mine in any way that would make our circles take notice. We were friends, full stop.

Massimo shook his head. "You should not even consider it. Killing that barista was stupid but not really relevant in the great scheme of things, but attacking someone from the Camorra's racing crew was even stupider, but still not causing any major ripples. But if you start killing off our own men, that won't go unnoticed. Our soldiers will demand an explanation, and I fear you won't have one that's acceptable for anyone without your erratic disposition. So if you leave, you must accept that Rory might move on with someone from our world, and you'd be unable to do anything against it."

By Frenzy I Rain

I didn't say anything because Massimo wouldn't have liked my answer. Maybe he knew it too because his eyes were full of warning.

The following day, Massimo, Alessio, and I had to visit two of our less productive drug labs to increase their motivation.

After finishing our jobs around eight in the evening, I decided to grab dinner and head for Aurora. "Where are you going?" Massimo asked when I dropped him and Alessio off at the mansion but didn't get out myself.

"To Aurora, where else?" Alessio said.

It would be futile to deny it as I'd be caught on camera anyway. "Just bringing them dinner and making sure they're safe."

"We could come along," Massimo said.

"You've been attached to my hip all day. I need some me time away from you fuckers."

"Sure, that's what it's about." Alessio rolled his eyes, then he gave a shrug and lit up a cigarette. "Not that I have any interest to go there. Mom made lasagna, so I'm going to stuff my face, then chill in my room."

"When I asked Carlotta if I should come over to make sure everything's okay, she told me she and Aurora didn't need any help. So why do they need you?"

"Jealous?" I asked with a laugh. Massimo wasn't the jealous type, but he'd never had something he was invested in. Lotta seemed to have gotten under his skin in a way I hadn't thought possible.

"Carlotta disapproves of your action and dislikes your personality, so no."

"Thanks for the heads-up. I'm not going there for Lotti. I have things to discuss with Rory." I threw my door shut and reversed out of our driveway. Massimo, Alessio, and I had never had secrets. I didn't enjoy deceiving them, but I had no choice right now.

After picking up Asian takeout, I went over to Aurora's apartment. I thought she expected me to visit daily, so I was dumbfounded to see her angry face as she opened the door for me. Her hair was disheveled as if she hadn't found time to brush it yet. She still looked gorgeous. She was in sweat shorts and a white tank. To my disappointment, she had on a white sports bra underneath.

I raised the bag with Chinese takeout. "I bring dinner."

If looks could kill, I'd be ashes.

"It's nine o'clock," she said pointedly.

"Won't you let me in?" I asked when she made no move to open the door farther.

She released a sigh and stepped back so I could walk in.

"Did you tell him it's nine o'clock?" Carlotta shouted from somewhere in the apartment. Her voice sounded as welcoming as Aurora's face looked.

I wasn't sure what their problem with nine o'clock was. Maybe it was girl code for something I wasn't aware of.

I headed into the kitchen, turned on the light, and set the bag on the table. Aurora didn't follow me, so I returned to the hallway, and when I didn't find here there either, I went to her bedroom. She was inside and lifting Battista out of his crib. He was crying softly, not the full-blast screeching some babies were masters at.

"We already ate dinner," Aurora said when she turned to me with him on her hip. "I was trying to get him to sleep when you rang the bell and woke him from his almost slumber, ruining forty minutes of my singing and rocking efforts."

"Maybe you should give him a Valium."

Aurora glared and stomped past me. "Very funny. In case you don't know, dinnertime with a baby isn't nine o'clock. We ate at seven, and since then, I've been busy getting him ready for bed. He's been fussy all day. I think he's teething. But of course you wouldn't know any of this since you haven't asked about him since you visited us for breakfast yesterday morning."

"We saw each other last night. I'm sure you would have told me if something was the matter with him."

"You should ask about him. He's your son. Even now, I don't think you're here because you want to see him."

She was right. I was here because I wanted to see Rory. "I'm here. That's what counts."

She shook her head, rocking him, but he looked wide awake as he stared at me. "You promised you would try to take responsibility. But I don't see that."

"What do you want?"

"I have to start working in two days, and my first shift begins at six in the morning. Carlotta has courses, so I can't ask her to watch him."

"I'll sleep over tomorrow, then I can watch him for you," I said, even if I doubted it was a good idea. I'd never had a calming effect on kids, and it seemed to extend to my own son too.

Aurora nodded slowly, but she didn't seem too happy about that either.

"I'm heading to bed now. I have to get up early," Carlotta said from the doorway to the kitchen. She was in a fluffy bathrobe.

"Sleep tight," Aurora said with a tight smile. After a scathing look at me, Carlotta left.

"She's pissed at you."

"I wouldn't have guessed," I said dryly.

"Do you want to hold him a bit? Maybe he'll fall asleep in your arms."

I stared at the kid who looked perfectly comfortable pressed to Aurora's breasts. I would have been too. "If you want him to have nightmares, sure." I glanced down at my black tee. "I can't promise that there isn't blood on my shirt."

Aurora pressed out air. "Fine. Then don't. I'm heading to my room to get him to sleep. You know where the front door is."

"Rory!"

She stalked away, turned off the light in the kitchen, and locked herself in her bedroom.

I sank down at the kitchen table and unpacked the takeout boxes. I opened the first box, chow mein, and started eating it with the plastic chopsticks in the dim light streaming through the window.

I still heard Battista's cries for a while, but then silence fell over the apartment. A few minutes later, a lock turned, and soft footfalls sounded.

"I told you to leave," Aurora murmured as she settled on the chair across from me.

"You said I know where the front door is."

"Do you have General Tso chicken?" she asked. Even in the dim light, I could tell how exhausted she looked.

"I do." I pushed one of the boxes and chopsticks over to her. "I know it's your favorite."

She nodded and silently began to eat with a plastic spoon that had also been inside the bag.

"There are sticks and even a fork inside. Spoon-feeding the kid seems to have rubbed off on you."

She pushed another spoonful of chicken into her mouth and chewed thoughtfully as she regarded me. Since our messed-up night at the party, her demeanor toward me had changed. She could look at me without blushing or making a fool of herself. She twisted the spoon around and, after swallowing, said, "I don't trust myself with pointy objects around you tonight. I've fantasized about stabbing you with chopsticks while I lie beside Battista in the dark."

I grinned. "You could kill me with a spoon too."

"Have you ever killed someone with a spoon?"

I leaned back in the chair. "Not yet. I never thought about it. I'll put it on the list."

Aurora ate another spoonful of chicken. "I shouldn't be helping you. You haven't given me any reason yet to believe you'll change anytime soon."

"I told you I'll watch him tomorrow."

Aurora got up and grabbed a glass of water. She leaned against the kitchen counter with a look of worry. "He's your son. Watching him once won't suffice. Sometimes I wonder if you're just not telling anyone, so you can bind me to you. I can't avoid you as long as I'm taking care of your son."

I pushed to my feet and walked over to her. She tensed but didn't otherwise move. "I told you before that you're in my head, and there's no escaping from there. With or without Battista, I'd make it very hard for you to avoid me."

"I can't even put into words how furious you make me," she whispered as I stopped right in front of her.

I cupped her cheeks and pushed my fingers into her hair as I gazed down upon her. "I can see the fury in your eyes, and it's fucking sexy."

She slammed the glass down on the counter and gripped my forearms, but she didn't push me away. "I don't like the person I become around you. I don't want to be her. I don't want to be consumed by anger."

"Then allow yourself to be consumed by lust."

By Frenzy I Pain

She glared up at me. The battle was clear in her eyes. I slammed by lips down on hers before reason won over. I kissed her like I'd wanted to do for a while, like I'd dreamed about. I stole her breath, ravaged her mouth, my fingers in her hair keeping her in my control. Her nails dug into my forearms as if she was about to shove me away, but her lips moved against mine, her tongue as eager as mine. Even her body was torn by differing emotions.

I dropped my hands from her silky strands, grabbed her by the hips, and lifted her up on the counter, without ever stopping our kiss. The moment I broke our connection, I'd lose her, I could tell. Aurora pushed her palms up against my chest in a slight resistance, but it wasn't convincing.

I pressed into her, my body coming alive with a hunger I was wholly unfamiliar with when it came to anything but killing.

Aurora ripped away from our kiss and leaned back on her arms to put more distance between us. "Go away," she breathed out. The fire in her eyes only kindled my own.

She shoved my chest. "Go away. I'm so mad at you and at myself."

I stepped back, even if it was the last thing I wanted. "Why are you fighting this?"

"Because I won't be your babysitter with benefits or whatever it is you have in mind for me."

"I wouldn't be the only one reaping benefits, trust me," I said with a smirk. Provoking Rory, when her reactions were so very entertaining and seductive, was impossible to stop.

Something in her eyes snapped, her expression bursting with rage but also despair. "What is it you want, Nevio? Do you want to fuck me a second time? Will you lose interest, then? Then fuck me. I'm here, have your way with me. I lay crying beneath you once. I can do it again!"

Aurora

My chest heaved, and my throat felt raw from the words that had ripped from it.

Nevio's eyes burned with an emotion I couldn't read. He jerked me against him, shoved my shorts and panties aside, and slid his index finger over my pussy, finding me still wet from our making out. My body sprang to life at the contact even as my brain shouted warnings and expletives at me.

"You wouldn't cry this time, except from coming so hard. You'd be begging me for more."

I gripped his wrist. Part of me wanted to keep him there and make good on his words, but the other remembered last time and what came after, remembered the last few months of his stalking, his brutality to make sure nobody got close to me, and now his irresponsibility when it came to his son.

I pushed his hand away, but he resisted. His gaze hit me, a dare, a provocation.

"I don't want your touch."

He smirked.

"If you don't accept my boundaries, then whatever's left of our friendship is dead."

He lowered his hand and stepped back. "I thought our friendship died the night I took your innocence." The way he said innocence as if I didn't understand the first thing about it stirred up my fury.

It's what I told him. And I thought it was true back then, but then he called me to help him with his son, and somehow this made me feel special, as if I were his confidant, when I was probably the only person stupid enough to say yes to his plea for help. "I helped you with Battista. If our friendship were dead, I wouldn't have done it, right?"

Nevio smiled in the strangest way. "You're a kind person. You always help people if you can. I thought you helped me for Battista's sake."

"For his and yours."

"Is it so bad that I want you, Rory? I thought that's what you wanted all along."

"You want my body. You want to chase the next high, no matter the price. I want more. I don't want a mad ride that never ends. I want trust, steadiness, commitment." I shook my head at the look on Nevio's face as if he could not grasp what I meant. I glanced at the kitchen clock. 11:00 p.m. It wouldn't be long before Battista would wake for his bottle. "I need to sleep."

Nevio didn't stop me when I jumped down from the counter and walked past him. My body yearned for his touch, willing to take what he could give even if it would never sate my heart and soul. "Don't come tomorrow if you intend to touch me again. Come to be a father for Battista and a friend who honors his promise."

I didn't wait for his reply. Without looking back, I went to my room and closed the door. I leaned against it and listened with bated breath. I didn't dare breathe again until I heard the front door click shut and the lock being engaged through the code panel outside.

This arrangement couldn't go on forever, not like this. Nevio would use every chance he got to touch me, to seduce me, because I promised to be a high he needed. Once he had me, he'd chase the next one.

Maybe that was the trick. I just needed to let him have me, and remember it, so he could move on.

Chapter Twenty-Seven

Aurora

Giving Nevio what he wanted. That idea had been ghosting around my head all night. It seemed like the easiest solution, one where part of my heart might be salvaged. Unfortunately for myself, I couldn't bring myself to consider that option—yet. I wanted to believe this was so he'd get more time to develop fatherly feelings for his son because I suspected he wouldn't try to form a bond if I weren't pushing him.

Carlotta noticed my sour mood, but for once, I didn't divulge last night's make-out session to her. I felt ashamed of my actions, ashamed of my lack of restraint.

I didn't leave the apartment all day. Poor Battista hadn't left it since Nevio brought him here. I didn't want to sneak him out in a cardboard box again, and I didn't have an idea how else to do it. When I wasn't busy entertaining Battista, I tried to read a book that would have been part of my nursing curriculum.

Nevio was on time for once, seven o'clock, with Indian takeout. Carlotta had dinner with us, which allowed me to relax as I was in no immediate danger of succumbing to my desires again. Battista was in his crib, gnawing on a teething ring. Nevio barely glanced at him during dinner as if he could pretend he wasn't a father.

Carlotta left for her room after dinner to study for her courses tomorrow.

"So will you give me the rundown of what I need to do?" he asked with a nod toward his son.

"You could start by taking him out of his crib. You haven't held him in a while."

Nevio got up and rubbed his palms over his legs as if they were sweaty from nerves, which I couldn't imagine, considering everything Nevio had experienced. A baby was hardly something to be scared of. Though, I had to admit that some of Battista's crying fits had me break out in a sweat too.

Nevio walked up to the crib and stared down at him with furrowed brows. Then his eyes slanted to me. "Do you think he'll be like me?"

I rose to my feet and moved to his side, even if his proximity always posed a risk. I wondered what exactly Nevio meant by this. Battista had Nevio's eyes and shared some of his facial features. Only his hair was a few shades lighter. "He needs a loving home, then everything will be okay."

Nevio shook his head, his dark eyes piercing mine. "I had a loving home, the fucking best family one could wish for in our world and beyond, but nothing is okay, trust me."

"Maybe you just tell yourself it's not because it's easier than working on yourself."

"Maybe," he murmured, but I could tell he didn't think it was the case.

Battista had stopped biting his ring and was now staring up at us with interest. I smiled at him, and he returned the smile. He only had two teeth so far, his upper incisors.

"He's going to cry if I pick him up."

"He won't ever react otherwise if you don't form a bond with him."

Nevio reached into the crib and lifted Battista out of it. For a few seconds, Battista only stared at him, then his lower lip began to tremble, and a cry burst out of him. Nevio immediately turned to me as if he wanted to hand his son over to me.

I stepped back and raised my palms. "You promised to take care of him. If you always give up immediately, that won't work."

Nevio nodded. "Go to sleep. I'll handle him. I suppose I have to sleep on the sofa. Or will you share your bed with me?"

I gave him a half smile. "The sofa is comfortable. You can find everything for his bottles on the counter. He usually wakes three times at night for his bottle. Sometimes he wants to play a little before falling back asleep, especially after his last bottle."

I turned around, even as Battista's cries tugged at my heartstrings. When my bedroom door fell shut behind me, I took a deep breath. I had to get up at five at the latest, but I wasn't sure if I'd get any sleep if Battista kept crying like this. Nevio needed to talk to him and show Battista that he was safe. Would he be able to do it?

I wasn't sure. I got ready for bed and lay down. Battista kept crying for another fifteen minutes, but then he quieted. I finally fell asleep.

I was woken in the middle of the night by cries. Usually, Battista signaled his hunger with mewl and soft cries. For him to cry this loudly, Nevio must have ignored those first signs. I got up and crept into the living room. The lights were on. A Nintendo Switch lay on the coffee table with some ego shooter. Battista was still in his crib, but Nevio wasn't there. I took him out and followed the light into the kitchen, where Nevio was preparing a bottle. He was only in his boxers, displaying the muscles on his upper body and legs, but something else drew my attention this time. He was wearing headphones, and I could hear loud heavy metal blasting from the speakers even from a few steps away. No wonder he hadn't heard Battista if he'd had those on the entire time and been busy playing computer games.

Nevio turned around with the bottle. His eyes scanned me from head to toe with a slow smile. My pulse picked up in anger. I didn't take the bottle. Instead, I handed Battista to him, then I tugged the earphones from his ears and tossed them on the table. I couldn't even say a word. I was so angry with him.

I whirled around and stalked back to my room. I was so agitated, I doubted I'd be able to fall asleep anytime soon. At least, Battista's cries stopped almost instantly.

I stared up at the dark ceiling, wondering why I shouldn't go to Remo and Serafina tomorrow and tell them the truth. Nothing pointed toward Nevio becoming a responsible parent soon. I couldn't do this alone. It wasn't my responsibility. In the short time I'd been taking care of Battista, he had already grown on me, but I was only eighteen. I couldn't become an adoptive mother.

My door creaked, and Nevio appeared in the dim light from the hallway.

"If you think I'm going to make out with you now, you're crazy," I whispered harshly.

He walked over to me and sank down on my mattress. I was determined to slap him if he made a move.

"Where's Battista?"

"He fell asleep in his crib after he had his bottle. The crying must have exhausted him."

"That's not how tonight was supposed to go."

"Rory," Nevio murmured as he leaned over me. I prepared to slap him, but as if he anticipated the move, his fingers clamped around my wrist, fixating my hand against my pillow as his thumb traced my palm. "You want a tame version of me that doesn't exist."

"I know who you are. I've known you all my life, and you are more than the monster you like to play. You can be funny, caring, and loyal. You can be so much more than what you limit yourself to be."

He came even closer until I felt his breath against my lips, but except for his fingers still holding my wrist, he wasn't touching me. "I'm not playing the monster. The only time I truly feel like myself is at night when I hunt and kill. That's who I am."

"Maybe it's easier to be him, but in the end, it won't make you happy."

Nevio chuckled without humor.

"If you're so sure you're only a monster, then why are you here? Why won't you just give your son to your parents so they can raise him?"

"Maybe I want to play family with the only girl who ever got under my skin before I succumb to the darkness."

I scoffed. "This isn't playing family. This is me being a babysitter and you the irresponsible parent. I think you can't stand the fact that you don't remember having had me, and now you won't stop until you've had me again to get me out of your system."

"I wish it were as easy as that. Fuck, if I knew how to get you out of my body. I wish it were as easy as bleeding you out. If bloodletting was the solution, I would have slit my wrists a long time ago. I want you out of my system, but there you are, the blinding light at the back of my darkness." He released a low breath. "Maybe you should go to my parents. It would be the final straw for my father. You'd be rid of me one way or another. If that's what you want, then you need to tell them the truth because I won't ever set you free."

He pushed to his feet and left.

There was no way I'd fall asleep again now.

The next few days were hell. Getting up early for my internship with our medical team proved almost impossible after being awake most nights with Battista. After the first night of Nevio taking care of Battista, I decided not to have him spend the night again. He'd been hardly any help. Instead, he came over in the morning whenever Carlotta didn't have time to watch Battista. Slowly, I was finding a tentative rhythm with Battista but it didn't make the situation easier.

Carlotta and I sat on the ground with Battista while he played on his blanket on the ground. His favorite toy was a whisk and a mirror.

I stroked his cheek when he accidentally smacked his forehead with the whisk, looking torn between crying and puzzlement. He gave me a grin.

"Every day he stays here makes it harder to say goodbye to him," Carlotta said. "You need to put a stop to this soon. Nevio won't become the father he needs to be. Not anytime soon. Maybe never. Battista should be raised by his family. Hoping for a miracle won't help you or him."

"Says the girl who goes to church every Sunday."

Carlotta pursed her lips. "I don't think any of Nevio's actions are God's doing."

"Definitely not. I'm the devil, Lotta," Nevio said.

I let out a surprised screech, not having heard him enter. Battista stared at me wide-eyed, the whisk covered in his spittle as it was pressed to his mouth.

"Just because you have a key doesn't mean you should enter unannounced," Carlotta voiced my thoughts.

She pushed to her feet and smoothed her skirt. "Antonia is picking me up in five minutes. I should head down."

She breathed past Nevio, grabbed her handbag, and left. It had become harder and harder to avoid visits from our family members. It was only a matter of time before they'd get suspicious and come over unannounced. I wasn't sure how we'd keep Battista's existence from them then.

Nevio squatted beside Battista and handed him the whisk he'd dropped. After a moment of hesitation, Battista took it and shoved it back into his mouth. He looked impossibly cute, and my heart warmed. Carlotta was right. It would only get harder the longer I took care of him. "I think we need to discuss Battista again. We can't go on like this."

Nevio's gaze hit me. "I know."

I was surprised and a tad suspicious by his reply. "I need to know when you'll talk to your parents. This can't be an arrangement without an end."

Nevio nodded again. "It would be best if my parents adopted him, or maybe Kiara and Nino."

"Don't you want to be a father to him?" I asked, my heart feeling heavy. Battista peered up at me as if he understood what I was saying.

"No," he said firmly. "For him, I'm going to make the right choice."

I glared, not convinced. "You just don't want the responsibility. Be honest."

He shrugged. "I'm twenty-one, and that's not even the main problem."

"I'm eighteen and have been taking care of him for you. It's not a matter of age."

"He'll be better off without me as his father, Rory. Nobody's going to contradict me on that point."

"I'd be better off without you too, but you don't care about that."

Battista started fussing, his lower lip wobbling. We shouldn't be having this discussion with him in the room. He was only a baby, but he could pick up on our agitation.

Nevio's expression became hard, then his lips pulled into a sharp smile. "With you, I'm not doing the noble thing. I want you too much for that."

I shook my head, annoyed but also maddeningly flattered, which made me even angrier. I didn't want to fall trap to Nevio's manipulation. I picked up Battista, pushed to my feet, and moved to the doorway. "I'm getting him ready for bed now. You can leave."

I turned, hoping he would be gone when I returned to the living room.

It took me almost two hours to get Battista to sleep. I should probably have tried to catch some sleep too, but I was still too agitated by the argument, and my sweet tooth was calling to me for a treat.

I trudged out of my room, past the thankfully empty living room, and into the kitchen where I froze. Nevio sat at the table, his feet propped up on another chair, watching something on his phone while eating Nutella straight from the glass with a spoon. That should have been my treat.

I lost it right then, right there, because of a bit of hazelnut spread. I staggered toward him and ripped the glass from his hand. It had been half full last time I'd checked. Now only another spoonful was left.

"Why can't you just leave me alone? Instead you make my life more miserable by the day. You haven't done a single nice thing for me yet."

I turned and grabbed a spoon from the drawer, then ate the remains of the Nutella, glaring at the kitchen counters.

"Who would have thought Nutella would be the last straw."

His sarcasm only fueled my anger. "It was the only thing that might have made a shitty evening better, and you ruined it."

It was unreasonable to be this mad because of food, but Nevio had been trying my patience for too long.

The chair scratched over the floor, and his steps sounded behind me. I whirled on him.

"There's Nutella on your face," Nevio murmured, reaching out for the corner of my mouth. I snapped at him and bit his finger. His grin became feral as he calmly wiped me clean before licking his thumb.

"I could make this evening better, far better than a glass of Nutella ever could."

"History says otherwise," I muttered, but something in his eyes called to me. He cupped my neck and jerked me toward his body. "Let me prove it to you." His lips claimed mine. I had every intention to shove him away, but he tasted of Nutella, of sin and dark promises, and I kissed him back. My entire body was aflame. Nevio was a master arsonist, and I was too willing to be set on fire by him.

His palms mapped my back, then grasped my hips and lifted me onto the counter. He stopped our kiss, to my utter surprise. His chest was heaving, so was mine, and desire swam in his dark eyes, so his ending our kiss made even less sense.

"This time, you won't escape me. I won't give you time to run."

I didn't understand what he meant.

Nevio dropped to his knees, taking me by surprise. It brought him to eye level with my knees and, thus, my most private area. Alarmed, I opened my mouth to protest, but he shoved my legs as far apart as they would go and hooked a finger under the crotch of my pajama shorts, pulling it aside. I never wore underwear under my pj's, so I was completely bare to his eyes. My pussy glistened with the first hints of arousal, a fact that made me feel ashamed. "You'll always remember me. My tongue in your pussy."

I pushed my palm against his head despite the deep need surging through my body.

I'd sworn to myself not to sleep with Nevio again. Of course I'd also sworn to myself to never have any physical contact with him at all, and I'd failed constantly at the latter. I was worried I'd fail at the former too because despite my anxiety when I thought of our first night together, not just the pain but also the emotional turmoil, I still wanted to be with Nevio in every sense. My body yearned for his closeness.

"Rory, I'm going to lick you. We both want it."

I swallowed because my core clenched when I imagined Nevio's tongue and lips on me.

My arm muscles softened, allowing Nevio to move, and he didn't need another invitation.

He pushed between my legs, his shoulders pressing into my thighs, and dove right between my pussy lips, swiping over my ass cheeks, my opening, and up to my clit.

My mouth fell open, and I gripped Nevio's hair. I wasn't sure where this would lead. It was nowhere good, but I couldn't resist.

Chapter Twenty-Eight

Nevio

The moment Rory didn't push against my head anymore, I used my chance and pushed her legs farther apart. I took it all in. Her round ass cheeks, her beautiful opening and pink pussy lips, her tiny clit. I licked along her slit. I wanted to taste every inch of her. I wanted to make her come so hard tonight that she'd squirt all over the countertop This was the only form of redemption I could offer her.

Rory tugged at my hair and moaned. This was only the beginning. I curled my arms around her thighs and pulled her to the edge, then I focused on her clit. I teased it with my tongue, lick after lick, and twirl after twirl, and it peeked out more. Rory had her eyes closed, her chest was heaving, and she was breathing heavily. This didn't do.

"Open your eyes, Rory, and watch me eat you out."

She opened her eyes and flushed even redder.

I pressed my cheek against her inner thigh and rubbed her little clit with my thumb, spreading my saliva and Rory's arousal. "You'll watch every second, understood? I want you to see me licking you, making you drip and come."

"As if I could ever forget it was you," she whispered with a hint of reproach.

I grinned because after tonight she'd definitely never forget how it was to be with me.

With my cheek still pressed against her inner thigh, I stroked the tip of my tongue along her puffy pussy lips, gently parting them to swirl her clit before I moved back down. Aurora's face was flushed as she watched me with parted lips. I pushed against her other thigh, parting her legs farther and revealing more of her pussy. My tongue dipped between her labia again, brushing over her smooth but tight opening. Her arousal coated my tongue. I hummed and started circling that perfect little hole that had welcomed me once before.

I pulled her down on my face, sucking her clit. She cried out in surprise and pleasure as I ate her out messily, smearing her juices all over my chin and cheeks. She leaned against the counter, both of her hands in my hair, her eyes wide and disbelieving as my mouth and tongue tasted her lips, clit and opening.

Her arousal wasn't a small drizzle anymore. It coated my tongue as I stroked her opening.

Her thighs tensed, her pussy clenched, and her face contorted with pleasure, then a loud moan fell from her parted lips. I gripped her ass cheeks, my fingers digging in as I pressed her pussy tighter against my face. She shuddered, her nails scratching my scalp. Her scent intensified. I groaned and shoved my tongue into her tight opening. Her arousal coated my tongue, and I eagerly lapped it up as I fucked her with my tongue. I wanted to claim every part of her, with my tongue, my fingers, my cock, even my fucking favorite knife. I wanted to imprint myself on Rory's body and mind.

"I can't. No more," she gasped after a while. I pulled my tongue out of her. My chin and mouth were covered in her lust. She licked her lip, her expression stunned and embarrassed.

After I'd shoved down her now soaked pajama bottoms, I gripped her hips and hoisted her back up on the counter, then pushed between her legs. My cock strained against my pants, but I had a feeling it wouldn't get its turn tonight.

"What—" Rory's eyes widened when I pushed my middle finger into her opening. She tensed, expecting pain, but despite how tight she was, and she was amazingly tight, she was so dripping wet that I slipped in easily. I looked down at my finger as it parted her pink pussy, glistening with her arousal. I curled the tip of my finger and pressed the heel of my palm firmly against Rory's engorged clit, then stopped moving.

"So tight," I said triumphantly. "Nobody's been in that pussy since me, and nobody ever will."

"I hate you," she whispered. But her eyes didn't convey hate, at least not only hate. She hated me, for good reason, and probably herself too. I was familiar with hate, with its ambiguity. It was the emotion dearest to my heart. It was also an emotion I'd never manage for Rory.

"I know," I murmured and dipped my head. I lowered my gaze from Rory's fiery eyes to my finger still buried deep. I opened my hand so my palm no longer pressed against her clit and darted my tongue out to caress it, then I moved lower and licked around my finger, teasing her sensitive flesh.

She tugged harder at my hair. Maybe she hated this power I held over her body, but not enough to stop me. If she knew how much power her existence held over my body and mind, she'd realize I was the doomed one in this.

I could have watched her forever, the subtle rocking of her hips as they met the thrusts of my finger and my teasing tongue. Her pants, the heaving of her chest, and flushed state of her face.

Soon, she shook with her second orgasm. She would have been so ready for me to fuck her. "I need to be inside you."

"You're crazy," she said.

Crazier than she thought. "I hurt you."

"You did," she confirmed.

"That's why I'm not going anywhere near you with my cock." Not tonight.

She frowned, distrust battling with curiosity on her face.

"But I need to claim you. Fuck, it's all I can think about. You know you're mine. I don't even remember our first night properly, and I want to make up for it. Tonight, I want to be the one to bleed and hurt as I claim you."

Her confusion only grew. I couldn't blame her, and I wasn't sure she wouldn't run away screaming if she found out what I had in mind. Fuck, I wouldn't even blame her, but this idea wouldn't leave me since I'd dreamed about it a few weeks ago. It was the perfect way to give Rory pleasure and me pain, and to claim her with a part of me that wasn't part of my body.

I unsheathed my knife.

Rory's eyes widened in alarm.

I flung the knife in the air and caught the blade. My grip was still loose, but the sharp blade already scratched at my skin. My calluses from fighting and Parkour didn't give in easily, but today, they would.

"This is insane," Rory whispered, but she hadn't moved. If she was frozen from shock or anticipation was also in the mix, it was hard to tell. She only watched me with utter shock. I licked over her thigh, then I raised the intricate leather handle of my knife to her pussy. "This is calf leather. It's soft, and the embossing will massage your inner walls. It's smaller than my cock, so it'll be perfect." I slid the round handle end over Rory's opening, coating it with her juices before I parted her with it and rubbed it over her clit.

Rory was frozen as she watched. I rubbed round and round over her clit, watching her face, loving the lust and fear there. Fear not of me. Fear of what I made her desire. Fear of the forbidden. But fuck, the forbidden fruit was always the sweetest.

"I'm taking you to hell with me, Rory. I warned you, but you wouldn't listen. Now it's too late."

I slid the leather handle lower and pressed it against her opening. There was a hint of resistance before her walls gave in and allowed the first inch inside her pussy.

"Fuck," I groaned as I watched the pink of Rory's pussy against the black leather of my knife.

Rory shook her head, still shell-shocked. "You're bleeding," she gasped.

I lowered my eyes from her face to my hand gripping the blade. A droplet of blood meandered over my wrist, and the hint of burning told me my knife had cut through the thick layer of my calluses.

"If it hurts you, it should hurt me as well," I rasped as I moved the handle up and down, still only an inch in.

"That's insanity," she whispered. "And it doesn't even hurt. It just stretches me."

"Last time, it hurt. Don't worry about me, Rory. Just relax and feel. Really feel the leather inside you."

She shook her head but didn't protest. I pushed a bit deeper and leaned forward to lick her clit. She panted as I circled my knife handle and her sensitive flesh.

I'd buried this blade, and many other blades, in so many people, had relished in their cries, but claiming Rory with my knife handle, giving her pleasure with the very thing that only brought pain to others, and receiving pain through my own blade as I gave her pleasure, that would go down as a highlight in my life.

Aurora

I would go to hell for this. No doubt.

I wasn't sure why I wasn't screaming and running away. Why I was sitting here, watching as Nevio fucked me with his knife.

It shouldn't feel good. But it did. The way Nevio watched me with rapt attention and pure hunger sent spikes of lust through my body I'd never experienced before.

He brushed the rounded handle along my seam back and forth. "You're very quiet. I take that as a good sign," he mused. "Now that your body has handled the first shock, I'm going to fuck you properly with my knife so you bathe my handle and mouth with your lust."

He gripped the blade harder and pushed the handle farther into me. "Is that a yes?"

I panted but didn't reply. I couldn't agree to this. I couldn't push him away either. I was lost between my desire to let this happen and my conscience telling me to stop it.

He pushed in slowly until the handle was about halfway inside me and became thicker, then closed his mouth over my clit again. I relaxed as pleasure surged through me from his tongue's magic work. I loved the soft feel of it, the heat of Nevio's breath on my pussy. My inner walls were very sensitive from my orgasm, and the softness of the leather soothed and teased them at the same time.

"More," Nevio murmured, and I hissed as he pushed deeper, my opening stretching around the growing girth of the handle. I hadn't been penetrated by more than my own finger and Nevio's tongue and finger since Nevio took my virginity.

My chest clenched with memories of the night and guilt over what was happening now. Nevio's tongue circled my clit, then stroked along my opening and lower. My eyes rolled back, and lust overrode guilt. I swallowed thickly, as stretching turned to a subtle pain as the handle conquered more of my pussy.

"Rory."

I lowered my head.

His dark eyes hit me. "Don't fight the pain. Savor it. Relax. Accept it."

I tried to do what he said, and when the handle was all the way inside me, I breathed out. Nevio leaned back slightly, his chin shiny with my juices, and watched my pussy. His fist curled around the blade, pressed against my pussy. Nevio uncurled his fingers. They were covered in blood and so was the blade.

I closed my eyes. I couldn't own up to the reality of it, to how good the leather felt inside me, of how sexy Nevio's reaction made me feel.

"Damn, Rory, seeing my knife sticking out of your tight pussy makes me horny as fuck. You can hate me all you want."

My heart pounded in my chest.

"Do you want to come all over my knife, Rory?" Nevio asked in a low, strained voice.

"No."

"No?" he murmured. He began to fuck me slowly with the hilt. In and out, slowly, gently. The leather caressed me, the end brushed a sweet spot deep inside me, and then Nevio's tongue brushed along my clit. My breathing hitched.

Lust dripped out of me as my body rang with sweet pleasure. I was getting closer.

I put my hand on Nevio's head, wanting to push him away, but his lips closed around my clit and began sucking, and I didn't.

I swallowed harder. Hating myself, hating him for what he made me lust for.

"Rory, look at me."

I opened my eyes, and I shuddered with another wave of arousal. The intensity of Nevio's gaze, the friction of the leather inside me, and his lips massaging my clit were all too much. My hips rocked against the knife, against Nevio's mouth, wanting more even if it was already too much.

"Almost there," Nevio growled. I gripped the counter as my heels pressed into the cabinet, and my toes curled. My pussy began to contract around the knife. Nevio pulled back, rubbed my clit with his thumb, his face still close to my aching flesh.

I came, my body convulsing uncontrollably. Lust dripped out of me, ran down my ass, and gathered under me. Nevio watched me with a smile that made me shiver. He leaned forward, his tongue following the trails of my arousal. I shuddered harder as another wave of pleasure captured me.

My chest heaving, I froze. Slowly, Nevio pulled the hilt out of me, causing me to tremble again. He regarded the handle with utter triumph. The leather was covered with my juices and a hint of something darker. Nevio darted his tongue out and licked the pink off. "A hint of blood."

I shook my head but couldn't say anything. Then he pushed to his feet and held the hilt up to my mouth. "Taste your pussy." I parted my lips, unable to resist Nevio's commanding tone. The tangy aroma of my arousal hit my tongue. Nevio's gaze became all-consuming, making my core clench again, even if I'd just come hard. "Suck it clean like you've been dreaming of doing with my cock."

My eyes grew with indignation. Of course, I'd dreamed about Nevio, and only very few of these dreams had been nightmares.

"Come on, Rory. Show me what you'd do to me."

I closed my lips around the handle, took more of it into my mouth, and hollowed my cheeks as I sucked on it. I gave it my all under Nevio's watchful gaze. Swirling my tongue across the tip of the handle, then sucking it into my mouth. How had my fury led to this?

Nevio's erection pressed against his pants, and I couldn't help but smile triumphantly around the handle. Nevio gripped my neck and leaned in, his lips brushing my ear. "That's what you do to me, Rory," he rasped.

He moved back and slowly pulled the knife handle out of my mouth, then he brought it to my pussy once more. He gently slid it all the way in, and I released a shaky breath because I couldn't take any more, even if it felt good. He extracted it once more and regarded the leather once again covered in my release.

The bling of the elevator on our floor let my heart rate spike. "Carlotta!"

Nevio stepped back and lifted me off the counter, then he calmly returned the knife into the sheath.

I tried to smooth my clothes and find my shorts. The keys scratched the lock when I finally managed to pull them on. Nevio leaned against the counter and watched me, his pants still bulging.

"What are you going to tell Carlotta when she sees this?" He pointed at the small puddle of my release on the counter.

"Oh God." I raced toward the cupboard with the cleaning supplies and grabbed a hygienic cleaner and emptied half of it on the counter, then started rubbing at it fervently with a rag I'd definitely throw away later.

"I'm back!" Carlotta called. She never did that, so maybe she suspected she might see something she didn't want to see. My face burned with mortification.

I didn't turn around when I saw Carlotta enter the room in my peripheral vision. I could only hope that Nevio's erection wasn't obvious anymore, or that Carlotta wouldn't notice.

"Everything all right?" Carlotta asked suspiciously.

I cleared my throat. "Sure." My voice was too high and scratchy.

"Splendid," Nevio said calmly.

When I was happy about the state of the counter, I turned to Carlotta with a forced smile. "I spilled some—"

"Juice," Nevio finished, and I could have killed him with that stupid knife of his. Though that would have probably been his dream.

Carlotta glanced between Nevio and me, her eyes lingering on Nevio's bloody hand, and sighed. "I assume Battista is asleep?"

I nodded. "You're back early." I wasn't even sure what time it was, but I definitely hadn't expected her yet.

Carlotta pursed her lips. "It's almost midnight. Dinner with Diego and Antonia usually isn't an all-night thing. Next time, I'll call. I think I'll go to my room until you're done with whatever it is you're doing."

"We're done," I said firmly. Carlotta was definitely offended, and I couldn't blame her. First, I let a baby move in with us, and now Nevio was here all the time.

Nevio didn't comment. He only gave me a look that made me feel hot all over.

"Nevio has to leave."

I walked into the hallway, just wanting to get out of the kitchen. Could you smell sex in a room? Luckily, Carlotta was completely innocent, so I probably didn't have to worry.

I was so going to hell. Nevio followed close behind me, and a shiver slithered down my spine. I wondered what was going on in Nevio's head right now. I stopped at the door and opened it. Nevio stayed in the doorway as if he knew I would have closed the door right in front of his face if he'd stepped out into the hallway. Right at this moment, I just wanted him to leave. I didn't want to own up to what we'd done. I needed more time to wrap my head around it.

I looked away from his penetrating gaze, but my eyes only caught on the knife in his leather holster. He rarely wore it this openly. Heat crawled up my neck, and my core tightened once more. I could almost still feel the silky leather inside me. I dropped my gaze, then frowned at the droplets of blood on the floor. My gaze followed its trail back to the kitchen. Nevio must have cut himself deeper than I'd thought.

I reached for his hand and turned it around. The cut in his palm was long but not overly deep, but it definitely needed stitches, especially since I knew he wouldn't go easy on it. He'd probably already be cage fighting tomorrow afternoon. "That needs proper treatment."

"It was worth it," Nevio said in a low voice, leaning closer. Our eyes met, and I exhaled, feeling the pull it was almost impossible to resist. "And I would cut myself even deeper if it meant seeing you come on my knife again."

I peered over my shoulder to make sure Carlotta wasn't close by. "Do you want me to put a bandage on?"

"I think you need a bit of alone time, Rory. Don't let your conscience ruin this."

It wasn't my conscience I was worried about but my heart. Nevio finally stepped back.

Nevio leaned close and kissed my cheek like a friend would, a show for the cameras in the hallway, because I could still smell myself on him. He turned and stalked away.

I closed the door and leaned against it.

"Should I be concerned?" Carlotta asked from her spot in the kitchen doorway.

I raised my eyebrows. "Did you eavesdrop?"

She made an appalled face as if that was the last thing she would do. "I'm too worried about what I might overhear."

I laughed bitterly. "Yeah."

She came over to me slowly, her face flashing with disgust as they registered the blood on the floor.

"I'll clean it," I said.

Carlotta leaned against the door beside me, her shoulder touching mine. She studied my face. "Are you okay?"

I hesitated. I wasn't really sure what I felt right now. "I'm not sure yet."

Her brows pulled together. "Did you sleep with Nevio?"

"No," I said, then bit my lip, my skin flaming. "It wasn't like that." Or did what we had count as sex? It was a form of sex, but Carlotta probably meant the classic version, not the twisted and perverted one Nevio had in mind.

"Looking at your face, I don't think I want details."

"You definitely don't want them." Carlotta would need an immediate appointment for confession if I told her what had just happened, and she'd probably ask for a new kitchen too.

"Are you okay with what happened?"

"Part of me is. Part of me definitely isn't."

Battista let out a cry, and I was glad for the distraction.

"It's almost as if Nevio can sense when Battista is awake and always leaves before," Carlotta said.

"That's not possible," I said as I walked into my room, where Battista had been sleeping the entire time. I got what Carlotta meant. So far Nevio's interactions with Battista had been few and far between. They hadn't built a connection yet, and after our conversation today, I knew Nevio preferred it that way. I knew that some fathers had a hard time building a bond with young kids, even if they'd watched them grow up from birth, but I wasn't sure that was the case with Nevio or if something deeper and darker held him back.

I picked Battista up and pressed him to my chest. Funnily enough, I had absolutely no trouble building a connection with this little boy. Just like his father, he'd captured my heart.

Chapter Twenty-Nine

Nevio

Few things got my heart rate up, but Rory did, and fucking her with my knife… My heartbeat had set a new record. I couldn't stop grinning as I headed to fight training. I was already late because I'd been up all night, but I couldn't care less. I really needed to get myself off. Just thinking of Rory's pink pussy and my knife made me hard again.

When I walked into the abandoned casino that the Camorra used as their gym, I could already hear the sounds of fists making impact and the low grunts of suppressed pain.

Stepping into the vast hall with the fighting cage in the center, I spotted Alessio and Nino sparring in it.

Massimo, Giulio, Fabiano, and Davide were watching and warming up by skipping rope. Of course, Massimo immediately noticed the cut

By Frenzy I *Pain*

in my hand. I hadn't bothered bandaging it yet. He stopped skipping, dumped the rope on a bench, and came over to me. "What did you do?"

The way he worded it made it sound as if I had been up to no good, which was, of course, the truth.

"Just some innocent knife play," I said.

Massimo gave me a look that suggested I was full of crap. "Show me."

"My knife play?"

He held out his hand with a no-nonsense expression, and I turned my hand over so he could see my palm. He prodded it without mercy, but the pain gave me nice flashbacks to what had happened, so I didn't protest. It confirmed I hadn't dreamed this.

He dropped my hand and stalked over to the cabinet with the first-aid kit. By now, the situation had attracted more attention, and Davide and Giulio came running. "What happened?" Davide asked excitedly. "You weren't in bed this morning when I tried to wake you for fight training."

I'd been outside, roaming the city, restless but at the same time strangely fulfilled.

"I got into a knife fight and had to defend myself."

"By holding his knife the wrong way? I doubt it," Massimo muttered. "This isn't a cut from defending yourself against a stab."

"Huh?" Davide and Giulio exchanged a look. By now, Fabiano had joined us too. Only Nino and Alessio were still fighting.

Of course, Massimo had to keep spewing his extensive medical knowledge. "He gripped a blade, and the cut suggests it was a sawtooth knife like his. Seems too big a coincidence."

I sent Massimo a look that told him to shut the fuck up. While I had no problem with him knowing the details of my adventure, I definitely didn't need Fabiano to find out. Things would get very, very tense between the Scuderis and the Falcones if he knew what I was up to with his daughter. Fuck, he might even try to put a stop to it, and Aurora would probably even follow his decision.

I didn't need the additional complication of having to figure out how to get rid of Fabi.

Fabiano raised one eyebrow. "What the fuck did you do now?"

I grinned. "I can't tell you with the kids around. Let's just say that a bit of pain makes me shoot fireworks much faster."

Let them think I needed to cut my own palm to get myself off.

Fabiano sighed and shook his head before he returned to skipping rope, obviously tired of my antics.

Davide and Giulio followed him after a moment. They'd seen Massimo stitch me up before, so it wasn't that exciting.

"If Fabiano finds out you're messing with Aurora, things will get very complicated," Massimo said in a low voice as he pulled out a bottle with clear liquid from the first-aid kit.

"Didn't you listen? I was involved in a fight."

"I listen to your bullshit all the time," he said, dumping half of the liquid over my hand. It burned like hell, and I gritted my teeth in annoyance. There were plenty of disinfectants that didn't sting, but Dad insisted we use the old-fashioned ones as additional punishment for getting injured in the first place. "My knife was clean, no need to disinfect the wound."

"I smell pussy on you, so cut the bullshit and let me do my job," Massimo said.

"Did you turn into a bloodhound since you're deprived of the smell of pussy?"

He ignored me and pulled out a needle and thread. I hadn't seen Massimo with a girl in a while, and knowing Carlotta's stance on sex before marriage, I doubted he'd gotten anywhere near her holy grail. Before Aurora I would have said no pussy was worth waiting for.

Alessio jogged over to us, covered in sweat and sporting a blooming bruise on his cheek. "How did you fuck up this time?"

"Not sure you can handle the truth. You've been a bit touchy recently."

"Fuck you," he muttered. "Just because I'm not quite as psychopathic as you two doesn't mean I'm being touchy."

Massimo jabbed me with the needle. I bared my teeth at him. "Your condition is defined as sociopathy, which is hardly more desirable," Massimo said to Alessio, unimpressed.

"Did Aurora try to stab you because she couldn't stand your annoying stalking?"

I just grinned, but I didn't really want to share any details.

Alessio glanced at Massimo, then back at me. "I probably don't want to know what kinky shit you were up to."

He jogged back over to Nino. Massimo regarded me intently. "Something is definitely up, and I don't think it's your usual nonsense. I haven't seen Carlotta and Aurora together since they moved into the apartment. They used to be inseparable. And suddenly, you are with them all the time."

"I think you've been reading too many conspiracy theories."

He narrowed his eyes. "Alessio, you and I have overcome many hurdles together. It makes me wonder what is so bad that you'd keep it from us."

I shoved my hands into my pockets. Maybe I should confide in them. Massimo was right. Alessio and Massimo were my ride or die.

I ran a hand through my hair.

"How about you move your ass into the cage and fight me?" Fabiano called.

I raised my injured hand, which had never stopped me. His so-what expression conveyed he didn't care.

"I'll go easy on you."

"No, you won't," I said as I pulled my shirt over my head. I shoved down my pants, leaving me in my boxing shorts, and turned to Massimo. "The French girl is the mother of my child, and she left him with me. I didn't know what to do with a baby, so I called Aurora, and she's been babysitting him for me since she moved into the apartment."

Massimo stared at me as if he thought I'd finally lost my mind, but I didn't give him a chance to question me. With a shrug, I turned around. "You can tell Alessio." I jogged over to the cage and got inside.

Fabiano and I had fought against each other in the past, but his expression today told me he had a bone to pick with me. This would get interesting.

"Why the pinched expression?" I asked as I faced him in the cage.

His mouth tightened. "You've been visiting the apartment every day."

"Like I said, I'm a good friend. I'm sure Aurora told you the same. You should know your daughter. She's a good girl and wouldn't lie to you."

"She is, and under normal circumstances, she wouldn't unless someone compelled her to do it."

"And I suppose that someone would be me." Fabiano only stared at me with raised eyebrows. "Let's stop the chitchat and get this fight going."

The words had barely left his mouth when he charged toward me. Soon, we were caught up in a heated fight. Fabiano was fueled by anger, which made up for his age.

"It's enough!" Dad's voice boomed through the casino. Fabiano stepped back, panting. I dropped my arms, my own chest heaving. I was covered in sweat and blood. Some of it was mine, some of it was Fabiano's. He was bleeding from his nose and a cut over his eyebrow. My mouth swam with blood, and my hand was bleeding profusely again.

Fabiano wiped his forearm over his eyebrow, smearing blood everywhere.

I spit out blood, then turned to Dad with a grin. He stood in front of the cage with a thunderous expression.

"What's the matter, Dad? I thought you want us to take fight training seriously?"

"This looked a bit too serious for my taste," he muttered.

I glanced at Fabiano, who'd given up on stopping the blood flow from his eyebrow. My ribs hurt too, and from Fabiano's stiff movements, I suspected it was the same for him. Fabiano walked toward me. "Good fight," he said, less tense than before the fight. Maybe he'd gotten his anger out of his system with our fight. For me, that trick never worked. "But this is nothing to how I'm going to kick your ass if I find out you're messing with Aurora."

"I'm going to be Capo. Many fathers would love to give me their daughters."

"I'm not one of them," he said as he headed out of the cage. I followed him.

Dad sent me a hard look, as if this was only my doing.

Grabbing a towel, I steered toward the changing room where Alessio and Massimo had disappeared a couple of minutes ago.

They sat across from each other, straddling the bench.

Alessio tipped an imaginary hat. "Every time I think you can't fuck up more, you raise your game. Cudos for still managing to shock me after I've seen you use the head of a corpse as a hand puppet."

Massimo motioned me forward and grabbed my hand. "I don't know why I bother treating your wounds."

"Fabiano wanted the fight."

"A kid, really? Ever heard of condoms?" Alessio asked.

"Why don't you scream a little louder so everyone can hear it."

Massimo got up. "You should tell them. This isn't a small secret. This is a child. You need help with this. You aren't equipped to take care of a child."

"Trust me, I know, which is why I asked Aurora for help."

"What's wrong with the girl that she can't say no to you, for fuck's sake?" Alessio asked, pushing to his feet.

"Ask her," I said with a shrug. Then I became serious. "You can't tell my parents or anyone else about this."

Massimo and Alessio exchanged a look. "You can't keep it a secret for long. Aurora can't play babysitter forever. Your father will rip your head off if he finds out you kept a child from him."

"He'll rip my head off either way." In this case, Mom would probably resort to violence too. Fathering a child with a woman I'd fucked once was definitely not something she'd accept.

"This is serious," Alessio said.

I glowered. "I fucking know that."

"I seriously doubt that, or you would have told our families right away. This is probably just your way to bind Aurora to you. The girl was trying to get away, but you couldn't let her," Alessio muttered.

"I know your stance on Aurora and me."

"Why don't you show us your son?" Massimo asked.

"Give me a sec to shower." I stepped into the shower stall after telling Aurora we would be coming over.

Thirty minutes later, Alessio, Massimo, and I knocked at the apartment's door. I was pretty sure that Massimo's interest in my son was only an excuse to see Carlotta.

Aurora opened the door, looking slightly disheveled, her cheeks flushed. I'd left her in a similar state yesterday, and the memory made me smirk. Aurora avoided my eyes as she let us in. "Carlotta and Battista are in the living room."

We followed her inside and found Carlotta and Battista on the floor on a blanket, playing with all kinds of kitchen utensils.

"So you finally decided to tell someone," Aurora said as she stopped beside me while Alessio and Massimo settled on the sofa beside Carlotta. She didn't look at me, though, keeping her eyes firmly fixed on the others.

"Alessio and Massimo are loyal. I should have trusted them from the start," I said.

"I guess I should feel honored that you considered me trustworthy enough to confide in me."

"You really should," I said honestly.

"I don't suppose they'll help with child care, though?"

"They might." I wasn't sure I wanted those two to take care of my kid. I leaned closer to Aurora to whisper, "Won't you look at me?"

She turned to me with narrowed eyes, but the blush on her cheeks was exactly what I wanted to see. "You're not the only one around."

She moved to the sofa and sank down beside Alessio. Her hair was in a high ponytail, revealing her beautiful neck I wanted to mark as mine. I'd never left a hickey on anyone, but with Aurora, I couldn't wait to change that. I would have loved to tease her a bit more about our kitchen adventure yesterday, but I had a feeling she'd avoid being alone with me.

Massimo got up and came over to me with an analytic expression. He crossed his arms over his chest. "You didn't even go over to the kid, and he barely reacted to your presence, so I suppose you two haven't bonded yet."

"I'm not sure if it's a good idea to bond with him at all."

"You don't want to be part of his life? Then why keep him here? Why not tell your parents about him and let them or my parents adopt him."

"I don't think I should be a father, and I don't think I want to be. If I tell them, they'll make me choose right away, but I want more time to consider my options."

"Or more time to spend with Aurora."

Aurora glanced our way as if she'd heard our conversation. I visited daily because of her, not because of my kid. Maybe he'd eventually grow on me. She dragged her eyes away again.

Massimo's gaze moved from Aurora to Carlotta.

"You always say you don't believe in deities," I muttered.

Massimo's gaze slanted over to me again, and he cocked an eyebrow in a mix of annoyance and boredom. "Didn't you give up on drugs?"

I rolled my eyes. "You don't believe in anything. Sex is merely a bodily outlet for you. And you despise religion and conservative views, yet you regard Lotti as if she were the most revered goddess on your altar."

His brows furrowed, jaw setting in a tight line. "I simply admire the perfect angles of her face. It's rare for nature to follow the perfect geometrical patterns to create something this pleasing to the eye."

I could admit that Carlotta was pretty, but Aurora was in a league of her own. Where Carlotta was sweet, Aurora was stunning in a memorable way. "Whatever. You can't fuck her before marriage, and you'll have to marry in a church if you want to pierce her hymen, so better find someone else with good geometrical patterns."

"A hymen can't be pierced in most cases—"

He cut himself off, seeing my expression. "It's not logical to postpone sex to marriage."

"You don't have to tell me." I wanted nothing more than to sleep with Aurora, but a part of me wondered if I wasn't making things worse. I couldn't date Aurora. Already this commitment of coming over daily felt like being on a leash. The Camorra and my family already limited my freedom. I wasn't sure if my frenzied brain could take more.

Aurora

In the five days that followed Massimo's and Alessio's surprise visit, I quickly realized that not much had changed. I had managed to avoid being alone with Nevio the one time he'd come over to help out with Battista. Though his help really only consisted of him buying everything Battista needed and bringing takeout.

When I was invited over to the Falcones for dinner with my family on the third day, I considered telling them, but I simply couldn't bring myself to break Nevio's trust, which didn't even make sense, considering how much turmoil he'd spread in my life since our night at the party.

Both Dad and Nevio still sported bruises. Alessio had hinted at their training fight having gotten a bit too enthusiastic. But Dad hadn't questioned me about Nevio again. Only Mom had once again emphasized that I could talk to her about everything, which made me feel even more horrible for lying to them.

During dinner, I pointedly ignored Nevio, though he tried to catch my eyes several times. I could hardly stop blushing with mortification when I thought of what we'd done, and looking at him would have only worsened my reaction. I didn't need to give Dad more reason to be suspicious.

I wished my body wouldn't always heat with longing whenever I thought of how Nevio had claimed me with the handle of his knife. Even just thinking about it again made my thighs clamp up, and my core tighten.

When Kiara and Serafina got up to clean up the dishes and take them to the kitchen, I did as well. I was glad for the distraction as I helped them.

I loaded the dishwasher while Kiara filled the sink with hot water to clean the pans.

"I love my son, but I know he's quite a handful, and that's putting it mildly," Serafina said suddenly from behind me, almost giving me a heart attack.

I straightened with a tight smile. "I've known him all my life. I know who he is." Yet I had to admit part of my previous perception of Nevio had been grounded on infatuation. Unlike in my fantasy, Nevio hadn't miraculously turned into a doting and loving boyfriend. He'd become the insistent, obsessed hunter more fitting for his personality.

Kiara dried her hands and came to Serafina's side, both of them bestowing me with understanding smiles. "We know you do. We just want to make sure you know we won't judge you if you want a bit of distance from Nevio."

I swallowed hard, wondering if they knew what had happened. Serafina touched my shoulder. I nodded. "I'm fine, really." I focused on the dishes once more. They probably wouldn't judge me this kindly if they found out I'd helped Nevio keep his child from them for weeks or possibly months.

After the conversation, I was glad when my parents, my brother, and I left the Falcone mansion. We crossed the premises as there wasn't a fence between our land and theirs, but I was too agitated to go inside yet.

"I'd like to stay outside for a bit," I said.

Dad glanced at his watch. "It's getting late. You should stay the night, and I'll take you to your place in the morning."

I couldn't do that to Carlotta. Battista's sleep pattern was still erratic. "No, I promised Carlotta I'd be home. She's still a bit hesitant about being alone in the apartment overnight."

"I could call Diego."

"No, please don't. He's already overprotective. Carlotta would kill me." She definitely would because she had no problem staying in the apartment alone.

Mom gave me a smile. "I don't mind taking you to your apartment later. Take as long as you need."

Dad gave her a look that made it clear he wouldn't allow it. "I'm not letting you drive around the city by yourself at night."

"Everyone knows my car and me. I highly doubt anyone's going to give me trouble."

"There's always a first for everything." He turned to me. "I'll take you home in an hour."

"Thanks, Dad," I said with a smile and stepped on my tiptoes to press a kiss to his cheek.

"You and your mom have me wrapped around your fingers."

Davide rolled his eyes. "Can we go inside now? I paused my game for dinner, and I want to finish this before midnight."

"You're lucky I don't confiscate your Switch."

Dad and Davide moved into the house, arguing about the stupid games my brother enjoyed, while Mom stayed with me. She touched my cheek. "I really wish you'd confide in me. I can tell something's bothering you."

What was currently bothering me was definitely not something I'd ever talk to Mom about.

"Sorry, Mom."

She nodded and went inside as well. I headed toward the pool and sank down on one of the lounge chairs, staring at the luminous water surface. I lost myself in whirring thoughts of my twisted relationship with Nevio, the myriad of lies I had to remember, and my growing feelings for the little boy I had agreed to babysit.

The next time I looked at my watch, forty minutes had passed. I rose from the chair and headed to my parents' house when a twig broke behind me. I knew who was following me. Had he been watching me at the pool? I walked faster, desperate to get into the house before he reached me. I doubted Nevio would follow me inside. Even he had to have a sense of self-preservation because my father would kill him if he found us in a compromising position. When I'd almost reached our terrace, fingers curled around my wrist and I was jerked backward and dragged away. My surroundings briefly blurred before me, then my back bumped against the house wall, and Nevio took shape before me.

Chapter Thirty

Aurora

My back pressed against the wall by Nevio's body, I craned my head back to look at his face. We were on a dark side of the house. Light only reached us from around the corner, where it illuminated the patio and living area.

Nevio's face appeared foreboding, angry even in the twisting shadows. "You've been avoiding me."

He was right. After the incident with the knife, which still brought up an equal amount of shame and desire in me, I couldn't be around him anymore. Our relationship wasn't going in a direction I'd envisioned in my fantasies, and I was worried I'd lose myself and what I really wanted along the way.

"I needed time to think. I still do," I got out.

Nevio bent down, bringing us even closer. He smelled good, like sin and temptation. Musky and fresh. He wasn't wearing a shirt, only low-cut workout pants. He must have been on his way to the gym when he saw me outside. My nights had been filled with fantasies about Nevio, things I wanted to do to him and wanted him to do to me, everything I tried to suppress during the day.

"You can't escape your desire or me," Nevio growled into my ear. The little hairs on the nape of my neck rose as his hot breath hit my skin. He was in a strange mood tonight, erratic and on edge. His lips pressed against the skin below my ear, then he scraped the same spot with his teeth, making me shudder.

I pressed my palms against his chest, wanting to push him away before he left a hickey. He felt perfect. Strong, his muscles firm and hot beneath me.

"Rory, I can't stop thinking about you, about how wet you were, how my knife looked in your pussy."

I didn't want him to voice what had happened. It made it too real and sent a new wave of mortification through me. "If you don't stop, someone will find out," I gritted out, but I hadn't taken my hands off Nevio's chest yet.

Nevio cupped my neck, his thumb against my pulse point. "About us," I added a little breathless.

Nevio's intent gaze had little to do with concern over being caught. In the distance, I could hear Gemma and Kiara laugh, soon followed by Mom and Serafina.

"Nevio," I pressed out, trying to move past him but his lips came down on mine. His tongue met mine, and his fingers around my throat closed possessively. I kissed him back, my hands moving lower to his abs with a mind of their own, feeling his heat and strength, growing high on it.

My body came alive violently, my core pulsing with a terrifying need that my own fingers would never be able to satiate.

Nevio's kiss demanded full surrender. I lost myself, lost track of time and our surroundings. His hand slid under my shirt and cupped my breast, his fingers tugging hard at my erect nipples. Nevio kissed me even harder, then ripped away from my lips, shoving my shirt up higher to reveal my bare breasts. Fabric ripped, and then his lips latched onto my nipple, sucking hard. I gasped, my eyes squeezing shut as I tried to keep down my sounds. Nevio's thumb stroked along my throat, and he nipped at my nipple, making me jump from the pain. I gripped his head to shove him away, and he sucked my nipple slowly, now sending spikes of lust through my body, right down to the already damp spot between my legs. Who would have known that the nerve endings in my breasts were so closely linked to my pussy? I sank my teeth into my lower lip. I wanted this; there was no denying it. That I also wanted more seemed inconsequential to my body.

I needed to shove him away. I needed to stop this, whatever insanity it was. Nevio licked, bit, and sucked my nipple while one of his hands twisted and teased the other.

Soon, I wasn't sure if I was trying to drag him away or keep him in place. He fell to his knees and pulled me toward him with one hand as his other ripped my panties off, leaving me bare under my skirt. His mouth covered me, his tongue shoving between my pussy lips and licking me out. My legs trembled, so he hooked them over his shoulders until I was only kept up by my back pressed against the wall and Nevio's shoulders. His face was buried in my lap, his tongue alternating between teasing my opening and flicking over my clit.

I could hardly breathe, my pants coming too quick, my body pounding with pleasure I'd never thought possible. My heart throbbed madly in my chest, from pleasure but also from fear of being caught. I held Nevio's head, my core beginning to tighten in a giveaway sign…when I heard Mom and Dad's voices as they stepped outside.

Cold fear washed over me. Nevio must have heard it too. He was the hunter, after all, but he only pressed harder against my pussy and slammed his tongue into my opening while his thumb rubbed my clit. I tugged at his hair hard to get him to stop. I didn't dare say anything for fear that Dad would overhear me.

That would be the ultimate catastrophe.

Steps crunched on the patio. Mom and Dad were just around the corner.

I opened my mouth to tell Nevio to stop right this moment, even if that posed the risk of being overheard. Then we might still have time to jump apart, and I could maybe put my clothes back in position. Everything was better than being caught with Nevio's tongue inside my pussy. Before I could utter a sound, Nevio's hand clamped over my mouth. His lips

By Frenzy I Pain

closed around my clit, and two fingers took the place of his tongue, slamming into me.

My body started spasming, my orgasm unstoppable despite the situation. I tore at Nevio's hair, my lips parting against his palms, my eyes squeezing shut and then pleasure pounded in my clit, my core, up through my entire body. My walls trembled around Nevio's fingers, and he kept pumping into me and sucking my clit, intensifying my orgasm.

"Do you think I should check on her?" Mom asked. "She seemed upset when I left."

"She obviously doesn't want to share whatever's bothering her. I'll go to the pool and see if she's there. If she wants to go back to her place, we need to leave soon."

"Okay," Mom said quietly. "I'll wait for you inside." The sliding door sounded, and steps crunched. Then I could see Dad's back as he headed down to the Falcone part of the huge garden.

Nevio kept his hand on my mouth as I slowly came down from my high, my thigh muscles trembling. Nevio put me down on the ground and bit the inside of my thigh, then soothed the spot with his tongue before he licked back up to my pussy. I shuddered at the new onslaught. I loosened my hold on his hair, a little shell-shocked. Staying away from Nevio wasn't going well.

Nevio

I smirked against Aurora's pussy as I tasted the remnants of her arousal. My own need pounded angrily in my pants. This was only the starter.

I shoved to my feet, my hand still pressed against her mouth. I lowered it and grinned at her stunned face, but then I kissed her. I couldn't stop kissing her.

"If my family finds out, they'll force me to move back in with them to keep me away from you, then I won't be able to babysit Battista for you anymore."

"There's not enough blood left in my brain to worry," I said. "This is the third orgasm I've given you, and you haven't returned the favor yet."

The thought of having Rory blow me behind her parents' house made my cock even harder.

Aurora shoved my chest. "It's only fair after my shitty first time, and I never asked you to do that."

She couldn't even put into words what had happened. Adorable.

"I have to go inside before Dad comes looking for me here. This isn't a game," she hissed. "Give me my panties back."

With a smirk, I bent down, enjoying the sight of her glistening pussy under the hem of her skirt as I picked up the remains of her panties. I held them out to her.

She picked them up with two fingers, her eyes widening in realization. "You ruined them."

I leaned toward her. "I love ruining your underwear in every way possible. But what I love even more is ruining every shred of your innocence, sweet Rory."

She tossed the panties at me and slipped away. This time, I didn't chase her and allowed her to escape into her parents' home.

Stuffing her ripped panties into my pocket—I'd add them to my collection—I strolled away from the Scuderi mansion.

Luck would have it that Fabiano crossed my path.

He barred my way, his expression one that would have spiked my hunger for violence with a stranger. "Where's Aurora?" he demanded in a hostile tone.

"I'm doing a nightly workout. I haven't seen Rory," I lied easily.

"And your workout led you into my garden?"

"I wasn't aware that I wasn't allowed on your premises."

He moved closer. I had half a mind to show him Rory's ripped panties. I was fucking tired of his obvious aversion to me being around her. Sure, I was bad news, but that didn't mean I had any intention to hurt Rory.

"I don't care if you're on my premises, but it's strange to find you here when I can't find Aurora anywhere."

"Dad?" Rory called from the patio.

"See, your daughter is safe and sound."

Fabiano glanced between Aurora and me.

"If you don't mind, I'd like to do my workout now," I said sarcastically.

Fabiano gave a terse nod before he headed toward Aurora, probably on a mission to interrogate her. As expected, Aurora ignored me, but her flushed face made up for her lack of acknowledgment.

I headed toward the pool for an unplanned swim exercise, which would also serve as a cool-off after another encounter with Rory that left me with a case of blue balls.

Rory thought I'd lose interest once I'd fucked her, but every encounter with her only left me hungry for more. Rory wanted more; she wanted parts of me that I didn't want to share with anyone, but I wondered if maybe we actually had a chance if I tried hard enough. Maybe following my demons was really just me choosing the easy way.

Alessio came to the pool when I did my last lap and squatted beside the edge, a cigarette dangling from his mouth. "Massimo and I are wondering when you want to head out tonight."

"I think I'll pass tonight."

Alessio raised an eyebrow. "We didn't go on raids for two nights because business kept us busy, and you want to go without for another night?"

I swam toward him. "You sound as if I'm addicted to it."

"Your actions indicate you are. You are addicted to the highs it gives you. The thrill of the hunt and the torture is your drug."

"I'm not a fucking pussy. I can control my urges. They don't control me."

"That's probably a phrase an addict would say," Alessio said. He pushed to his feet and stomped his cigarette out with his steel-tipped boot. Admittedly, seeing the shoes he always wore during our raids made me eager for the hunt.

"Is this your attempt to better yourself for Aurora? If so, kudos to you for even trying."

His tone made it clear I wouldn't succeed.

I sat up with a hoarse roar, sweat covered and with my knife clutched in my fist. Where was I? I shoved to my feet and turned on the light, searching my surroundings for signs of the horrid scene I saw playing out mere moments before.

My room wasn't covered in blood, not a single droplet. I ran a hand through my damp hair, my heart slamming into my rib cage.

"Fuck," I breathed out and stared down at my hands, turning them around. Of course, they weren't stained in blood and neither was my knife, but it wasn't difficult to imagine they were. I'd lost count of the times my skin had been sticky with blood. But the image of Aurora's and Battista's blood hit differently.

A knock sounded, and a second later, Dad poked his head in, a look of weariness on his face. "I heard your scream."

Had I roared that loudly? Fuck. What a goddamn nightmare. I didn't believe in premonitions. If a fortune teller tried to tell me my future, I'd end theirs. Still, I couldn't stop staring at my hands.

"Nevio?" Dad asked as he stepped into the room. He too was holding a knife in hand. My scream must have really worried him.

I shook myself and gave Dad a twisted smile. "I guess all the killings are getting to me."

Dad came toward me. "You're pale. Do you need me to pull you from your current tasks?"

It had been a while since Dad hadn't looked at me with anger in his eyes. His honest concern was a nice surprise. Of course, I was fucking undeserving of it, considering the nature of my dream.

Would it help me to stop killing? Or would it only lead to a frenzied killing spree I'd be unable to control. The last time I'd had a vivid dream like this had been in the months before my twelfth birthday, before my first kill. My dreams had been filled with images of carnage, and when I'd told Dad about it, he'd decided to gift me a victim for my birthday.

"I'm fine. I wanted to kill long before you made it part of my duty as a Made Man."

Dad regarded me with narrowed eyes, as if he might extract the true nature of my dream from me.

"Maybe you should spend more of your nights actually sleeping instead of creating mayhem with Alessio and Massimo."

"Sleep's a waste of time."

"Lack of sleep drives even the sanest person to madness."

"That's a very Nino thing to say."

"Go to sleep." He turned and left, but I could feel his worry radiate off him in waves.

And fuck, even I didn't share his worry. This had been a major mindfuck of a dream—nightmare.

Blood everywhere. Screams. My heart pounding, pulse racing. Bloodlust, eagerness, the thrill of the hunt.

But in the end, the two people in the puddle of blood had set my veins on ice: Aurora and Battista.

I didn't know if I'd killed them, but I was almost certain I had. What did my subconscious want to tell me with this shit show of a dream? That deep down the crazy fucker part of me wanted to kill them and everyone else I cared about? Or was this my subconscious manifesting my biggest fear?

I wasn't sure. I left my room and strolled through the quiet and dark house. It was three in the morning and everyone was asleep or at least in their bed, even Dad hopefully too. I knew every corner of our home, so I crept through the dark hallways, wondering when my heart would stop pounding.

I wondered if Dad had ever experienced nightmares like that when his life had been in upheaval after he found out he had two kids. I wished I could talk to him, but things had been too tense between us in the last few months, and my dream would probably only confirm his own worst worries, that I was a ticking bomb about to tear apart this family, possibly in the literal sense.

Chapter Thirty-One

Aurora

My phone lit up the room, alerting me of the bell, which I always muted at night. I slid out of bed and tiptoed toward the front door. It was the middle of the night, and nobody ever visited at this hour.

I glimpsed through the peep hole, my fingers clutching my phone, ready to speed dial Nevio so he could come and chase away whoever waited in front of the door.

My lungs deflated, my heart beat tripled, and for a moment, I couldn't move. I unlocked the door and opened it.

Nevio stood in front of me. A baseball cap was pulled down his face, and he was dressed in a long black coat which hid most of his body—a good thing considering what I saw beneath. He was covered in blood, from head to toe. Even his lashes were clumped with blood. He wasn't wearing

By Frenzy I *Pain*

a shirt or shoes, and his skin and the clothes he was wearing were covered in blood too, though their black color made it hard to see.

Smudges of blood now covered my white door too and bloody footprints led from the elevator to my door. If Dad saw this on the security camera, we'd be in a ton of trouble.

"What happened?" I whispered. I couldn't see any obvious injuries, nothing that would explain the amount of blood, except for a couple of bruises here and there. Tonight, hadn't been a cage fight.

The stench of blood quickly became oppressing in the narrow hallway. Considering my line of work, I wasn't sensitive about blood, but this was more than usual.

"I'll grab a shower," Nevio said, and I simply nodded, wondering why he was here. Maybe I should have sent him away. He had to be on edge. This was his doing, no doubt. He'd slaughtered one or more people tonight, and now he was here. Maybe I should have been afraid, maybe I had reason to be, but after the initial shock, my pulse was already slowing.

I stepped past him and opened the bathroom door for him so he wouldn't have to touch it, then I did the same with the shower. Nevio came in and unbuckled his belt. He didn't wait for me to leave. He simply shoved down his pants, and I merely stood in the middle of the bathroom, feeling a little lost. When he got out of his boxers, I didn't blush like I usually did. Blood had trickled down even to his penis. It had gathered in the ridges of his six-pack.

Nevio stepped into the shower and turned it on. Soon, the water washed away the first layers of blood. I backed away, but I didn't leave. I closed the door, in case Carlotta woke. If Battista started screaming, I'd hear him. I was glad he was too little to get up on his own and roam the apartment. He didn't need to see the blood, even if he'd probably think it was paint. Nevio washed his hair but his eyes were on me as I leaned against the door. Steam slowly filled the room, creating a visible barrier in addition to the one I could feel between us tonight. There had always been a push and pull between us since that night, but no matter how hard I'd pushed the pull had always been stronger. Tonight, it felt different. It felt as if we were on the verge of a push that would pull us apart farther than ever before, and I didn't think the push would be coming from me.

Maybe it should, maybe seeing Nevio covered in the blood of his victims should have been the final straw—and maybe in a day or two it would be, when it had sunk in—but right this moment, I felt drawn to him. I was attracted to someone whom many people would call a monster, and I feared it was his monstrous side that made out part of his appeal.

In less than ten minutes of showering, no trace of the carnage remained. Nevio was clean and he shut off the water, then got out of the shower completely naked.

Droplets of water meandered along his muscles, caught on them and the scars that covered his chest and stomach. One wayward drop traveled lower and caught in his trimmed pubic hair.

Nevio didn't bother drying off. He stalked straight toward me. His hair dripped down his face, making it appear as if he were crying, but I'd never seen Nevio shed a tear, and I doubted anyone else had either. I wasn't sure if he was capable of it. Nevio stopped close in front of me.

"You are pure light," he growled.

I didn't say anything.

Tears filled my eyes. Nevio brushed his thumbs along my cheeks, catching the droplets. "I don't know why I'm crying," I whispered.

His lips pulled into a bitter smile. "I think you do, Rory."

I bit my lower lip, the tears now coming harder.

Nevio's darkness was impenetrable.

I'd always known Nevio carried plenty of darkness. You couldn't know Nevio and not know. But I'd always thought the darkness was a small part of him. Over the past year, though, it had become clear that the Nevio I loved was part of a dark even he couldn't control. Or maybe he just didn't want to control it. The dark meant freedom for Nevio. He didn't try to control his nature, he lived it.

"I'm not made for companionship. I'm better off alone, free to go bump in the night."

I shook my head. "That's not true. Look at your bond with Alessio and Massimo. You've been best friends all your lives."

"They joined me in the darkness but they never quite needed it as much as I did."

"Nevio—"

His lips came down on mine. I opened up. I didn't want any games, any push and pull, not tonight, not when this felt horribly final. I wasn't even sure why I knew, and why did this make me so sad. I had tried to get Nevio off my trail for months, and now that it felt as if he might be backing off, it crushed my heart.

His fingers still lightly held my cheeks as we kissed, a slow, gentle kiss that accentuated the finality of this moment. Nevio pulled back an inch. Waters from his hair dripped down on my face and cleavage, droplets chasing each other down the valley between my breasts and soaking my camisole. The fabric clung to my breasts, and my nipples hardened.

"Rory." The word was dark, almost agonized. Nevio gripped the hem of my camisole and pushed it up. I lifted my arms so he could pull it over my head. He tossed it to the floor, then cupped my cheek and pressed his lips to mine again.

His eyes were on mine as if he sought a connection to ground him. More water dripped down on me, and goose bumps rose on my skin. Nevio pulled back and lowered his face to my chest, his warm tongue chasing the drops along the swell of my breasts, then over my nipples.

I arched, my hand gripping the back of his head, fingers tangling in wet hair. His tongue meticulously licked up every drop of water from my chest. Every time he brushed my nipple, my core clenched. I felt on edge, oversensitive in a way I'd never experienced. A few drops of water escaped down my belly, and Nevio's tongue pursued them. When the tip of his tongue passed my belly button, I tensed, my fingers flexing against his scalp. I knew this wouldn't end where our last encounters had ended. This time, I'd give even more of myself to Nevio, physically and mentally, and I feared it would ruin me for good.

Nevio gazed up, part of his eyes covered by his dripping wet hair. A smirk pulled at his lips, reminding me of my Nevio, of the man I still wanted by my side.

By now several droplets had trailed down my thighs and over my pubic bone, some catching in my trimmed hair, others resting between my pussy lips or in the ridge between my labia and thigh.

My body was as taut as a bow, ready for Nevio to catch those wayward drops too, full of desire and longing but also apprehension. Kneeling in front of me, he slid his tongue along the groove between my thigh and pubic bone, then along my outer thigh and inward. His eyes caught mine again as he dipped his tongue between my pussy lips to catch the water that had gathered there. His hair kept dripping, and Nevio lapped up every drop that caught on my pussy.

"Water never tastes this sweet," he rasped. He parted my folds with his thumbs and bent over my pussy so more cold water dripped on my heated flesh. Every drop against my clit left me shell-shocked and desperate for more. Nevio covered my pussy with his mouth and really dove in. His licks became almost feral as he gathered more than just water. My cheeks heated from lust and embarrassment as I watched him devour my pussy. I was close; my legs tensed but Nevio pulled away.

I tried to shove his head back, but he was too strong. His eyes made me shiver with lust. One of his fingers traced the seam of my pussy, far away from my clit.

"Do you ever fantasize about the feel of my knife? How it claimed the part of your innocence that my cock hadn't?"

More heat raced into my face as it always did when I remembered that incident. I still couldn't believe it had actually happened, and I had enjoyed it.

Nevio smiled when I didn't reply. He gripped my thigh and shifted it to the side, then pushed two fingers into me. I let my head fall back but kept my head tilted down so I could watch. His forehead pressed against my lower belly, the cold a shock to my system. He fingered me faster and deeper, and his lips closed over my clit. I came with a violent shudder, my lips pressed together to stop myself from making a sound. He shoved to his feet and cradled my face, his dark eyes full of need. "Rory."

It was all he said, but even that one word carried his desire. I met his lips, letting my own need take over.

He lifted me off the ground, and my legs came around his waist. He walked backward, then lowered himself to the ground with his back against the bathtub and me straddling his belly.

With his eyes locked on mine, he gripped my hips and guided me so his tip pressed against my opening. "Take all of me, Rory. I want to watch your face. Want to see the lust, the pleasure, the pain as my cock takes whatever innocence is left."

I began to lower myself. The knife handle had been much smaller, and the memory from that first night had already faded. Tonight felt as if it was our first time. Nevio cupped my neck, his thumb on my throat as his other hand pressed down on my hip. I sank down despite the intense stretching sensation, my lips falling open as the air left my lungs. "To see pain mix with pleasure on your face is the biggest turn-on I've ever had. Nothing compares to it, and at this moment, I want to believe it could be enough."

I sank all the way down until our pubic bones touched. My eyelids fluttered shut from the intense fullness and dull pain I felt. I didn't want to think about his words, not now.

Nevio pulled me toward him, his lips claiming mine. His hand moved from my hip to my ass, fingers digging into my ass cheek. The kiss was unhurried, but I could feel the rising need in Nevio, and my own body called for more, even if it still hurt.

I rotated my hips, allowing Nevio's cock to slide out halfway only to sink down fully again. Nevio brushed his thumb over my lips, his intense gaze making me shiver. He wanted—needed—more.

I moved faster as we held each other, as his lips slid over mine, and Nevio's heart beat pounded against my chest. Slower than mine, and I wondered if the horrors of tonight had made his heart pound faster.

Soon, Nevio's fingers dug harder into my flesh, and his hips jerked upward, driving his cock deeper into me. My core tightened as the first sparks of my orgasm lit up my body until a firework of pleasure took hold of me. I sank my teeth into Nevio's shoulder to keep my scream in, and he let out a harsh groan. His own release was close.

Even as waves of pleasure still flooded me, my body still high on dopamine, the first dark clouds of regret and even shame overcame me. I had sworn to myself not to become Nevio's babysitter with benefits, friend with benefits, whatever you wanted to call it, but I had allowed myself to be shoved into that mold, and I had no way of escaping it.

I needed to put a stop to this, needed to set firm boundaries. I didn't want to lose sight of my own happiness and eventually of myself, but the path Nevio and I were on right now would ultimately lead to that result. It had to stop now.

Chapter Thirty-Two

Nevio

Some crazy primal part considered spilling my come inside Aurora's pussy, and impregnating her. Having Rory carry my child made my cock harden even more and my chest swell. Fuck it. I already had Battista and hardly knew what to do with him. I couldn't do this to Rory, even if I wanted to lay claim to her in every way possible before I had to make a hard decision. I barreled into her even harder, desperately. Aurora's hot breath hit my shoulder before her teeth sank into my flesh again, upping my pleasure.

She came around me with a harsh cry, her pussy squeezing my cock so tightly I saw stars and needed every ounce of my self-control not to shoot my load into her. I lifted her up, my cock sliding out and set her back down on the ground. Rory had lost every sense of our surroundings. She was lost in pleasure, like I was lost in her. I slammed my lips against hers, kissing her full of need. "Rory," I groaned. I needed to come.

By Frenzy I *Pain*

Fuck, I was burning up with need ever since I'd fucked her with my knife. I couldn't take much more. She curled her fingers around my cock and began rubbing me. I wrapped my hand around hers to increase the pressure. I pressed my lips to her ear. "I want to come inside you."

Her lips pressed against my chest, then down my pecs. Fuck. I couldn't take it. I needed even more. She finally dropped to her knees. I grabbed her neck and pushed her closer to my cock. Maybe a good guy would have given her time to explore, but I needed to fuck her mouth now or lose my last shred of sanity. Her lips parted around my cock, and I threw my head back with a groan as her hot mouth and tongue engulfed me. I came hard.

My chest was heaving, my cock still pulsing inside of Aurora. Then she looked up at me.

Fuck. Something was up, and it wasn't good.

Aurora wanted to talk emotions—her expression left no doubt about it—but after last night's nightmare and tonight's frenzy, I couldn't be what she needed. I pulled her up to her feet, gripped her neck, and kissed her hard. "Don't."

I wasn't sure if she knew what I meant, but stubbornness tightened her face, mixing with the first traces of regret.

People often regretted having met me. Naturally, Aurora would be no different.

"I'm a detonation about to happen, Aurora," I snarled. My grip on her neck tightened even more and she winced, but the stubbornness remained in her eyes. Fuck, she needed to stop hoping. I wished she could see into my brain just for one day to realize I wasn't kidding.

"Fight it, fight it whatever it is. Fight it for me, for your family, for Greta, for your son," she whispered. I wished she hadn't uttered those words because they made me want to try, but trying would hurt people I cared about. I could sense it deep in my bones.

I kissed her, smiling bitterly against her lips. "If you knew the chaos in my head, you'd give me up."

"Like you so easily do with me because I'm inconsequential to you." Her voice was harsh, and she was trying to make her face seem that way too. Rory was many things, but harsh wasn't one of them. She wasn't a good liar either, which made it even worse that I forced her to lie constantly.

"You aren't inconsequential to me, Rory," I said harshly. If she were, I wouldn't be scared shitless of what I might do.

"Your actions speak louder than your words."

She pulled away, but I wouldn't let her. I tightened my hold on her. "What do you want me to do?"

"I want you to try. You're not even trying. You just follow your impulses. You don't try to be a father to Battista, and you're not trying to give us a chance." Aurora's lips thinned as if she regretted her own words.

I leaned my forehead against hers. "You shouldn't ask that of me."

"Why not?" she asked angrily.

"Because for you, I might actually do it. For you, I'll try."

Not even twenty-four hours after I'd given Aurora my promise to try for her, to allow something between us to bloom, to take responsibility not just for Battista but also for my emotions and for her, I'd gone on one of the biggest killing sprees of my life. Maybe it had been inevitable.

It was as if my monstrous side had feared being caged in and gone rampant to prove who was still running the show, and it was definitely a side of me that wasn't fit for a relationship of any form.

Battista and Aurora deserved better. My family deserved better. Hell, even the Camorra deserved better.

I was covered in blood from head to toe, could feel it stick to my face, my eyelids, my lashes. The world around me was cloaked in a pink mist because blood even covered my goddamn eyeballs.

I watched the droplets of blood dripping from my soaked pants and dropping to the floor.

A police officer stepped up to the cell. Young. Overmotivated. Arrogant. Maybe a bit sadistic. I watched him from the corner of my eye. Police had picked me up at the scene of the carnage. I'd sat among the dead bodies and allowed the police to take me with them. I'd been high on adrenaline. If you could overdose on bloodlust, then that had definitely been the moment, but other than with drugs, I hadn't died. At least not my body.

Maybe a part of me had, though. Who could really say? My brain was still too much of a mess to analyze anything.

"We should hose him off," the young officer said. "Get him out of those clothes and give him a long cold shower." The excitement in his voice was unmistakable.

"I won't go in there," the older officer said. He'd avoided me as if I were the devil. They probably thought I was possessed. "And you better not either."

"Come on. We're armed, and he's not. He's a spoiled brat, but without his dad here, what can he do? He's at our mercy."

I watched their interaction through half closed eyes.

"Bernie, you need to learn a thing or two. You're new."

Bernie scoffed. "You mean bow down to the mob?"

The older officer sighed. "Just don't go in there." He turned and walked out of the cell block, leaving young, naive Bernie alone with me and a couple of drunkards in neighboring cells.

Bernie stepped closer to the bars with a nasty grin. I didn't move and stared at my blood-covered hands. "Not so loudmouthed now?" he taunted. I didn't remember being loudmouthed. Usually, I was silent and lethal.

"You should listen to your colleague," I murmured.

He grabbed the keys and pulled the taser gun. Unlocking the door, he pointed the taser gun at me and stepped into the cell. Without warning, he shot the taser at me. The wire shot out and the two darts hit my shoulder. My muscles flexed uncontrollably as electricity coursed through my body. My teeth clanged together, and the metallic taste of blood filled my mouth as I tried to regain control over my body. My breathing stuttered as I fought to stay on the bench and not topple over.

With a grunt, I forced one arm up and ripped the darts from my body. One of them hadn't penetrated my skin fully, which was probably why I could move and didn't have to wait for a break in the electric impulses.

I jerked to my feet and pulled at the wire. Bernie stumbled forward before the wire tore apart. In two steps, I was by his side, grabbed his arm and head and flung him toward the wall. His shoulder blade and chin bone collided with a satisfying crunch with the concrete. His answering roar of pain made me smile. I jerked his head back so his agony-stricken eyes met mine. "Time to play, motherfucker."

Steps rang out, and the first officer came rushing into the corridor.

I kicked the door to my cell shut with a high kick and the lock clicked in place. Two more officers came rushing in. The first fumbled with his keys as I grabbed Bernie once more and wrapped the taser wire around his throat. I pulled it tight, but after a few seconds of gasping from Bernie, the wire tore apart again. "Shame," I drawled. He spluttered and clawed at my hands.

I smiled at him and smashed my forehead against his nose, causing blood to surge out of his nostrils. He cried hoarsely.

Guns pointed my way, and one nervous finger pulled the trigger. I used Bernie as a shield, and the bullet hit him in the thigh. He screamed again.

"That was close to his artery." I tsked. "If you want to kill Bernie, you'll have to give this another try."

Finally, the door to my cell opened, and another officer staggered in. I shoved poor Bernie toward him. They collided, and I jumped at them with another kick, sending them both flying to the floor. I landed beside them, and within a flash, I held their guns and pointed them at their heads. The prison was filled with more and more officers, and all of them worried that my trigger finger was better than theirs—for good reason. I bared my teeth at the officers at my feet. "Next time, you better listen to your colleagues, Bernie."

"Enough," someone roared.

I froze when Dad, Nino, and Savio walked in. The police officers parted. "Down with all of the guns," Dad ordered.

The police officers didn't hesitate, and I followed suit.

Slowly, I straightened and tossed the guns away.

"He comes with me. Don't mess with my family."

Neither Dad nor my uncles said a word when they led me to their car. I suddenly felt exhausted. I leaned my head against the window and must have dozed off because when I looked around again, I was in a bare-walled room without windows. Nino leaned against the wall across from me, straight in my line of vision. He regarded me from head to toe without a word. His expression was blank, and sometimes even I got goose bumps because of my uncle. "You are lacking control," he drawled.

"He's lacking more than that," Savio muttered who appeared at Nino's side. "Empathy, restraint, reason. The only thing he's got an abundance of is craziness."

I flashed him a grin. He shook his head, for once not in the mood for jokes.

"I'll talk to him alone," Dad said in a low voice. My eyes sought him. He leaned against the wall to my right.

Nino touched Dad's shoulder, and they exchanged a look that reminded me of Massimo and Alessio. Something passed between them that I wasn't supposed to be privy to.

"Get a grip, man," Savio muttered as he came toward me, his fingers digging into my shoulder, his eyes imploring.

I bared my teeth. "You never saw me lose control."

"That's what we fear," Nino said. He searched my eyes, then he only nodded and walked out with Savio.

I glanced around, realizing where we were. This was where enemies and traitors were taken to be tortured and killed.

I cocked an eyebrow at Dad. "Do you really think you can?" It was meant as a provocation and a joke.

Dad stared into my eyes, and my grin died. I chuckled, then nodded. He stalked toward me and gripped my face, resting our foreheads against each other, his eyes burning into mine. Sometimes I saw the same insanity and hunger for destruction in them that always burned inside me. "I love you more than my life. But sometimes I think you are punishment for my sins, a way to throw my own faults back at me. I never knew what Nino had to put up with until you came into my life."

I wasn't hurt by his words. Very few things in my life hurt me, physically or emotionally. They were true. "Greta got everything good Mom and you got to give, and I inherited all the bad. It's the way it is. That's yin and yang for you."

"It's not funny," he roared.

"No, it's my life," I growled. "It's who I am, Dad. You, unlike the others, never asked me to change or to control myself. You only asked me to channel it."

"Because I know you can't control it."

I smiled bitterly.

Dad dragged a chair across the room and sat down across from me, regarding me like a rabid dog that his owner couldn't put down even though he knew the monster would kill again. "Las Vegas is under my control. The West Coast is. But at some point, even my control won't be enough. Even the strongest empire can fall if the king doesn't make sure his subjects feel safe." His voice shook with restraint. He wanted to kill me, and he knew he should.

"Is anyone safe, Nevio? Is there a limit to what you're capable of because recently I fear there isn't."

I should have lied, but I didn't want to. "I don't know. I wish I did, but I don't, not one-hundred percent." I shrugged. "Are you absolutely sure you'd never hurt the people you loved?"

"Yes," he said firmly. I wondered if his certainty really came from conviction or because he thought by saying it aloud, it would become true.

"If I thought I could ever hurt our family, I'd leave and never come back, Dad," I said finally, because it was true.

"You better do," he murmured. His eyes reflected pain. "Don't force my fucking hand. It would kill your mom. It would kill Greta." He swallowed, his hold on my throat tightening. "It would kill me."

"You know how good I am at killing, Dad," I said.

Chapter Thirty-Three

Aurora

I glanced at my watch once more but there was still no sign of Nevio. He was running late. Thirty minutes late, to be exact. I had to leave for work in about twenty-minutes and Carlotta in about ten minutes for college. Diego was picking her up as usual and taking her there.

"He hasn't even received my text yet," I muttered, glaring down at my phone.

A stupid part of me worried something had happened to him that stopped him from being on time, when I knew it was simply Nevio being Nevio. I could see his promise to give us a real chance slipping away. I wasn't sure if he couldn't do it or if he didn't want to. It was probably a combination of the two. My heart ached and my belly felt hollow as I considered what this meant. I'd made my boundaries very clear to Nevio, and I wouldn't budge this time. I didn't care if my body burned up for his touch or my dreams replayed the pleasure he'd given me. I didn't care if this meant giving up on Nevio and me for good because the other option meant giving up on me. I wouldn't do that, not even for Nevio. He had done nothing to deserve it, and I doubted there was ever a moment when someone was truly worth it to give up on everything that makes you you.

Carlotta put down her backpack on the counter with a quiet sigh. "Maybe this is what you feared, that he's pulling back completely, that he got cold feet after he promised you progress. Maybe him ghosting you is really the sign you need."

"I don't need another sign to know that a relationship between Nevio and me is not going to work. I need someone to watch Battista, and that someone should be his father."

Carlotta nodded, her expression compassionate, but I could tell she also thought it was partly my fault. And she was right. I should have kept the promise to myself after the party. Instead, I'd fallen prey to Nevio's seduction. Who knew that stalking me and driving me to the brink would turn me on?

I pressed my lips together, then I nodded. "You're right. I made excuses for him for far too long. I enabled him to stay irresponsible because he had me for his responsibilities."

Carlotta came over to me and hugged me. "If he doesn't show up today and doesn't have a very good excuse, you need to tell his parents about Battista."

I nodded, and Carlotta pulled back. She kissed my cheek. "I really need to go or Diego will come up. He's already suspicious about why I never invite him in."

"I know. And thanks for always having my back."

Carlotta smiled, then she turned and went over to Battista in his playpen to kiss his forehead before she grabbed her backpack and left. Battista pulled himself into a very unsteady standing position and looked at me hopefully. I went to him and picked him up, then blew a raspberry on his chubby cheek, which caused him to giggle uncontrollably. I'd be late for my internship, and Doc Gentile wouldn't be impressed at all. I set Battista down despite his protests and picked up my cell phone to call the hospital. After I'd closed the kitchen door to avoid Battista disturbing me, I called in sick.

I could hear that he thought I was faking it, and of course, he was right. I went back into the kitchen where Battista had started bawling because I'd left him alone. He stopped once I picked him up again. Singing "Wheels on the Bus", I tried to call Nevio again, but the call didn't go through.

Battista babbled along with the song, a bit of drool running down his chin thanks to his teething.

"Your father is an idiot," I murmured.

Battista chortled as if I'd told him a joke, which unfortunately wasn't the case. My phone rang, and my eyes widened thinking it was Nevio. Instead, "Dad" flashed on my screen.

"Oh no."

"Hey, Dad—"

"Are you okay? The doc called me."

I bit my lip. I should have known Dad would find out, but this was quicker than I thought.

"I'm fine, just a headache."

"I'm coming over. Something's up."

"Dad—"

"No," he said firmly. "After Nevio's last visit, I'm done believing things are fine."

Of course, Nevio leaving bloody footprints and looking like death himself had left Dad very concerned. Nevio was causing me way too much trouble.

"If he hadn't disappeared from the face of the earth, I would have beat the truth out of him."

"He's gone?"

"Not the first time he's taken off, and probably not the last time either. Maybe Remo will have to save his sorry ass from another police cell again."

I shook myself. "Can you send Mom over? Please."

Silence on the other end. "Aurora, what's going on. Are you able to talk freely?"

"I'm not in a hostage situation, Dad," I said. "I just need Mom."

"Fuck. Now you really have me worried. I'll drive your mom over, but I'm coming with her. No way am I going to let her go alone as long as I don't know what's going on."

He hung up.

I stared at Battista. "Everything will be okay."

Suddenly, my heart felt heavy thinking of having to let him go. We'd become a good team, and he was really attached to me.

When the door rang, I put Battista back into his playpen to open it. Mom and Dad waited in front of the door. Dad held a gun in his hand as if he was ready for war. Mom looked upset and concerned.

I was already in scrubs. Dad scanned me from head to toe.

"I'm not injured," I said, opening the door wider so he could see nobody was behind me.

"Is anybody with you?" Dad asked.

I hesitated. Because technically there was, just not in the sense that Dad meant. But my hesitation was too much for Dad. He gently pushed me aside and rushed into the apartment, checking one room after the other until I heard him curse.

Mom's expression tightened. "Aurora, what is going on?"

I motioned her to follow me and once inside the kitchen, she too let out a startled curse upon seeing Battista. He had started crying when Dad entered the room. I picked him up and soothed him with gentle words.

Mom and Dad stared at me in horror.

"What the hell? When did this happen? How did you hide this from us? It's Nevio's. I just have to look at those eyes. I'm going to kill him for touching you."

It took me a moment to realize Dad thought Battista was actually my son.

"Aurora wasn't pregnant," Mom said, but I could hear the barest hint of hesitation in her voice.

"How could I have hidden a pregnancy? You saw me in bikinis all the time," I said with a laugh.

Neither Mom nor Dad laughed, but they looked relieved when they realized I said the truth.

"So he's not yours," Dad said.

"He's not mine. Nevio asked me to take care of him."

"Of course that's what he did," Dad gritted out. He paced the kitchen, the gun still in his hand as if he hoped Nevio might show up.

"Can you please calm down? You're scaring Battista."

Dad stopped abruptly, but he didn't appear calm at all. His blue eyes burned with fury. Mom came toward me. "You've been taking care of him since you moved in here, right? That's why you wanted to move in so quickly. Four weeks. That's a long time for someone as young as yourself."

"Many women in our circles aren't much older when they give birth," I said. Battista watched Mom open-mouthed.

"I know." Mom nodded, regarding me with admiration which slowly morphed to reproach. "You've lied to us."

Dad scoffed. "Nevio made her do it. That's his special talent." He came closer but stopped when Battista started bawling again.

"Shhh, it's okay," Mom whispered, but Battista pressed his face into my chest, and I rubbed his back until he quieted.

Dad fixed me with a hard look. "Answer me one question, why?"

I shrugged. Even I didn't really have an answer to that question. "I suppose I wanted to help Nevio."

"Has he touched you?"

"Dad—" I blushed.

"Don't 'Dad' me now. Answer my question. Has he touched you?"

"Fabiano, I really don't think that's our business," Mom said gently, but I bet she would have asked me the same question once it was just the two of us.

Dad moved closer, and this time, he didn't stop when Battista started crying.

"Aurora, I want an answer. If you don't answer me, I'm going to take your blushing as a fucking yes, and I'm going to hunt him down."

"She's probably blushing because that's a very personal question."

I swallowed. Mom defending me made me feel even worse, but she had a point. My sex life wasn't Dad's business. "Nothing happened against my will," I said.

Dad let out a roar and kicked one of the chairs so it flew across the room and smashed against the wall, losing a leg. "I'm going to rip his balls off."

"Fabiano!" Mom said, wide-eyed.

"No, you're not. What happened between Nevio and me is only my business."

Dad's head was almost purple from fury. "It's my business if he compels you to have sex with him!"

"You had sex with Mom before marriage, if this is about having sex out of wedlock." My cheeks burned. Talking about sex with Dad was the absolute last thing I wanted, but he didn't leave me a choice.

"It's not about some conservative world views," Dad gritted out. "This is about you being with Nevio fucking Falcone. He's not someone you should be close to. And I had serious intentions with your mother. What about him?"

I didn't say anything because I wasn't sure of Nevio's intentions. I doubted even he knew.

"You were unsure about us when you started pursuing me. Maybe it's the same with Nevio," Mom said, touching Dad's upper arm in a calming gesture.

He met Mom's gaze, and for once, she didn't get through to him. "I sure hope not. I don't want him with Aurora. I won't allow it."

"I'm here, you know. And I have no intention to be with Nevio," I said. This was my life, and though I'd admitted I made some very bad decisions when it came to Nevio, I now had a new resolve to ban him from my life once and for all.

Dad pulled his phone from his pocket. "I need to call Remo now."

I took a step forward. "Wait."

Dad frowned. "It's his grandson. He needs to know so he can rip Nevio a new one."

I bit my lip. I wasn't sure why I was suddenly so scared to tell Nevio's family about Battista. They had a right to know. They were his family after all. Mom gave me a reassuring smile. "It'll be all right. Remo won't be mad at you for helping Nevio keep this secret."

"He'll be mad as he should, and I'm mad as hell," Dad said, giving me a stern look. "Lying about everything, that's not who we raised you to be."

"You taught me the importance of loyalty. You don't always agree with Remo's decisions but you have his back."

"He's my Capo."

Mom gave him a look but she didn't contradict him.

"He's your friend first," I said. Though friend really wasn't the right term. Fabiano considered Remo almost as his brother, but I couldn't bring myself to see the Falcones as family, especially now that I'd slept with one of them. That would be too weird.

"Which is *why* I'm going to call him now. The secrets end now."

Not all of them.

"Maybe we should tell Remo in person," Mom said in her lawyer voice. "That way, he can't build up his rage."

"He'll have more than enough if we tell him in person, but this might be news that's really better told directly." Dad lifted the phone to his ear. After a few rings, Remo picked up. "I need to come over to talk to you. It's important." Pause. "I'd rather not tell you over the phone." Pause. "Yes, it's linked to Nevio." Dad lowered the phone, then he met my gaze.

I swallowed. "This isn't going to go over well."

Chapter Thirty-Four

Nevio

I never thought I'd leave Las Vegas, not for long, not without a definite return date. Yet today, I'd purchased a one-way ticket to Naples.

I hadn't talked to anyone about it, not even Greta or Aurora. There was enough commotion in my brain as it was. Nobody could take this decision from me because nobody knew how messed up my thoughts were right now. I needed time to get a grip—to grow up how Dad would call it. Maybe that too. But who'd ever heard of a serial killer growing out of his murderous urges.

The problem wasn't even the latter—being a good killer and loving it was the best condition to be a Made Man. The whole male side of my family were murderers. Some liked it more than others, but we were all good at it. Problem was that it had become an addiction. After a kill, I

By Frenzy I

was already thirsting for the next kill. I lived for my nightly hunts and needed to get a grip.

I wanted to. I wanted to manage my dark side like Dad and Nino did, something I'd never admit to them. I admired them for how they handled a family life and the darkness that they harbored.

Sometimes I wanted to hurt everyone, but there were certain people I always wanted to save a little more than I wanted to hurt them. Save them from me. The problem was, every day I was a little less sure who held the reins, me or the monster.

When I left the Falcone mansion in the morning, I wasn't sure when I'd return or if I'd return. I could die helping the Camorra in Italy. I could decide my darkness simply wasn't controllable.

The hardest part was not saying goodbye, especially to Aurora. She wouldn't forgive me for this, and she had every right to hate me. But she'd be able to hand Battista over to my parents, and they would take better care of my son than I ever could.

My first stop after landing in Naples wasn't the local Camorra headquarters or my great-uncle's villa outside the city.

I went to the best tattoo studio in Naples. When my plan to leave had formed in my head, I'd known I wanted to take Battista and Aurora with me in any way I could, so I decided to ink them into my skin. Aurora because of the feelings I had for her, and Battista because of the feelings I should have for him.

I didn't have an appointment but managed to get in anyway. I showed the tattoo artist an image of an aurora borealis. Aurora's name couldn't have been more fitting to how I saw her. A bright light against the dark sky. Her light even managed to brighten the blackness inside me. Maybe one day I would reach my personal equinox, and maybe one day my dark and light would be even. The aurora borealis always shines brightest on the night of an equinox. As long as my darkness overweighed the good inside me, Aurora's light would always burn a little less in my presence. I didn't want that.

The tattoo artist created a few quick drawings of aurora borealis tattoos. I didn't want a backdrop of a forest or mountains. I wanted the sole focus to be on the northern lights and the night sky behind them. I picked a black night sky as the background and bright green and turquoise lights. I didn't have many tattoos, not as many as Alessio and Massimo, only two so far: the Camorra tattoo of the eye and the knife, then a Joker tattoo on my back with his smile and *Why so serious?* in blood red beneath it followed by a string of HAHAHAHAHAHAHA. The A's didn't fully close at the top because every vertical stroke stood for one life taken, like a tally list. There were many haha's by now, becoming smaller and smaller as they meandered down my back. I had a feeling I'd eventually have to give up taking tally. Both tattoos were held in black and red. Both colors I appreciated for their deeper meaning to me. Now the first dash of color would be added to the list.

"Where do you want the tattoo?" the tattoo artist asked after I'd picked the design. I motioned to the center of my chest, then slightly to the left. "I want the lights over my heart," I said.

The tattoo artist nodded but didn't comment. Good for him. I pulled my tee over my head.

"Great artwork," he said when I turned my back to him. Nino had done a fabulous job of the Joker tattoo and the bloody tally list. I showed the guy the Camorra tattoo on my wrist was equally as good.

"My uncle did them."

"Impressive. Why didn't you choose him for these tattoos?"

"I didn't want to. Are you worried your art won't be as good as his?" I raised my eyebrows at him. "Because I'm putting my trust in you, and these tattoos are very important to me."

He swallowed. "It's going to be my best work."

I stretched out on the chair and held out my forearm to him. "Let's start with the letter." The tattoo for Battista would be simple. A red B over my wrist because he was my blood. I'd wanted to pick a tattoo with a deeper meaning like I'd done for Aurora, but I simply didn't know him well enough. I hoped if I'd ever get the chance to do so I could add more detail to the tattoo. For now, I'd carry his initial with me as a constant reminder that Aurora wasn't the only one who needed me to face my demons and shackle them. After less than an hour, the red B decorated my skin. The moment the tattooist touched the needle to my chest, I closed my eyes, allowed the burn to invade my body. It felt as if it almost touched my heart, as if the ink buried itself deeply enough to reach that part of me, just as Aurora had done.

After three hours, the hum of the needle died down for the last time. I opened my eyes and stared at the tattooist.

His forehead was sweaty, probably not just because he'd worked three hours straight.

He grabbed the mirror from his workstation and held it out to me so I could see his work. The black of the night sky over my heart made it look like there was only a black hole in my rib cage, which was fitting, but it was illuminated by meandering light strokes in green and turquoise.

I gave a terse nod. It was how I'd imagined it. I swung my legs off the chair and got up.

"You did good," I said. I wanted to leave, felt the need to be alone with the strange sensations this manifestation of Aurora on my body created.

I grabbed my shirt and put it on, then on my way out, I tossed a wad of cash onto the reception desk, way too much for his work, and then again, not. I didn't wait for him to count it.

My heart pounded in my chest, and I felt restless, hunted. I had expected a reaction to the tattoo, which was one of the reasons I hadn't picked Nino for the tattoo. He would have seen something in my eyes or face, something I didn't want to share with the people who knew me. I could only imagine what Alessio and Massimo would say if they saw the tattoo. Know-it-all Massimo would put two and two together. He definitely knew what the tattoo showed. Aurora borealis.

Aurora.

The fucking light in my life.

Chapter Thirty-Five

Remo

"I HAVE A FUCKING BAD FEELING," I MUTTERED.

Nino narrowed his eyes in thought. "You think he knows about the party incident?"

"Fuck if I know. He sounded pissed."

"Maybe we should tell him that we've known about the incident for a while," Savio suggested with a shrug. "Better than keeping up the lie and having it explode in our faces later." He let out a chuckle. "Who would have thought that Nevio would be the one to cause a sex scandal. It should have been me."

"You could still cause one, but Gemma would rip you a new one, and I'd help her," I said. I'd never thought Savio could be faithful at all, but Gemma seemed to be what he needed.

"The only sex scandal I'm up for is being caught having sex in public with Gemma."

"How about we return to the matter at hand?" Nino asked.

I gave a terse nod. "Tell your sons to get their asses over here. Maybe they know more. Or have heard from Nevio. Serafina is starting to worry, and I'm getting pissed."

"You weren't before?" Savio asked with a cocked eyebrow.

I didn't remember the last time I wasn't pissed at Nevio. He had an uncanny talent to cause trouble. I really hoped it would grow out of him soon. He needed to be more responsible if he wanted to become Capo one day.

Massimo and Alessio entered the room after Nino a few minutes later, both with unreadable expressions. I wasn't kidding myself into believing that their loyalty to me trumped their loyalty to Nevio. These three were usually attached by the hip.

"What's going on?" Massimo asked, glancing from Nino to me.

"Nevio is in trouble, and so by proxy, you two are probably as well," Savio said.

Alessio and Massimo exchanged a look, one I couldn't decipher.

"We suspect that Fabiano found out about the party incident," Nino said, eyeing his son closely. "Or is there something else that might upset Fabiano?"

"I'm pretty sure nothing could upset Fabiano more than Nevio taking Aurora's innocence. Isn't that enough?" Alessio asked with a sarcastic laugh.

Nevio always found ways to make an already bad situation worse. He lived for mayhem.

"So you two are unaware of further developments that might cause us trouble?"

Another look passed between them. Sometimes they reminded me of twins. Nevio and Greta, too, had shared looks that no one but them could read.

"I'm about to lose my shit. If Fabiano tells me something you two should have warned me about, then there will be hell to pay."

"Your loyalty to Nevio is admirable, but first and foremost, your loyalty should be with Remo."

The door ripped open, and Giulio stomped in. "Fabiano is here with Aurora and Leona, and a baby that looks like Nevio when he was little." His voice was eager as if he could smell that trouble was afloat. He too lived for it. My genes had really gone all in with my sons.

Then his words registered, and my heart started pounding in my chest. "A baby?"

Giulio nodded with a grin. "Like a little Nevio."

"Fuck it," I growled. I definitely hadn't fathered a kid, so that left one conclusion. My son had impregnated someone. "Don't tell me Nevio impregnated Aurora!"

"If their first sexual interaction had been at the party, she couldn't have had his child," Nino said, as if I couldn't do math.

"Who knows if they didn't have sex before!" I stalked toward Massimo and Alessio looking from one to the other.

"It's not Aurora's child," Massimo said, looking calm and composed.

I had half a mind to grip his throat, but he was Nino's son, so I controlled my first impulse. "How long have you known?"

Quick female steps came closer, and Serafina appeared in the doorway, her eyes wide with shock and her face flushed.

I ran a hand through my hair. I really wished I could have kept this from her, but one look at her told me she'd just seen little Nevio. "I think we should all talk to Fabiano now."

"Remo," Fina said slowly.

I touched her lower back. "I don't know any more than you."

When we entered the common room, Fabiano was pacing back and forth with a look of agitation on his face. Leona sat beside Aurora on the couch, and the latter had a baby on her lap. Dark hair and eyes. And the typical Falcone features.

"Fuck it!" I snarled, causing the baby to burst into tears.

"You still got it," Savio said with a chuckle as he walked past me to get a closer look at Nevio's kid. He let out a whistle.

I motioned at Aurora and the baby. "Would someone care to explain what the hell I'm seeing here?"

Fabiano stopped and stretched out his arms to both sides with a bitter laugh. "Apparently, your son got a girl pregnant, who then dropped the kid off, and he decided it was a good idea to let Aurora take care of the baby for weeks."

Gemma came in with a look of confusion. "What's going on?"

Giulio perched on the backrest with a devilish smile. "Nevio's in trouble!"

Gemma looked at the baby and blew out a breath before she walked over to Savio. I shook my head.

"Maybe someone should get Kiara so she can be in on the fun," Savio said with a laugh.

"This isn't funny!" I growled.

"Maybe not for you, Grandpa," Savio said. I had half a mind to kick his ass. I still remembered the times when he'd driven me crazy with his antics, but in comparison to Nevio, he'd been a saint.

"Maybe we should allow Aurora to tell the story since she seems to be the one who knows the details," Nino said in his usual logical manner.

I motioned at Aurora to start. She swallowed, still rocking the child on her thighs. The words of what had happened since the boy's mother had abandoned him rushed out of her. She didn't mention the party, or if there had been any other similar encounters between Nevio and her, but I had a feeling the party hadn't been the end of it. That wasn't my main concern right now, though. I was fucking relieved that Fabiano didn't know about that yet.

"So you took care of Battista for six weeks?" Serafina asked softly and walked over to the sofa. She sank down beside Aurora, but Battista had his face buried against her chest.

"You should have told someone," I gritted out. I was torn between anger over this major secret that she'd kept for Nevio and admiration for taking care of a baby that wasn't even her own, when she was only eighteen. That girl was a better mother figure than many much older women, such as the kid's actual mother.

"Do you know where Nevio is?" I asked.

She shook her head with a look of anger. "He was supposed to watch Battista today, but he never showed up."

"I assume he left most of the work of taking care of the baby up to you?"

She nodded. "He tried to be there for us, but it was difficult for him to accept that he was a father. Carlotta helped me with the babysitting."

Was she actually defending him? After all the shit he pulled.

When I'd found out I had kids, I had known one thing for certain: that I would take care of them, that I would take full responsibilities and that their needs would trump my own.

The kid looked at me, and it hit me like a fucking sledgehammer again. "Fuck him!" I snarled.

"Remo," Serafina said reproachfully because Battista had started crying again. She rubbed his back, but he pressed closer to Aurora. He was obviously very attached to her.

"Poor baby has gone through so much," Serafina murmured. I could see her motherly instincts rearing up again, but this kid wasn't our child. It was Nevio's.

Still, I could already feel my own protectiveness rise. This boy was now a part of our family.

I turned to Massimo and Alessio. "Where is Nevio? No more lies. This is too serious for your loyalty bullshit."

"We don't know," Alessio said with a shrug.

"He disappeared without a word. We haven't seen or talked to him in more than twenty-four hours. Maybe he's on a raid to clear his head."

I doubted it.

Our last conversation flitted through my mind.

I'll leave if I ever fear of breaking my promise. Was this the case? "Check his room. Are his clothes gone?"

Massimo and Alessio left.

"Do you think he'll be gone for longer?" Fina asked quietly, her eyes wide with concern.

"Running away from his responsibility," Fabiano said with a scoff.

I hadn't told Fina about my conversation with Nevio. It would only make her worry more. "He'll be back." I didn't feel the same conviction that my voice conveyed.

"How long have you known about this?" I asked Fabiano.

"Today. If I'd known before, I would have told you and kicked Nevio's ass for burdening Aurora with a task like that. She's pretty much a child herself."

"I'm of age. And I've been taking good care of Battista."

"Nobody doubts that," Nino said. "But it shouldn't have fallen upon you to take care of Nevio's child."

"Exactly," Fabiano said, then his eyes met mine. "Did you know that Aurora and Nevio had sex?"

"Dad!" Aurora cried, her cheeks blushing furiously. "I never said that."

"Do you think I was born yesterday? One look at your face and I know it's true," Fabiano growled. "I've interrogated too many people not to be able to read expressions."

"I would prefer torture to this mortification," she muttered, avoiding everyone's eyes. Leona patted her knee.

Fabiano crossed the room and stopped in front of me. "Did you know?"

"Yes," I admitted, even if it would hurt Fabiano's trust in me. But if I kept lying, it would only make things worse.

"What about the promise we made after our death battle? I took it seriously. You obviously didn't."

"Our children's sex life is a private matter, so I guess Remo didn't want to break Nevio's trust," Leona said.

Fabiano scoffed. "Yeah, I'm sure that's what happened. How many more of you knew?" He looked around.

"Great! So everyone knew except for me?"

"I didn't know!" Giulio said quickly.

"Did you know as well?" Fabiano turned to Leona, who gave him a stern look. "I didn't. But if Aurora had confided in me about something like that, I wouldn't have broken her trust by telling you. She didn't, though." She gave Aurora a look, which made the latter sink even lower into the cushions.

"The only sex I care about is the one that created that baby!" I muttered, but one look at Fabiano's face told me he definitely wouldn't drop it easily.

"I don't know anything about the mother, except that she's not from the States and probably already fled the country," Aurora said quickly, obviously glad for the topic change.

"Figures," I muttered.

Alessio and Massimo returned. "Some of his clothes are gone, but none of his weapons," Massimo said.

"What does that mean?" Fina asked, a hint of panic in her voice. She rose to her feet and came over to me.

"That he's taking a flight," I said.

Fina gripped my arms. "But where could he go?"

"We'll find him," I said firmly, kissing her mouth, then gently prying her off.

"We should give Adamo a call in case Nevio shows up there despite the evidence hinting to another scenario," Nino said.

I doubted that would be the case, but Nino was right, and Adamo needed to know anyway. "Do that." Nino took out his phone and went over to a corner of the room to have quiet.

"Maybe he's with Greta," Fina said. "I'll give her a call."

"Don't say anything about the kid yet."

She nodded slowly. Greta couldn't carry children because of her injuries, and Nevio had a kid that he obviously didn't want.

I fixed Aurora with my eyes. The baby had fallen asleep in her arms, one of his hands clutching her right thumb. "Battista has lost too much in the last few weeks. If you take him from me now, it'll be too much for him. You're all strangers to him."

I nodded. I could tell that Battista and Aurora had formed a bond, and the boy needed someone he trusted for now.

"You can't return to the apartment. While I hunt Nevio down and make sure he gets a fucking grip, I want you to keep watching the baby like you have done so far."

Aurora hesitated. "But if I move out, Diego will insist that Carlotta moves back to his house, too."

That wasn't my problem. "I won't have my grandson anywhere but inside this mansion."

She nodded. And I tried to wrap my head around the fact that I was a fucking grandpa. What a mess. I didn't feel old, and I could still kick anyone's ass, but now I had a grandchild. Greta and Amo had discussed having children, and Fina had even agreed to help them once they felt ready, but I hadn't thought I'd become a grandfather this soon.

"She won't move into the Falcone mansion. Her home is our house," Fabiano said firmly. His stance was aggressive, and I could tell he wouldn't budge on this. Usually, this would have made me absolutely raging mad, but I had something to make up to him. Not to mention that our two mansions were very close together.

"I'll let her live with you," I said. "But she needs to come over with Battista daily."

"He's not with Greta either," Fina said once she returned from her call with Greta.

I hadn't expected him to be. Nevio felt volatile, and even he knew that going into Luca's territory when he felt unstable wasn't the best idea.

My phone rang. It was the head of the Italian Camorra. My first impulse was to ignore his call. He probably needed help and money again, but then I had a suspicion. "Alvize, what do you need?"

"Remo, your eldest son showed up on my doorstep today. Did you send him to help us?"

Of course, Nevio would go there. The Camorra in Campania was at war on several fronts. This was the perfect place for someone like my son.

༄

The black sheep of the family.

Maybe every fucking family had one. Maybe some would consider Nevio our black sheep. Maybe he did too.

It was bullshit. The Falcone family was a herd of black sheep, with a few gray and even fewer white ones in between. Nevio thought he was the wolf in sheep's clothing, a risk to us, but he wasn't. He could fit in if he really tried, but he didn't want to.

He chose the excitement of a war-torn Camorra over the responsibilities piling up in Las Vegas. And I would tell him exactly that once I saw him in Campania. I'd boarded a flight to Naples two days after I'd found out about Battista and Nevio's flight.

Naples was where the head of the Camorra in Italy had resided for over a century and where the majority of their business was still conducted, but Alvize, the over seventy-year-old Capo, was hiding away in an estate in the countryside in Campania, and Nevio was there right now.

༄

I was angry.

Fucking furious.

I hadn't been to Italy, and the Camorra there in a long time. I didn't see a reason too. Sure, it was where my ancestors had once come from. But the Camorra in Italy right now was a mess, fighting among each other, struggling with the Italian police and Europol. It was a cesspool of intrigue and envy.

They hadn't given us a second glance when the Camorra in the US had been struggling and weak. Now that we were strong, stronger than they could even dream of right now, they came running, hoping for help, hoping for money. Fuck them.

And still I was heading there now. To kick my son's ass. The son who had a son himself.

I couldn't wrap my head around it.

I had never felt ready to become a father, but the moment Greta and Nevio had entered my life, I had been. I had taken responsibility by the balls.

Nevio had run. He was younger than me when I'd been thrown into fatherhood, but not by much. He was less controlled, and what really mattered was that he didn't have the boy's mother at his side.

Serafina had been a lioness of a mother. She had been a shining beacon. I'd admired her for it and had wanted to be an equally worthy parent. Battista's mother was a bitch who abandoned him.

I'd already taken care of my brothers, had fought for a territory and won. I'd lacked control, true, but I'd been better at channeling my violence because years of responsibility had taught me to do so.

Nevio had always had the freedom to follow his violent desires and live them as freely as our lifestyle allowed.

Maybe I should have forced him to restrain himself, giving him more responsibilities and a purpose.

Becoming Capo was in his future, but it was too far off for him to hold on to as an incentive to become a more restrained version of himself.

⁂

I didn't text Serafina or Aurora the outcome of my conversation with Nevio. This was something that needed to be said in person.

By Frenzy I *Pain*

Of course, words weren't needed when I entered the mansion without Nevio by my side. My face was probably a dead giveaway too. I felt like exploding.

Serafina closed her eyes, but when she opened them, a new resoluteness entered her expression. "Our main concern should be Battista right now. He needs a family and love." She and Kiara exchanged a look, motherly concern filling their faces. What neither of them probably noticed was how Aurora's arms tightened around the boy.

I wasn't sure why she'd agreed to help Nevio with a task like this, but from the way the little boy sought her closeness, she'd done a good job.

"What are your thoughts on the matter, Aurora?" I asked. It was strange to think that after meeting my children several months after their birth due to the circumstances, the same thing now happened with my grandchild too. Fuck. I never thought I'd be a grandfather at my age. I really wanted to kick Nevio's fucking ass.

Surprise crossed Aurora's face. She swallowed and squared her shoulders. "Battista has lost his main attachment figure only two months ago and had to get used to me and Nevio as his new caregivers. Now Nevio left too. I don't want Battista to lose another person in his life. Right now, I'm the only one he is attached to, so taking that from him would be cruel."

I seriously doubted the kid's mother had been any kind of attachment figure. If anything, she'd probably caused the kid attachment issues for life. He was better off without her.

But fuck Nevio for not being up to the task of being what the boy needed.

"Do I understand correctly that you want to keep caring for the boy for now?"

Fabiano walked back and forth in the room, his face on the verge of an outburst. I got it. He must be pissed about the situation. His eyes slanted to me, and I could see the same anger in them as five days before. I couldn't blame him. Nino and I had kept things from him, important information about his daughter. I was glad he hadn't packed his bags yet. That he was still here and willing to work on a solution for a fucking nightmare of a situation showed how loyal he was.

"This is insane. You're eighteen. You have your whole life ahead of you. This isn't even your child, and even if it were, nobody would blame you if you handed his care off to someone else. You're almost a child yourself. You should live life to the fullest, not be bound by this responsibility."

"I'm not a child, Dad. Growing up in our world makes it impossible to stay a kid for long, not just the boys who become Made Men."

Leona sat there silently. She was generally a more quiet participant whenever arguments arose between our families, which had happened rarely. "I'm sure Serafina and Remo would gladly take care of Battista as his grandparents. That way you could move back to your apartment."

Fina nodded enthusiastically. She had already bought clothes, toys, and furniture for the kid. "Of course, we would raise him until Nevio returns."

Fabiano scoffed. "If he returns. And let's be honest here, he still won't be father material then. He's a fucking mess. He's lucky I haven't bought a ticket to Naples yet to end his sorry ass for what he did to Aurora."

I gritted my teeth. Threatening my son, the future Capo, was something that didn't sit well with me, but fuck, Fabiano had every reason to hate Nevio right now. As his father, even I wasn't happy about any of this. He'd messed up royally, and I wasn't sure he'd ever redeem himself.

"Ultimately, it's your decision as the head of your family if you're willing to have Battista stay under your roof, but like Aurora said, the boy needs consistency. She can live here."

"You know full well that this isn't about the boy living under my roof. It's about Aurora. Nevio has done nothing to deserve Aurora's sacrifice."

I nodded. I wasn't blind to Nevio's many faults. I met Aurora's gaze. "I think we can all agree that he doesn't deserve you."

"I know," she said. "Maybe one day he will."

"You really think that?" Fabiano growled. "You are too clever to be foolish."

"First and foremost, I'm doing this for Battista, not for Nevio, so it doesn't matter," she said defensively.

Aurora reminded me of Fina in some ways. Like me Nevio seemed to be drawn to the light when it came to women. And like me, Nevio had given up said woman. Fina had returned to me and I'd won her back. I hoped Nevio would manage to do the same.

Chapter Thirty-Six

Nevio

5 days prior

After my tattoo appointment, I decided to head for Alvize's estate in the countryside. I didn't want to announce my visit to one of his three Captains in Naples, all of whom were married to his daughters and hoping to become the next Capo for want of a son.

His mansion was near the Vesuvius National Park, and the volcano's foreboding cone loomed on the horizon. Massive cast-iron gates and an old stone wall barred my way onto the premises. I got out of my rental car and approached the gates. There was a security camera at the top. I looked up so whoever watched the footage would get a good look at my face. "I'm Nevio Falcone and here to support my great-uncle."

For a while, nothing happened. I gripped the steel bars and looked inside. Over boarding bushes with pink flowers, huge olive and fig trees, and extensive rosemary shrubs filled this side of the garden. Farther up, I could see the red shingles and white top floor of a villa.

Steps crunched on the asphalt, which was ripped where the unrelenting sun had worn the material down. Two guards with machine guns came into view. They shouted at me in Italian with a Neopolitan dialect.

"Put your hands behind your head and lie down."

What a warm welcome, but I did as they said. If I killed them, Alvize might be less inclined to let me stay.

The sun had heated the ground to a degree that I had to hold back a hiss when my chest pressed against the surface. My tattoo was still fresh. Maybe the foil the tattoo artist had put on it would burn itself into my skin.

One of the two patted me down for guns while the other pointed the barrel of his machine gun at my head. "All clear." The two men grabbed me by the arms and legs, then carried me inside. I relaxed in their hold.

Alvize stood on the last step of the stone staircase leading up to the wood double doors of his villa. He was a fat man, though I doubted anyone dared to describe him as such. They probably called him sturdy or imposing. And what the hell was up with his hair? He had hardly any left except for something that resembled a tonsure. He wore a suit, sunglasses, a hat and wingtip shoes. I had trouble stopping a sarcastic comment. He was like a caricature of a mobster. But this was his kingdom, and even if he was a miserable king, I had to show him respect if I wanted to play here.

His men dropped me off at the base of the stairs. I sent them a hard smile.

"Nevio Falcone?" he asked doubtfully.

I straightened. "The one and only. I thought my welcome here would be warmer."

He stepped down the last step. "True. My men can be somewhat overcautious. These are dangerous times."

"Indeed," I said. The two baboons stayed close as if they thought I'd come here to off my great-uncle. Did they think I wanted his place? I could become Capo of a functioning empire, I didn't need one that was in shambles."

"Did your father send you? Are you here to help? I thought he'd send a few more soldiers, not just one."

"Trust me, I'm worth more than just one man." I ignored his question about my dad. For one, it would have made Dad look weak if I'd gone without his permission, and it might have led to him sending me back.

"I've heard the stories." He motioned at the door. "Why don't you come in for a drink and I'll give your father a call to thank him."

I nodded, not batting an eye. Dad wouldn't admit that I'd gone without asking him. The two guards followed us inside. I cocked an eyebrow at them. Alvize was obviously scared of being alone with me. That wasn't a good thing for a Capo. Dad was capable of defending himself as any Capo should.

"We're family," I said.

Alvize cackled. "That doesn't mean much, does it?"

"For my family, it does."

"Then why are you here? Shouldn't you help your family in Vegas?"

My chest tightened with an unfamiliar feeling. "They don't need help."

Yet I knew right at that moment that I'd do anything to return to them as quickly as possible, especially to Aurora and Battista, even if both probably didn't even want me to.

Alvize asked me to stay at his villa for a couple of days before I was supposed to leave for Naples to get in the thick of things.

I'd known Dad would be majorly pissed when he found out, but I hadn't expected him to cross half the globe. When Alvize told me my father was on his way to the villa from the airport, I had trouble hiding my surprise.

Dad rarely bothered hiding his emotions, especially his rage. Sometimes he toned it down for Mom's benefit, but when he stepped into the living room of the villa with Alvize by his side, only his eyes revealed his fury. His face was a mask of control while Alvize droned on and on about the current state of the Camorra in Campania.

Dad didn't like the guy, so I knew it cost him extra effort to restrain himself.

"I need to talk to my son alone for a bit," Dad said.

Alvize nodded. "You can stay here, and I'll give you some privacy."

"We'll head into the gardens for some fresh air," Dad said, motioning me to lead him outside. I wouldn't have stayed inside these walls for a private conversation either. I bet Alvize had eyes and ears everywhere.

The moment Dad and I were outside, hidden between the massive olive trees, his controlled mask slipped away. "I don't even know what to say to you."

That was a first. "I told you I'd leave when I felt like I was losing control. Going here and helping the Camorra somewhere else seemed like a wise choice. I didn't ask you for permission because it wouldn't have changed anything."

"This isn't even why I want to slam you against this fucking tree," Dad growled.

I nodded. "Ah. Is this about Aurora?"

Dad got in my face. "It's about the fucking son you didn't bother telling me about!"

I wasn't mad at Aurora for telling my family. I'd failed her and Battista. She had no reason to take care of him for me anymore. She wanted her freedom and her life back.

"I've known about him for only two months."

"Then you should have told me two months ago! Instead, I find out you made Aurora take care of your son while lying to all of us. Fabiano is pissed, and that's an understatement. I wouldn't turn my back on him if I were you."

"I needed to figure things out for myself before telling you."

"And this is how you figure out being a father?" Dad motioned around us. "Running away to Italy?"

"Trust me, everyone's better off with me here. I need to get a grip before I return."

"You sure as fuck will get a grip. I did and so can you."

I glared. "But I'm not you, Dad! I have to figure things out for myself."

"And while you figure things out, you expect everyone else to take over your responsibilities."

"I bet Mom and Kiara love to take care of Battista while I'm gone, and all the other tasks can be done by Massimo and Alessio now that they get their beauty sleep at night again."

"I think Aurora wants to keep taking care of your son. I don't know what you did to that girl's head but she's obviously willing to sacrifice a lot for you."

I was stumped. I hadn't expected Aurora to keep watching Battista. I'd always thought she would hand him off to my parents the moment she got the chance. I had to admit my heart doubled in size thinking about it. I touched the tattoo without thinking about it.

Dad gripped my shirt and shoved it up, revealing the aurora borealis tattoo. He scanned it briefly before he narrowed his eyes at me. "Is this what I think it is?"

"I'm not good at reading your thoughts."

"If you care about Aurora, running away and abandoning her, certainly sends the wrong message."

"You sent Mom back to the Outfit, even though you cared about her. That was even more stupid. She could have married her fiancé and you would have never seen her again."

Dad grabbed my shoulder. "As you like to point out, you're not me. Will you be able to see Aurora move on? What if she's with someone else when you return?"

"She won't be," I said firmly, possessiveness burning through me. The mere idea of anyone touching Aurora made me want to maim and kill them.

"Considering your actions of the past, she would be stupid not to move on."

"Mom didn't move on, even though your actions were even worse than mine." I hadn't kidnapped Aurora or tried to destroy the people she loved, so I really wasn't sure why Dad was so pissed at me.

"Your mother was busy being pregnant and raising twins," Dad said.

"But you didn't know that when you sent her away. I can't imagine you being okay with someone else being with Mom."

"I knew she wouldn't move on with someone else," he said.

"And if she had."

His face gave me an answer. "See, and I would do the same. Just because I'm here doesn't mean I won't find out if a guy makes a move at her and then he'll quickly back off."

"Maybe Aurora deserves to move on, especially if you are gone for years."

I scoffed. "Please, don't pretend you had it in you to be noble, I certainly don't. I'm a murderous, possessive asshole and Aurora knew that when she fell for me. Now that she's in my head, she must know what that means."

"And apparently not just in your head," Dad said with a wave at my chest.

I didn't comment. My feelings were volatile and elusive, I preferred not to dwell on them.

"Does Greta know?" I asked, changing the topic. I had reduced my contact to her to a bare minimum since I'd found out about Battista. Maybe it was guilt. While she wanted children but couldn't have them easily, a son had been thrown in my lap, and I didn't even want him.

"Your mother didn't mention Battista to her yet, but it's not something we can keep from her for long."

I nodded. "She'll be sad that we kept it from her at all." I shoved my hands into my pockets. "I need to stay here. I need to figure things out and battle my demons."

"You should figure them out with the help of people who care about you."

"Does that include you?" I asked, bracing myself for the answer.

His fingers on my shoulder tightened. "It does, but that doesn't mean I don't want to strangle you for the pain you're causing your Mom and everyone else. Your strength, your dedication to the Camorra and your fight skills have made me incredibly proud in the past, but nothing would make me prouder than seeing you become a good father to your son, and a good man for Aurora."

We returned inside after that, and Dad left the next day without me, only leaving me with the burden of his words. Yet I was glad he'd said them because they'd showed me he still believed in me, and I sure as fuck wanted to become both—a good father for Battista and a good man for Aurora.

Chapter Thirty-Seven

Aurora

Dad's anger filled the room as we sat at the breakfast table. It had been five days since he'd found out about Battista, since I'd moved back in with my parents, but he still barely talked to me. Most of his anger was directed at Nevio, but a small part was for me too. He felt betrayed, not just by Remo and Nino, but also by me. I had lied to him and Mom, so many lies. Nevio wouldn't come back, not anytime soon. Remo hadn't been able to bring him back. Nevio didn't want to be here, and I doubted anyone, not even Remo could force him.

I rocked Battista on my lap. I had been taking care of him for two months now. Two months of spending every waking moment bonding with him and hoping that Nevio too would find a bond to his son.

He hadn't. Instead he'd decided to remove himself fully from not only Battista's life, but also mine. Remo had said he did it because he was on the verge of losing control, that he was too erratic, too volatile, too much in need of the thrill of the kill to take over any kind of responsibility.

Maybe one day he would be. I worried it would be too late for Battista, and I was certain it would be too late for us. I wouldn't press pause on my life for Nevio, not this time. I had to move on because he obviously did. Even if it broke my heart for my silly younger self who'd dreamed of a future with Nevio, for the boy on my lap who deserved a father.

I was seething at Nevio for letting me deal with this on my own. He should have told his parents about his son and not dropped it on me.

"I'm sorry, Mom," I said when I saw her expression. I'd already apologized to Carlotta several times, and she always responded with "Don't be", which had made me feel even worse because her understanding made me feel like a miserable friend. She too had to move back home because of me. Our brief taste of freedom and adulthood had quickly been ripped away again.

Mom patted the hand that wasn't holding Battista. "I admire your strength, but at the same time, I worry about you more than I can put into words."

Dad regarded us without a word. Since Remo had returned from Italy last night, his mood had soured further. He had barely talked more than a few words with me. I got it. This wasn't a simple fib, and it would take time to build trust between us again.

Davide turned to Dad, his mouth full of half-chewed cornflakes. "Are you going to challenge Nevio to a death fight now?"

"He won't," Mom and I said simultaneously.

"I'd rather just kill him. He has lost my respect, so I don't see why I should pay respect to him by offering him the same chance his father once had."

"He probably won't return anyway," I said, not sure if that was what I really wanted.

Leond

As a parent you always hope to raise children that are good people. Well, I supposed Fabiano's wishes for Davide were of a different kind, but beyond their life as part of our cruel world, I wanted both my daughter and son to have a good heart.

Aurora harbored an abundance of kindness, and a heart so incredibly huge that she took a child that wasn't even her own under her wing when she herself was only eighteen.

She was still a child in my eyes, my baby, my firstborn, in need of my protection, yet here she was rocking a baby on her lap and making soothing sounds. She looked grown-up at that moment, and it was hard to wrap my mind around it.

When she noticed me watching her, her smile became tighter, apologetic. She'd lied to us for months. Helping Nevio with his son wasn't the beginning of it. I had a feeling the root of it was around the time of the party when she'd insisted on sleeping over at Carlotta's. I wondered if I'd failed as a mother for her not to confide in me. Fabiano chose to focus on his anger, which I supposed was easier in some ways, but I simply didn't feel enough anger toward Aurora to do that.

I hoped he'd feel relieved of some of his anger once he returned from the gym with Davide. I was also glad for the time alone with Aurora that their trip gave me.

"Don't look at me like that," Aurora said softly. "I told you I'm sorry."

"How am I looking at you?"

"Full of sadness and disappointment."

"I'm just wondering if I'm a bad parent."

Aurora's eyes widened. "How could you ever think that? I want to be a good mom like you one day."

My eyes heated. "I think you already are." I motioned at Battista who had fallen asleep against her chest, his mouth open, dripping drool on her shirt. Aurora's eyes darted down to him then she got up and carefully put him inside his bassinet.

"But I'm not his mother, and I don't know what I'm doing."

"Oh, I didn't know what I was doing when you made me a mom. I think few people really know when they become parents. You figure it out as you go, and that you take care of him even though he isn't yours makes it even more special."

Aurora gave a shrug. "In the beginning I did it mostly to help Nevio. I don't even know why."

"I think you do," I said gently. I wasn't sure why she'd fallen for him. Remo scared me on occasion, though I'd learned to handle him over the years, but I wasn't sure if I'd ever get used to Nevio's kind of darkness. It was one that felt far more volatile than his father's ever had. "Will you forgive him once he comes back?"

"I don't want to forgive him," she said. "I want to move on. Maybe find someone else, someone who doesn't stalk me and kill any guy who shows interest in me."

I raised my eyebrows. I hadn't heard that tidbit before, but I couldn't say I was surprised.

"If you want to move on, taking care of Nevio's boy seems counterproductive."

Aurora bit her lip. "Perhaps. I don't know. Right now, I'm still too wrapped up in everything that happened to consider dating ever again." She moved to my side. "Do you think I should move on?"

"I want you to be happy, that's all I wish for. I don't know if you can be happy with Nevio."

"I don't know if I can be happy without him," she whispered, sounding almost scared.

I got up and wrapped her in a tight hug. "You deserve happiness, and I know it'll find you in whatever form you need. You have a family that loves you more than anything, and we have your back no matter what you choose to do."

"I doubt Dad is in favor of me forgiving Nevio."

"He's not, but even he'll eventually come to terms with it, if Nevio proves himself worthy, which he hasn't so far. You should make him redeem himself. He has so much to make up for once he returns."

She nodded against my shoulder. "Thank you, Mom. It means so much to me that you allow me to make my own decisions, and I promise I won't give Nevio another chance unless he finds a way to make it up to me and Battista, which I doubt he's capable of."

I hugged her tighter. I wanted to protect her from harm, but I knew giving her freedom was equally important. I wasn't sure what to wish for. Nevio's return? Or that he stayed in Italy. One thing was sure, I'd keep reminding Aurora of her promise to make it hard for him.

Chapter Thirty-Eight

Nevio

The first few weeks in Italy passed in a blur. I really threw myself into every battle and job Alvize had for me, no matter how risky. Killing became an all-consuming job, one that filled me with excitement and fulfillment, but a nagging voice remained at the back of my head. A voice that called for Aurora's closeness, for my family, even Battista.

Did I feel ready to return? No.

I had avoided all calls from my family, even Greta in the weeks since Dad had left. I needed this time to figure things out, to see if I could be someone worthy of Aurora and Battista.

Today, I decided to answer Greta's call. She could be stubborn if she wanted to be, and she wouldn't give up until I finally talked to her.

"Hey, Greta," I said.

"Nevio." The relief in her voice was unmistakable. "I'd given up hope you'd ever answer my calls."

I didn't say anything because I didn't have a reason for avoiding her except fucking cowardice. Her disappointment always hit me hard. I had a feeling she knew about Battista by now, which made me even less eager to talk to her.

"I miss talking to you," she said softly.

"You ran away first."

"I didn't run away. If anything, I ran toward Amo. What did you run from?"

"Myself," I said with a dark chuckle.

"That's impossible."

"Maybe. But I ran from the part of me I was supposed to be."

"Hmm," Greta murmured. "You should be with our family."

"You too."

She sighed. "I love our family, but now Amo is my family too. And you have your own small family now too."

"Battista?" I asked warily.

"Him and Aurora if you figure out a way to make her forgive you."

"Any tips? Not that I'm returning anytime soon. I need more time here to get my shit together."

"I know how it feels to succumb to darkness, but I also know it feels better to choose the light."

"Comparing us doesn't work, Greta. But I want to run toward the light, believe me." Aurora was my light at the end of the tunnel, the one I was trying to run toward. If I didn't make the walls collapse around me before.

"Maybe you don't believe it, but I know you can be a good father. What distinguishes you from men like Luca, Dad, and Nino is simply that you haven't made the choice to be a good father yet."

Was I crazier than any of those three? Considering what Luca had done to the bikers, how Dad had slaughtered his enemies, and what Nino had done to Kiara's abuser, it seemed unlikely.

"Have you talked to Aurora in the last few weeks?"

"Once. She seems really close to Battista. I could hear how much she cared about him."

That was Rory for you, being a better mom than the actual mom and taking over my job as dad too.

"Did you talk about me?"

"We did, but that's confidential. I don't want to break her trust."

I grimaced. "I'll send her a beautiful present for Christmas."

"I don't think she wants presents from you. She wants you to be there for Battista and prove to her that you really care about her."

"That's what she said?"

"That's what any woman would expect from a man."

Aurora never reacted to the present I sent her. I had a feeling she'd either thrown it away unopened or pushed it to the back of her wardrobe.

Greta was probably right. What Aurora wanted from me couldn't be paid with a black American Express.

Maybe a fucking idiotic part of me had even hoped she'd give me a call. Instead, Fabiano had. His words repeated in my head ever since.

"*Don't come back if you're the same crazy, irresponsible motherfucker that you are now. Aurora doesn't need you to ruin her life more than you already have. We all don't need you to stir up shit like you used to do. The man you're now is not worthy of becoming Capo of the Camorra, so unless you become a worthier man, which I fucking doubt, then stay there and don't come back to Vegas. Your father fought the same, maybe even worse demons than you, but he fucking stepped up to the task of raising his brothers, to claiming his territory, and even becoming a better father than anyone could ever hope for. He's Capo of the Camorra. You're not, and I don't see that changing. If you have a shred of decency, you'll let her go.*"

His words had hit their mark. He'd voiced some of my own thoughts of the last few months.

But letting Aurora go was simply not an option. Even from Italy, Alessio and Massimo kept me updated on her life despite their initial protests.

Aurora

I wasn't sure what I'd expected when Nevio had left. That he'd be back by Christmas? But two months after he'd run off to Italy, he was still there. I made sure not to pay attention when Alessio and Massimo discussed what he was up to. I didn't want to hear about possible female conquests or how he had the time of his life killing for the Camorra there.

On Christmas morning, I glared at the present that Massimo was holding out to me. He'd been clever enough to hand it over to me before my family and I met with the Falcones for our traditional gift exchange and breakfast. Though handing over wasn't the right term as I refused to take the small parcel wrapped in expensive-looking blue gift wrap.

"It's for you." Massimo held it closer to me. Battista, who I was holding on my hip, made a move to snatch it up. He'd turned a year old a few weeks ago. I'd picked a date for him for lack of knowing his real birthday. Nevio had even sent him a present too. I bet Serafina had told him what to get, and Battista had been excited about the Ferrari ride-on car. But I definitely didn't want a present from Nevio.

"I don't want it," I said. I could hear Mom and Dad talking upstairs, and it sounded as if they were about to come down. If Dad saw the present, his mood would go downhill. Just the mentioning of Nevio usually brought out his anger. "Shouldn't he have bought something for his son?"

"That's under the Christmas tree in the common room like all the other presents, but I thought it prudent to hide Nevio's present for you from our families as it might cause some aggression."

I snorted, which made Battista's eyes light up, and he giggled.

Why did Nevio even think I wanted a gift from him? It only made me furious.

I was trying so hard not to think about him. A task which was made almost impossible by the small boy who resembled him more and more every day.

"I'm not taking it back," Massimo said simply. "I can leave it here on the patio or I can give it to you."

I ripped it from his hand. "All right. But I won't look at it."

"Can you give this to Carlotta? I can't visit her in the hospital." He held out another parcel to me.

"Sure," I said in a less hostile tone. "She'll be very happy about it."

Carlotta had been struggling with her health in the past few days, and it had gotten so bad that she'd be spending Christmas in the hospital to keep a close eye on her oxygen saturation. Dad and Mom entered the kitchen at that moment.

"I hope that's not a gift from Nevio," Dad growled.

I gave him an annoyed look. "It's from Massimo for Carlotta."

"Oh, that's sweet," Mom said with a smile at Massimo, who looked as if he'd rather be somewhere else.

Dad's anger disappeared. Of course, he then spotted the other present. "And what about that one?"

"That's from Nevio, but I won't open it if that makes you happy."

"Happy? No. I'd be happy if he stopped bothering you." Dad stalked toward Massimo. "You shouldn't support his bullshit. You should know better."

Massimo cocked an eyebrow. "I'm doing a friend a favor. It's not my place to judge the morality of it. And neither do I care, if I'm being honest." He glanced at his watch. "Gift exchange starts in five minutes. The kids won't be happy if we're late." He turned around and moved across the garden toward the Falcone mansion.

"Do you want me to throw it away?" Dad asked, picking up Nevio's present. "I could burn it."

I narrowed my eyes at him. "I can handle it myself. Just leave it here."

"Come on, Fabiano. Let's not be late," Mom said. She put her hand on his arm, and he finally put the present down. "It's Christmas."

Together, we moved toward the Falcone mansion. Mom and Dad chatted quietly and soon Dad's face became less angry. Gemma opened the glass door to the common area for us. She wore an incredibly ugly Christmas sweater over workout tights. Huge red pom-poms were positioned right over her breasts and jiggled when she moved. Seeing my expression, she rolled her eyes. "Savio picked it for me. The girls wanted to make ugly sweaters a tradition for Christmas." Her smile became wicked. "But I found a good sweater for him too."

I glanced at Savio who watched as his daughters searched the presents for their name tags. His sweater showed the back of Santa Claus, who was pulling his pants down and flashing his very pale ass at everyone. "Good one," I said. Gemma made faces at Battista which made him shake with laughter.

"Thinking of having another one?" Dad asked Gemma as we entered the house.

"I don't think I want to give birth a third time," she said with a grimace.

Kiara came toward me, beaming. She held out her arms and I handed her Battista. She had taken care of Battista often when I couldn't, and Serafina was busy with Giulio. Now that Battista was being pampered by Kiara, I went over to Amo and Greta who were in conversation with Serafina.

Greta gave me a warm smile. I wasn't sure when she'd last talked to Nevio and was half tempted to ask, but decided against it for my sanity. "He looks like Nevio," she said with a nod toward Battista, whom Kiara was showing the red ornaments at the tree. Caterina and Luna soon joined her to entertain him too.

I tried to keep my face neutral. Christmas wasn't the time to bad-mouth someone, and right now, I only had bad things to say about him.

"He should be here with us on Christmas," Serafina said heavily. "He shouldn't be spending that day alone."

I wondered if he was alone. Maybe he'd found a girl to bang or was busy torturing a poor soul.

"Time to open the presents!" Kiara announced. Giulio and Roman, who had played chess with Nino, dashed toward the tree. Davide rolled his eyes and crossed his arms as if he was above such childish displays when he too had been like that a year or two before.

Caterina, Luna, Battista, Roman, and Giulio were the youngest Falcones, and all of them still believed in Santa Claus, though at almost nine, Giulio had started asking tough questions.

Serafina went over to Kiara, and they helped Battista unwrap his presents together.

"I think we should make ugly sweaters a Falcone Christmas tradition," Savio said loudly, motioning at his sweater.

"Over my dead body," Alessio said. He and Massimo lounged on the couch.

Savio shrugged. "That can be arranged."

"It's Christmas. No violent thoughts welcome," Serafina said.

"Then you need to kick out your husband. I doubted he's ever not felt violent in my presence," Amo said.

Remo didn't contradict him, only flashed a dark smile. Greta huffed.

Soon, we all settled around the dining table which was loaded with breakfast casseroles, charcuterie, cheese platters, panettone, and many more delicacies.

I caught Greta's eyes across the table. In hers, I could see a hint of sadness. Nevio should have been here. Part of me was relieved he wasn't.

Chapter Thirty-Nine

Aurora

Six months later

I chased Battista across the lawn. He was surprisingly fast with his short legs. He stumbled over a bump on the ground and went flying. He didn't cry, only peered up at me with a look of puzzlement. "Not so fast," I said with a smile as I picked him up, dusted him off and set him back on his feet.

My eyes slanted to movement on the patio in front of the Falcone mansion. It was early on a Sunday, and usually, the only people awake at that time were Massimo and Nino for their morning swim. But it wasn't them.

Nevio stood on the patio in swim shorts and a black T-shirt that stuck to his wet skin.

I froze. Nobody had warned me that he would be back, that he was right here in Las Vegas. When had he returned? I'd spent the day before with Carlotta in the hospital as she recovered from pneumonia, so I hadn't been over at the Falcone mansion. Serafina had watched Battista all day, and Mom had picked him up in the evening for me.

I hadn't seen or talked to Nevio in nine months. I wasn't sure what exactly he'd been up to in all this time while I'd taken care of Battista like a mother. He'd probably fucked his way through the Italian girls.

I'd never asked Remo. I hadn't wanted to know. Nevio had decided to extract himself from my life, from Battista's life, and I had decided to do the same with him as far as my subconscious allowed, because my dreams and nightmares were still filled with him.

And now he was back.

His eyes slanted to me. Something had changed about him. He seemed even taller, more grown up, harder in a sense but also more serious.

I kept on walking, following Battista who made a beeline for the sandpit. I wasn't going to make a big deal out of his appearance. I didn't want it to be. I'd worked my hardest to forget him. I knew I'd have to interact with him because of Battista, if Nevio wanted to see his son, which I truly hoped even if part of me dreaded how close that would bring Nevio and me again. Part of me was even scared. What if Nevio had found someone? A nice Italian girl to marry who wanted to raise Battista with her. He wasn't my son, but he felt like it, and I was terrified of losing him. Few people understood why I'd so easily adapted to a life full of responsibilities at my age, but I'd never been a party girl.

Steps followed me, and I took a deep breath, knowing what was to come. I'd prepared for this moment for months, had replayed what I'd say, but now his sudden appearance threw me off completely.

"Rory, wait." Nevio's voice sounded deeper, more adult. How was that possible in less than a year?

Battista had reached the sandpit and played with the sand molds. I turned slowly, keeping my expression neutral. Nevio stopped right in front of me. He had a new scar on his chin, a white line in his otherwise tanned face. He must have spent plenty of time enjoying the south Italian sun.

"You're back," I said, sounding surprisingly unemotional. It was a good thing Nevio couldn't see into my heart, though, because that one was a complete mess.

Nevio's eyes traveled the length of me. Droplets of water trailed down his face. His shorts clung to his body, accentuating every inch of his abs. "You look even more gorgeous than I dreamed about."

My heart skipped a beat hearing those words. He'd never said anything like it before. Instead of letting his praise mollify me, I scoffed. "Really? You never once called, and you probably got it on with countless girls, and now that you're back, you want me to believe that you dreamed about me? I'm sorry, maybe past Aurora was this stupid, but I'm not, and I'm not going back to being like her."

Nevio nodded and took a step closer. "I never lied to you, Rory. And I won't start now. If I tell you I dreamed about you every fucking night, then that's the absolute truth." His voice had a slight growl to it that sent a shiver through my body. It reminded me of past encounters that a part of me desperately wanted to relive, but I wouldn't let that part of me win this time.

"And about me fucking countless girls…You are the last girl I fucked, and if I get my will, you'll remain the last girl until I die."

I didn't allow his words, words I'd so desperately wanted to hear a year ago, weaken my resolve. "So you intend to stay abstinent for the rest of your life?" I congratulated myself silently at how tough and sarcastic I sounded. A quick glance at Battista showed that he was so immersed in his sand play that he didn't pay attention to us. He didn't recognize Nevio, that much was clear.

One corner of Nevio's mouth pulled up in a sly grin, and he chuckled. "I guess I deserve that."

"Oh no, you deserve far worse for the shit you've put me and, worse, Battista through. And I wasn't joking. I won't sleep with you. It caused a mess last time, and it'll cause a mess again. I don't want that. I don't *need* that in my life."

His eyes flickered with bitterness. "Oh, Rory, I know you don't need me or the fucking mess I was and probably still am in some ways. You're tough as steel the way you took care of Battista. The way you handled everything. But you know what?" Nevio leaned down so we were almost at eye level. I tensed, ready to shove him away if he tried to kiss me. He didn't.

"I need you. I want you. And I will stop at nothing until I get you. Until I've proven to you that I deserve you. At absolutely nothing."

His eyes darted to Battista. "And I'll prove that I can be a good father for my son too."

"What makes you think I'm still available? You were gone for a year. What if I moved on and am dating someone?"

Nevio shook his head. "You want to get me out of your head, but I'm still in there. I can see it in your eyes. And I know you wouldn't have moved on to someone else so quickly, especially not when you had Battista to take care of."

I glared. He was right. I hadn't had time, or the mind frame, to see anyone. Battista, my work at the Camorra hospital where I'd started to learn everything I needed to work as a nurse, and Carlotta's health problems had kept me busy. "You probably had Massimo and Alessio give you updates about my love life anyway, so you could fly in and ruin it if you felt like it."

"I'm not a good guy. I'm a very, very bad guy, trying to be a slightly less bad version of myself. Letting the girl that I want more than anything in the world see other guys isn't part of my self-improvement strategy, I'm afraid. So yes, if I'd found out a guy would have made a move on you, I would have made sure he regretted it."

I wasn't really surprised. I wasn't even as annoyed as I should have been. Part of me loved Nevio exactly for that reason, no matter how crazy it sounded. Maybe it was in my genes. Mom had fallen for Dad, even though she hadn't even grown up in the mafia world, even though she'd known he was bad news and even after he'd killed her father. Falling for bad men seemed my fate. Could you evade fate?

"Battista wants to play in the sand for a bit. I can bring him over once you've changed into dry clothes so you can spend some time with him, if that's part of your self-improvement strategy?" I cocked an eyebrow like he liked to do.

Aside from my anger for how he'd treated me, I was even more furious for how he'd just abandoned Battista, his own son, when he needed him most. I wasn't sure how he ever wanted to make up for it. Battista was still young, not even two years old, so maybe he'd eventually forget that his father had missed so much of his early life.

"I'm going to step up now, Rory. I'm not going to half ass it again. I'm here to stay, here to take responsibility for my son, for you."

"You don't have any responsibility when it comes to me, Nevio. We're not a couple. You left. You moved on." I smiled tensely. "But I'm glad you decided to finally be a father for your son. He deserves a good father."

Battista briefly looked up from the sand, probably because of my tense voice, but after a smile from me, he focused on the sand castle in front of him.

"From what I hear, he has a good mom already," he said, his dark eyes softening.

I swallowed hard. "Someone had to take care of him. He's been abandoned often enough in his short life."

"You didn't have to. You could have handed that responsibility over to my parents. They wouldn't have expected you to help them."

"That responsibility is a little boy who already lost his mother and then his father because they both didn't want him. By the time you left, Battista had formed a bond with me. Handing him to your parents would have been another hard hit in his short life. I couldn't do that. Not before I was sure he wouldn't suffer."

"You still haven't. You're still taking care of him, and Dad said he started calling you Mom."

My heart swelled thinking of it. It had shocked me to my core when Battista had called me Mom one morning when he'd woken beside me in bed, and he'd kept doing it ever since. "I didn't make him. He just started it."

"Because you act like a mom should."

I didn't say anything to that. I felt like Battista's mom, which was strange because I'd really never intended to let it happen. What had been meant as a temporary solution, had turned into something I didn't want to lose. Battista had become part of my life. I supposed that what he and his father had in common. They'd both wormed their way into my heart and simply wouldn't leave.

He motioned at my clothes. "You even wear matching outfits." Battista and I both wore short denim overalls, which had happened by accident.

"When you bring Battista over, I thought we three could spend some time together," Nevio said.

My first instinct was to say no. I didn't want to spend time with Nevio. But I was also worried about how Battista would react to Nevio trying to spend time with him, so I nodded. I squared my shoulders and narrowed my eyes. "Battista was left twice. Once by his birth mother and once by you. I hope you're one-hundred percent sure that you've come to stay and not run off again, because I'm sick of picking up the pieces after you. I don't want Battista to get to know you again, to spend time with you again, only to have that taken from him yet again."

Nevio gave me a strange smile. "This is exactly why I won't stop until you're mine, why I left Battista in your care. There's no better person in this rotten world than you." He kissed my cheek, startling me. "I won't run. I'll stay, because of Battista, because of you." He pulled back. I took a few steps back and cleared my throat. "You should probably go inside before you catch a cold, and I'm sure your family wants to talk to you."

"Except for Dad, no one knows I'm back, and he only found out last night when he ran across me in the common room. But I'll give you some time to yourself now." He headed for the patio and disappeared inside. I let out a shaky breath and walked over to Battista. He showed me what he'd build so far, and I smiled in response, even if it cost me. My thoughts were a mess. I needed time to wrap my mind around it.

Nevio

My decision to return home had been spontaneous. I'd felt ready for a few weeks, but then one day I'd simply known it was time. I was still a messed-up motherfucker, but I felt like I wasn't haunted by this irresistible urge to kill anymore. I felt more centered.

Twenty-four hours after my decision, I had already been on a plane back home. I hadn't told anyone, except for a text to Alvize before I'd boarded.

When I entered the code to the Falcone mansion after midnight, I felt a sense of belonging that I hadn't in a long time. This house and city were my home. I'd missed both, but especially the people who made this place special. My family and Aurora of course.

The house was silent when I stepped inside and made my way into the common room.

I sank down on the comfy couch and crossed my arms behind my head, letting out a sigh. Fuck, this felt right.

Steps sounded. Heavy, male steps.

"You better be a burglar because if this is who I think it is, I'm going to have to kick his ass for another solo run," Dad muttered.

I opened my eyes with a tired smile. He towered over me, in pajama bottoms, and with a stern look. But he wasn't really angry. I knew all of his angry expressions, and this wasn't one.

"It's good to be back."

Dad didn't say anything for a while, then asked, "Are you back for good?"

"I am," I said. "This is where I belong."

"Took you a long time to realize it. Your mom will be ecstatic to have you back."

I pushed to my feet. "And you?"

Dad pulled me against him and patted my back hard. "You belong here." He moved back. "I think you know that not everyone is going to be excited about your return."

"Aurora."

"And Fabiano. He's still pissed at you."

"I'll talk to him. I'm sure I can make him see reason."

"You are not the person I'd pick to make someone see reason without torture."

I smirked. "I've gone through some self-improvements."

"I hope those updates are better than the ones on my phone because those are making me murderous."

"I should probably head to bed. I want to beat jet lag and get up early."

Tomorrow would be a busy day, and one with many emotional ups and downs.

I ran a hand through my hair when I entered the mansion after my morning swim, after having met Aurora again.

I hadn't expected to see her yet. It was only seven in the morning. I went into the kitchen for a coffee and a protein shake. Dry clothes could wait.

I hadn't even finished my first coffee when Mom's voice made me jump.

"Nevio!" I turned, only for her to fall into my arms and hug me tightly. I rested my chin on Mom's head and waited for her to calm. When she pulled back, she slapped my chest hard. "Don't you dare leave again."

"I won't."

She looked down at her now wet bathrobe, then up at me. "You're dripping water all over the floor."

"I missed your early morning nagging the most."

She slapped my chest again. "Get out of your shirt at least, if you don't want to go up and change."

I pulled my shirt up over my head and draped it over a chair. Mom's eyes immediately registered the tattoo on my chest.

"What—" She went silent as realization settled on her face. "You have a lot of work ahead of you if you want to win her over."

"I know."

The door banged open again, and Alessio and Massimo walked in. They both noticed the tattoo of course.

"Back to cause trouble, I see," Alessio said with a shake of his head and clapped my hand before he pulled me in for a brief hug. Then it was Massimo's turn. His expression remained tight. I supposed the thing with Carlotta troubled him.

"Good work," he said. "Even Dad couldn't have done a better job."

"I would have tried to talk him out of this emotional display," Nino said as he came in followed by Kiara. My return must have made the rounds.

"You have emotional tattoos," I reminded him, which he pointedly ignored.

"You didn't stop him when he disfigured his privates with a bull," Gemma muttered from the doorway with a head toss toward Savio behind her.

Fuck, how I missed the Falcone banter. Always a little too honest. With a howl, Giulio barreled into the kitchen and flung himself at me. I grunted from the impact and chuckled at his excitement. The little shit drove me up the walls more often than not, but he was my favorite to do so. "You missed your favorite prank victim, I see."

He grinned up at me. I'd probably fall victim to him often in the next few days.

Being reunited with my family made me realize why I'd often felt this hollowness in my chest while I'd been away. It was almost gone now, and what remained could only be filled with Aurora and Battista.

Chapter Forty

Aurora

After his midday nap, I cuddled longer than usual with Battista. Maybe I was overreacting, but I was really worried the Falcones would decide to take him from me so he could live under the same roof with Nevio. Eventually, I couldn't postpone Nevio meeting his son anymore, and deep down, I knew it was the only right thing to do, to give these two a chance to form a bond. So far in his short life, Battista had spent hardly any time with his father, and I really hoped it would change now. Dad was such an important part of my life. I couldn't imagine being without him.

Battista was good on his feet, so he and I walked over to the Falcone mansion, his small hand secured in mine. My stomach coiled tightly when I slipped through the open French windows into the common room where Nevio waited for us. He sat on the sofa, bent forward, his arms propped up on his thighs, looking thoughtful. This side of Nevio was new and surprising. I really hope it meant he'd grown up.

He looked up and smiled a honest smile, then pushed to his feet. "Hey, Battista."

Battista didn't remember him, which wasn't surprising as he'd only spent very little time with Nevio in his life and hadn't seen him in a while. At Nevio's attention, Battista pressed himself against me and tugged at my clothes, his request to be picked up. I bent down and lifted him into my arms. He pressed his cheek against my chest and regarded Nevio from there.

Nevio didn't try to approach us. "You don't remember me, right?"

Battista only stared. He wasn't a talker, could only say about twenty words, and never when you expected him to. His motor skills were definitely his strength.

I wasn't exactly sure what to say. Should I introduce Nevio as his father, or would that confuse Battista at this point and make everything worse? I'd often told him stories about his dad, that he had to leave for a while—something I'd always hoped—to be a hero. A white lie because Battista needed a hero in his life, even if Nevio hadn't gone to fight for a good cause. He'd gone to help the Camorra in Italy. He'd also run, but Battista didn't need to know that.

Nevio motioned at something beside the armrest of the sofa, a ride-on car that looked a bit like his Ram. "I hope you like trucks."

Battista lifted his head off my shoulder, definitely interested. "He loves cars, and diggers, tractors, forklifts, trucks…" I grinned down at Battista. I would have never thought I'd ever spend so much time looking at images of construction vehicles and dinosaurs…

When I looked up, I caught Nevio staring at me.

"Do you want to ride it?" he asked after a moment.

Battista gave a small nod, so I put him down on the ground. He grabbed my hand and tugged me toward the car. Once there, he mounted it and started racing through the living room with it. He bumped against pretty much every piece of furniture, but that only seemed to make him happier, judging by his boisterous laughter.

"That reminds me of you as a little boy," Serafina said from the doorway.

By Frenzy I Pain

I hadn't noticed her before. She leaned against the doorframe with a soft smile as she watched Battista race around. She wore a long flowy dress that hid her bloated belly. She had started taking hormones so she could eventually carry Greta's babies for her.

"You never had this angelic smile on your face when I barreled into furniture." Nevio scoffed.

"It's different," she said with a shrug, and her eyes caught mine. I could tell that she felt as emotional as I did. Serafina and Remo had stepped up as family for Battista from the moment they'd found out about him. They'd supported me without hesitation. Remo appeared behind his wife and also watched the scene unfolding in the living room. I wondered if they expected me to leave so the four of them could share a moment. I wasn't part of the Falcone clan, but I couldn't leave Battista.

He took a turn around the sofa too sharply and toppled over with the ride-on car so his forehead bumped against a leg of the side table. He immediately burst into tears, his eyes seeking mine. "Mom! Mom!"

I rushed over to him and knelt beside him. I picked him up and blew on the already forming bruise. It wasn't too bad, more of a shock than anything else, but I kept blowing until his cries eased and he only sniffed, already giving the ride-on car a side-eye. "Ready to try again?" I asked with a laugh.

He nodded enthusiastically, so I helped him right the ride-on car and settle on it. Nevio came a bit closer and cheered Battista on, who visibly relaxed over time.

"I'll prepare snacks for Battista," Serafina said with a smile at me. Did she want me to join her so Nevio could be alone with Battista?

I nodded. "I'll help you."

Remo moved toward Nevio to watch Battista as I headed for Serafina despite my reluctance. It was stupid of me to be this attached. Remo and Serafina, and also Kiara, Nino, Gemma, and Savio had watched Battista without me before. Even Massimo and Alessio had on occasion kept an eye on Battista for a short time.

"Mom!" Battista called.

I turned. He'd stopped racing and watched me leave with big eyes. "No go!"

I raised my arms in surrender, relief surging through me. "I'll stay."

"I'll help Fina," Remo said and walked out with her. I focused on Battista, not Nevio, still unsure what I felt about his return. I was glad for the constant visits of other Falcones, especially when Massimo and Alessio showed up and settled on the sofa to play blocks with Battista. It prevented Nevio and me from having another private conversation.

Battista didn't leave my side while he and I spent a few hours with Nevio. Serafina and Remo came in twice more to check on us, obviously curious how things were going, and Kiara brought us cookies after Battista had finished his fruit and vegetable platter.

I wondered if Nevio being back meant his family would insist on Battista moving into the Falcone mansion. I couldn't imagine being separated from him, but what could I really do if they decided that was what should happen.

Serafina

What my daughter Greta so desperately wanted—a child—had been thrown into Nevio's lap, but he hadn't been willing and able to accept the responsibility that came with it.

Seeing him trying to form a bond with his son, who didn't even remember him anymore, tore at my heart. I still wasn't sure he was ready for the task, that he was 100 percent willing to do what needed to be done to be a father. Sacrifice and thoughtfulness came with the task.

I still wanted to protect Nevio. He was my son, and I would always feel a deep sense of motherly protectiveness for him. But I felt even more protective of Battista because he needed my protection more than his father did, because he was helpless and in need of love. I worried that Nevio felt that I wasn't on his side, which wasn't true, because deep down, I knew that one day he'd realize protecting his son was also protecting him from a world of guilt and regret.

It was an hour past Battista's bedtime when I went over to the Scuderi mansion. I'd seen worry and fear in Aurora's eyes tonight. Through the patio door, I could see Leona sitting in a silk dressing gown at the dining room table, bowed over paperwork. I knocked at the French window,

By Frenzy I *Rain*

and she looked up disoriented. When she spotted me, she got up with a worried expression and opened the door for me. "Hey Fina, what's up?"

"I'd like to have a word with Aurora, if she's awake?"

Leona regarded me with growing concern and the protectiveness I knew too well. "Battista took a long time to fall asleep tonight. She's on the treadmill now. Today was a lot to take in for Battista and for Aurora. She's been giving everything for this boy since day one."

I smiled understandingly. "I'm not here to take anything from Aurora. She's like his mother, and nothing in this world would ever make me separate a child from a loving mother."

Leona nodded and finally stepped back, allowing me to enter. We had been friends for a long time, and I didn't blame her one bit for how she'd just acted. I would have done the same, and I appreciated her even more for it.

"Is Fabiano still working?" I asked. He had been gone all day, which was probably for the best, considering his fury toward Nevio, but eventually, those two would have to settle their disagreement.

She let out a sigh. "He's not ready to come home, knowing that Nevio is here. He's holding a grudge."

We both knew that was the understatement of the year. Fabiano was furious, and if Nevio wasn't Remo's son, I was sure he would have tried to kill him. Aurora hadn't given us any details, but we all realized that something had happened between Nevio and her, and it was pretty clear that Nevio had broken her heart. Again, I couldn't blame Fabiano for feeling murderous. If someone had broken Greta's heart... I would have become a fire-spitting dragon.

And I liked Aurora. Scratch that, I adored her. She was kind and tough, and responsible despite her young age. She was someone I wished at Nevio's side. I wasn't sure I wished it on her to be with him, though. I loved my son, but I wasn't blind. Aurora deserved better. Had Nevio changed enough to be deserving of her? Today, he'd tried to bond with Battista, giving Aurora the space she needed. But I wasn't stupid. What happened when those two were alone would determine their chances.

I eventually found Aurora in the gym. She had headphones on, but I could still hear the fast beat of the music as she raced on the treadmill at what must have been full speed. She wasn't working out for the sake of it.

She spotted me, surprise then worry flitting across her red and sweaty face. I waved and smiled, hoping to reassure her I came in peace.

She slowed the treadmill to a stand, then wiped her face and took the headphones off before she stepped down. "Serafina," she said hesitantly. "What's wrong?"

"I want to talk about Battista with you."

I could see her walls coming up, could see her body tensing, her mouth setting in a thin line. She was preparing for a confrontation, and if I'd come here to take him from her, she would have put up a fight. I stifled a smile. She'd really become a true mother to this poor child. My conversation with Kiara rang in my ears, how quickly she had felt like Alessio's mother, and I could tell it was the same for Aurora even if their stories were vastly different. Aurora hadn't been ready for a child. She'd been on the cusp of figuring out her own life, but she'd put it on hold and made Battista the center of her life.

"Nevio wants to be Battista's father. He still has a long road ahead of him. Today proved that. But I want you to know that even if Nevio's bond with his son grows, that doesn't change the fact that you're Battista's mother. Nobody in my family would ever consider taking the boy from you. I want Nevio to see his son, but unless you and him move in together, I would never suggest Battista living with him. The boy should always live with you as he's been doing since Nevio gave him to you. Remo and I agree on this, so please don't worry that anyone's going to doubt your right to this child."

Aurora stared at me and swallowed hard. She gave a terse nod then walked over to a bench and sank down. She buried her face in a towel and her shoulders began to shake as she succumbed to sobs.

I rushed over to her, plopped down beside her and wrapped an arm around her. "I'm sorry that this has been weighing so heavily on you. I thought you knew that Remo would never consider taking Battista from you."

Aurora rubbed her face with the towel then peered up at me with swollen eyes. "He's a Falcone. On paper and by blood."

"And by heart he's yours," I said softly. "I'm gladly his grandmother, even if it's still hard to stomach that I'm old enough to be one."

Especially since I was trying to carry a child for Greta soon.

Aurora laughed along with me. "You don't look it, if that's a consolation."

I sighed. "I know you probably have no reason to believe it, but Nevio loves you. I see it in his eyes, and even if I probably shouldn't talk to you about it, he admitted it to me when he first came back. I know he's more than most can handle. I know he has many faults. I know in many people's eyes, he's beyond redemption, but so was his father. Still is in most people's eyes. I hated him for a while, then hated and loved him, then wanted to hate him, and eventually I just loved him. It hasn't always been easy, but I never regretted becoming Remo's wife, or accepting his love, and who he was and will always be."

"To be honest, I could never understand how you forgave him for kidnapping you."

I laughed. "To be honest, I don't always either, but I did, and not just because of Nevio and Greta. It's hard to explain, but I guess love always is. I know Nevio hurt you too, even if I don't know what exactly he did, and I'm not telling you to forgive him. I just ask you to listen to your heart. I know you're the person Nevio needs by his side. I know having you and Battista in his life would make it easier for him to become an even better version of himself. But I want you to know that I won't blame you if you won't or can't give him another chance."

I got up and squeezed Aurora's shoulder. "Sleep well." I turned and left. I'd said what I wanted to say, and now things were out of my hand. I wasn't sure if Aurora would give Nevio another chance.

Remo was in bed when I came into the bedroom. His expression tightened with concern upon seeing me. "I hope Nevio didn't do anything to cause this look."

He was angry. He'd never understood why Nevio had left. For him, Nevio should have fought harder to maintain control and taken responsibility. Seeing how wary Battista was of Nevio had awakened his anger again.

"I talked to Aurora."

"I hope you didn't try to talk her into forgiving our son. Because I'm not sure he won't fuck up again."

I gave him a stern look as I changed into my nightgown. "He won't,

Remo. I talked to him. He's determined to win her back, to be a father for Battista, to take over more responsibilities in the Camorra."

"Just took him a year. A year he won't get back with his son. I always regretted not getting to experience many first with the twins, and he just threw the chance away."

"He did, but I think he did it out of responsibility. He knew he was on the verge of something bad and didn't want Battista and Aurora to be affected by it."

"He and I, all of us Falcone men are always potentially on the verge of something bad. It's in our blood, in our nature. He can't always run. He'll have to face his demons and shackle them."

Chapter Forty-One

Fabiano

After I was done with two high-profile debtors in the early afternoon, I called Diego to tell him I'd take over a few of his customers. He was glad for the free time that gave him so he could visit his sister. I couldn't return home right now, knowing that Nevio was back, that it would be so easy to kick his sorry ass. I needed more time, and I needed to get rid of some of the violence that filled every fiber of my being.

I sent Leona a short message so she wouldn't worry, though she probably would anyway, then I drove to the first address that Diego had given me.

I hardly felt less violent when I eventually entered our mansion shortly before midnight. Leona had fallen asleep at the kitchen table with her head on her work folders. Her maroon hair was a mess, having fallen out of her ponytail. A pen was still clutched in her fingers. I gently pried it from them then lifted her in her arms. She stirred but I shushed her and carried her upstairs. After I'd put her down on our bed, I went to pull the curtains shut but spotted light in the former ballet studio on the Falcone premises.

Nevio, no doubt. I jerked the curtains shut and stormed out.

"Fabiano?" Leona called drowsily but I didn't stop.

When I reached the ballet studio and ripped open the door, it wasn't only Nevio who was inside. Of course not. The Unholy Trinity was finally reunited and was up to no good again. They sat on the ground. Alessio was smoking a cigarette while Nevio and Massimo drank beer.

"Fabiano," Nevio said with a tight smile. His eyes were vigilant. Seeing him back in this place, already looking as if he had never been gone in the first place only multiplied my anger.

"I hope you're not drunk. Kicking your ass will be less fun if you're inebriated."

Massimo put down his beer and got up, opening his arms in a disarming gesture. "Fabiano, this is something Aurora and Nevio have to settle."

"Don't interfere. This isn't your business."

"You two can leave. Fabiano and I will talk about this like adults," Nevio said as he put down his beer and rose to his feet too.

"Now you're trying to be the reasonable adult?" I growled.

Alessio and Massimo left the studio. I hoped they wouldn't run off to their father.

Nevio pushed his hands into his pockets. I stalked toward him, but he remained like that, as if he didn't have a fucking care in the world.

"The only reason I'm not killing you is that you have a son who needs you, if only to show him how not to behave, and because I'm loyal to your father."

Nevio nodded, and smiled tensely. "The reason you won't kill me is because I won't let you."

Wrong thing to say. I smashed my fist against Nevio's chin. His restrained demeanor vaporized like I knew it would. It felt good to kick his ass. I wasn't sure how much time passed before Leona's voice rang out and then strong arms wrapped around my chest and dragged me back, while Alessio did the same with Nevio. Nevio was bleeding from his nose and a cut in his hairline. My mouth quickly filled with blood too and every inch of my body felt bruised. I definitely had a one or two broken ribs, and I hoped it was the same for Nevio.

"What's wrong with you?" Leona seethed as she stepped between us, still in her dressing gown.

"The list is long. Even if he likes to think otherwise, Fabiano is a messed up killer like myself," Nevio said, wiping his forearm across his nose and smearing blood across his cheek.

"So that's what this was? You were trying to kill each other?" she asked, her wide eyes darting between Nevio and me.

"If they were intent on killing each other, they would have pulled their knives," Massimo said with a nod toward Nevio's knife at his hip. I had briefly considered pulling my knife. But if I'd done it, I might have taken something from Aurora I had no right to take. She had to settle things with Nevio, as Leona never grew tired to emphasize. Plus I honestly wasn't sure I could beat Nevio. I'd probably die in an escalating fight too, and I couldn't do that to Leona and my children. I'd once made Leona watch a death fight and she'd often told me how terrified she'd been.

"I still need to talk to him," I said, then spit some blood on the floor.

Leona shook her head. "I won't let you two alone. This is madness."

"We won't fight again," Nevio said firmly. "But Fabiano is right, we need to talk."

"We'll stay in front of the door," Leona said, giving me a warning look. She, Massimo and Alessio left the room and closed the glass door.

"So now let's chat," I said.

Nevio nodded. Blood had started flowing out of his nose again, and my mouth was filled too. I spit out once more.

"What are your intentions toward Aurora and Battista?"

I didn't only feel protective of Aurora, I also cared about the little boy who had lived under my roof for almost a year.

"I want to be a decent father for Battista. I want to make up for the lost time, and I want to prove to Aurora that I deserve her. I want to be with her. I want everyone to know that she's mine."

"And that you're hers. I won't watch you cheat on my daughter."

"I have been hers for a while." He lifted his shirt, revealing a tattoo I had trouble figuring out in the dim light but then I realized what I was seeing. The aurora borealis right over Nevio's heart.

"Grand gestures are fair enough, especially to impress a woman, but they don't mean anything if your actions don't match."

He lowered his shirt with an acknowledging nod. "I know and my actions will show the truth behind the gesture and the words."

"Has Aurora seen the tattoo yet?"

"No. There wasn't the right moment yet."

I'd known Nevio all his life and found many of his antics amusing. He'd reminded me of Remo when I first met him, and even the recklessness of my younger self. Remo and I had grown up. I wanted to give Nevio the benefit of the doubt, that he too had grown up enough to make up for his past fuckups.

Nevio stepped close, his expression serious, no sign of the trademark smirk. "I'm serious about Aurora. I'll stop at nothing to prove to her that I'm ready to commit, that I want her and no one else."

"You better succeed. If you mess up again, I can't promise you I won't try to kill you, even if it means we'll both die."

"If I fuck up again, my parents will be the first to kill me. They love Aurora."

"Do you?" I asked. I wasn't sure if Nevio was capable of love, but I'd thought the same about Nino and Remo, and both had proven me wrong.

His expression was hard. "I think I've said enough. The rest is only for Aurora's ears. I respect you Fabiano, but that doesn't mean I'll pour my heart out to you."

"I'm still not convinced you have one," I said but most of my anger was gone.

"For a long time, I wasn't either."

Chapter Forty-Two

Aurora

My mouth parted in surprise upon seeing Dad's face when I entered the kitchen. He sat at the kitchen table and was sipping his coffee with a swollen lower lip. A bruise bloomed on his temple and his stiff movements suggested he had more injuries.

Mom's annoyed expression told me she wasn't impressed.

"Do you need me to check your injuries?" I asked, ready to hand Battista over to Mom.

"I'm fine," Dad said.

"Sure." I grabbed a cup of coffee for me and sank down beside Mom. "Let me guess, you met Nevio. Is he alright?"

Dad shook his head with a scowl. "Glad you're concerned about his health."

"I'm concerned about yours too, but I can see you're not seriously injured."

Dad's mood lifted obviously. "So you think I kicked his ass?"

I doubted Dad could beat Nevio in a fight, but I kept my thoughts to myself.

Mom huffed and set down her cup with force. "Alessio and Massimo had to separate them."

"You don't need to punish Nevio on my behalf, Dad. I can handle him, okay?"

I took a few pancakes from the stack in the middle and put one on Battista's plate with some fresh berries and yogurt.

"Can I kick his ass too?" Davide asked from the doorway where I hadn't noticed him before. He had begun styling his blond hair with gel, which always made him late for everything.

"He'll wipe the floor with you," I muttered.

"She's right. You still need to improve your fighting skills if you want to be a match for Nevio," Dad said.

Mom sighed. "Can we not talk about violence at the breakfast table?"

Dad and Davide exchanged a look. They'd probably go to the gym for fight training later. Dad probably should have taken the day off, considering his injuries, but it would have been futile to tell him that.

I didn't have to work today, so I wanted to enjoy the warm weather at the pool. After breakfast, I changed into a bikini, then covered myself with a pink beach dress before I dressed Battista in his cute shark swim trunks and headed out.

Battista's hand in mine, I went over to the pool—he loved our almost daily swims—but I froze when I saw Nevio, Alessio, and Massimo in the water. I let out a small sigh. If I turned on my heel now and returned inside like I wanted to do to avoid Nevio, Battista would throw a fit. He was currently discovering his emotions and had tantrums over the smallest things, like a banana cut the wrong way or picking the wrong color for his spoon. Canceling our swim would equal a screaming rage.

Squaring my shoulders, I kept on walking to the pool. I wouldn't allow Nevio's return to mess up my life. It had taken considerable effort to build up a routine and figure out my life when he left me with his child.

His back was to me, presenting the twisted Joker smile that still gave me the creeps. His tally list hadn't grown, which surprised me. From what I'd read in the news about the mob wars in Italy and what I'd overheard

By Frenzy I *Rain*

Dad and the Falcones discuss, the death toll had been great. I didn't believe for one second that Nevio hadn't been responsible for quite a few of those kills himself. Maybe he'd waited to be back home so Nino could ink him. Eventually, the space on his back would run out, though.

Massimo nudged his chin in my direction and said something to Nevio, who turned halfway.

His expression was hard to read, almost anxious. It wasn't a look you saw often on his face. Alessio clapped Nevio's shoulder, and they both left. I almost called for them to return. Had I looked like I wanted alone time with Nevio?

It was too late. They were already on their way to the mansion. I gave Nevio a tight smile and focused on putting water wings on Battista. I stayed in my beach dress for the time being, not wanting to expose myself in front of Nevio. He'd seen it all. Hell, he'd been inside me with his fingers, tongue, cock, and even knife. Still, he felt like a stranger after our time apart. I had changed, and from the little glimpses of him that I'd gotten, he had too. I wasn't sure yet if it was for the better.

I set Battista down, and he stormed toward the shallow part of the pool to play with his toys. Nevio headed over to me. "I can go into the pool with Battista if you want to sunbathe for a bit."

My attention was on the tattoo on his chest, and he allowed me to get a good look as he waited in front of me silently. It took me a while to figure out what I was seeing, and even then, I still had trouble believing it. The northern lights. Aurora borealis.

My heart picked up its pace, and my throat became tight, unwanted reactions I wanted to suppress.

Nevio followed my gaze, then tilted his head up to regard me with intensity. "You know what that is?"

"A beautiful phenomenon?" I didn't want to consider why he'd tattooed said phenomenon I was named after on his chest.

"I couldn't have said it better," he said in a low voice that raised goose bumps all over my body.

"Did you visit them while you spent time abroad?" My voice was strangely scratchy. Nevio wasn't the type to get tattoos of pretty travel destinations.

He shook his head, his intense gaze still on me. "No. And if I ever do, the woman who inspired this tattoo will be with me."

"Maybe I'll meet her one day," I said.

He smiled strangely and moved even closer. My eyes darted to Battista, who sat on his bum and played calmly. Why couldn't he cause trouble when I needed him to?

"You know this tattoo represents you," he said. He was close enough that I could have touched the vibrant swirls of the northern lights on his chest. The tattoo on his chest was even more beautiful this close-up. I'd never seen a more beautiful color scheme for the lights before. Then my eyes caught on something on his wrist, a red B tattoo. I swallowed hard.

He turned his arm, showing me the tattoo. "Once I know Battista better, I want to add details representing him."

I swallowed. "It's not as easy as getting a tattoo. You ran because you were scared of the responsibility. Now you have to prove yourself."

"I wasn't scared of the responsibilities, Rory. I was fucking scared of myself, or what I was capable of."

I searched his face. Everything about him was honest. "Then running away didn't really make sense, did it? You can't run away from yourself, and looking at the headlines in Italy, you kept going there where you left off here."

"I knew I couldn't run from myself. That wasn't the point."

"What was it then?" I had trouble keeping my voice down and even. I didn't want Battista to pick up on the tension between his father and me.

"The point was that I left the people behind that I wanted to protect from myself. I didn't care about the collateral damage I left behind in Campania."

"So killing more people without any responsibilities in Campania made you change?" I asked doubtfully. It seemed he'd fed his demons, not starved them.

He shook his head slowly and tugged down his swim trunks a few inches. I tensed. "I just wanted to show you something."

I remained wary until two angry red, round scars beside his hip bone and over his pubic bone came into view.

"Almost dying changed me. I was hit by two bullets about a month ago. They got me good, and I almost bled out before I reached the hospital."

"How come your father didn't tell anyone?" Or did they just keep it from me?

"He doesn't know. Nobody does. Alvize was too scared of Dad's reaction, so he was happy to keep it a secret when I asked him. When I lay there in my own blood, I realized that I'd missed so many opportunities, not to kill and torture, but to spend time with you and Battista, to show you what you mean to me, and I realized I needed to go home to you and my family."

I licked my lips nervously. His words hit me right in the feels, but I didn't want to dissolve into an emotional puddle.

Nevio pointed at the lights tattoo then at the B. "I didn't get these tattoos to impress you and make you forgive me. I got them because they were my only way to take you and Battista with me safely. To remind me of why I was trying to get my demons under control."

Battista waited beside the pool, watching us expectantly. I was glad for his presence, for the distraction it offered, because part of me wanted to sink into Nevio's strong arms after his words.

Nevio leaned closer. "If I could have tattooed you onto my heart, I would have done it. I would have cut open my own rib cage so the tattooist could reach it," he murmured, then pulled back and moved over to Battista, leaving me there to catch my breath.

"Do you need my help with the water wings, buddy?" Nevio asked as he squatted beside Battista, who sent me a questioning look. He'd removed his water wings as he often did. I gave him a smile then nodded, and he handed Nevio his water wings in reply. I turned my back on them, trying to calm my racing heart.

I didn't have any tattoos of Nevio or Battista on my skin, but I carried them with me anyway.

"I'll catch you, don't worry," Nevio said, followed by a loud splash and Battista's high-pitched laughter.

I glanced over my shoulder. I never allowed Battista to jump into the pool. All the men in the Falcone and Scuderi household always joked I was hovering too much like a mother hen. My first instinct was to say something to Nevio, to make my standpoint on water safety clear, but Battista was his son, and if he really wanted to step up and be a real dad, I needed to give him room to do so.

I sank down on the sun lounger and watched them play wildly in the water. They seemed to enjoy the same boisterous activities.

Nevio's words kept replaying in my head. I'd sworn I wouldn't forgive him. But thinking about how he'd almost died, my throat felt tight. I didn't want to live without him. That didn't mean I would forgive him easily, but I would give him a chance to prove himself one last time.

Nevio

Patience wasn't my strong suit, and it would never be. I burned up with desire for Aurora, wanted nothing more than to bury myself in her again, but she wanted to see if I was really willing to commit, and jumping her like a randy teenager even if I felt like one, wouldn't get the right message across. I'd just have to live with my blue balls for a while longer.

I allowed her a few days to come to terms with my return and used the time to resume my position in the Camorra, and prove to Dad that I was up for whatever task he had in mind for me. I spent time with Battista every day, first under Aurora's watchful eyes—she obviously didn't trust me with him yet, but today I got the chance to be with him on my own for the first time. Aurora had to work in our hospital, where she'd started her training as a nurse. I was glad she had chosen to stay within our world and not start college for a nursing degree.

"Are you sure you'll be fine?" she'd asked around a half dozen times before she'd finally left me with Battista.

I was nervous. It wasn't as if I didn't have experience being around small children. I'd watched my nieces Luna and Caterina, and my brother Giulio as toddlers all the time, but I'd never babysat them. I suppose Mom and Dad, and Savio and Gemma had never considered me a valid option. Not that I had ever wanted to be a babysitter. And now I sat on the floor beside my almost eighteen-months-old son and played with toy fire trucks and tractors.

I staged a crash between two tractors with plenty of sound effects, causing Battista to giggle before he became serious as he rolled the fire trucks toward the crash scene.

"Have you ever ridden in a fire truck?" I asked.

Battista looked up from the toy cars curiously. I wasn't sure if he understood what I meant. He was probably still too young to get it. "Do you want to ride in a fire truck?" I asked instead.

He nodded enthusiastically. That was enough for me, even if I still wasn't sure he got what I meant.

I pulled out my phone and called the fire department. At first, they thought I was a prank caller. I had to repeat my name several times before I was told I could come over. I stood and held out my hand. "Come on, let's go ride a fire truck."

Battista looked up from his toys then he stumbled to his feet, one truck under his arm.

I grabbed my car keys on the way out, then paused because I almost forgot the child seat. After I'd taken the child seat from Mom's car and put it in mine, Battista and I could finally head out.

We were on the road for fifteen minutes when Battista signaled that he was hungry and thirsty. Of course, I hadn't packed anything. I hadn't even thought of packing his diaper bag. Grimacing, I headed toward Whole Foods because that was what Aurora would have wanted, so I bought Battista some watermelon, fruit pouches, a bottle of water, and a cheese sandwich.

Ten minutes later, Battista was satisfied, and his clothes ruined with watermelon juice, blackberry stains, and bread crumbs. Half of the water had soaked my shirt too. "All right. I suppose we need to go clothes shopping."

I sent Aurora a photo of Battista and asked where I could buy clothes for him.

She called immediately. "Is that blood?"

I rolled my eyes. "It's watermelon and blackberry."

"Oh," she said, sounding embarrassed.

"I know I've been a horrible father so far but do you really think I'd get Battista covered in blood the first time I watch him alone?"

She cleared her throat. "There are spare clothes in his diaper bag. And why aren't you home?"

The worry in her voice was unmistakable. "I forgot the bag, and we're heading to the fire department to watch and ride the fire trucks."

Silence on the other end. I could imagine the concern on Aurora's face. I supposed that wasn't something she would have done with Battista. "Well, then you'll have to buy clothes I suppose, also a sun cap, sun screen, diapers, rash cream…" She trailed off. "The sirens might be too loud for Battista so they can't turn them on."

"Where's the fun in that?"

"His ears are sensitive."

"All right, Rory. I'll make sure Battista will be in one piece when you come home tonight. Don't worry."

"Nevio, do you really think that's a good idea. You could go to a playground with him. There's one—"

"It'll be fine," I said, then hung up. Rory needed to see that I didn't do things like her but that I could still do them well.

After a quick visit to two more shops to buy everything Rory had said plus ear protectors, Battista and I finally arrived in front of the fire department.

"We're here, buddy," I said, turning around in my seat, only to find Battista fast asleep. A glance at the clock in my dashboard showed it was his nap time.

I put my head against the backrest with a chuckle. My phone vibrated in my pocket. It was Mom. Before she could say anything, I said, "Has Aurora set you up to this? Battista is fine."

Mom let out a laugh. "Okay. But if you need anything, call me."

"I'll be fine!" I muttered. Fuck. Next Dad would probably show up here to help.

"Have fun," Mom said with a hint of amusement.

I grabbed a fruit pouch and emptied it then ate the second half of Battista's sandwich. I'd forgotten to grab food for myself.

"Wow," from the back seat made me turn around. Battista stared out of the window at the fire department with huge eyes. Two fire trucks were parked in the huge entry.

I got out and grabbed Battista. One of the fire fighters was an illegitimate son of a Camorrista. He was the one who showed Battista and me the fire truck. I took a few photos of Battista behind the steering wheel, then sent them to Aurora, before we headed out with the truck with blaring sirens. Battista sat on my lap and clapped excitedly.

Thanks to the ear protectors, Battista could listen to the sirens safely and had the time of his young life. And I had to admit, I had fun too. I'd thought spending time with a young kid would be boring as fuck but there were lots of fun things to do, and seeing him so excited was a bonus. I sent Aurora a video of Battista screaming in delight as we drove around with the sirens.

She sent back a thumbs-up smiley, which was a fucking let down. Maybe she still disapproved of me doing this, but I wasn't going to do boring ass shit all of a sudden. This was my kid and if he was anything like me, he'd soon want to do crazy stuff like riding fire trucks on a whim.

When we returned home in the later afternoon after a quick stop at Shake Shack to grab a burger and some fries, Battista looked ready to fall asleep. And I felt tired too.

"Don't tell your mom about the fries," I told Battista with a wink when I picked him up. Though, considering he smelled as if he'd fallen into a bucket full of fries, it would be difficult to keep it a secret. I didn't dare giving him a bath without help.

Mom sat in the common room at the sewing machine. She'd taken up sewing a couple of years back after Gemma had shown her how to do it, and now she sewed most of her dresses herself, and sometimes did custom pieces for the women in our family.

She held up a onesie with small fire trucks all over it.

Battista rushed over to her with a big grin and she hugged him tightly. "I smell fries."

I shook my head. "Can you help me bathe him before Aurora returns?"

"She won't be mad that you gave him fast food."

"At the moment she likes to be mad at me," I said.

Mom didn't say anything but her expression told me she was on Aurora's side in this. But she helped me give Battista a quick bath before I settled on my bed with Battista to read him a book.

I wanted to show Aurora that I was ready to take responsibility, and I felt like I had done that today even if she didn't approve of my methods. Fuck, I hoped Aurora would see it too.

Chapter Forty-Three

Aurora

GIOELE, THE NEWEST DOCTOR WHO WORKED FOR THE Camorra, dropped me off in front of my home. He'd done so a few times because it was on his way and I didn't want Dad to pick me up like a little kid all the time.

The moment I was inside, I searched for Battista and Nevio, but they weren't there. Maybe they were still at the Falcones, so I headed there. I was practically living there too.

Nevio wasn't in the living room, though. Serafina was there, bent over her sewing machine with a look of concentration. She was working on a skirt and was busy attaching lace to the hemline. She always created beautiful boho-style clothes. Maybe if I ever married, I'd ask her to sew a dress for me.

"Where's Nevio?"

"He and Battista are in Nevio's bedroom because Battista was tired."

I frowned. "Is everything okay?" It was still early for Battista to go to bed.

Serafina gave me an understanding smile. "It was an exciting day, for both of them."

I nodded. "Can I go there?"

"This is practically your home too."

I bit my lip. Despite spending so much time over here with Battista, I didn't dare go into Remo's wing without permission.

When I knocked at Nevio's door a little later, nobody answered. Worried, I opened the door and froze.

Nevio was stretched out on his bed with Battista cuddled up against his side, one small arm thrown over Nevio's chest. A book rested on Nevio's stomach, and one of his arms was curled around Battista protectively. His eyes peeled open when I stepped inside. I gave him a small smile, feeling guilty for having been so worried, but given Nevio's past escapades, I couldn't help it.

Nevio extracted himself from Battista and got up. We went into the hallway. Nevio's hair was tousled. "Do you want to check on him to see if he's got a pulse?" he asked with a sarcastic twist of his mouth.

I flushed. "This was your first time being alone with him, and you chose to make a whole trip out of it, of course I was worried."

"Everything went well."

"Except for the ruined clothes, the missing diapers, the lack of healthy snacks, and the ruined bedtime routine."

He took a step closer, backing me into the wall. "Except for that, yes," he said in a low voice. "But I doubt Battista cared about any of those things. He won't remember that I forgot to pack his bag, he'll remember riding a fucking fire truck and having a great time with me."

To my surprise, I detected a hint of hurt in Nevio's eyes.

"You're right," I admitted grudgingly. "But being a parent isn't only about doing the fun things."

"Fuck, Rory. I know, and I'm doing my best. Maybe it's not up to your high standards yet, and maybe it won't ever be, but I won't ever be like you. I'll always only be the father I can be. Maybe I won't do things how you would have done them, but that doesn't mean I'll do a bad job."

"Battista looked happy on the pics you sent me. Thanks for thinking of me," I said as a sort of peace offering. Actually saying I'm sorry to Nevio wasn't an option at the current time.

His eyes seemed to grab me by the throat. "I always do."

I looked away, clearing my throat.

Nevio's gaze traveled along my body. "I like you in scrubs. They look sexy on you."

I shrugged, pretending not to care even as my body heated. "They're functional." I slipped away to bring more distance between us. "I need to figure out a way to get him into his bed."

"I can carry him."

"I need to change him into his pajamas."

"He's actually in his pajamas. I changed him after we arrived."

Surprise washed over me, followed by suspicion. "What did you wash off him?"

Nevio sighed. He grabbed my wrist and tugged me closer. "You're really good at giving me a hard time."

"This isn't me giving you a hard time."

He smirked. "All right then. How about we two go on a date?"

I began to shake my head, but Nevio kept talking. "An innocent date, without any knife play or other kinky stuff. And no other fun activities involving our nether regions either, unless you want to."

"I don't—"

"I washed the smell of fries off him, okay? We had our dinner at Shake Shack, and I forgot to brush his teeth after."

I couldn't help but laugh. "And you think that will make me say yes to a date?"

"I thought honesty would," he said. His smile still promised trouble, and I had serious doubts Nevio would manage a whole date without trying to seduce me, but I felt myself nodding. "Okay, but no funny business."

"We won't have any fun, if that's what you want," he said with a smile.

I sighed. I really hoped I wouldn't regret this.

Nevio carried Battista over to my home. He was so exhausted he didn't even stir when I put him in his bed. I accompanied Nevio downstairs where we met Dad. His expression was furious. "What were you doing upstairs?"

Nevio's answering smirk promised trouble.

"Nevio carried Battista for me," I said quickly before things escalated.

Dad relaxed, but he still fixed Nevio with a hard look. "Did Gioele drive carefully when he brought you home today?"

I pursed my lips. "Of course, why…" Then I got why Dad had mentioned Gioele. Nevio's intense gaze rested on me. I sent Dad a glare before I pushed Nevio outside, away from Dad's provocation.

"Who's Gioele?"

I rolled my eyes. "He's a doctor in the hospital, and he occasionally lets me ride with him so Dad doesn't have to pick me up."

"How nice of him." Nevio's voice was hard, and his eyes promised violence.

"It seems some things haven't changed…"

"I'm still me, Aurora. The murderous asshole you fell for. I haven't turned into a fucking domesticated housecat so if some asshole thinks he can make a move on you, he better know about the consequences. I don't share you."

My heart picked up. "You can't share me because I'm not yours."

He didn't say anything but his face made one thing very clear: I was his.

"Gioele is married, so you don't have to hurt him."

"As if marriage has ever stopped anyone."

"He hasn't done anything, so please stop it!"

"I'll stop it, and I won't even kick his ass if you'll let me pick you up in the future."

"And what if you are busy?"

"Then I'll send someone I trust."

I huffed. I couldn't believe his audacity but at the same time I got a sick thrill out of knowing Nevio was jealous. "We're not dating," I reminded him.

"But I'll do everything in my power to change that. I'll make up for the shit I pulled in the past until I'm worthy of calling you mine."

He turned and stalked off, leaving me with my heart pounding in my chest. Nevio was still as intense as he'd been before he'd left despite the notable changes I couldn't deny. Even if I'd never admit it to him, I was glad he hadn't changed completely. That fact probably made me as crazy as him. Thinking of our upcoming date, my belly fluttered with butterflies. I'd never been on a date. What Nevio and I had done in the past had hardly qualified as one.

Nevio

I picked up Aurora at the hospital the following day. Fabiano had driven her there in the morning. Because I'd had to visit a couple of casinos for the Camorra, Mom had watched Battista until early afternoon, and I'd taken over after that. By now, the little man had gotten used to me, and every moment I spent with him he grew more on me too.

"Gioele wasn't at work today. Not as a doctor at least. He was admitted last night as a patient because apparently someone ran over him with a car."

I bared my teeth. "It's a dangerous world."

Aurora narrowed her eyes. "It was you."

I shrugged. "I'm still me, Rory. I put on my civil mask more often for you, but beneath it, there's still a monster that hungers for blood, especially when men don't keep their distance to you."

Aurora shook her head. "You could have killed him!"

"I ran him over with my car so I wouldn't feel tempted to kill him because if I'd felt his blood on my skin, I would have ripped his heart out."

Aurora blinked and slowly turned around to Battista as if she remembered his presence just now. "Did you have fun today?"

He nodded enthusiastically. His curly dark hair bobbed all over the place.

"He and I took a quick dip in the pool."

Aurora gave me a small smile. I could tell she was still a little pissed, but she knew what she was getting herself into.

"You sure you want low-key?"

I'd given her the choice between fancy and low-key for our date, and of course, Aurora being Aurora had picked the latter.

"Definitely. No dress up or stiff settings."

"Nothing will be stiff, promise," I said with a devilish grin. Aurora sent me a warning look, as if Battista would get my innuendo.

I dropped them off at Fabiano's mansion so Aurora could change out of her scrubs (though I really liked her in them and would have loved to remove them myself) and put Battista to bed before I picked her up for our date.

Two hours later, I rang the bell. Of course, Fabiano opened the door. He barred the doorway with a hard expression, arms crossed in front of his chest. He looked like a bouncer. "I don't think I have to say anything."

"I'll behave and bring her back before curfew," I said in my best everyone's darling voice. "Promise, *Sir*."

"I don't know why an intelligent, nice girl like Aurora picks someone like you," Fabiano muttered.

"Bad boys do it better."

Luckily, Leona and Aurora appeared behind Fabiano at that moment or he would have punched me in the face. And while I was always eager for a bit of sparring, I was really looking forward to my date with Aurora. That alone showed how Aurora had changed me.

Aurora wore a short black overall dress, a white T-shirt beneath, and her favorite white Converse. I smiled. This was Aurora, and I hoped she'd never change.

She tapped Fabiano on the shoulder until he finally stepped back to let her pass. She scanned my shirt with raised eyebrows. I wore a black T-shirt with the KISS band logo, black cargo pants, and black Converse. "Since when do you like KISS?"

"I started listening to them in Italy."

"Be back at ten," Fabiano interrupted us.

"Midnight is good," Leona said.

"I'm of age."

Fabiano scowled at me, not her. "And you live under our roof, so you play by our rules."

Aurora sighed as she followed me to my truck. I touched her lower back, but she moved away so my hand slid off. Fair enough. I still had a lot of work to do before Aurora would forgive me. I led her to my Ram and opened the door for her, then held out my hand to help her climb inside. She took it with a mumbled thanks and got in. The glimpse of her gorgeous legs immediately quickened my pulse, but with the utmost effort, I kept my comments to myself. Aurora wanted the good-boy version of myself today, and I'd try to give him to her.

When I sat behind the steering wheel, I said, "This is my first date."

"I know."

"No," I said firmly. "I've never been on a date with a girl."

Surprise flashed in Aurora's eyes and a small smile played across her face, making her even more gorgeous, and making it ten times harder for me not to lean over and kiss her. "I guess then we need to make it count."

"I'm doing my best," I said as I started the engine and pulled away. In the rearview mirror I could see Fabiano still in the doorway. I had to admit I had been sure he'd put a bullet in my head but that he actually allowed me to take Aurora on a date made me really want to prove to him and everyone else that even if I was fucked up as hell, I had it in me to be what Aurora deserved.

"Where are you taking me?"

"KISS world mini golf."

Aurora laughed. "Really?" Her blue eyes sparkled with amusement. "That's why you're wearing the shirt?"

"Yep. Trying to get in the mood." I let my gaze travel over her. "And I really like that our clothes are matching without even trying."

Her hands rested in her lap and she was playing with her fingers. I put my hand on the center console, palm upward. Usually I would have just taken her hand without asking but I really wanted to give Aurora the time she needed this time even if it went against my nature.

Her gaze darted to my hand but she didn't take it.

Biting back my disappointment, I kept my palm where it was in case Aurora changed her mind.

Aurora's eyes lit up when we entered the KISS-themed miniature golf. It glowed in the dark in neon colors.

"I don't even remember the last time I played miniature golf," she said.

"I think it was about three years ago with Carlotta, Greta, Massimo, Alessio, and me."

She nodded thoughtfully. "Right. Massimo beat all of us, but you came in second."

"Tonight, I'll win."

"We'll see," she said with a smile.

By Frenzy I *Rain*

Aurora let out a sigh when she missed the hole again. The ball had to roll up the red tongue of a Gene Simmons figure, but Aurora either used too much force or too little, and she grew frustrated.

"Let me help?" I stepped up behind her and she gave a small nod. Pressing my front to her back, I put my hands over hers, my arms wrapped around her. "You need the right amount of force," I said close to her ear to be heard over the music. "Not too hard, but not too gentle either."

Aurora shivered in my hold, and then together we moved and hit the ball with the golf club. The ball shot up the red tongue and dropped into the hole.

Aurora beamed. "Let me try it on my own."

I stepped back even if it was the last thing I wanted. Behind us a couple of people were waiting but one look from me and they backed off.

Aurora flushed. "Sorry. Just one more try!"

"Take all the time you need," I said firmly.

But she hit the ball with the right amount of force on the first try this time and hit the hole. She jumped up with a big smile and hugged me. My arms came around her at once, holding her against me. She beamed up at me and then the KISS song came on that had been on repeat in my car when I'd been in Italy.

I was made for loving you.

I leaned down. "Rory, you were made for me, and I was made for you." Our eyes met and Rory swallowed hard. I forced myself to pull away to give her the space she'd requested, then nodded toward the next hole. Aurora followed me without a word as the next song came on.

After that we got In-N-Out burgers and vanilla soft serve and ate it in the car on a hill overlooking Las Vegas. Aurora had requested the spot, and I got why. "Is this low-key enough for you?" I asked once we'd finished the soft serve.

She gave a nod and sank against the seat with a satisfied smile. Fuck, she looked perfect at that moment, especially because of a smudge of ice cream on her cheek. It was so fucking Rory.

I reached over and wiped the ice cream off. "Ready to go home?" It was half past eleven, and I wanted to get Rory back within the time Leona had given. This was a new thing for me, but if this meant Aurora realized I was fucking serious about her, then I'd be the good guy for once.

Surprise flashed in her eyes. A moment of hesitation followed before she said, "Yeah."

I started the engine, and like I'd done on the drive at the beginning of our date, I put my hand in the middle. Rory glanced at it, then put her palm in mine, and I closed my fingers around hers.

Fucking perfection.

Before I dropped her off, I turned to her, our hands still linked. "I don't think I've ever enjoyed a night that didn't involve blood more than tonight."

"I enjoyed our date as well," Aurora admitted.

"So you'll go out with me again?"

"Yes."

"This is probably breaking protocol but I don't care. I need to do this." I tugged her toward me and kissed her, then with a monumental effort, I pulled back.

"Thanks," Aurora said quietly as she stepped up to the front door.

"Thank you for giving me a chance I didn't deserve."

Chapter Forty-Four

Aurora

Nevio had surprised me with our date. He'd nailed it. Maybe some women wanted a fancy restaurant and all that stuff, but for me, low-key made me feel like myself.

Nevio had broken my no physical rule by kissing me, but the kiss had been so sweet and chaste, so un-Nevio-like, that I couldn't even be mad at him, especially because I had almost lost control and deepened the kiss myself.

But this time, I wanted to do things right and not allow my desire for Nevio to overrun everything else.

Nevio and I went on two more dates that he planned, another fun evening at the Play Playground with games for adults like a doctor game, and the second time, he even took me to a museum I'd once mentioned to him, which definitely wasn't his thing.

I appreciated the thoughtfulness of the dates, especially as each one showed that he knew my taste better than I'd ever thought possible.

I decided to organize our fourth date, a movie night at the apartment with homemade tacos and Nevio's favorite sour beer.

"Are you thinking about moving back here?" Nevio asked as we settled on the couch with our tacos. I turned on the TV to watch the horror classic *Nosferatu* that Nevio loved. I wasn't a huge fan of black-and-white movies, but I enjoyed the occasional masterpiece from the past, and this was one of them.

I looked around the small, cozy living room. It had felt good to live here with Carlotta, but with her complicated health situation and me taking care of Battista, it didn't seem clever to move out of my home anytime soon. The support from my parents plus the Falcone clan made daily life with Battista so much easier. Of course, now that Nevio was back, we'd all have to figure out a new routine.

"I don't think so. I wouldn't want to live here alone. I really appreciate everyone's support."

Nevio nodded. He and I sat very close, our shoulders touching. "I could move in with you."

My eyes widened. "You want to move out of the Falcone mansion, away from Alessio and Massimo, to live in this small place? Why?"

His eyes were serious, and it was still strange to see him this responsible and thoughtful. "I'd do it for you. And that way, we could work out how to be a family with Battista."

My throat became tight and my chest felt as if it might splinter from the force of my heartbeat. I cleared my throat, trying to find words. "Shouldn't we figure out how to be a couple before we live together and try to be a family?"

"Aren't we on our way?"

It felt like we were. "It's still too soon to say." I could see the disappointment, maybe even frustration in Nevio's eyes. I understood him. I too wanted to speed up things, to throw myself headfirst into this, but the past had taught me caution, especially when it came to Battista's well-being. "I don't want to give Battista a family he might lose."

"He won't lose it, Rory. I want you, and I'll do everything to make us happen. I know we can be a family for Battista. Maybe not the one you see in cheesy commercials. We'll always be an unconventional family, but unconventional doesn't mean bad. My family is a bunch of weirdos, and I loved growing up among them. Fuck, I couldn't have wished for a better family."

I chuckled. "They are great, and you gave them a hard time over the years."

"I did, but they handled it as best as anyone could. And if Battista is anything like me, he'll need a family to have his back."

"I want us to be a family," I admitted. "Let's work on us a bit more before we think about including Battista, okay?"

Nevio nodded slowly. I turned on the TV. After a while, Nevio put his arm around my shoulders. I snuggled against him, allowing the closeness because my body yearned for it more than I could put into words.

"I think I'll open your presents tomorrow," I whispered. His Christmas and birthday presents for me were hidden in the back of my closet. I hadn't had the heart to throw them away, and now that Nevio and I seemed to be working on our relationship, I was glad for it.

Nevio pulled back slightly to peer down at my face. "I worried you'd thrown them away."

A small smile tugged at my lips. "I wanted to. Well, part of me did, but I couldn't bring myself to do it even though you deserved it."

His expression became more intense, and his eyes darted down to my lips. "I'll kiss you now, and it's not going to be the chaste kiss from last time, so if you really don't want it, you should run. Now."

I should have run. His lips crashed against mine, following up on his warning, and dragged me down into a whirlwind of sensations. I'd missed this, the fire only Nevio could ignite in me. Only this time anger wasn't the dominating emotion, and it felt even better. Nevio dragged me closer until I half lay on top of him, his arm wrapped possessively around my back. His palm stroked up my back, over my sensitive neck and higher until his fingers tangled in my hair, his fingers against my scalp. I moaned into the kiss, desperate for more. Despite the burning need in my body, I pulled away. "We're missing the movie."

Nevio let his head fall back, eyes squeezed shut. "I don't give a fuck about *Nosferatu* right now."

I smiled at the strain in his voice and kissed his cheek before I sat down beside him. I pretended not to notice the bulge in his pants, but seeing it gave me great satisfaction. If Nevio had removed my pants, he'd found the results of our make-out session too.

"Let's watch the movie," I said firmly.

Nevio grabbed the last taco, which had to be cold by now, and stuffed it in his mouth, then washed it down with a few swigs of beer.

After a few minutes, he relaxed against me, and we kept watching the movie. Close to the end, he leaned down to my ear. "Sitting beside you, knowing you're wet and not being able to do anything about it is pure torture, and people call me cruel. They haven't met you yet."

I rolled my eyes.

When Nevio brought me home that night, he gave me another chaste kiss. My body wanted more, and I wondered if I was punishing myself as much as I was punishing Nevio. Battista had fallen asleep beside Serafina so I had the night off. It was strange to be alone in my bedroom. I went to my closet and grabbed the two packages. Perched on my bed, I opened the one from Christmas first. It was a beautiful pendant that shimmered like the aurora borealis. My birthday parcel had the matching bracelet inside. Both were incredibly beautiful.

With a sigh, I let myself fall back on my bed and stared up at the ceiling. My cell phone beeped with a message. When I saw that it was from Nevio, I grabbed it.

Tonight was great. I enjoyed every single one of our dates. It never gets boring with you, Rory. Sleep well. I'll dream of you.

I don't think I can sleep. I'm reliving our kiss.

You could get a repeat performance and more. One word from you and I'm there to give you everything you want.

I bit my lip. **You would have to sneak into our house.**

There wasn't a reply. I felt disappointed. Maybe I'd hoped for some sexting? Though that would have posed the risk of someone reading our messages. I got up and went into the bathroom to get ready. Fifteen minutes later, I returned to my bedroom in my nightgown and slipped under the covers, then turned off the lights. As soon as I closed my eyes, the kiss replayed vividly before my mind. My core tightened with longing.

With a resigned sigh, I slid my hand down my body to relieve some tension. A hand clamped down around my wrist through the covers while another hand covered my mouth to hold in my startled cry, then a hot breath fanned over my ear. "That's my job, Rory."

I relaxed, and my still widened eyes took in Nevio's outline as it came into focus in the dark. He lowered his palm from my mouth. I licked my lips, my throat suddenly dry. "How did you get in here?"

"Through the basement. The same way Greta once did. Of course, the codes have changed by now, but as a future Capo, I have access to all relevant security information."

I could hear the smugness in his voice but also eagerness that only kindled my own.

"Dad will kill you if he finds you in my room."

"I'm sure that's what he'd like to do," Nevio murmured, his face still right over mine. "But he won't find out because you'll be silent when I make you come, won't you?"

My thighs twitched in anticipation, and the heat between my legs had reached unbearable dimensions. "I thought you like it if I made a noise."

"Oh, I do, and there'll be plenty of opportunities to make you scream, but today, you'll be a good quiet girl."

I shivered. His lips brushed mine, full of promise, and I almost begged him to touch me where I ached. Instead, I watched in anticipation as he turned on the lamp on my nightstand, casting us in a soft glow.

"I need to see you when I claim you tonight."

He tugged the covers off me. My hand still rested above my pubic bone. Nevio pushed it away and climbed on top of me for another searing kiss. His lips on mine, his hands roamed my body, tugging my nipples through the thin fabric of my nightgown. I arched into him, my own hands mapping his strong back where the proof of his depravity was inked into his skin.

His fingers clamped down on my hip when I arched up again, growing impatient. By now my panties were soaked, and I needed Nevio to relieve the unbearable tension.

He chuckled, a sinister sound that only made me wetter. "Patience, Rory. Weren't you the one who wanted to wait with the physical part of our relationship?"

I sank my teeth into his lower lip, nicking his skin. "Oh shut up."

He chuckled again, but this time his hand finally moved down where I needed him. His fingers slipped under my panties, and his answering growl when he felt just how much I needed him made me smile. His fingers teased my clit, and his lips on mine dimmed my moans. I was already strung too tightly, ready to burst from months of only fantasizing about this moment. I was getting closer and closer, my breathing erratic, and when he pushed two fingers into me, I exploded with a choked cry that Nevio swallowed with an all-consuming kiss.

Nevio didn't give me time to catch my breath.

He pushed to his feet and ripped his shirt over his head, revealing a body I'd dreamed about in my darkest nightmares and my most lustful fantasies. The sight of the aurora borealis tattoo made my heart throb even harder in my chest. Nevio followed my gaze and briefly pressed his palm over the tattoo, his eyes conveying a message I hardly dared to decipher. Then it was gone and replaced by burning desire. With hurried moves, he shoved down his pants and underwear, then kicked them off.

Nevio half fell on top of me, parting my legs wide with his thighs, his dark eyes like that of a hunter as he slammed his lips against mine. I touched his cheeks, and his eyes returned to mine. The frenzy in them eased, and he slowed. His kiss became gentler. With our gazes locked, he entered me until he settled all the way inside me. My eyes closed, really feeling him. It felt perfect.

His lips brushed my ear, his voice raw. "This feels like a fucking rebirth."

Nevio

Nothing had ever felt better than being inside Aurora, to be connected to her in such a profound way. Not just in the physical sense but because with one look from her, I felt like she held my heart in her hand.

With every thrust, she felt more like mine. That I was hers wasn't even a question anymore. She lived in my head, my heart, even my black soul. She was the voice at the back of my mind keeping me rooted.

I kissed her like she was my salvation, and maybe she was. She started to tremble, her walls tightening around my cock until stars danced before my eyes, and then we both exploded at the same time. Our fused lips swallowed our moans.

Eventually, I pulled back, and our ragged breathing filled the room. That it could even be heard over the pounding of my heart was a miracle.

Aurora's blue eyes pierced mine, filled with questions and hopes.

"You know what I want," she whispered. "I want commitment. I want love and fidelity. I want forever."

"I want the same, Rory. You are my forever."

"I am?"

I pressed her fingers to the tattoo of the northern lights. "I want to be the person you deserve."

Fuck. I wanted nothing more than to be that person for Aurora. But I was a monster. I knew it. I relished in it, but on occasion, I channeled my monster. Most days, I liked being a monster. Rarely I didn't. Most of these occasions involved Mom or Greta, and Aurora. The only times I ever felt guilty for being a monster were when Greta, Aurora, or Mom weren't quick enough to hide their fear from me. Fear, not of what I would do to them, because they knew I'd die before I'd ever hurt the people I cared about. Fear of losing me to the darkness, and of what I could do to everyone else. Maybe my darkness scared them more than Dad's because mine hadn't been born from childhood trauma. I had been born a monster. It was in my genes.

"But I'm a monster and that won't ever change."

Aurora nodded. "I know. I've known you all my life, and from the moment I overheard Dad telling Mom about how you killed a man for your twelfth birthday, I knew you were a monster, but it never changed how I felt about you…"

Alessio and Massimo knew my monster, but they didn't mind, Massimo because he was a monster too, a different kind, but a monster nonetheless, and Alessio because he wanted to be a monster to silence the demons that haunted his nightmares. Mom and Greta knew it to, but they preferred to ignore it and to pretend I could be better. Dad and my uncle knew all about my monster, but they, too, were too monstrous to care—a monster was useful in our world.

Aurora, however, knew my monster, but didn't ignore it, didn't like it, didn't use it. She accepted it because she loved me.

I could see love in her face and eyes. For a long time, I hadn't been sure if my messed-up brain could feel a pure emotion like love. But if this feeling I had for Aurora wasn't love, then what was it? When I was with Aurora, I wished to be better. No one had ever made me feel that way.

I'd been high on alcohol, high on adrenaline, high on anger, lust, and pain.

Today I was high on Aurora.

I wasn't sure if it was enough. If it could carry me through the thunderstorms that ravaged my brain sometimes. For a long time, too long, it had made me pull away from Aurora, waiting for a moment of certainty. But when was there ever absolute certainty in life?

The only thing I was sure about were my feelings for Aurora right now. "What does it say about you that you made a monster fall in love with you?"

Aurora's eyes widened a fraction, her breath halting. She swallowed noisily, and a small smile tugged at her lovely lips. "What does it say about me that I fell in love with a monster?"

I cupped her cheeks and kissed her. "If you knew how crazy I was about you, you'd run, Rory."

"I think I do know. You killed a man because he flirted with me."

"And I'll do it again. You have my fucking heart, and that kind of shitty gift comes with a lot of baggage."

Aurora laughed. I kissed her again. "You know what's the worst about loving you?"

She shook her head, eyes wide and expectant. "For the first time in my life, I fear death because it would mean I'd lose you."

"Then you better try not to get yourself killed in one of your crazy adventures."

Chapter Forty-Five

Aurora

"How is she?" I asked Diego as I followed him upstairs to Carlotta's room. I didn't believe her insistence that she was fine.

"Her heart is giving us reason to worry. She probably needs another transplant."

I nodded slowly. I'd feared that was the case. Maybe telling her about Nevio and me wasn't the best idea, but she was my best friend, and I wanted her to know.

I knocked on her door and stepped inside. She sat at her desk, probably studying for her college classes. She looked pale, even her usually pink lips were pale as if the color had been washed from them.

I went over to her. "How do you feel?"

She sent Diego a scowl. "I hope he didn't exaggerate. I'm fine." She turned to me with the same scowl. "Don't look so worried."

I tried to relax my facial muscles but it was difficult. When Diego closed the door, I said, "I came here to tell you something, but now I'm not sure I should."

She shoved my leg. "Stop it." She scanned my face. "You and Nevio, right?"

I nodded. "We're dating. I know you don't like him…"

Carlotta pushed to her feet and put her hands on my shoulders. "I don't like how he treated you."

"He's changed, Lotta. He really showed me that he wants to be with me."

"If he keeps treating you like you deserve, then I'm fine with him."

I grinned and hugged her. "Now I just have to tell my parents…"

Carlotta chuckled. "Good luck. Your dad's the toughest nut to crack."

"No, that was you."

We both laughed.

"Can I talk to you?" I asked as I stepped into the kitchen with Battista on my hip where Mom, Dad, and Davide waited for me to have breakfast. Two weeks had passed since Nevio admitted his feelings for me, and since then, he'd snuck inside my bedroom almost every night. Nobody knew anything. They thought we only spent time together during the day with Battista.

Davide leaned back, arms crossed over his chest. For the first time, I realized how much he'd grown, and how much he looked like Dad. If only he weren't such a pain in my ass. "This is going to be fun. She looks fucking guilty."

"Language," Mom admonished as she took Battista from me and put him into his high chair. I sank down beside him. I wanted Mom and Dad's approval, but I doubted I'd get it, especially from Dad.

Dad sipped at his coffee and raised one blond brow. "Yes?"

Mom gave me an encouraging smile. Maybe I should have started with her and told her about my relationship with Nevio.

"Coffee?" Mom asked as she lifted the thermos.

I gave a terse nod. "You know I love you, and I still feel guilty for having gone behind your back—"

"So you chose to go behind our backs again?" Dad asked with narrowed eyes.

I stared. "No! I mean… I didn't really go behind your backs." Did they know about Nevio's nightly visits? I couldn't imagine Dad being so calm if that were the case.

"Your dad and I know you're dating Nevio," Mom said.

Dad grimaced. "My worst nightmare come true."

Davide laughed, obviously delighted.

"How?" I asked.

"Davide saw you kissing Nevio in the garden a few days ago."

I glared at my brother. "And you had nothing better to do than to tell on me?"

"I could have kicked Nevio's ass for touching you, but I like him. And I went to Mom first. If I wanted to cause you trouble, I would have gone to Dad. Then Mom couldn't have held him him in check."

Dad scowled. "Your mom doesn't hold me in check."

Davide and I exchanged a look, because she definitely did. Mom cleared her throat, trying to hide a smile. "We know you're seeing Nevio, but we would have wished you'd told us right away this time."

"Nevio and I needed to figure out things first," I said. "Are you going to be okay with it? I really need your support."

"You always have our support," Mom said.

I glanced at Dad. He was the one I really worried about.

He nodded and took my hand. "I'll always support you, even if I'm not exactly happy about your decision."

"But you like Nevio, right?"

"I liked him better before he started something with you."

I laughed. "He's been really trying very hard to make me happy since he returned from Italy."

"I'll be impressed if he keeps it up a year from now. I seriously hope he's serious about you."

I smiled. "He is. He asked me to live together so we can become a family for Battista."

Mom and Dad looked at each other with obvious surprise. "You're moving out?" Mom asked. "Back to the apartment?"

I shook my head. "Nevio and I agreed that it would be best to live with our families. We're both young and need all the help we can get with Battista, and we want him to experience the same big family support and craziness we had."

Nevio

I went in search of my parents and found them both in Giulio's room, doing homework with him. If they both joined forces, then Giulio was in serious trouble. Nobody could play good cop/bad cop better than Mom and Dad. When it came to schoolwork, Mom was usually the bad cop. Dad probably didn't see the value of calculus once Giulio became a Made Man.

They looked up when I entered. Giulio's face flashed with relief.

"I need to talk to you," I said. I'd already told Greta about my relationship with Aurora, and she had been happy for me. She probably thought it was fate. Since she knew Amo, believing in fate was her most annoying character trait. Though part of me had to admit that Aurora felt like my fated mate. Fuck.

Giulio jumped up from his desk chair. "I'll give you privacy."

Dad grabbed his shoulder and pushed him back down. "You stay where you are. Another suspension and we'll have no choice but to homeschool you, and trust me when I say that no one in this house wants that."

Giulio pouted but didn't protest again. Mom and Dad followed me outside and closed the door.

Once we were in the hallway, I said, "I'm dating Aurora and I want everyone to know."

"That's wonderful," Mom exclaimed, hugging me as if I'd won a Nobel Prize. Rory was worth so much more than the Swedish trophy.

Dad clapped my shoulder, his expression hard. "Don't fuck this up. Finding a good woman is like winning the lottery, especially for men like us."

"I know, Dad, don't worry. Which is why I want to show Aurora that I'm 100 percent invested. We decided to move in together with Battista."

"Where?" Mom asked. She was probably worried about losing her grandchild and son at once.

"Adamo's part of the house is empty. That's enough room for Aurora, Battista, and me."

"And even more kids in the future," Mom added.

"Let's try to keep Giulio in check before we plan more offspring with my blood."

"That's not your decision, Dad." I chuckled. "So can we have Adamo's old rooms?"

"Of course!" Mom smiled.

"Great."

Dad released a sigh. "I rule over the West, but apparently, my ruling doesn't extend to my own home."

Mom touched Dad's arm with a grin.

My phone beeped with a message from Aurora. I immediately clicked on it and released a sigh of relief when I read that her parents were okay with us.

"I can't believe you're going all domestic on us," Alessio said when we painted one of the rooms in light blue and cream. It would become Battista's nursery. Carlotta who was good at painting helped Nino draw balloons, clouds and animals on one wall as decoration. Massimo hovered around them half of the time instead of helping us.

"I'm a father, and I want to be with Aurora so this is the logical choice." Massimo glanced my way upon hearing one of his favorite phrases. He tilted his head in agreement.

"I couldn't imagine being a father right now."

"It wasn't my plan but I want Battista to have a father he can look up to."

Alessio gave me an approving look. "I didn't think you had it in you."

"Don't worry. I'm still the same fuck up when it comes to our raids at night. I won't give them up completely."

"I didn't think you would," Massimo said when he joined us.

Aurora came in with Battista on her hand. His eyes lit up when he saw the drawings on the wall. "It's beautiful!" Aurora said.

"Not my doing. You got Carlotta and Nino to thank for that."

Battista raced toward me, and I picked him up, then carried him over to the wall art. "This is your new room."

Aurora came up to me with a pleased smile. "This is so exciting."

Two days later, Aurora and I spent our first night in our bedroom. Battista was in his crib beside the bed because Aurora was worried the paint in his room was still too fresh. I wouldn't have minded having sex once he was asleep, but Aurora wasn't having it, so she was cuddled up to my side, her head on my shoulder.

"I can't believe we have our own place." She paused. "Well, kind of. It feels like we have our own place."

"Minus any kitchen duties because Kiara and Gemma love to do that."

Aurora laughed. "We should help them more."

"I doubt anyone wants to taste what I cook."

"You could clean the dishes."

I groaned. "If I'd known this was part of the deal, I would have declined."

Aurora slapped my chest hard. I rolled us over until I was on top of her. "People have lost their lives for less than hitting me."

She rolled her eyes. Then she became serious. "Are you worried about this? About us living together?"

"No," I said, and it was the absolute truth. "I know you, and you know me."

"We know each other as friends, and we've gotten to know each other as a couple, but being a family is a new challenge."

"I like a challenge, and I know we'll master it."

Aurora smiled. "We will." She ran her hand along my shoulder blade

By Frenzy I *Rain*

then down my back in a very distracting way. "The conservatives will definitely gossip about our new living arrangements."

"Let them talk. Nobody will dare say anything to your face, trust me." I searched her eyes. Things between us were still fresh but in my mind, there was no doubt that Aurora and I would grow old together, if I didn't get myself killed before then. Maybe she wanted me to pop the question? I didn't really see the necessity of marriage. It had always seemed like such a superfluous arrangement. Why did anyone need a marriage certificate to be happy? But if Aurora wanted us to make it official in that way. "We could marry if that would make you feel better."

Her face twisted with shock, but not the good kind. "I don't want to marry because of societal pressure or because you think I want it. I want us to marry because we both want it."

"Then we might never marry because I just don't see a reason for marriage."

Aurora swallowed, but the stubborn gleam remained in her eyes. "Then I'll be okay with that. I want us to marry for the right reasons, and I want a real proposal!"

I chuckled. "Promise, if I ever find a good reason to marry, then I'll knock you off your socks with my proposal."

I arrived for our weekly business meeting ten minutes early. The surprise on Dad's, Fabiano's, and Nino's faces, who were already there, made it clear that they still hadn't gotten used to my responsible side. It wasn't only Rory who needed to see that I was more than a crazy killer. Dad needed to realize that I'd one day make a good Capo and not cause the Camorra to implode with my craziness.

I sank into the armchair across from Fabiano. He and I had a sort of truce, but he definitely liked me a little less since I started dating his daughter. "I should probably give you fair warning that I might one day ask Rory for her hand."

The words slipped out before I could think them through. I still wasn't sure about marriage.

Fabiano's expression twisted with confusion, not the shock I'd expected. "And you're telling me now?"

"So you can make peace with the idea," I said with a grin.

Dad and Nino exchanged a look that showed they were more shocked than Fabiano.

"If I hadn't made peace with you and my daughter, you would know by now. And I always expected you to be serious about her, so why would I need to get used to the idea of marriage?"

"I'm serious about her. But that doesn't mean it has to end in marriage. People can love each other without being married."

Fabiano narrowed his eyes. "Not in my world."

I chuckled. "I don't see why we should marry without a good reason."

"Then find a reason."

Dad rolled his eyes. "You took a while to find a reason to ask Leona for her hand."

"But I did find one, so it's irrelevant."

Nino opened his mouth. He was as skeptical about marriage as I was. Fabiano raised his palm. "Don't bother. I've heard all of your logical arguments, and I'm over them. Nevio will find a reason to marry Aurora."

I stifled a laugh. Fabiano's scare tactics were directed at the wrong person, but I had no doubt that Rory would make me want to marry someday.

Chapter Forty-Six

Aurora

I scanned the ground below us. Where the scenery had been brightly lit when our flight had taken off, darkness spread below us as our airplane slowly descended for landing. In the distance, I could make out a spattering of light. At least, there seemed to be some kind of civilization where Nevio was taking me.

"Won't you tell me where we're going? I'll eventually find out," I said. I'd asked Nevio countless times since he'd practically kidnapped me from the breakfast table this morning. I'd only had time to say goodbye to Battista before Nevio and I had driven to the airport where the private Camorra jet had been waiting. Nevio had even packed my bag, which was one of my main worries right now. I doubted Nevio had any clue what kind of clothes I'd need. I hoped he'd at least asked a female family member for help with the toiletry bag. My other worry was how Battista would fare. This was the first time I'd be gone for more than a few hours. He would turn four this year and he loved spending time with his grandparents and his uncle Giulio so my concern was completely unfounded.

Nevio crossed his arms behind his head with a satisfied grin. "Can't you guess?"

"Well, considering our flight time and the landscape below, I'd guess we're somewhere in Europe, most likely up north."

"Good detective work, Sherlock."

I moved over to him and sat on his lap. "We're supposed to stay buckled in," he said with raised eyebrows, but his hands grabbed my hips as I straddled his thighs.

"Then you should consider telling me or risk my health."

"I like you on my lap. What's life without a little danger?" He kissed me, his fingers tangling in my hair.

I sank into the kiss when the buckle up sign binged again. Nevio moved back with a sigh.

I returned to my seat with an expectant expression.

"All right. Lapland."

My eyes widened. "We're here to watch the northern lights?"

Because of Nevio's obsession with the lights, I'd started researching them, and the photos I'd seen had made me want to experience them in real life.

"I thought it would be the perfect way to spend our second Valentine's day as a couple."

"It is!"

The hotel that Nevio had picked for us was in Northern Lapland and consisted of small round cabins with a glass roof over the bed. Our cabin even had a Jacuzzi on the patio. Everything was covered in snow, making the area look even more magical. Having spent most of my life in Las Vegas, the temperatures were a shock to my system, but Nevio had bought snow attire for both of us in preparation for the trip.

"Admit it, you got help with my clothes."

Nevio didn't even try to deny it. "Kiara helped me."

By Frenzy I *Pain*

Despite the jet lag and exhaustion, I begged Nevio to ride a dog sleigh through the snowy landscape. In my thick layers of clothes, I couldn't have walked the area for long without falling over like a Michelin man.

The dog handler showed us how to steer the sleigh, but the dogs got nervous around Nevio, their howls and barks rising high above the crowns of the firs around us. I understood them only too well. Nevio was a force of nature, a predator of his own right, one who had haunted my nights for a long time—nightmares and dreams, both equally passion-filled. When Nevio and I had both taken position on the sleigh, with Nevio's arms pressing against mine as we held the handle, Nevio let out the call that told the dogs to run. I would have toppled backward if Nevio hadn't been behind me. The dogs raced past trees, whirling up the snow, as if the devil was after them.

It was incredible, and I couldn't stop laughing in absolute joy.

That night and the following nights, Nevio and I watched the northern lights from our bed, wrapped in each other's arms, and the sight never got boring. Whenever I thought I'd already seen every color scheme, nature surprised me again. The night sky flared with luminous waves, turquoise and pale blue, pink and fiery orange. My breath halted as I watched in awe how the darkness lit up above our heads. It was a mesmerizing display I'd never dreamed of witnessing, but here I was with a man who hadn't let me run from him. I felt Nevio's gaze on me as if I was more interesting than the aurora borealis.

Nevio

The colorful lights of the northern lights reflected in Aurora's eyes, illuminating her hair and awed face.

"You must watch the lights, not me! You can watch me all the time!" Aurora said indignantly, never taking her eyes from the sky.

I got it. It was difficult to look away from something this beautiful. For me the sky came only in second place though. Still, I finally tilted my head back to watch nature's display. Aurora pressed her head against my shoulder and released a small, pleased smile.

I leaned over to the nightstand and removed the box I'd carried with me since we left Las Vegas. Now was the perfect moment to give it to Aurora.

Eventually, she lowered her gaze from the sky and beamed at me. "This is just incredible. I won't ever forget this moment. Thank you for taking me here."

"I had to," I said roughly. Aurora's brows pulled together. "I had to because I wanted you to understand how I feel when I look at you. I want you to understand what you do to me. This Nordic sky is nothing to the darkness inside me, but you still manage to shine your light on me in a far more awe-inspiring way than the aurora borealis."

"Nevio," Aurora whispered, her breath creating small puffs between us.

My fingers around the box tightened, and I raised it so Aurora could see it.

Aurora's eyes moved down to my hand and widened before they darted back up to my face in disbelief. "Nevio?"

I untangled myself from our warm nest and walked around the bed, then got down on my knee on Aurora's side and opened the box. The lights became particularly bright at this moment as if they wanted to match the ring I showed Aurora. A piece of jewelry I'd spent a long time searching for until I'd ordered a goldsmith to create it for me. The stone looked as if I'd condensed the aurora borealis inside of it.

Aurora sat up slowly, her lips shaped an O, and her eyes glistened with tears that only magnified the glow of the northern lights in them. She took my breath away. The past few days with her here, I was fucking content. I didn't need the thrill of a kill, of a hunt, of blood and torture. With Aurora, my destructive urges could rest for a bit. I knew they'd always be there, and these brief respites would always just be that, brief pauses in my otherwise dark nature, but it was more than I'd considered myself capable of.

I took her hand. "I told you before, but I know I should do it more often. I love you. The light side of me, which I never thought existed, but also the darkest, most depraved corners of myself, love you, Aurora, every fucking thing about you. Most of all how you keep shining brightly no matter the darkness I throw at you. I can't let you go. I won't let you go. I want you to be mine forever because in my heart, in my head, even in my damned soul if I have something like that, you will always be mine. Marry me."

Did my words leave Aurora a choice? I wasn't sure she had one. I hoped she didn't need one. I hoped she felt the same painful desire to spend her life with me until the very last breath I took. Because she'd better survive me. I wouldn't live a single moment without her.

Aurora bit her lip with a soft smile as she nodded. "Of course, I'll marry you!"

Before I could push to my feet, Aurora slid down from the bed and fell into my lap, her arms around my neck, her lips against mine. She clung to me as I sank down full on the warm sheepskin and hugged her to me, returning her kiss with every bit of love I felt.

Soon, her tears wet my face, and I pulled back to wipe them off.

The idea of tears of happiness had always been a mystery to me. Hell, I hadn't even cried tears of sadness as far as I could remember, but seeing Aurora's obvious joy, I understood tears of happiness finally, even if I'd never cry them myself.

"I guess you aren't mad at me for making you cry this time?"

Aurora let out a choked laugh. "No!" I took her hand and slid the ring on her finger. Aurora shook her head as if she couldn't believe it.

"What changed your mind about marriage?"

"Every day I spent with you did. Maybe marriage isn't necessary, but so many things in life aren't. I just wanted to call you my wife. It's as fucking simple as that. And your name will sound fabulous. Aurora Falcone."

I kissed her again, and then I made love to her under the luminous night sky.

THE END

Please consider leaving a review. Readers like
you help other readers discover new books!

Printed in Great Britain
by Amazon